A MAID'S FRIENDS AND FANTASIES: SHORT STORIES

T0352260

A Maid's Friends and Fantasies:
Short Stories

DEVLIN O'NEILL

BLUE MOON BOOKS
NEW YORK

A Maid's Friends and Fantasies
Copyright © 2005 by Devlin O'Neill

Published by
Blue Moon Books
An Imprint of Avalon Publishing Group Incorporated
245 West 17th Street, 11th floor
New York, NY 10011-5300

First Blue Moon Books Edition 2005

ISBN 1-56201-473-0

9 8 7 6 5 4 3 2 1

TABLE OF CONTENTS

A Note from the Author   vii

SECTION I

Fence Mending 101   3
Teresa's Ill-advised Shopping Trip   12
A Hot Day in Tuscany   25
The Office Assistant   44
Speed Hurts!   57
Teresa's Illness   79

SECTION II

Devlin's Cure for Gwen   117
A Doll Story   144
Preparing the Way   172
Forgetfulness   189
The Unfortunate Disagreement   212

Table of Contents

A Note from the Author vii

Section I

Fence Mending 101 3
Teresa's Ill-advised Shopping Trip 12
A Hot Day in Tuscany 25
The Office Assistant 44
Speed Hurts! 57
Teresa's Illness 79

Section II

Devlin's Cure for Gwen 117
A Dull Story 144
Preparing the Way 172
Forgetfulness 189
The Unfortunate Disagreement 212

A NOTE FROM THE AUTHOR

Some people write for a generic audience that is conditioned to read bestsellers; some target a sub-set of tastes. I belong to the latter category and write erotic spanking fiction, like the *A Maid for All Seasons* series. My preference, however, is to write for an audience of one, one whose specific taste I know well. This approach is artistically and emotionally fulfilling, but apt to keep an author's royalty income on the low side of zip point nothing if that's all he writes.

Still, I have been lucky to find two such singular audiences; two women who not only fulfill my emotional and artistic needs but inspire me to greater creativity. These Muses, spiritual cousins of Lisa Carlson and Beth Trelawny, have shared with me their wishes and desires, and shown me exactly how and where they want a story to go. I borrowed their moist dreams, and their *voices,* and with their collaboration, inspiration and dedication I wrote the pieces that follow.

This book's first section belongs to Teresa Wagner, the *nom de plume* and on-line persona of a woman who lives overseas. When I posted a web story that later became part of the second *Maid* novel, she read it and e-mailed to say how much she enjoyed it. Teresa intrigued me from the start, since I never had a *fan* before, but our author/admirer relationship blossomed into something much more complex. In fact, it was she who encouraged me to make the leap from storyteller to novelist. We began to write the stories *she* wanted to read and as our connectivity grew, so grew our fantasy world, populated, quite naturally, by our fantasy selves and whatever fictional or semi-fictional adjunct characters we thought necessary.

Other fans appeared as I posted more web stories, and I reveled in not only the attention but in the unique opportunity to hear and absorb the fantasies and suggestions of people all over the globe. The ether-net's anonymity allowed even the shyest person to be open about his or her dreams, and as a dialogue

unfolded I was able to create fiction tailored to a specific preference, and also hone my skill through long hours of practice at a truly delightful, and well appreciated, task.

One such delightful task has been writing with Gwen McKenna, another of Lisa and Beth's spiritual cousins. Our connectedness is, was and shall continue to be *exactly* the equal of that which I share with Teresa. (I know you two are reading this so please note my emphasis on *complete* equality.) Gwen resides, geographically, much closer to me, only 3,000 miles, airport to airport, but we have so far missed meeting each other even though we live on the same continent. Stories I wrote for and with her comprise the second section of this book. They are different in style and tone from Teresa's because each voice is unique, although the premise remains the same: naughty girls get spanked, and all girls are naughty . . . those who inhabit *these* fantasy worlds, at any rate.

When we wrote these pieces, I had in mind to include similar characters in the *A Maid for All Seasons* novel series, which I ultimately did. I want to emphasize the word *similar,* because the Gwen and Teresa who appear beginning with *Maid, Volume III* are not exactly the same as the ones here; that is, these are not sequels, prequels or spin-offs to the novels, but rather may be considered sketches for those characters.

Our stories are works of fiction, as noted in the legal disclaimer, and we wrote them with zeal and pleasure. They also are labors of love, conjured from fertile, lascivious imaginations to be shared with a deeply significant other, then polished and perfected, but never purged of their breathless, heartfelt immediacy, to be presented in this format. A story conceived, nurtured, and sent into the world as these have been assumes a life of its own. Such tales are *true,* even if they didn't happen, and my coauthors and I hope you approve of our children.

—Devlin O'Neill *et alia*

A Maid's Friends and Fantasies: Short Stories

SECTION I

SECTION I

FENCE MENDING 101

Fence Mending wasn't *the* first Teresa story but it came quite early in our relationship. I used her suggestions and bits of our e-mails to write this, and she wrote the actual beginnings of later stories. The *I/you* point of view and present tense are approximations of the way people act out their fantasies in instant messages on the web.

The setting here is purposely nebulous . . . an upscale home somewhere in Southern California. Our earlier scenes took place in Devlin's cyber-space apartment, a device that overcomes not only time and space but any objections. (Thank you, Elwood P. Dowd.) Teresa could jump on the ether-net bus at her home in Germany and be there instantly, but then one or the other of us decided that we needed an actual *locale* for our stories, otherwise readers would be perplexed by the red e-mails and fat blue JPG files that constantly flew past the apartment window.

"Teresa . . . how nice to see you. Please come in."

"Thanks." You bite your lip, and clasp your hands at your back as you pass me.

"It's good of you to come, sweetie."

You pout and look at me from the corners of your eyes. "Yeah, right, Uncle Devlin. Like I had a choice."

"Whatever do you mean?"

Your pout deepens and you stamp your foot. "If I didn't show up you'd come looking for me . . . with a *switch*."

I smile and steer you to the sofa. "Yes . . . I probably would have done. All the same, it's good to see you. Will you join me in a glass of port?"

You smooth the back of your skirt and your eyes twinkle as you sit. "Do you think we will both fit?"

I laugh and lean over to kiss your forehead. "That's a very old joke. What I *should* have said is, would you care for a glass of port?"

"OK." You dig into your purse and pull out a small, flat box. "I . . . I got you a present, Uncle Devlin."

"You did? What a *sweetheart* you are."

I pour amber liquid into two cordial glasses and carry them to the sofa.

"Open it." You smile as I tear paper and read the label on a plastic jewel case.

"The Oxford English Dictionary . . . complete on two CDs. You are very kind, Teresa."

"Now when I use words you do not understand you won't have to refer to that clunky old Webster's you have had since college."

I raise my index finger, then lower it and smile. "No, I suppose I won't . . . and I'll be happy to share this with you, should we ever come across a word *you* are unfamiliar with."

You grin and raise your glass. "Cheers."

"*Prost!*"

Crystal chings and we sip.

"Mmmm . . . tastes like . . . pecan syrup, Uncle Devlin."

"Really? I thought it was more . . . walnutty."

You sip again. "No . . . definitely pecans."

"Possibly. Either way, it's very good over vanilla ice cream." The empty glass clunks when you set it on the coffee table. "Another?"

You shake your head. "Uncle Devlin?"

"What is it, sweetie?"

"I'm glad you're not mad at me."

"Of course I'm not mad at you. Why would I be?"

Your shoulders heave as you take a breath. "Because I made such a mess at your pool last weekend."

I smile and take your hand. "I'm not angry, sweetie . . . but I *do* have to spank you very, very hard tonight."

"*No!* If you are not *mad,* why *must* you?"

"Because you *need* to be spanked. If I don't spank your naughty bottom I would be derelict in my duty toward you. You understand that, don't you?"

"No I *don't!*" You fold your arms and stare at the coffee table. "Why not just tell me not to do it anymore and I *won't?*"

I chuckle, take the empty glasses to the bar and fill them. "I *know* you better than that."

You glare when I hand you a glass and sit beside you. "But . . . I didn't do it on *purpose.*"

"I know . . . but the damage *was* your doing and you have to pay for it."

"Can't you just take it out of my allowance?"

"It has nothing to do with *money.* Your tender little bottom will pay for cleaning up after you."

"How . . . how *much?*"

You sip port as I look at the ceiling.

"Let me see . . . forty-two fifty American for the maid service to bleach the merlot and suntan oil out of the tiles . . . that's what? About sixty thousand Deutschmarks?"

Port sprays as you laugh into your hand. "No *way.*"

I give you a linen napkin. "That comes to thirty thousand spanks per cheek."

"Uncle Devlin!" You giggle and wipe your hand and chin. "You will spank my fanny right *off.*"

"That would *never* do . . . it's such a *cute* fanny. Tell you what . . . we'll reconvert to dollars. That would be um. . . ."

"Twenty-one point twenty-five."

I raise my eyebrows. "Languages *and* math . . . I'm impressed."

You lean over and cuddle my shoulder. "Uncle Devlin?"

"Hm?"

"Why don't we just look up some naughty words in the OED?"

"Later, perhaps. Finish your drink and get over my knee."

Air hisses through your teeth and you kick the coffee table. "You are such a meanie!"

"We'll add the removal of your black toe mark from the table and make it an even twenty-five per cheek."

"Nooo! It was an *accident*. My foot slipped. *Please* don't!"

"Over my lap right *now*, young lady, or I'll get the hairbrush."

Your face pales and you jerk to your feet. "No! I mean, no *sir*. *Please?*"

"Raise your skirt."

Your lower lip curls out as you scrunch khaki linen with both hands. The hem rises like a slow curtain and lacy white drawers peek at me beneath the crumpled material. I smile and you stamp your foot.

"It isn't *fair*."

"Over my lap, sweetie."

You stomp around to my right side and lie across my thighs. I tug the skirt up your back and pat your lace-covered bottom.

"That's a good girl."

"Then why do I have to get *spanked?*" you say to the sofa cushion.

"I meant you're a good girl to wear such lovely panties."

You look over your shoulder and wipe your eye with the heel of your hand. "Do you like them?"

"Very much."

"So I can keep them on while you spank me?"

I laugh. "The port has addled your mind, little girl. When have I *ever* spanked you with panties on?"

You smile and shrug. "It was worth a try."

"Indeed . . . now lift up so I can take down your pretty drawers."

You squirm and push with your knees. The frilly white shorts tighten around your full, ripe bottom. I smile and tug the waistband down your thighs.

"Not *real* hard, OK, Uncle Devlin?"

"When have I *ever* . . . ?"

You slap the sofa arm. "I *know*." Your voice timbre drops an octave. "When have I ever not spanked you *hard*, Teresa?"

I shake my head. "You'll rupture your vocal cords doing that . . . now hold still. Two hundred fifty per cheek, wasn't it?"

"It was twenty-five!" You glare at me over your shoulder.

"Ah! My mistake . . . but I'm an author, not a math genius."

"You're a mean old man and I don't know *why* you like to spank my poor bottom so much."

I smile and stroke your firm mounds. "Then probably I should tell you."

"I'm not sure I want to know."

"Of course you do, sweetie. There is a cosmic symmetry to the female bottom that. . . ."

"But not the *male* bottom?"

"Hush and let me pontificate."

You cup your chin in your hand, wriggle your behind and glare at the sofa arm. I clear my throat.

"Let's see now . . . cosmic symmetry, um . . . oh, yes. Its round plumpness is the model for the St. Valentine's heart and its . . . oh bloody hell. You've thrown off my rhythm."

I raise my arm high and smack hard on your right cheek. You grunt and clasp your hands. I slap the other cheek and you whimper. Warm, pink blossoms burst high on your smooth bottom flesh, and you whisper the count while my hand bounces off your adorable behind.

"Fifty!" You reach back, grab my left hand, kiss my fingers, and then use them to wipe a salty streak from beneath your eye. "I . . . I'm sorry I messed up your pool deck."

The hot, sweet bloom on your right cheek quivers when I kiss it, and then I scoop you up to cuddle you. "You're forgiven," I whisper in your ear.

You moan as I rub away the sting. "I . . . I don't really think you are *mean,* Uncle Devlin."

"I know. Do you feel better now?"

"Uh huh. Can . . . *may* I have some baby oil on my fanny?"

I smile and raise your chin so I can kiss your ripe-plum lips. "Sure . . . but first I have a present for *you.*"

Your eyes gleam. "Really? You didn't *have* to."

"It's in the coffee table."

You grin and twist away from me. The linen skirt bunches at your waist and you display two inches of plumber cleavage as you

sit on the sofa and lean over to open a floor-level drawer. You drag out a box covered in red, white and blue foil paper that you immediately shred to bits. Your jaw drops as you shake open the box.

"Uncle Devlin!"

The box falls to the floor and you chew a pinky finger.

"Don't you like it?" I reach down and pick up a short black paddle. "Look . . . it's real Italian leather. I thought you'd be pleased."

Fire burns in your green eyes as you stand, pull your panties up, straighten your skirt and grab your empty glass. You stalk to the bar and pour two ounces of port into the glass and three ounces onto the countertop, then drain the glass and refill it. I set the paddle on the table and join you. You turn your back to me and I hug you from behind.

"What's *wrong*, sweetie?"

I hold you close while you whimper and squirm.

"Uncle *Devlin!* You . . . you're not going to spank me with that . . . that *thing*, are you?"

"Yes . . . you *still* owe me for the lost masonry work."

"But I . . . I didn't *mean* to be naughty." You weep and turn around to hide your face in my chest.

"Shh . . . it's all right . . . but Southern California *isn't* Western Europe. We still think bare female breasts are remarkable, and showing them to the hired help is simply *not* done."

"You . . . you sound like a stuffy old Englishman."

I smile. "Which is exactly what you thought I *was* when we first met."

"But now I *know* better. You are a kind and loving American uncle who would *never* spank his favorite niece with a nasty *paddle*."

"That's *partly* right, sweetie."

You look up at me. "*Which* part?"

I kiss your moist lips. "The kind and loving American part."

"Uncle Devlin!" You stamp your foot. "Can't you just spank me with your *hand?*"

I hold up my right palm. "Do you see how red this is?"

You kiss it and then bite your lower lip. "It is only a *little* red."

"No, it's *very* red and it probably stings worse than your naughty bottom does. Have you been working out?"

"I . . . I walk a lot." You drain your glass.

"Yes, I'll *bet* you do. Go to the sofa."

"Uncle *Devlin*." The bottle gurgles when you slosh more port.

"Right *now,* young lady."

"But . . . if those workmen *are* from Samoa, they should not have been distracted from building your wall! They see bare breasts all the *time*. It is a cultural thing."

I nod and cross my arms. "Yes, I believe it is . . . but they see their wives' breasts . . . their sisters' . . . their neighbors'. *Not* voluptuous, alabaster bosoms such as yours."

You huff and curl out your lower lip. "That's kind of racist, Uncle Devlin."

A growl rasps my throat and I grab your wrist. Port drenches the counter when you drop the glass. I set it upright and you squeal as I pull you to the sofa.

"No, *please?* I'm *sorry*."

I sit, throw you across my lap and raise your skirt. Hot pink glows beneath delicate lace and I take a deep breath as I once more lower your knickers.

"I didn't *mean* it, Uncle Devlin!"

The leather paddle handle feels cool and smooth in my port-sticky hand. I pop your pink bottom with thirty centimeters of Italian leather and you yelp.

"*No!* Owee!"

Your full, round behind bounces when I smack again and leave a bright red blotch that spans the deep crevice.

"Are you *ashamed* of showing your bosom to those workmen, Teresa?"

"Owee! I . . . *yes!* I . . . I am *heartily* ashamed."

I swat hard, just where you sit down, and you shriek. "Then *why* did you tell me it was no big deal?"

"Naiiiee! *Please!*"

"You said on the phone you had no *idea* they were watching you."

"I . . . I didn't I *swear*."

"You *said* you just wanted to even your tan lines." Leather sears your bare flesh.

"*Ja!* It's *true*. I'm innocent, honest!"

Your round cheeks flatten as the paddle fans warmth into your bottom.

"Why don't I *believe* you, Teresa?"

"Aiee! But you *must*! Please not so *hard!*"

"Does your fanny burn, young lady?"

I wrap my left arm around your waist and raise your behind. You kick the sofa cushions and shriek while your right hand scrabbles to protect your rear. I slap the knuckles with the paddle and you jam your fingers into your mouth.

"*Please?*"

"I asked you a *question*, Teresa Luisa."

The paddle cracks like a pistol shot across the center of your cheeks.

"*Yes!* It *burns! Stop!*"

"Do you think it burns like those poor workmen's eyes did . . . when you teased them like that?"

You sniffle and pant to catch your breath while I caress your behind with warm leather.

"I . . . I don't *know*, Uncle Devlin!"

"No? I think you *do* . . . I think you taunted them with your plump, ripe breasts for your own amusement."

"But I *wouldn't!*"

I slap your tight redness hard and then throw the paddle to the floor. You wail when I turn you over. Hot tears streak your face, and crimson streaks your bare bottom. You quiver as you hug me and sob into my neck.

"It's all right, Teresa."

"I . . . I'm *sorry*, Uncle Devlin." You twitch when I lay a gentle hand on your sore behind.

"You were naughty, weren't you?" A quick shrug quivers your shoulders. "And you got spanked really hard." You nod and wipe your eyes. "So now you're forgiven."

"You . . . you *promise?*"

"Promise."

"I . . . I didn't *mean* to tease those men," you whisper.

"All right . . . but you were lucky you didn't have three 200-pound Samoans all over you, sweetie."

"Yeah."

"Or did you *want* three 200-pound Samoans all over you?"

You sniffle and glare. "Don't be mean, Uncle Devlin."

"Do you want baby oil?"

"Yes, please."

"Can you reach the top drawer in the table?"

You twist and bend. Your bottom arches as you lean forward. I touch the hot, red flesh with my fingertips, and you scowl at me over your shoulder as you pull out a plastic bottle. You hand it to me, and watch while I fill my palm with oil. I slick coolness down your sore fanny and you moan.

"Uncle Devlin?"

"Yes, sweetie?"

"Am I a good girl now?"

I smile and kiss the back of your head. "Of course you are. Why?"

"Um . . . because I made reservations at Chez Henri for eight o'clock."

My hand stings when I swat your scarlet behind. "You little *minx*."

"Owee! But I always *wanted* to go there. It's four or five stars, you know?"

"I assume you made the reservation in *my* name."

"Of course . . . you've got that platinum card."

I lean over and kiss your lips. "Yes, and I'll probably get a call from the American Express people tomorrow, wanting to know if I really spent five hundred dollars at a restaurant."

You grin. "But I'm a *good* girl. Don't I *deserve* truffles and champagne and filet mignon *once* in a while?"

I smile. "Every day of the week."

You screech when I squeeze a flaming red bottom cheek.

TERESA'S ILL-ADVISED
SHOPPING TRIP

Shopping Trip was Teresa's first *story start,* where she wrote a two-page set-up and I continued from there. It is a sequel to an incident that became part of *A Maid for All Seasons III* and stands well on its own.

Teresa always wanted a rich, handsome American uncle, which she told me is not an uncommon desire among young German women, but *her* fantasy uncle had to be strict and demanding as well. A rich, handsome American college professor fits her needs exactly.

Her first language is German, but she works as an English translator and also speaks fluent Italian and Spanish. Still, it took a giant leap of faith to overcome her reluctance to write a story in English, especially one that would be read by her strict and demanding author uncle, and I was very proud of the result.

Uncle Devlin is a bit worried. He hasn't seen much of Teresa the past few days. Most of the time she stays in her room, shifting papers or working on her computer, and she has gone shopping a lot. Devlin does not even want to think of her credit card bill that is due to arrive soon. He sips coffee and opens the morning

paper. Sometimes it is not easy to deal with his adopted niece. He wonders what would become of her if not for the benefit of a guardian who keeps her on track and gives her the love and discipline she so obviously needs.

After a few minutes Teresa swirls into the room, a huge, happy grin on her lips.

"Good morning, Uncle Devlin!" She bangs the door shut and runs to give him a kiss. "How are *you* this bright and sunny morning? The weather is *beautiful* and I can't *wait* to get out of the house."

He puts down the paper, raises his left eyebrow and then can't suppress a smile. "Good morning, sweetie. I am fine . . . you're right, the weather is beautiful . . . and you look as if you've caught spring fever. Perhaps I should take your temperature before you leave for school."

Teresa scowls and blushes. "*Really*, Uncle Devlin . . . I *don't* have any fever. I am just excited because the sales start today and I will go to the mall with Laura. We are going to meet in an hour or so."

"You're going to the *mall?* What about your classes at university?"

"Umm . . . we *have* no classes today. They need to do some renovation work in the ladies' rooms . . . and . . . they told us it would be better if we stayed away and studied at home today . . . and tomorrow, too!" She flashes a brilliant smile and quickly sits on his lap. "Uncle Devlin?"

"What is it, sweetie?"

"Has my credit card bill arrived yet?"

"No . . . why do you ask?"

Teresa bites her lip and gives him a guilty look from under her lashes while she unconsciously rubs her bottom. "I . . . I was just curious. I think I had better get ready now. I want to buy a few nighties to leave in your apartment. I cannot always use your tee shirts when I am sleeping over . . . and your flannel shirts will be too warm in summer, anyway."

Uncle Devlin shakes his head and makes a mental note to contact Professor Bender. The bathroom story sounds too fantastic to be true.

"All right, sweetie . . . I want to send that story to the publisher today. Did you say you checked it?"

"Yes . . . it was perfect, except for two missing periods and one or two typos. I left the edited printout on your desk. I really need to run now!"

She gives him a really tight hug and a long, sweet kiss, and feels something hard against her thigh.

"*Men,*" she mumbles as she skips out the door.

• • •

Almost exhausted by her day at the mall, Teresa pushes open Devlin's front door. She drops eight plastic bags, shrugs off her coat, and tosses it in the closet without bothering to put it on a hanger. It is just over an hour until sundown. She scrabbles in the bags to find the nighties she bought on sale. There are three diaphanous gowns, pink, blue and green, and three warm cotton shifts, also pink, blue and green. She stacks them and then searches for the two sets of baby doll pajamas, one with teddy bears and one with ballerinas, and a Dr. Denton sleeper with its built-in feet and rear drop-flap so she doesn't have to take it off to use the toilet in the middle of the night. She grins when she finds it, and wonders what *else* Uncle Devlin will find to do with that flap in the middle of the night.

Bags, tags and plastic wrap shush beneath her feet as she tip-toes across the living room to peek into the study. Uncle Devlin has his headset on so she knows not to interrupt. She grins, blows him a kiss and sits in the guest chair in front of his desk. He holds up a finger and points to the earpiece.

"Yes . . . yes . . . I will . . . and thank you," he says. "No . . . that's quite all right. I appreciate your candor, Professor Bender. Good-bye."

A thousand manic butterflies careen through Teresa's tummy when Uncle Devlin switches off the phone, removes the headset and glares at her. She bites her lip, slides off the chair and backs toward the door. He watches her but says nothing until she is almost out of the room.

"Teresa Luisa!"

"Oh, shit!" she mutters.

"*What?*"

"I . . . I said *shoot* . . . I forgot to lock the front door. I will be right back, OK?"

He stands, shakes his head, and her knees turn to jelly. Her heart throbs as he rounds the desk and stalks toward her. She bites a fingertip while he takes her arm and sits her in the chair.

"They . . . they must have repaired the restrooms early, Uncle Devlin."

His eyebrows arch. "Don't try that with *me,* young lady. Did you think I wouldn't check on your story?"

"No! I . . . uh . . . that's what they *told* me, Uncle Devlin! We . . . we couldn't go to class because of the repairs to the water closet."

"Oh? Professor Bender tells me that there are *three* ladies' rooms in the building, so renovations to one would scarcely have an effect on class schedules. He *also* told me of your continual inattention in class . . . *and* he mentioned that today was the deadline of his *extension* on your mid-term paper, which you should have given him two weeks ago."

"But Uncle *Devlin,* I . . . I *have* it . . . mostly!"

Devlin scowls while hot butterflies dart like tracer bullets in Teresa's tummy. "*Mostly?* As in, you have the rough draft I looked at three weeks ago?"

"*No, I* . . . I worked on it since then, I really *did.*" She wrings her fingers, blinks, then smiles. "I got some very pretty nighties at the sales. Do you want to see them?"

He sighs, then leans over the desk and presses two buttons on the telephone console. The speakerphone clicks, hums and beeps a number.

"Professor Bender's office, may I help you?"

"Elena, this is Professor O'Neill again. Sorry to bother you but. . . ."

"That's OK, Professor. Daddy's still here and I don't think he's very busy. Do you want to talk to him?"

"Please."

"Sure . . . I'll get him. Teresa was naughty again, wasn't she?"

Devlin's jaw muscles twitch. "If you would just. . . ."

"Daddy nearly had a *fit* when you told him what she did. I could hear him growling all the way out here. I'm glad it's *her* heinie that's going to. . . ."

"Elena! We're on the speakerphone. Could you please patch me through to . . . ?"

"Yes, sir . . . sorry, sir. Go ahead, please."

Teresa whimpers and bites her lip. Her bottom squirms as the speaker clicks and whirrs.

"Hello again, Professor O'Neill," the machine says.

Teresa sobs and wipes her eyes with her knuckles.

"I don't like to trouble you," Devlin says. "But you wanted to know when she came home."

"Uncle *Devlin,*" Teresa whispers.

"Indeed," Professor Bender says. "I only wished to make sure she enjoyed her day off . . . and I want to see her in my office tomorrow."

Devlin nods toward his frightened niece. "As well you should . . . but I'd like to ask if . . . were Teresa to have the assignment completed by that time . . . you might reconsider giving her a failing grade."

There is silence on the line for ten long, painful seconds. Tears well in Teresa's eyes as she stares at Devlin. Her jeans tighten across firm bottom cheeks when she wriggles. The wad of credit slips in her back pocket burns tender flesh, and she whimpers while she blinks silent pleas.

Uncle Devlin, for God's sake just spank me and get it over with! I know I was bad and I promise I won't do it anymore. Why are you even talking to him? This is so embarrassing!

Professor Bender clears his throat. "I wish I could accommodate you, Professor O'Neill . . . but Teresa's problem is ongoing and seems no closer to resolution than it was a few weeks ago. I'm afraid there must be consequences or she will learn *nothing* from her error. I mean *really* . . . telling you the school was shut because of lavatory repairs?"

"I understand perfectly, sir. One would have thought her last lesson in your office would have taught her *something,* and I truly hate to take advantage of your good nature, but if I could impose upon her the same sort of consequence as last time. . . ."

"As you said, Professor . . . her previous lesson seems to have been less than effective."

"Yes, it appears I wasn't strict enough, and I do *not* propose to be as lenient this time."

"Uncle Devlin!"

"*Hush,* Teresa."

Tears flow from her eyes. "But Uncle *Devlin!*"

"Not another *word.*" Devlin huffs and turns. "Professor Bender, I propose to punish her quite severely, and I would see it as a great personal favor if you will grade her paper as is, but deduct a suitable penalty . . . say one letter grade . . . for her tardiness in presenting it."

Another hellish silence is punctuated by Teresa's sobs.

"Very well. My office, first thing tomorrow," Bender says.

"Thank you, Professor . . . but I anticipate she will be at her task through the wee hours of the morning and I think working with a sore bottom will keep her awake. I would like to suggest that I punish her in your presence but over the phone. Will that be acceptable?"

"Uncle Devlin, *no!*"

He scowls and Teresa buries her wet face in her palms. Professor Bender chuckles.

"Justice *heard* to be done, eh?"

Uncle Devlin smiles just a little. "Exactly."

"All right. I think I know you well enough that you won't attempt any deception."

"Thank you, Professor Bender. You may rest assured I won't, but you have my permission to inspect the affected area before class tomorrow."

"I appreciate the offer . . . perhaps I will do. Please proceed."

Uncle Devlin nods to the speakerphone. "Thank you, Professor. Teresa, remove your jeans and bend over the desk."

Her heart pounds like a trip-hammer; her hand trembles as she reaches out to him; her lips move but no sound emerges. Devlin opens a drawer and takes out a 30-centimeter plastic ruler. Her eyes pop wide and she gasps.

"Nuh . . . nuh . . . *no!*"

He shakes the ruler at her. "Right *now,* Teresa Luisa . . . and tell Professor Bender everything you're doing."

"P-p-*please,* Uncle Devlin, not with a. . . ."

Devlin drops the ruler on the desktop, strides around and takes hold of her arm. She squeals as his hand collides with her tightly denimed behind a dozen times.

"Your *jeans*, Teresa."

"OK, OK! Geeze!"

Numb fingers fumble with the buttons.

"What are you doing, Teresa?"

"I am *doing* it . . . why are you . . . ?"

"Then tell *him!*"

Teresa gasps, sobs, and drags a sleeve across her eyes. "I . . . I am unbuttoning my jeans, P-Professor," she whispers.

"*Louder,* girl." Devlin swats her backside.

"Ow! This is not *fair!*"

"Teresa!"

"OK! I am un . . . unbuttoning my jeans, *OK?*"

Devlin scowls, points an index finger and jerks it forty-five degrees toward the floor. She whimpers and seesaws the snug pants down her hips. He raises his eyebrows and nods toward the speaker. She stamps her foot and bites her lip. Devlin crosses his arms and glares.

"All *right* . . . I . . . I am taking off my jeans." She looks down when he points again. "And my shoes."

She kicks off her loafers and pushes soft denim to her ankles, then steps out of the jeans and pouts at her uncle. He nods toward the desk.

"But Uncle *Devlin,*" she whispers.

He picks up the ruler and smacks his palm. Butterflies with steel-tipped wings crash about inside her tummy. She bends, rests her palms on polished oak, and sobs as the rear wedge of red string-bikini panties snugs into her cleft. The tiny wisp of material highlights more than it conceals her round cheeks. Her ear is next to the speaker and she hears Professor Bender shuffling papers.

"What are you doing, Teresa?" Devlin says.

She rubs her eyes and kicks the carpet with a cotton-socked toe. "I am bending over the desk, *OK?*"

"Don't take that tone, young lady!"

The ruler cracks the naked swell at the base of her bottom and she squeals. A sharp sting races up her loins and explodes in her bosom.

"*Ow!* I . . . I'm bending over the desk . . . sir!"

"Is you naughty bottom bare, Teresa?"

"Uncle Devlin! Owee! Nooo! I . . . I have panties on!"

Professor Bender chuckles. "Not from the sound of those last two swats. What *was* that, anyway?"

Teresa bites a fingertip and looks at the phone. "A p-plastic ruler, Professor."

"I see. Sting a bit, did it?"

"Ye-yes, sir."

"Tell Professor Bender what *sort* of panties you have on, Teresa."

"*Devlin,* nooeow! *OK!* They . . . they are bikini panties."

"And where is most of the material at the back of those panties?" Devlin raises the ruler.

Teresa moans. "In . . . in my . . . cleft," she whispers.

"That could be uncomfortable," Professor Bender says. "Perhaps you should ask your uncle to remove them."

Tears roll from her eyes. "Oh, *God!*"

"What did you say, Teresa?"

"P-*please,* Uncle Devlin?"

"Please *what?*"

"Please don't *do* this to me. I am so *ashamed.*"

Devlin nods. "As well you *should* be. But I thought you meant, please remove my panties . . . or would you rather do it yourself?"

"No! *Please,* can I . . . may I leave them *on* this time?"

"They certainly don't cover anything of consequence, but I do think you'd be more at ease without the material stuffed into your bottom crack."

She wails and yanks the flimsy underpants to her knees.

"What are you doing, Teresa?" Professor Bender says.

"I am taking the damn things *off,* if it's any of your busin*eeeow! Devlin!* Owee! Nooo!"

Devlin presses a hand to her back while he fans her squirmy behind a dozen times with the ruler. Tears pool on polished oak as the sting grows to a crisp burn.

"*What* have I told you about that sort of language, Teresa Luisa? And this certainly *is* the Professor's business!"

"Ow! Ow! Owee! I . . . ow . . . I'm *sorry! Please!*"

She whimpers as Devlin plucks tissues from a box next to the computer screen and puts them into her hand. Teresa sobs and wipes her face.

"How . . . how could you suh . . . *say* that about . . . about my *bottom crack*, Uncle Devlin?" she whispers.

"How could *you* ask to leave your panties on when I punish you, young lady? Whatever were you thinking?"

She sniffles and blows her nose. "I . . . I don't *know!*"

"That's as may be . . . but I want you to tell Professor Bender why I am about to give your bare bottom a good thrashing."

She turns teary eyes to her uncle. He glares at her and hides the ruler behind his back so she won't see his hand tremble.

"P-please, Uncle Devlin?"

"*Now*, Teresa."

"Be . . . because I fibbed to you and went . . . went shopping instead of going to class."

Devlin shakes his head. "No, Teresa. I will discuss *that* with you later. Your concern with Professor Bender is the history paper you have not yet turned in, and *that* is why he is present to witness your correction."

Teresa moans and Devlin nods toward the speaker. She sighs and wipes her eyes with the clump of tissue.

"I . . . Uncle Devlin is going to correct me be . . . because I didn't do my homework, Professor."

"That's better, Teresa. How?"

"*What?*"

"*How* will I correct you?"

"You . . . you're going to s-*spank* me."

"Where?"

"On . . . on my . . . *bottom*."

"On your . . . ?"

Shameful tears drip into Kleenex. "On my buh . . . *bare* bottom."

His left hand heats her back through a red cotton sweater and pink silk blouse. She trembles as he holds her firmly against the desk and raises the ruler. He takes a deep breath and blinks. Her heart thuds and her pert young cheeks clench and relax as she wriggles. The ruler clacks, quick and sharp, across the center of Teresa's firm, round behind.

"Owee! Not! Ow! So! Ow! Har-*ow!*"

Devlin starts at the top of her cleft and paints four-centimeter bands of sting down her bottom to its base, then begins again at the

top. His arm rises and falls like a metronome while she squeals, kicks and pounds the desktop with her fists. Professor Bender clears his throat three times while Devlin spanks the girl, and the speaker crackles as the man fidgets in his ancient, squeaky roll chair. Devlin stops after thirty-six swats, when Teresa's cheeks have turned light red. The deep divide opens and shuts as she writhes, and the tiny red panties lie in a tangle beneath her feet.

She sobs as Devlin lifts her from the desk and hugs her. Tears wet his tie while he strokes her sore fanny.

"Shh . . . almost done." He turns her toward the speaker. "I believe you have something to say to Professor Bender, Teresa."

Her lips quiver as she takes ragged breaths. "I . . . I am sorry, P-Professor Bender. I . . . I will finish the paper tonight, I promise."

Bender clears his throat once more, and the chair squeaks. "Yes . . . well . . . I certainly *hope* so, young lady. You should thank your uncle for being so persuasive in your behalf. Mind you, the paper had better be worthy of an A, and even so you only will receive a B."

"Y-yes, sir. I understand. I will do my best."

Devlin kisses her forehead. "We won't keep you any longer, then, Professor . . . and we appreciate your cooperation."

"Glad we could sort this out. Always happy to oblige when I can."

"Thank you, sir. Have a good evening."

"Good night, Professor O'Neill."

The speaker clicks. Devlin reaches over to shut off the phone, then sits in a straight-backed chair and takes her on his lap. Teresa squirms until her thighs rest on his, and then reaches back to rub her bottom with both hands while he cuddles her.

"I hated to have to do that, sweetie."

Teresa nods and leans into his hard chest. "Me too! That was the worst spanking you ever *gave* me."

"I hope you learned something this time."

"I did, Uncle Devlin. It was so *awful* to get spanked in front of him again, even if he *couldn't* see me. And why did you have to tell him all about my . . . ?"

"Shh . . . it's over now, so I can forgive you. But you have to forgive *me*, as well."

She raises her chin and he kisses her lips. "I just wish you wouldn't tell people about the state of my *panties*."

He smiles and kisses her again. "I won't."

"Thank you."

"Unless I think it necessary."

"Uncle Devlin! That is *not* very reassuring."

"Probably not . . . so the best thing *you* can do is not to put me into a position where I have to make a show of your naughty little heinie, hmm?"

He squeezes her and she pouts.

"I almost wish I *had* taken the failing grade, instead of you telling him my undies were stuffed in my crack. I thought I would *die!*"

"But you didn't . . . and now you have a second chance at the paper, and possibly even passing the course. And you *know* how unhappy I would be if you failed, sweetie. So can we let that go?"

She gives him a teary half-smile. "I get to forgive *you?*"

"Of course. Don't you want to?"

"Well . . . yes. It just seems funny . . . but OK . . . I forgive you. Can I have cold cream now?"

"May I . . . ?"

"*May* I have some?"

Devlin nods and kisses her forehead. "Do you want it before or after your spanking?"

"*What?*" She squirms and hugs his ribcage with all her strength. "But you already spanked me very *harshly.*"

"Not as badly as all *that*. The ruler weighs barely an ounce so the sting is all on the surface and should fade quickly."

She pouts at him. "Yeah, but it is *my* surface and it hurts like hell!"

"Don't be cheeky. You know you've got to be punished for fibbing to me."

"But *Devlin!*" She hides her face in his chest.

"Shh . . . come along. I'll spank you on the couch so you don't have to bend when I take you over my lap."

"You . . . you will not use that ruler?"

"No, sweetie. Now get up."

"But my bottom is so *sore!*"

She clings to his neck as he stands, cradles her in his arms and carries her to the living room. Sunset gleams through a double casement and colors low, fluffy clouds the same pink as Teresa's

fanny. Devlin smiles, rolls her onto her tummy on the sofa and goes behind the bar. He pours five ounces of merlot and two ounces of Glenfarclas and carries the glasses to the coffee table. She takes the wine and drinks half of it.

"I . . . I want cold cream before *and* after." She twists around to inspect her warm, sore behind. "I don't know *why* you are so mean to me."

He sips whisky, sets the glass down, kisses her pout and goes into the bedroom. She sighs and rubs her fanny. Quivery tingles shoot through her tummy as the sting fades. She lifts her hips and slips a finger between plump, damp labia. Wet lightening flows up her belly and into her breasts. She hears the thump of his shoes on the carpet and yanks both hands to her bottom.

"Teresa? Are you all right? Why were you whimpering?"

"I . . . um . . . it hurts *real* bad."

Devlin sits, uncaps the Pond's jar and draws her across his lap. "I don't think it's quite *that* awful, sweetie. I'll put a *little* on before I punish you. You know how much it stings when your bottom is damp."

She moans when his fingers, slick with cold cream, caress overheated cheeks. Wet lightening strikes anew when she squirms her vagina against his thigh. Hard nipples burn beneath a skimpy bra and she bites her finger to stifle a squeal. He massages the quivery mounds while laser bolts flash through her brain. She jerks, twists, screams and grabs his neck. He holds her tightly as she pants and trembles through the aftershocks.

"My *goodness*, sweetie!"

Teresa swallows hard and takes a deep breath. "Guh-goodness had nothing to *do* with it."

He laughs, kisses her and puts her across his thighs. "I have no doubt of *that*, you naughty girl. But since you have it all out of your system, perhaps you will pay attention while I spank you for fibbing to me and skipping class, hmm?"

"But I won't *do* it anymore, I *promise*. You already spanked me real *hard* and *oweee!*"

Toes pound sofa cushion while he slaps her achy behind. Ruler sting reawakens and he drives it deep inside. Her vagina throbs with remembered pleasure and she tries to focus there, but gives up and shrieks as his palm claps, over and over, and fans a blaze

that burns away her guilt. His hand goes numb and he stops. Shrieks turn to piteous wails as he scoops her up and cuddles her for ten long, slow minutes. He caresses her scorched bottom while salty repentance wets his tie, then he lays her down and spreads big dollops of cream across crimson handprints. She moans and pushes her rear cheeks higher so he can coat the deep inner surfaces.

"Mmm . . . th-thank you, Uncle Devlin."

"You're welcome, sweetie. Now you've already had your fun for this evening so go put on your pajamas and some slippers and get to work."

"But, *Devlin!*"

He picks her up and kisses her. "Don't argue with me or I'll start over."

"*No!* Won't you just put your fingers . . . ?"

"Shh . . . all I will do right now is forgive you for being so naughty about the shopping trip . . . but I'll help you with your paper as much as I can."

Teresa huffs and then kisses his lips. "OK . . . but I am *hungry.*"

"I'll make supper while you get set up at the computer. You brought the paper on disk, didn't you?"

"Yeah."

"Then get started while I see what there is to eat."

"Very *well* . . . but you are very silly if you think I can work when I am this *horny.*"

"Teresa!"

She giggles, kisses him again then jumps off his lap and runs to the bedroom. He sighs and finishes his whisky while she stands at the open door and puts on a flimsy blue nightgown.

A HOT DAY IN TUSCANY

Tuscany is the longest, five or six pages, and by far the most detailed of Teresa's story starts. The *I/you* point of view and her fondness for and familiarity with the setting make it very personal and provocative.

I love the hot, lazy summer days and nights in Italy, with long siestas while the shutters are closed to keep the heat out. Devlin lives in California, where they have air conditioners in the houses, which is very comfortable, I suppose, but for me the idea of making love in an ancient villa during siesta is very stimulating. Just to look at such a home at that time of day brings erotic scenes to my mind . . . . light lunch with salad, *frutti di mare,* iced melon and chilled *vino rosato* . . . sultry looks across the table while outside life seems to have come to a halt.

There is silence in the garden and in the streets. You look at me and realize that I am probably the only source of restlessness in the whole neighborhood. I am not able to find a comfortable position on my chair because I am still sore from the punishment you gave me only two hours earlier. Not even spankings take place during siesta time. It is an appropriate activity for the mornings,

or for after dinner in the case of an erotic spanking. You give me a wicked smile while you sip your wine.

"Are you ready for cold cream now, sweetie?"

I am glaring at you because I think you really overreacted when you punished me for canceling my dentist appointment last month. You know how much I hate going to the dentist, so a simple spanking would have been enough.

It is a mystery how I could do something stupid like this and think you would never find out, but at that time it *seemed* to be a good idea. I called at the dentist's office, telling them that I am your secretary and that you asked me to cancel the appointments for Teresa Wagner because she went home for the rest of the summer. It was so easy! And then I told you everything was fine with my teeth and you had no reason to doubt it. However, when you did my quarterly bills this morning you could not find the statement from the dentist. When you called them to check, the whole miserable story came out. I blush furiously when the morning's scenes come rushing back to me.

• • •

"Teresa Luisa! I want to see you in my study *now*. "

I was reading my e-mails but something in your voice told me that it would be wise to follow your kind invitation immediately. The look on your face when I entered the room made me hurry even *more*. You pointed at the chair in front of your desk and I sat down.

"We need to talk about your visit to the dentist last month."

"Yes, Uncle Devlin . . . but *why?*"

"As I recall, you told me everything was fine."

"It . . . it *was*. Why are you asking?"

You frowned when I gave you a puzzled look. "Come here."

The tone of this simple command made me wince, and then it dawned on me that something had gone terribly *wrong*. I walked to your side of the desk, already shielding my bottom with both hands.

"Young lady, you are in enough trouble so don't make it worse by continuing to lie. I want you to tell me why you never went to the dentist, and I want the *whole* story, is that clear?"

When you said *lie* the tears began welling up in my eyes.

"I . . . I am sorry, Uncle Devlin, I didn't *mean* to be bad, only . . . I was so *afraid* of the dentist . . . and I thought it wouldn't hurt anyone if I told a little white lie."

"There is no such *thing* as a little white lie, at least not in your case. I can't *believe* you pulled a stunt like this. What am I to do with you?"

"*Please* not a spanking! It didn't seem so bad to me until you *said* it. I won't do it again, I promise!"

"I think you're right, Teresa. Just a spanking won't do."

I was surprised that you gave in so easily, but then I realized you had said *just* a spanking, and my tears of sorrow changed to tears of fearfulness!

"What . . . what do you mean, Uncle Devlin? What are you going to *do* to me?"

You held out your hands and I hesitated for a long time before I sat on your lap. Usually I feel so safe when I am sitting there, because you are protecting me, but today my guiltiness would not let me feel protected, and that made me cry even harder. You hugged me while I cried, and softly patted my bottom, but that only made things *worse*. And *then* you announced what you were intending to do, and I thought I would faint!

"You have been a *very* bad girl so I have to be very strict with you."

I was trying to speak, but I could not because of my crying, and because of those horrible butterflies that always awaken in my tummy when I know you are going to punish me. They are sometimes not so bad, when I only have been a little naughty, like if I am merely impertinent to you, but I know that you think lying is very wicked and so the butterflies in this case were almost *painful* to me. I wanted to tell you how sorry I was and to beg your forgiveness, but the words were stuck in my throat. You were holding me tightly so I heard everything you said yet I could not believe you were *saying* it.

"Teresa, we will go into the bathroom where I will wash all the lies out of your pretty mouth, and then you will receive a very big enema to clean you out completely."

And you were saying that so *calmly*, Uncle Devlin! As if you were telling me that we would go to a nice restaurant and afterward

to a film, instead of announcing that you intended to give me the most embarrassing punishment I could imagine! How could you be *doing* that to me? Somehow I found the ability to speak, or at least to scream, but you did not care in the least that I was kicking and trying to get away from you . . . you merely stood up and carried me to the bathroom. My face was *so* red, and the tears *would* keep coming from my eyes while I was glaring at you, but you put me down in front of the big mirror over the basin so that I could see that my face was in *such* a state!

I was wiping the tears away while you were getting some things from the cabinet, and I thought if I could just get back to the bedroom, take off all of my clothes and lie down on the big bed, that you would see me naked and ready to make love, and perhaps you might change your mind regarding all those horrible things you said. Yes, Uncle Devlin, I know that those were silly thoughts, but you must understand that you were frightening me very much, and I did *not* like the look on your handsome face *or* that awful enema bag you were taking out of the cabinet.

"Where do you think you're going, Teresa?"

You did not even look at me when you said that, but I was standing very still while I was only halfway out the door. My heart was pounding and I could not move my feet.

"It . . . it is almost lunchtime, and . . . and I only wanted to see if Maria has come with the shopping, and um . . . would you like a nice glass of port before lunch, Uncle Devlin? P-perhaps we could lie down for a bit and have a glass of port in bed before lunch. It is already so warm out so I *know* you would like that."

My heart was pounding even harder when you turned around and looked at me.

"It is only ten-thirty and Maria never arrives before twelve, you know that. Now come here."

There was a warm breeze blowing through the bathroom window high up on the wall, and it made my cotton dress begin to flutter. I was shivering in spite of the summer heat and I wrapped my arms over my breasts while I inhaled the scent of orange blossoms and oregano. Signora Portallo must have been cutting herbs from her porch garden across the way. I was beginning to regret that I did not put on a bra, and I was wearing only the smallest of pink bikini panties underneath my cream-colored dress with the

violets on it, so I already was feeling almost naked and *very* vulnerable. Then you pulled the vanity chair beside the basin and crooked your finger at me.

"Uncle Devlin, *please? I promise* I will never do this again."

"Teresa Luisa!"

New tears flowed down my cheeks while I was shuffling across the ancient tiles and then sitting on your lap. You were leaning over the basin and dribbling water and hand-soap onto a face flannel, and also ignoring my pitiful whimpers and the pleading looks I gave to you. I could not believe my eyes when you wrapped a hand towel like a bib around my neck!

"You won't *really* wash my mouth with soap, will you?"

"When my girl fibs to me I am forced to be very stern. Now open your mouth. If you behave yourself this will only take a minute."

Oh, *God*, it was horrible! You were holding tight to my shoulders while you pushed that soapy cloth into my mouth! It tasted so *nasty*, Uncle Devlin! I was gurgling and kicking my feet and trying to spit the cloth out of my mouth, but you just kept on scrubbing my teeth and my tongue and my lips, and all the time you kept *shushing* me and telling me to be a *good* girl. How could I be a good girl when you were doing something so *awful* to me? And I was *trying* to get away but you were holding me so tight, and that soap tasted *terrible*, and I was almost *gagging* with that nasty taste, and then you were pushing me over the basin so I could spit it all out.

Then you were petting me and rubbing my back, and I don't know where the bottle of Evian water came from but you were pouring it into my mouth, and I was just spitting and spitting and *spitting* all that icky, awful soap into the basin, and also *crying* because I was feeling very, very sorry for myself. Then you were putting me back on your lap and hugging me.

"Here, sweetie. Swish this in your mouth and spit it out. You'll feel better."

I was glaring at you but I took the little plastic bottle of Scope and put half of it into my mouth. It burned, but most of the soap taste went away when I leaned over to spit it into the basin, and then you made me rinse with the rest of it, and spit it all out.

"Th-thank you, Uncle Devlin, but you were very mean to *do* that to me."

"You were very mean to *fib* to me."

"But I said I was *sorry*. Why can you not forgive me?"

You smiled but you were shaking your head. "Because you haven't been punished yet."

"Nooo! I mean *yes* . . . you *did* punish me! That was so *nasty* and . . . it was so . . . Uncle Devlin, you cannot *possibly* be intending to punish me even *more*. I promise I will be good forever and I will never, *ever* lie to you again. Can't you just . . . ?"

I sighed when you covered my mouth with your lips, but I also was cringing because I *knew* you could taste the soap. Why did you *do* that when you know how much I enjoy your kisses? I will bet you did it to embarrass me, because what you did *next* certainly did!

"All right, sweetie. Stand up so I can take off your clothes."

"Uncle Devlin, *please?*"

"Right *now*, Teresa Luisa! Or do you want a spanking *before* your enema?"

"Don't do *that!* I mean . . . yes *spank* me, but don't give me a . . . a . . . just *don't*, please?"

You were so *awful* to me then! You made me stand and lift up my arms so you could pull my dress over my head, and you would not even let me cover my bosom with my hands, but told me to hold my arms at my sides so you could admire my breasts! Uncle Devlin, I may be only nineteen years of age but I know you well enough to realize that it is not my *breasts* you admire when I am naked. You were saying that only to embarrass me further, which you *did*. Sometimes I think the only reason you touch my breasts at *all* is because you know I enjoy it when you touch me *anywhere*, and that you would much rather be caressing my bottom than wasting time on my breasts. Well, it is the truth, and I have just spent a very long, very embarrassing morning learning to tell the truth, so you will just have to live with that!

I know that was very much beside the point, but I really do *not* want to think about what happened next. Even though I was hoping that my sad green eyes and my contrite attitude would have persuaded you not to punish me further, I was *very* much mistaken. You were scolding me all the while you were pulling off my panties; you were scolding me when you were leading me to the bathtub; you were scolding me because I was whimpering when

you were making me to kneel on the bath mat and push my behind up while I lay my head on the mat. Then you made me spread out my legs so that my bottom would be open for your inspection! It is just *terrifying* for a girl to show the insides of her cleft to *anyone,* Uncle Devlin! That is such a very private place and you just *looked* in there for such a long time that I thought I was going to die from shame!

"I will be only a moment, sweetie. Try to relax."

Then you merely walked away and left me naked, kneeling with my bottom open and vulnerable, while you mixed warm water and glycerin in that big rubber bag! I watched you through of blur of shameful tears, and even heard you *humming* while you were doing it. And you were putting such an *enormous* amount of water in the bag I just turned my head away and shut my eyes. I wanted so badly to get up and run . . . run across the lane to Signora Portallo's house, but I was naked and you *made* me naked, naked and *ashamed,* and even if I *had* gone running to her, I could not tell her why I was naked because she is such a good Christian woman she might have given me a switching herself for lying to you, like she did to Antonia the other evening.

Poor, *poor* Antonia! She is not a big girl for twenty-three years, but she is so plump behind that you would not think a slender olive twig would cause her to yell so loudly. No, I think I was behaving wisely not to run to Signora Portallo. If she would be switching her daughter so harshly merely for coming in half an hour late the night before, what would she do to *me* if she found out what *I* had done? Of course these thoughts did not help me to relax, but at least I was not thinking about what *you* were going to do to my bottom!

That is why I squealed and jerked my head up when you were kneeling down beside me and patting my heinie, Uncle Devlin. I was merely *surprised.*

"Shh. It's all right, sweetie. It will be over soon and you will be my good girl again."

"But I want to be your good girl *now,* and it is so *embarrassing* when you do this to me! I . . . I would much rather have a spanking! Will you . . . could you give me a spanking instead? I promise I will behave myself and not complain! I will be your good girl while you spank me very hard, but please don't put that awful thing in my bottom, *please?*"

Then my heart nearly melted because you *smiled*. You have such a lovely smile, and your whole face lights up when you are doing it.

"I will spank you *very* hard . . . right after your enema."

My melted heart froze at that moment and I thought that it would *stop*.

"Uncle Devlin, *no!* You *can't* . . . you *won't*. How can you be so *cruel* to me?"

"Hush, Teresa. I am *never* cruel to you, no matter how hard I spank you, but now I must purge all the lies from you . . . so lean forward and put your head down on the mat so I can apply some Vaseline to your bottom hole."

Geeze, Uncle Devlin, you did it *again*. It was just your smooth, deep, gentle voice, but you were telling me such horrible things! Why do you *do* that? I shut my eyes tightly, but that did not stop the tears from coming because you were reaching inside my cheeks and smearing slippery stuff all around my *anus*. Yes, Uncle Devlin . . . girls have *anuses*, not *bottom holes!* It is so *embarrassing* when you call it that. But I think you already *know* this and that's why you say it to me. Well, I hope you are proud of yourself because you *did* embarrass me very, very *much*. And *then* you put your finger inside of me!

I really do not mind so awfully much if you do this when we are in bed together, but when it is the middle of the day and you are doing it to punish me it is *horrible*. You make me feel so *exposed* when you do this. So I do not understand why you complain when I am squirming while you have your finger in there.

"Teresa, be *still*. The enema nozzle will go in much more easily if you are fully lubricated. Now stop being so naughty."

"But it is *nasty*."

"It isn't . . . and I see from the condition of your vagina that *some* part of you finds my finger anything *but* nasty."

"*Noooo!*"

But of course you were right, and I was being even sillier when I tried to close my legs so you could not see how wet I was down there. Yes, I know better and I should not have been surprised when you pulled your finger out of my anus and proceeded to spank me, but it really did *hurt*, Uncle Devlin, even though you did not spank very hard. The skin of my bottom was stretched so very

tightly because you had me bent over nearly in half, and I was already so *sensitive* from being impaled on your finger.

I did not *intend* to scream that loudly while you spanked me, or try to keep my legs together afterward when you were pushing them apart again, but I truly did *not* want for you to see how much *that* part of my body seems to enjoy what you are doing when you punish me. It is simply not *fair* that my body betrays me in this way!

"Teresa Luisa, behave yourself or I will get the hairbrush *right now.*"

"*Please,* Uncle Devlin! I . . . I *will* be good! Not the hairbrush, *please?*"

"All right, then . . . keep still while I put the nozzle into your bottom hole."

God, how I hate those words! And how much I wanted to rub the stinging from my behind, but you put your hand on my back and pushed me forward while you slid that cold *plastic* thing inside of me. It didn't hurt but it was so *awful* when it went in. It is such a helpless feeling for a girl, when she is naked and bending over like that and a man is looking inside her bottom! I heard the click of the little clamp and felt the first gush of warmth.

"Puh-*please?*"

"Please what, sweetie?"

"Please do not put very much in? I . . . I think that is *enough.* You . . . you can stop now because I am very sorry I lied to you and . . . and my tummy is very full *now,* so *please?*"

I looked over my shoulder and you smiled *again.* You leaned over to kiss me, all the while your hand was on my bottom, holding that awful hose so that I could not push it *out.* I whimpered as I was kissing you, but you were merely pushing down on my back so that my bottom was higher in the air!

"Don't worry, Teresa . . . it's only a liter. You can easily take it all."

"Nuh-*noooo.*"

You were leaning over me with your arm wrapped around my waist, and your hand was rubbing my tummy while it filled up with water. I moaned, not from the cramps inside me, but from the fact that your fingers were so *very* far from my wet pussy and I wanted so *very* much for you to touch me there, but you would not, and I whimpered with frustration.

"Shh . . . don't wriggle so much . . . we're nearly done. I'll just squeeze the bag so every drop goes in, all right?"

"But I . . . you . . . yeeeek!"

And you *did* squeeze every drop into me! Then you slid the nozzle out of my anus and pushed your thumb against it to help me hold the water while you were pulling me up onto my feet. My tummy was gurgling and sloshing, and I was moaning while you walked me toward the toilet and made me sit on it. I looked up at you with pleading eyes and you were smiling and turning toward the door, so that I thought you were leaving me in privacy to release the nasty water, but you were merely picking up the bag and taking it to the basin!

I could not wait any longer, and even though you were still in the room I covered my eyes in shame and let the water splash into the bowl! But I am grateful that the owners have at least installed a modern commode so that I did not have to reach up and pull a rusty chain such as are found in some of the villas, and I flushed several times before I felt empty. You were very kind and did not make a large production, but only sprayed the deodorizer mist discreetly while your back was turned to me.

"Are you feeling better now?"

"Yuh-yes, Uncle Devlin, and I . . . I am no longer naughty at *all*. The lies have been completely purged from my body!"

I was reaching for the roll of paper when you turned around.

"No, Teresa. Stand up and I will wash you."

My mouth dropped open and I stared at you because I could not *believe* you were saying this to me. "Uncle Devlin, *please?* I can do it *myself*."

You crossed the room and took my hand. "Yes, but if I am to spank your bottom I wish it to be as clean as possible. Now stand up like I told you."

"But it is so *shameful* that you will wash me that way . . . and . . . and you cannot *possibly* intend to give me a spanking after you . . . *no!*"

"*Hush*, Teresa."

Your palms felt very cool when you took hold of my hot hands, and then you pulled me toward the basin. I felt so soiled and so embarrassed when you were making me bend over the vanity table next to the basin. You took a warm, wet cloth and washed the

cheeks of my behind, and then spread them wide apart so that you could wash all the insides. Tears were dripping from my eyes and perspiration was running down my forehead, but you were being so gentle with me that I was whining and whimpering only a little.

But you made me to stay bending over while you were wetting a towel with cool water, and then sitting me on your lap when you sat on the vanity chair. I was squirming my sore, bare bottom on the slick linen of your trousers as you were bathing my face, my neck, my back, my thighs with the cool towel. You were kissing me when you were sliding the towel across my bosom, but the towel was no longer cool, or perhaps my breasts made the towel hot, because my nipples were *burning*. They were so hard that each time you touched me there a burst of flame was shooting down between my legs. I wanted to tell you to stop this but I could not!

"Duh-Devlin?"

"What is it, sweetie?"

"I . . . I love you."

"I love you, too . . . very much."

"Then . . . you will not spank me?"

You kissed me once more but you were smiling, as if I had said something funny!

"I spank you *because* I love you."

"Nooo!"

I was hugging your neck very hard while I was weeping into your shirt, then you picked me up and carried me into the bedroom while I was trying to tell you how very *wrong* it was to spank me after the awful things you had *already* done to my poor bottom, but you *ignored* me. I was wriggling and weeping because I did *not* want you to sit on the bed and put me over your lap, and I most certainly did *not* want you to reach over and pick up the hairbrush from the nightstand, but that is what you were doing, and it was so *unfair*.

"Hush, sweetie, *please*. I can barely understand a word you're saying and you know it would make no difference anyway. You told me a fib and your naughty heinie must pay the penalty."

"No, *please*, not with the hairbrush!"

"You are going to be a very sorry little girl in a few minutes, but you know you deserve this."

"Nooweeeee!"

And with one quick swat, that awful, nasty, hard hairbrush stung my fanny like a *hornet*. I was kicking and beating on the duvet with my hands while you were leaning your arm into my back to hold me, and my bottom was sticking so high up in the air, and it felt so horribly vulnerable, and the hairbrush was stinging it even *more*.

"Will you ever lie to me again, Teresa Luisa?"

"No! Ow! Never! Aiee! Please! Yow! Devleek! Not! Aiee! So! Eeek! *Hard!*"

The hairbrush was swatting my fanny and setting it on *fire*, but *you* did not mind. You merely continued *scolding* me!

"When you know you must go to the dentist. . . ."

"Yeeeowch!"

"Or the doctor. . . ."

"Haieee!"

"Or to class. . . ."

"Neeauuu!"

"Or do your homework. . . ."

"Aieeooo!"

"Or anything *else* you know you're supposed to do. . . ."

"Nahhahaowooo!"

"Will you ever! Ever! *Ever* tell me you did it when you *didn't?*"

"Neeeek! Neeooo! *No*, Uncle Devlin, I swear to *God* I won't!"

But you were *still* not satisfied, because you continued to spank me with that horrible brush, even though my bottom was already *burning*, and it was swelling up to *twice* its size, and I was screaming and kicking and begging for you to *stop*. It was like a thousand angry bees stinging me all at once, and I was bouncing on your lap, and then, finally, when I was thinking that you would spank me *forever*, you *did* stop.

"Shhh . . . it's all right, sweetie."

Suddenly you had your arms around me, and my sore, achy, *fiery* bottom was on your lap, and you were handing me bunches of tissue to wipe away the tears, and I wanted so *badly* to tell you how sorry I was, but I could not, for all the sobs that issued from my throat. Still, I think you knew what I was trying to say because you were kissing me and softly caressing the bitter sting that *you* put in my fanny! So I merely gave up and cried into your neck while you were holding me close. Your hand was so comforting on

my heinie, and your strong arms made me feel so safe and so loved, why did you feel the need to say what you said *next?* Once more, you were not being *fair* to me.

"Blow your nose and then go stand in the corner."

"Uncle *Devlin!* You cannot *mean* that! You have blistered my behind until I cannot sit *down* and I . . . I want cold cream! You cannot *possibly* . . . !"

I was blinking away tears and looking into your beautiful blue eyes, but they were still looking at me as sternly as they did when you took me into the bathroom, so I was sobbing as I buried my face in your shoulder. You caressed my scorched bottom for a few more precious seconds before you lifted me off your lap and pushed me into the corner by the chest of drawers. I was whimpering and stomping my foot, but you merely smoothed my disheveled hair and kissed my neck.

"Now I want you to stay here until lunch and think about what you did to deserve your punishment."

"But I *hate* standing in the corner! It . . . it is so *childish.*"

"Yes, because you *behaved* like a child . . . a very *naughty* child."

"Nooo . . . can't I . . . can't I think about it somewhere *else?*"

"Teresa, do you remember last winter when I had to punish you in Professor Bender's office . . . and then just a few days later, I had to repeat that punishment when he was on the speaker phone?"

More tears gushed from my eyes as I took deep breaths and wondered why you were bringing *that* up.

"Um . . . yes, Uncle Devlin. I . . . I remember it very well."

"Do you remember *why* you were punished?"

"Be . . . because I did not finish my History assignment, but I *always* did my homework after that because I *learnt* my lesson, honestly I did, and. . . ."

"I had to punish you *twice* for the same assignment, though, didn't I?"

"Yeh-yes, sir."

"And do you remember why I spanked you again *after* I spanked you the second time for missing that assignment?"

Why were you making me tell you that? You were being so cruel to me that I do not understand it, so I was pouting *very* hard when I finally answered.

"Be . . . because I said that the school was shut for repairs."

"And *was* it?"

I was barely able to whisper the words. "No. Sir."

"So, when you went shopping instead of to your class, you told me a . . . ?"

You said nothing further and I turned sad, weepy eyes to you. I truly, sincerely did *not* want to say what you wanted to hear, but I knew that I must.

"I . . . I told you a fib, Uncle Devlin." You were nodding your head and that made me angry. "But you already *spanked* me for this and it is not fair to. . . ."

A low groan came from my lips when you put your finger over them.

"Yes . . . and then I made you stand in the corner afterward, didn't I?"

"No, you only. . . ." Then I gasped. "*Yes* . . . yes, you . . . oh, God!" And then I whispered, "No, Uncle Devlin."

You were nodding again and I was squirming my feet upon the cool tiles.

"I'm not sure *why* I didn't, but obviously it was a mistake, so I don't want to hear another word out of your pretty mouth about standing in the corner. You will stand here for as long as I say, and you will *not* rub your bottom while you are doing it, is that clear?"

"But this is not *fair* to make me *ouch!*"

And then you were very kind because you rubbed a *little* of the sting from the harsh spank you delivered to my sore fanny, but I did not like the look in your eyes when I turned to glance over my shoulder.

"Face the corner, Teresa. I believe I just heard Maria come in with the shopping, so I will go and see about lunch . . . but I will check back from time to time and make sure you are where you're supposed to be. *And* I will leave the hairbrush out, in case I catch you rubbing your behind."

I was huffing and whimpering and crying, but you did not mind at *all*. You merely gave my heinie a soft squeeze that made me groan, and then turned around to walk away!

"Uh-Uncle Devlin? What . . . what if Maria is to come past the bedroom door? She will *see*. . . ."

"She will see that my naughty girl has got what is coming to her

. . . but I will make sure she stays in the kitchen while she prepares our meal. Now put your nose in the corner and *behave* yourself."

It was so *awful* to stand in that corner, Uncle Devlin! But I *did* try to be good, just like you *told* me. Meanwhile, I listened for your footsteps on the tiles because even though I was doing what you said and *not* rubbing my bottom, I was a bit concerned that you might think that rubbing something *else* that needed very badly to be rubbed could be considered naughtiness by some people, and I truly did *not* want anymore of that hairbrush! It makes my heinie simply *burn,* and then the burning somehow is transferred between my thighs, so I was leaning my hot forehead against the cool, ancient wall while I made myself feel better. Is that so wrong?

When you looked into the bedroom, I was merely wiping moisture from my face with tissues, so there is no reason to tell you what sort of moisture I was wiping away from *other* places. Then, *finally,* you came and told me to get dressed for lunch.

• • •

My bottom still stings and your suggestion of cold cream sounds *heavenly.* I snap back to reality and see that you are still looking at me, slightly amused. Maria watches me over her shoulder as she is carrying away our plates.

"Um . . . yes, Uncle Devlin. Cold cream would be very nice before we lie down for siesta. You . . . you are not still angry with me, are you?"

But you are smiling and my heart is fluttering.

"No, sweetie. I am never angry with you, but you know I have to punish you sometimes, even though neither of us likes it."

I am pouting while I nibble the last of the chilled melon, because I believe that now *you* are fibbing! "You did not *like* to put the enema nozzle in my anus, Uncle Devlin?"

Your mouth is very wide as you are glancing toward Maria's broad back, but she merely scrapes the dishes while you are coughing. "Teresa! Why do you *say* such things at the table?"

You drink from your glass of *vino rosato* and lick your lips. I look at you with my eyes very wide as I am trying not to smile, because you are blushing!

"I was only wondering. Did you not enjoy . . . ?"

"Teresa Luisa . . . *enough.*"

I am afraid perhaps that I have pushed the joke too far because your voice sounds very ominous, so I lower my chin and bite my lip while I am blinking my green eyes at you. I am smiling, however, because you are shaking your head and looking at the ceiling.

"Was I being naughty, Uncle Devlin?" I whisper.

You look at me as your lip is quivering, then you chuckle. "You *know* you were."

"Then . . . then you should send me to bed."

Your chair legs scrape on the tiles as you push away from the table and take my hand. I stand up and lean against you as you are looking toward Maria.

"Signora, you need not return this evening to prepare our meal. We will dine out instead."

She is turning around. "OK, *Signor Professore.* I shall be making the luncheon tomorrow, yes?"

You are nodding your head. "Of course . . . the *frutti di mare* today was delicious. Perhaps you could prepare that cold pasta salad with cheese I like so much."

"OK, *Professore!* No problem."

"*Grazie, Signora. Buona siesta.*"

"*Buona siesta, Professore . . . signorina. Ciao!*"

Maria hums softly as she does the washing up, and we walk hand in hand toward the bedroom. I have no panties on under my dress, so that the warm wind blows through the open arches of the portico and up my skirt where it plays with my bare behind like soft fingers. I sigh from such a tingly feeling in my sore bottom, all the while I am imagining how wonderful your very real fingers will be feeling in only a short time.

You close the door behind us, shutting out the light, the sounds, the reality of the outside world. There are only the two of us now, safe in our bedroom universe. The wide-bladed fan on the ceiling high above is the only thing that stirs the warm, dark air. Your skin feels damp when I open your shirt and rub my fingers through the thick hair on your chest. I am looking up into your eyes as you lean down to kiss me.

I sigh deeply as we lick each other's tongues. Your mouth tastes of melon and wine. You reach down and raise the hem of my dress

in order to stroke away the achy hotness from my bottom, but then you lift your head to look once more into my eyes.

"Where are your undies, sweetie?"

"Devlin!" I am pouting *very* hard. "You have spanked my poor heinie so hard that it is much too sore to be wearing any silly *undies* on it! Sir!"

You are chuckling as you pull my dress above my head and throw it toward the bureau. It floats in the thick air like a kite and then falls in a puffy heap on top of the wooden chest.

"Are you being impertinent, young lady?"

I am smiling as I look up at you. "Well . . . perhaps a *little*, but it is time for siesta and you would not spank me *now*, would you? It is much too warm and languid a time . . . besides which you must be very tired from all of the punishment you gave to me this morning."

"Perhaps, perhaps . . . in any case, you're right that it is too warm for that sort of exertion."

You are grinning as I remove your shirt and begin to unfasten your trousers.

"I am happy you agree with me, Uncle Devlin . . . but is it too warm for *other* sorts of exertion?"

The trousers fall into a heap at your ankles and you are kicking them off along with your sandals. Your eyes grow wide as you hug and kiss me, then you wrap your arm around me and pat my sore fanny as we walk to the bed.

"What *sorts* of exertion, Teresa?"

"Well . . . you know. Those sorts we have when we no longer pretend that you are my uncle."

I am almost floating when I throw back the quilt and lie on the cool, crisp sheet. Your penis waves free when you push down your shorts, and now you are stretching out beside me. I turn and cuddle into your chest. It rumbles beneath my fingers as you moan.

"I understand perfectly, sweetie. We ceased to be related the moment we got into bed."

"OK . . . but you will still be my *pretend* uncle forever after, won't you?"

You nod and kiss my lips. Our moist, hot bodies touch and I slowly stroke your neck and shoulder while your erection glows like a heat lamp against my tummy. What little is happening does

so in slow motion, like in a movie. My eyes close because the warmth is making me so sleepy I cannot keep them open, but now you are moving away from me and I am whimpering!

"Devlin?"

"It's all right . . . I'm only getting the cold cream for your poor little heinie."

Suddenly I am awake and scurrying toward you. "But Devlin, I want to. . . ."

"Shh . . . be still. Lie on your side and I'll hold you while I spread cream on your bottom."

"Oh! Oh, yes! Yes, *hold* me, Devlin."

And you push your left arm beneath my neck to cradle it while you are pulling me close to you. The stiffness between your legs is burning against my tummy once again. I shudder with delight as your firm hand caresses cool moistness over my sore cheeks, and takes away the ache and sting. You dip more cold cream and I gasp as your fingers slide inside my cleft. I kiss you urgently while your fingertip finds the rosebud deep within and now I am lifting my left leg up and over your thigh so the finger can slide *inside* me.

A bright, quivering charge of electricity pulses through my bottom and your tongue is licking my lips while I moan. Now, as if you are under water, you move your body a little ways down the bed, and as you slide back up toward me I gasp because your rod is slipping between the wet folds of my pussy!

More and more deeply the hot hardness fills my soft, clinging wetness, while all the time your finger pushes farther and farther into the smooth tightness between my cheeks. My head spins as you impale me from both directions and I want so badly to shriek my pleasure, but the air feels so thick around me that I cannot utter a sound. You pull back your finger the tiniest bit and my bottom follows the motion, as if it has a mind all its own, and then, when you push the finger back in, my hips thrust forward and I slide even farther onto your stiffness.

My arms tremble as I clutch your neck, and you moan into my ear while your member throbs inside me. I feel the strong, steady beat of your heart against my bosom, the tingly pulse of your finger in my bottom, and the hot, insistent fullness of you inside my vagina. No longer can I tell where *I* end and *you* begin. We float in a distant universe, but there is only one of us. I lie for

hours, days, weeks, within this universe, and then your arm moves against my neck.

Without a spoken word, I know what you wish me to do. You roll onto your back and I roll along with you, as if I am a piece of you, like your hand, your foot, your sweet mouth. My legs spread wide, just as you silently tell them to do, and a gasp comes from our lips. Our penis slides farther into us when we sit on top of it. As slowly as the tides, we retreat with our hips while stars and moons swirl about our head, then just as slowly we return together, and the stars and moons quiver and flash before our eyes while our hot member searches the depths of our moistness.

Somewhere in the distance, we feel the tingling of our finger in our bottom, like a trumpet counterpoint to a glorious brass choir. The horns wail their angelic chorus in our ears, and lilt, soar, arch toward their crescendo. Like molten lava piling against an earthen dam, the heat and the ecstatic pressure are building as we move our hips. Higher and higher it builds, until the earth can hold no more and the dam bursts asunder in a fiery wave of shuddery bliss.

The final, triumphant chord echoes in my head as I cover your wet face with kisses. Slow, massive after-quakes are quivering through our bodies while we moan in perfect bass and soprano harmony. You hold me as if you never will let go, and I squeal each time you flex the last precious droplets of yourself into me.

I watch you fall asleep, rest my head on your shoulder and shut my eyes.

THE OFFICE ASSISTANT

Office Assistant is really two stories that began with e-mail conversations and prompted Teresa's story starts. I included portions of the e-mails, which accounts for the unusually long speeches. The college referred to here is one we invented to fulfill our strict professor and naughty schoolgirl fantasies. Teresa named it Red Blossom College, a delightfully apt and evocative designation.

Teresa looks across the breakfast dishes at Uncle Devlin. His side of the table is covered with printouts of letters sent by fans after he published the first Teresa story last week.

"A lot of people enjoyed reading your story, Uncle Devlin. I am *so* proud of you, you know."

"Thanks, sweetie. I'm pleased that so many people out there agree with my methods of raising and educating young girls."

Teresa blushes as she walks around to sit on his lap. Her bottom squirms and she grins. Even though she does not always agree with his methods, which seem terribly old-fashioned sometimes, she cannot deny that she benefits from them in more ways than one.

"You will need an assistant to answer all those letters, Uncle Devlin. I didn't like your suggestion of my working at a hairbrush factory . . . the idea of getting spanked for test purposes is *not* very appealing! How could you ever *think* of something horrible like this! But you are right . . . I need to find a way to earn some extra money if you don't raise my monthly allowance. You know that a hundred Euros is ridiculous! Perhaps I could help you with your office work a few hours a week? I promise to look up all the new words in the dictionary, and you can proofread the letters before I send them out. *Please?* It would be so much fun!"

Uncle Devlin can't help but smile when she looks at him with big, pleading eyes. "All right . . . I'll think about it. But you would have to work hard and I will punish you if you mess up. We'll talk about this later. I really need to get some work done now, so off you go." He gives her bottom a loving smack and she gets up.

"OK . . . if you are busy this morning I will go shopping. I need a few new panties anyway." She hugs him from behind, presses her breasts against his back and kisses his cheek. "See you later, Uncle Devlin! Oh . . . may I have your golden Visa card? And don't adopt another niece when you answer your fan mail . . . I have no *idea* how you would be able to cope with another cyber brat! Ciao!"

Devlin takes a deep breath, drops his pen and turns. "Sweetie, *what* are you doing?"

Teresa bites her lip. "Only getting your credit card, Uncle Devlin. I have to buy. . . ."

He sighs. "Put it back in the wallet."

She pouts, jams the card behind his driver's license and then glares at him as she crosses her arms beneath her breasts. Butterflies invade her tummy when he crooks a finger and pats his knee.

"But Uncle Devlin, I really *need* some new undies and you said. . . ."

"I said I'd think about letting you help me but I *didn't* say you could have my card to go shopping. Now come here."

Her feet feel like lead as she slogs across the carpet. A hot blush creeps up her throat while she stands before him and bites a fingertip.

"I asked you *nicely*, Uncle Devlin, and when you didn't *say* anything I thought it was OK."

He takes her hand, leans back and smiles. "I didn't have a *chance* to say anything because you were rattling on so. Now . . . I thought you bought a whole truckload of panties just before Christmas."

She shakes her head like a spaniel with a bone. "Not *just* before . . . it was *ages* ago . . . like two or three months."

"Oh, *my*. I had no *idea* you were so bereft of underpants."

Teresa stamps her foot. "Don't be sarcastic, Uncle Devlin. I just need to get a few to replace the ones that are worn out."

Devlin smiles. "Why are you so hard on your panties?"

"*I* am not but *you* are." She grins as she sits on his lap.

His eyebrows arch. "Excuse me?"

"You *are* . . . you have such big fingers, and every time you pull down my undies to spank me, the elastic stretches."

"Isn't that what elastic is *supposed* to do?"

"Not *that* much. My school panties are all *droopy* now, and you don't want me to wear droopy panties to school, do you?"

He sighs, smiles, and kisses her lips. "You know there are plenty of extras in the cabinet at the college."

"Yeah, but . . . those are for the *other* girls. I should not be taking them."

"That's very considerate of you. Let's have a look at the ones you have on now."

Teresa frowns. "Why?"

"I want to assess the damage my huge fingers have caused in your unmentionables."

"Um . . . *these* are OK. You don't need to look."

Her knees quiver when he lifts her off his lap and slips both hands beneath her short skirt. She moans, deep in her chest, when he furls the light wool at her waist. A silky pink bikini almost covers her plump mound of Venus. She blushes hard and grips his arms with both hands.

"*This* is what you wear under a skirt that doesn't even reach mid-thigh, young lady?"

"Well, yes . . . um . . . that is why I need *new* ones, Uncle Devlin."

"I find it hard to believe you could find *nothing* more modest in your lingerie drawer this morning."

"But I . . . I am real careful to keep my skirt down so nobody will see them. Why are you being such a prude?"

She whimpers when he turns her to inspect the back of the panties. Half of her firm cheeks peek beneath taut leg bands. The waist snugs just under the top of her cleft, and translucent silk highlights rather than conceals the deep crevice that separates her plump mounds. He shakes his head and tries to scowl while his pulse rate increases.

"You should have worn cotton briefs, Teresa."

" I *cannot* wear schoolgirl panties under a miniskirt!"

He turns her to face him and she bites a fingertip. "If no one will *see* them, what difference can it make?"

"*I* would know!"

"Oh? And no one *else* would?" She shakes her head and stares at a spot on the wall. "Teresa, did you by any chance have a date to *meet* someone at the mall?"

Her face turns bright red. "I just . . . I only want to go *shopping*."

"Teresa?"

"What?" She chokes back a whimper.

"Did Pieter say he would meet you at the mall today?"

"No! I *told* you! I . . . I just . . . oh, *God*." She collapses onto his lap.

He strokes her hair while she quivers. "Sweetie? Look at me."

She shakes her head and buries her face in his neck. He smells of soap and musky aftershave, and her heart pounds beneath her breasts.

"Teresa, I don't mind if you meet the boy in public and in broad daylight, but I won't have you sneaking around to see him."

"I . . . I am *sorry*, Uncle Devlin." Moist green eyes plead with him as he cups her chin.

"Take your panties off."

Her heart leaps into her throat. "I . . . but . . . . OK, I . . . I will go and put on schoolgirl panties right now!"

She pushes against his chest but he holds her firm in his lap.

"*After* your spanking, sweetie."

A hot tear drips from her eye. "Please *no* . . . I am sorry and I won't do it *anymore*."

"I know you won't. Now take off your panties. We wouldn't want my big fingers to spoil the elastic."

"Noooo!"

He sighs, twists her around and deposits her, face down,

across his thighs. The little skirt curls about her waist. She wails as he nudges the waistband with his fingertips and rolls the tiny pants down her bottom. A silken strand, like a slender pink rope, hugs her thigh tops just beneath the under swell of her quivery bottom.

"You were very bad to try to deceive me like that, Teresa."

"I did *not* and . . . and I won't ever do it *again* so *please* don't spank me hard!"

"Just hard enough that you won't be in a hurry to show Pieter what's under your skirt."

"But I *wouldn't!*"

"Then why did you insist on wearing this little shred of nothing?"

"Be . . . because I . . . I wanted to feel *sexy*. You just don't understand!"

"Perhaps not . . . but if I *do* let you go shopping after this, you will have to make do with however *sexy* you feel wearing cotton undies. Now be still."

"Uncle Devlieeeow! Owee! Nahaaa! *Devlin! Not.* Ow! *So.* Haiee! *Hard!*"

His left arm holds her wriggly waist while his right hand spanks hot pinkness into her behind. The shadowy cleft widens and contracts as she scissors her legs. His palm stings like bright red nettles and she shrieks when the nettle-sting lances fire through the plump lips between her thighs. She kicks harder and moisture seeps from her labia.

He stops after twenty serious swats and rubs the soft bottom. She gasps, huffs, and then wipes her eyes with both hands as he lifts her and seats her on his lap. Molten lava boils under her. He presses a handkerchief into her sweaty palm and she weeps into it.

"It's all right now, sweetie . . . go ahead and cry."

"I . . . I am sorry, Uncle Devlin," she whispers.

"I know, and you're forgiven. If you still want to go shopping you may take the card . . . but behave yourself at the mall."

She shakes her head. "I . . . I would rather stay with you."

He smiles. "I'd like that too, but I have *got* to get some work done."

Teresa squeezes the handkerchief and looks up into his eyes. "If . . . if I promise to be real quiet while you work, can I watch?"

"*May* I . . . ?"

"*May* I watch? *Please?*"

"Yes you may . . . but I'm feeling a bit rumpled. Perhaps we should freshen up before I get back to work, hm?"

She grins. "That's not *all* you're feeling . . . is it, Uncle Devlin?"

His erection throbs when she squirms her hip. "Teresa! Go start the shower. I'll be there in a moment."

"OK . . . but *hurry.*"

He kisses her, pushes her off his lap, and smacks her squirmy, sexy behind to send her toward the bedroom.

• • •

Steam billows from the half-shut shower door when Devlin walks into the bath. He smiles and loosens the belt of his terrycloth robe. Teresa grins at him in the vanity mirror, which has started to mist from the steam. She sits on the padded stool wearing only a towel, snug beneath her armpits and knotted above full breasts. He rubs her shoulders and kisses the top of her head.

"Come along, Teresa."

Warm green eyes sparkle in the mirror as she simpers for only a second, then she grins and bounces off the vanity stool. The towel floats to the floor when she thumbs the knot. Devlin hangs his robe on a brass hook beside the shower stall and follows her inside. Teresa steps under the spray and then giggles as she turns to press her slippery bottom against his thighs. His penis hardens between hot, wet cheeks.

"Mmmm . . . will you wash my back?" she whispers.

He coughs and pushes her forward. She squeals as water drenches her hair.

"I'll blister your heinie if you don't behave, little girl." His voice is rough as a smoker's cough.

Teresa sputters and picks up a soap bar. "I am being *very* good . . . but *he* is not!"

She works the bar between her hands and grins. His member stands at full attention as he leans back to douse his hair.

"I have *told* you that it's impolite to comment on a man's involuntary reactions."

"Yes." She smears creamy lather across his chest. "But you tell me *lots* of silly things."

He sighs and wipes water from his mouth while Teresa swabs suds across his belly. She leans forward and rakes his ribs with hard, pink nipples. His erection, slick with drippy lather, wriggles against her tummy like a hot, naughty sausage. Devlin chuckles and reaches into a tiled niche to squeeze shampoo from a plastic bottle. Gooey lather erupts beneath his palm and Teresa moans when he rubs bubbly, iridescent foam over her bottom.

"Ooh, your hand is *so* nice when it isn't spanking my heinie."

His lips brush her forehead. "If you weren't such a naughty girl I wouldn't have to spank it so often."

She wriggles her behind and pouts as he slips a finger between her cheeks and slides it up and down the deep, warm crevice. "I don't *mean* to be naughty, and I know you will make me a better girl when I *am*. That's why I love you."

He smiles and kisses her pouty lips when she looks up at him. "I love you, too, sweetie. Now turn around so I can wash off the soap."

"No, I want you to rub my bottom some more. You spanked it very harshly and I . . . nooo!"

Her feet slap tile as he turns her toward the water. He laughs and holds her while he sluices mounds of lather into the drain, then wipes water from her eyes with his thumb and reaches behind the bottles in the niche to get a small tube. She looks at the tube and squeals.

"Since *when* do you keep K-Y Jelly in your shower?"

He shrugs and pops the cap. "Since my naughty niece decided she liked to have her little bottom hole filled up."

She sputters, throws her arms around him and turns away from the spray. "But I . . . I like it when . . . when we are in *bed* . . . all warm and toasty."

"It's very warm in *here*."

Teresa rubs her forehead against his chest and looks up, a sly, elfin grin on her lips. "You are a very bad man to even *think* such a wicked thing."

The tube cap snaps and he sighs. "I must have inherited *my* wicked thoughts from my wicked *niece*. Do you want me to shampoo your hair?"

"Devlin! You . . . I . . . how would we *do* it?"

He kisses her wet mouth and reopens the tube. "Here . . . turn around and grab the towel bar . . . that's it."

Her fingers clutch the ceramic rod. She looks over her shoulder and her knees tremble as she pushes her hips back. Manic butterflies careen about her tummy while she watches him dribble clear ointment onto his fingers. She slides her feet apart and moans as he coats her cleft and the tight bud inside with warm slickness. His finger slips into the tiny hole and she gasps.

"Are you all right, sweetie?" he whispers as he leans over to kiss her neck.

"Ahhh! Mmm! Y-yes. Put . . . put in some more, OK?"

"As much as you want."

She pants and stares wide-eyed at the tiles when his fingertip slides from her anus, then sighs as he pushes a fresh coat of jelly deep inside. He reaches around to cup her left breast and squeezes the firm, taut roundness while he fingers her bottom hole with slow, gentle thrusts and retreats. Her chin drops to her collarbone and she quivers as she takes long, deep breaths in time to the motions of his finger. Somewhere far away a bright light, like a porch lamp that signals the end of long journey, flashes and dims. Teresa swallows hard, blinks, and realizes that the light is the flash of warm fire that courses through her nipple each time his thumb caresses it. She pushes away from the bar and turns to hug him. His finger slips halfway out of her bottom and she squeezes her cheeks to hold him.

"Oh, *God,* Devlin," she whispers as she wraps a quivery hand around his erection. "I . . . I think I'm ready."

"Tuh . . . Teresa, *please!* Not so *tight,* OK?" He loosens her grip on his manhood. "I think you *are* ready. Can . . . can you bend over for me?"

Upper teeth slide across her lower lip. "Don't I *always,* Uncle Devlin?"

He gulps air and takes his finger from her tight hole. "Yes . . . you do. Now turn around . . . hold onto the bar. That's it . . . mmm . . . *yes.* Did you know you have the sweetest little tushy in the entire universe?"

The hot, spongy head presses her taut, throbbing ring.

"If . . . if you say so, Uncle Devlieeeaaaah!"

The shaft enters her tightness and starbursts glow around his head. She groans and pushes back with her hips to take him deep inside. Sparks fly past her eyes and she pants quick, hard breaths while she revels in the fullness. He draws back and she whimpers, then she moans as he plunges farther inside. Far in the distance they hear the spatter of water on tile. Her rear cheeks compress and relax as she squeezes him. He gasps, slides a hand up her thigh and finds the tiny button between the wet lips. Moist pink lightening flashes up her tummy, through her taut breasts, up her neck, then explodes in her head. She screams and pushes backward as he releases a torrent of passion into her bottom.

He opens his eyes and swallows hard as Teresa sighs long and deep. His arms wrap around her as they lean, crushed front to back, against the wall. She whimpers when his penis slips from her bottom, then moans and turns to him. Devlin reaches beneath the cold spray to turn off the shower. They shiver as he pushes open the door and leads her into the foggy bathroom. She wraps her arms around his neck and they kiss for a long minute. He picks her up and carries her to the heated towel rack, then covers her in a warm bath sheet.

"Mmmm . . . this is nice, Uncle Devlin. Can we go to bed now?"

His eyes narrow as he smiles. "It's the middle of the working day."

"I know . . . but if we go to bed, you can do that to me *again.*"

He laughs and swats the firm cheeks beneath the bath sheet. "You give me *far* too much credit and I do need to get back to work."

She pouts when he kisses her, grabs his robe and goes out the door. Warm, naughty chills shiver her bottom as she sits at the vanity table to dry her hair, and she giggles at the soft, lascivious expression on the face that looks back at her from the cloudy mirror.

• • •

The next Saturday Teresa spends three hours and several hundred Euros at the mall to get ready for her first day as Uncle Devlin's home-office assistant. The woman in the shop where she

buys her business suit is very kind and agrees to rush the tailoring for her, so she picks it up on Monday evening.

She floats into Devlin's apartment at ten o'clock Tuesday morning and goes to the study. A Mozart concerto drifts from wall mounted speakers and a log fire warms the room. She feels so professional, so purposeful in her new suit, but her elation is short-lived. There, on the small table Devlin has set up for her near his desk in the study, is a brief memo about an error in the introduction he wrote for a story. She peeks out the study door and sees him in the kitchen grinding coffee, so she boots up the computer and types a memo in response.

"I have just read your letter, and you are being *mega-unfair,* Uncle Devlin! You never gave me the final version of your intro that you published! I would have mentioned the strange combination of words because it didn't make sense to me when I read it the first time! If you want me to be a responsible assistant, you should make sure I get the edited files before you go and send them to the moderator of a kinky group and discuss with him intimate details of the state of my panties! Really Professor O'Neill! You will *not* spank me for this one! I will not go meekly over your lap or bend over some silly desk in this case! It was all *your* fault!"

She prints the memo, stands and rereads it, then becomes angry all over again. Medium-heeled pumps clomp the carpet as she takes it into the living room, puts it on the coffee table and simmers while she waits for him.

"Good morning, sweetie!"

He smiles, hands her a cup of steamy Jamaica Blue Mountain and sits on the sofa beside her. His eyebrows bristle as he reads the printed sheet, then he takes a deep breath and looks at her.

"Teresa Luisa, the *first* thing a good assistant learns is *not* to throw tantrums, even when her employer unfairly accuses her of an error. I didn't realize that you hadn't seen the final version, and I *never* would correct you for something that isn't your fault. *However,* this sort of histrionics in the workplace is *anything* but appropriate and you know I don't tolerate such behavior at home or at school, and I *certainly* won't have it in the office. Now, come along, young lady."

She gasps and bites a fingertip. It must have grown quite cool in the apartment because her nipples are very hard and they rub

against black satin bra cups while Devlin holds tight to her hand and leads her to the study. The gray, smartly tailored Ann Klein suit skirt feels very tight around her hips, and the big toe of her right foot cramps inside a black pump because she is not used to walking in two-inch heels. He leaves her to quiver in front of the desk while he steps around to open a drawer. She squeals when he takes out a clear plastic 30-centimeter ruler.

"Uncle Devlin, *no!*"

"*What?*"

"I . . . I meant . . . Professor O'Neill! I . . . I didn't *mean* to throw a tantrum and I will not do it anymore!"

"I would *hope* not . . . but the tantrum has been thrown, so I may as well take this opportunity to counsel you on office decorum."

"But I . . . I already *know* all that and . . . and you *cannot* spank me on my first day!"

"I never will spank you during office hours."

Teresa's eyes widen. "You . . . you *won't?*"

Devlin shakes his head. "One doesn't *spank* an employee. It's unprofessional."

She bites her finger. "Then . . . what are you going to *do?*"

"Counsel you regarding office decorum." He steps over to sit in the straight-backed chair next to the desk. "Raise your skirt."

Teresa winces when she stamps her foot. "But you said you wouldn't *spank* me!"

"That's too undignified a term for office use. I merely intend to counsel you on appropriate behavior."

"It . . . it doesn't matter what you *call* it . . . if you smack my heinie it's still a *spanking!*"

He stands and claps the ruler into his left palm. "Lift your skirt at *once*, Teresa."

Her knees turn to jelly and she whimpers as fierce butterflies race about in her tummy. Quivery fingers inch the tight skirt up smooth, nylon-clad thighs.

"But . . . but it isn't *fair*, Unc . . . Professor! You did not let me *proof* it before you. . . ."

"The error in the introduction no longer is an issue, Teresa. Your appalling behavior, however, *is* so come along."

He holds out a hand and she stumbles to him, her skirt bunched at her waist, her eyes damp with incipient tears.

"I . . . it was a misunderstanding, Uncle Devlin, and . . . and I'm *sorry* for writing that memo so you don't *have* to. . . ."

"You may apologize after you've been counseled." He takes her hand and squeezes it.

She stamps her foot, yelps, and kicks off her pumps. "How can a *word* be undignified when you are going to pull down my panties and paddle my bare bottom? How dignified is *this?*"

"Hush, Teresa, and let me help you out of your things."

"Noooo!"

He unbuttons her suit coat and she whimpers as he removes it and hangs it over the back of the chair, then she wails when he turns her around to thumb charcoal pantyhose down her plump rear. Black, micro-fiber panties snug the smooth contours of firm cheeks. The cotton-lined gusset, so dry and fresh only minutes before, moistens when he puts his fingers inside the waistband. She gasps as the tight fabric slides away to bare her creamy behind. He rolls the panties and hose a few inches down her thighs and then sits in the chair. Her jelly knees fold when he turns her. She moans, deep in her throat, and lies across his hard thighs. Trouser wool tickles the crinkly hair between her legs. She grabs the chair leg with both hands, bites her lip and turns her head to look at him. He rubs her bottom with the hard, cold plastic. A single tear drips from her eye.

"*Please?*"

"Please what, Teresa?"

"Will you spa . . . *counsel* me with your hand instead? *Please?*"

The ruler bounces when it hits the carpet and Devlin nods.

"Very well . . . since it *is* your first day. But don't expect such lenience in future unless you mend your attitude."

"I . . . I *will*, I promise."

"All right . . . now pay attention."

"Yes, sir."

He lifts her waist and settles her across his lap so that her bottom points at the ceiling as she stares at the carpet. His right thigh tenses and she whimpers when he raises his arm. The hard palm stings across her cleft, and she gasps and clutches the chair leg. Another hot clap flashes through her right buttock, and she yelps. He colors her twitchy bottom warm pink with a dozen sharp swats and then concentrates on the firm roundness just above her

SPEED HURTS!

Speed is based in fact. Teresa really did get a citation while we were in the midst of plans for Red Blossom College episodes. The event disturbed her so much she wrote the longest story start of her career, and even invented the handbook mentioned here. The scholarly pontifications, however, are mine.

Jill is Jilliane Scott, fellow author, web-site designer, good friend and confidant to Devlin, both in fact and fiction.

Teresa has been sitting at her computer for hours. Uncle Devlin wonders why it takes her so long to enter the few changes into the files he wants to give to Jill this afternoon. He knocks at her door and when there is no answer he quietly enters. She is squirming on her chair while she types very quickly. He hears a soft giggle and walks across the room.

"What on *earth* are you doing, Teresa?"

She almost jumps from her chair, then frantically closes chat room windows and opens Uncle Devlin's text folder. Her mind races to think of an excuse, and decides the best defense is a good offense.

"I *hate* it when you sneak up on me like that!"

"I knocked but you didn't answer so I thought I should check on you. I didn't know if you were asleep or sick or *what*. But that doesn't answer my question. What have you had been *doing* in here all morning? I assume my files are ready. Jill wants to go over a few things this afternoon and I'm on my way to her place, so if I could have them now, please?"

Teresa blushes and then gets very pale. "Umm . . . they are *almost* finished, but there is still a little problem with the format. They will be ready in an hour or so."

"*Format* problem? All I wanted you to do was enter the few changes we discussed yesterday. I'd like to leave now because I need to stop at the bank and settle a few things on my way to Jill's office. Could you just print a hardcopy for me? We can talk about the format later."

"Well . . . actually I haven't *finished* all the files. I tried to fix the format . . . and . . . well . . . *you* know!"

He shakes his head, crosses his arms and glares at her. "Yes, I'm afraid I *do*. You've been chatting on the internet all morning, haven't you? About sex, sex and *more* sex, I would guess."

"That is not true! I . . . I talked to a girl who sounded *very* depressed. She flunked her math exam and doesn't dare to tell her Daddy because he is going to punish her!"

"I don't see anything wrong with that. It's good to know that at least *some* parents are responsible, and you know what would happen to *you* if you got bad marks."

Teresa's hand creeps back to protect her bottom. "But . . . she was so *frightened,* and I could not *leave* like this! Don't you understand? So . . . um . . . why don't you go now and get your bank matters done, and I will meet you at Jill's office at two o'clock?"

Her eyes plead with him and Devlin heaves a sigh as he nods his head.

"All right . . . but be sure you're there on time *and* with all of the files. I'll spank you right in front of Jill if I hear another excuse."

"Yes, sir!"

At this point Teresa knows *exactly* how her cyber friend Lindsey feels. She quickly opens Devlin's file and starts to work. A few minutes later she hears his car leave the garage. She looks

at her watch and decides she has plenty of time for a quick visit to the chat room, so she logs on to #girlshavefun and meets some of her friends. They talk about fashion, boys and sex, and time is flying by. It is one o'clock when Teresa logs off and now she has to work quickly, but it takes her a little longer than she originally thought. She will have to hurry to get to Jill's office on time.

At one-forty she starts her car. Uncle Devlin was already annoyed with her and although she doesn't *think* that he really would spank her in front of Jill, she is not quite sure and doesn't want to find out. Her eyes are fixed on the clock so she doesn't even think of watching the speedometer. Suddenly a police car is overtaking her and she pulls to the curb. A policeman in his forties approaches her and demands to see her driving license and insurance documents.

"Do you know how fast you were going, Ms. Wagner?"

"Um . . . no, sir, I am afraid not."

"You went forty instead of twenty-five through a school zone so I'll have to issue a speeding ticket."

"No, *please,* officer! Could you just give me a warning? I *never* speed but I am in such a hurry today! I didn't even realize that was a school zone, and it is vacation time anyway so I didn't really endanger anyone!"

The man shakes his head. "The sign says the limit is 25 when children are present and there's a big soccer tournament today. You would have noticed all the cars and people around *if* you had been paying attention."

"But sir, I . . . yes, sir. I guess I should have paid more attention." She pouts and mutters while the officer writes in his book. *Oh, shit! Uncle Devlin will be so mad!*

"I will tell you something *else,* young lady. If my daughter was caught speeding in a school zone, she wouldn't sit comfortably for a *week.*"

She nods as he hands her the citation and shows her where to sign. Such might be her fate, too! The policeman tears out the ticket and gives it to her.

"Perhaps *this* will remind you to be more careful in future."

"Yes, sir," she says simply.

Teresa does *not* wish to discuss the policeman's methods of discipline at the moment. It is already one minute after two, so she

takes the ticket, puts it into her handbag and decides to think about this problem *after* she has explained to Uncle Devlin why she is late for their meeting. The officer waves her into the street and she is on her way once more. Perhaps she can go to the bank and pay the ticket out of her allowance. Uncle Devlin doesn't even need to *know* about it! Yes, that might work!

She arrives at Jill's office at two-twenty. Not too bad, really. Uncle Devlin will have chatted with Jill over a cup of coffee in the meantime. Jill answers the door.

"Hi, honey . . . where have you been? We've been waiting for you. Come on in."

Jill hugs her, but then Teresa sees Uncle Devlin's face. It has trouble written all over it.

"Hi, Uncle Devlin, I . . . I am sorry to be so late, but it was not my fault at *all* because there was an accident! A car ran over a cyclist and they had to wait for the police and the ambulance, and there was blood *everywhere* and I was so scared! I am still shivering thinking of it. Can I have some Coke, please?"

The words tumble out of her mouth before she has time to think about it. Uncle Devlin's eyes become soft and he walks over to hug her.

"Shh . . . it's over now, sweetie. I'm sorry you had to see that."

Teresa feels terrible because she knows she doesn't deserve his comfort, but she started this charade and now has to go through with it. Jill brings her a glass of Coke with ice and Teresa swallows a large slurp.

"Thanks . . . I think I am OK now. Let's get started with those files."

She slides a zip disk into the computer. Devlin pats her back and Teresa goes to sit in a nearby chair while he and Jill discuss the changes in Devlin's new *Handbook of Proper Education for Young Ladies at Red Blossom College*. Jill is confident that the book will be a bestseller within a few weeks. The publishing house has already received orders from boarding schools and private institutions all over the country. Teresa sips her drink, not really paying attention to what Devlin and Jill are saying until she hears the ominous words *punitive enema*.

"I agree, Jill . . . a good cleansing is suitable punishment for certain offenses and I've given quite a few, mostly for lying. But I *do* have to wonder if this should be discussed in a book read

mainly by teachers. I don't see how that sort of discipline is feasible in a formal school environment."

"In a *formal* school environment, sure." Jill shrugs. "But given the state of public and even private education these days, do you think you're the *only* one who wants to offer an alternative such as RBC to parents of young women in need of a guiding hand? We should at least *mention* it, Devlin. Our readers want comprehensive information on *all* your methods, since your program has proved its effectiveness."

Teresa gulps and excuses herself to go to the bathroom. She doesn't care for that kind of discussion right now because she still feels bad about the lie she told and doesn't want to think about what will happen if Uncle Devlin ever finds out. A long while later he knocks at the bathroom door.

"Sweetie, are you OK?"

She quickly washes her hands and opens the latch. "I am fine, Uncle Devlin . . . only a bit tired."

"You look a little pale." He palms her forehead. "Jill and I have done all we can for today, so let's go home and have a quiet evening. Do you want to ride in my car? We can leave yours here and get it tomorrow when I come back for a final review."

"But I really feel better and . . . and I would like to do some shopping before I go home. I need new jeans and panties and. . . ."
. . . and to go and pay the ticket and forget all about it!

"Not in your condition, sweetie. You've had a shock and it affected you more than I realized, so you're going straight home with me."

"But Uncle Devlin!"

"No *buts,* young lady. The subject is not open for debate."

Teresa knows *that* tone of voice and decides not to press her luck any farther. She can pay her ticket later.

"Yes, sir, but . . . I mean . . . can I drive my own car?"

He cups her chin and peers into her eyes. "All right . . . but stay close and no detours past the shops. Understood?"

She nods and goes to hug Jill good-bye. Uncle Devlin's gaze has awakened nasty, guilty butterflies in her tummy and she longs for the safe isolation of her little BMW. Once in the car, she taps her fingers impatiently and wonders how big a gap in the rush-hour traffic Uncle Devlin needs before he will pull into it. Finally,

he guns the huge Detroit engine and shoots down the block to the stoplight queue. Teresa grins and touches the accelerator. The BMW zips along right behind his Firebird and stops just a few centimeters from the rear bumper.

The light changes and they make a right turn. She sighs and watches her speedometer. It is so aggravating! He never exceeds the speed limit, yet they seem to fly along the boulevards toward his townhouse.

• • •

Devlin rubs his eyes, loosens his tie, and tosses his suit coat across the back of a wing chair. Teresa licks her lips and smoothes her skirt.

"Do you want a cup of coffee, Uncle Devlin?"

"That's a good idea. Will you make some?"

"Yes . . . right after I wash my hands and put on other shoes."

She runs to the stairs, stumbles over one of the cat's playthings and drops her handbag. It opens and the contents spilled on the floor.

"Oh, shit!"

"Teresa? Are you OK?"

He runs over to kneel beside her and help pick up the debris from her purse. She is searching for the folded paper with its ominous red stripe, but he grabs it first and she gasps.

"I am fine! Honestly!"

Teresa stands and quivers while Uncle Devlin picks up a few more of her things. He unfolds the red-striped paper and shakes his head as he rises. Dark furrows wrinkle his brow as he looks at her.

"Young lady, would you care to explain how you managed to get this speeding ticket while you were standing in a traffic jam waiting for the ambulance to take away the poor cyclist whose blood was spilled all over the road?"

She swallows hard and gasps because she knows the jig is up. Even *her* imagination has limits, and all she can do now is confess everything.

"Um . . . Uncle Devlin? Don't be angry, OK? I am sorry, I mean . . . I *didn't* mean . . . it just *happened* and I am so sorry . . . *please* don't punish me!"

His muscles are rigid with tension when she throws her arms around his neck.

Oh, why did this have to happen on Friday? If nothing else . . . and she dearly hopes there *will* be nothing else . . . he will ground her for the weekend so that she cannot go out with the Swedish girls to the club on Saturday, or even chat with her friends on the internet!

The red-striped paper rustles and she realizes he is still looking at the damn ticket! He is patting, or perhaps a bit harder than merely patting, Teresa's bottom beneath her faded blue-jean miniskirt. She squirms her hips and wishes she could think of something more to say, wishes *he* would say something, *anything,* to make her feel better. But all he does is to take her arms from around his neck and look at her, and that makes her feel even worse!

"Go put your pajamas on."

"But it is not even dinnertime! Why must I . . . . ?"

"Hush, Teresa Luisa! You *know* how much trouble you're in so do as I said and we'll discuss this later. Go on . . . I'll make the coffee."

"But I *said* I was sorry and . . . and anyway that policeman was not being *reasonable* with me! And . . . and he even threatened to *spank* me and *owee!*"

She stumbles backward and rubs harsh sting inside her skirt. Uncle Devlin scowls fiercely, so she decides it is a good time to do what he told her. Shoes fly off her feet as she runs upstairs and slams the bedroom door. Remorseful tears burn her eyes and she squeals when he shouts at her.

"Young lady, you know better than to slam that door!"

Her hand trembles as she opens it and takes a deep, shuddery breath. "It . . . it was an *accident,* Uncle Devlin! I will close it quietly now!"

"I want you in the living room, in your pajamas, in ten minutes, *understood?*"

"Yuh . . . *yes,* sir!" She gives the door an angry yank, then thinks better of it and eases it shut.

How can he do *this to me? Shouting at me like I am a ten-year-old child! It is simply not fair! I should call Felicia! She will let me stay with her until Uncle Devlin cools down. Mac will not*

mind if I . . . oh, God! It has been only a month since Felicia ran
through that stop sign and got a ticket, and her bottom still was
swollen the next day from the spanking Mac gave her. Perhaps if
Fel doesn't tell him why I must stay with them? No. She tells him
everything!

Bitter, exasperated tears stream from her eyes as she throws her
skirt, sweater and undies at the hamper. She goes to the bathroom
and splashes water on her face, dries, and then turns to look at her
behind in the mirror. There is the deep, bronze tan she got lying on
the nude beach with the Swedish girls, and she frowns when she
thinks how Uncle Devlin will soon turn the golden cheeks a very
sore and achy red. She cups her vagina with her right hand and
moans as she squeezes.

He is being completely unfair! I don't want him to spank me! It
is so . . . so awful when he is doing that to me! And why must he
do it on my bare bottom? He has no right to pull down my panties!
It is horrible when he sees me so naked and so vulnerable! God,
how I hate that muh . . . muh . . . maaan!

Teresa stifles a delighted yelp, and then gasps as she leans
against the wall. Quick, quivery spasms shoot through her pelvis
and bosom while she dabs guilty moisture from her lower lips with
a tissue. She takes a deep breath and runs to put on a light gray
sweat suit and her house shoes.

• • •

Devlin sits in his armchair and sips black coffee laced with
brandy. He pores over a hardcopy of the manuscript, searching
for typos, but he doesn't really see the words. Teresa's citation
lies on the table beside his cup. He glances at his watch and
shakes his head. The chair squeaks as he rises and goes to grab
the phone from the credenza. He dials and waits through three
rings.

"Hello?"

"Hi, Jill . . . sorry to bother you at home."

"Hi, Dev . . . what's up? Is Teresa OK? She didn't look so good
in the office today."

"There was a reason for that. I'll tell you about it later, but the
short version is . . . she got a speeding ticket."

"Oh boy. So um . . . how's her fanny right about now?"

"A whole lot better than it's *going* to be . . . but that isn't why I called."

"I kinda figured. You're never one to *talk* about it. You just do it and put the cold cream on later."

"Yes, well . . . what I wanted to ask is, how do you feel about doing a transcription for me?"

"Umm . . . like doctor's notes?"

"I know you've had some experience."

"Well, yeah . . . my first real job was in a gynecologist's office. Why?"

"Do you still want a chapter on punishment enemas?"

Jill laughs. "Well *duh,* Uncle Devlin! Do I dare guess *who* is going to be the case study?"

Devlin sighs. "I'm sure you already know, and I promise you'll have all the details your naughty little heart desires by Monday morning. Can you fit it into your schedule?"

"Hey, Unc, I'll stay up all *night* if I have to!"

"A simple *yes* will suffice. I put new batteries into the mini-recorder but the tapes are kind of old. I hope they're not too scratchy."

"Listen, Professor . . . you do the deed, I'll transcribe it, and we'll have that chapter done and indexed before the deadline, no problem."

"I knew I could count on you, Jill." He frowns. "Just don't get *too* wrapped up in the details, all right?"

"*Me?* No idea *what* you're talking about."

"Yes, dearest . . . I *know* how very indifferent you are to enemas and other squirmy medical procedures."

She chuckles. "I can be as professional as I need to be, Herr Professor. But I know you won't mind if I make a copy of the tape."

"I should have guessed. Just don't sell it to the *Enquirer,* all right?"

"No *way* . . . this is between you, me, and the nozzle, I *swear.*"

"OK, I believe you. 'Night, Jill."

"'Night, Dev. Don't do anything I wouldn't do . . . as *if!*"

He laughs and rings off, then looks at his watch and scowls at the stairs.

"Teresa!"

Her heart pounds when she hears his shout. She only wanted to put a little eyeliner on so she will look more sad and apologetic while he scolds her, but she sees that this has taken much too long and she throws open the door.

"I am coming!"

Bare feet skitter on the carpeted stairs and Teresa slows to a more demure pace, eyes focused on the floor, as she approaches her scowling uncle.

"I *said* ten minutes, young lady, and it has been over twenty. What were you doing up there?"

"Nuh . . . nothing, Uncle Devlin, I only . . . I had to use the bathroom, that is all."

He cups her chin in his warm palm and bright, scary butterflies dance inside her tummy while he gazes into her eyes. His scowl deepens and Teresa winces.

"That sounds very much like another fib, Teresa Luisa."

"*No,* I just . . . I only . . . I *was* in the bathroom, I *swear.*"

She moans as he leads her to the sofa. Her bottom tingles when he sits down, puts her beside him and wraps an arm around her quivery shoulders.

"Are you ready to tell me the truth about this afternoon?"

"But I . . . I already *told* you . . . the . . . the policeman was very unreasonable and has given me this ticket most *unfairly.*"

Devlin nods. "And he offered to spank your naughty bottom into the bargain?"

Teresa gasps. "Well . . . *yes,* he . . . he told me that if his own *daughter* gets such a ticket, she will not sit down for a month! That to *me* sounds like a threat!"

"Hmm . . . perhaps . . . or he wanted you to know how lightly you were getting off, after speeding through a school zone!"

"But . . . but it is *vacation* time! How am I to know there are children when the school is not in session?"

"Did you read his comments on the ticket?"

"There are comments on the ticket?"

He picks up the red-striped paper. "Right here, under Additional Circumstances. 'Driver says she took no notice of parked cars or persons around the school.' You must have been in a great hurry, Teresa."

"I . . . I only wanted to be on time for the meeting! You tell me always to be on time!"

"Yes, but those changes to the manuscript should have taken you an hour at *most*. You just couldn't stay out of those chat rooms, could you?"

"No! I mean, *yes!* Uncle Devlin! You are being so. . . ."

She sniffles and hugs his chest while he strokes her hair. Her heart throbs and she whimpers when he gets up and goes to the credenza. There is a small plastic box there, next to the brandy bottle, and he picks it up. A button clicks and he turns toward her as he speaks to the little box.

"We'll start here, Jill. Call it chapter X and I'll leave it to you when to start transcribing."

"Who . . . what are you *doing?* Is that a tape recorder? You are not going to give this to *Jill,* are you? Uncle Devlin, *no!*"

Teresa hugs her knees and curls into a ball on the sofa. Hot, silent tears drip from her eyes as he sits beside her. A desperate sob escapes her throat as he turns her around and pushes down on her legs.

"Sit up, young lady. Take a deep breath and tell me why I am so put out with you. *Now.*"

"Oh . . . oh . . . *geeze!* I . . . I *said* I was sorry to get this ticket and I will pay it from my allowance! Why must you . . . ?"

"Teresa! You know very well that's not why I'm upset with you. Now tell me."

Nasty, crampy butterflies whiz through her tummy and tears sting her eyes as she looks at him.

"Be . . . because I told a fib?"

Uncle Devlin nods, but he is not really looking at her, so she sobs when he hugs her to his side. He clears his throat.

"As mentioned in other chapters, the primary means of discipline for young ladies is to convince them that they must *own* their problems. A student has to acknowledge her fault prior to correction or the punishment will be meaningless."

Teresa whimpers and looks up. "Uh . . . Uncle Devlin? Who are you talking to?"

He smiles and kisses her lips. "To you, sweetie, among others . . . and that should be *to whom are you speaking?* Now . . . you know I have to spank you for telling a fib, don't you?"

"But I don't *want* you to . . . and . . . and turn off that stupid tape recorder, OK? This is just so . . . !"

"Hush! I have to spank your naughty bottom and you *know* that, so ignore the tape recorder. No one but Jill will ever hear it and. . . ."

"You are not *serious,* are you? I will be embarrassed to *tears* if Jill hears you spanking me! Why are you *doing* this?"

"I said to be *quiet.* You know how I feel about lying. I made that perfectly clear at the villa in Italy, but it seems I have to repeat the lesson and it annoys me to have to do it so soon!"

Teresa coughs and then swallows hard. "You . . . but . . . *no!* You would not give me a . . . do those awful things you did to me at the villa . . . while *Jill* is listening, would you?"

She hides her face in his chest but he picks her up by the shoulders and twists her across his lap. Shuddery sobs rack her throat when he puts his fingers under the waistband of her sweatpants. She wears no panties and he bares her bottom with one quick tug. Teresa gasps and rubs tears from her eyes while she tries not to speak out loud. She doesn't want Jill to hear her plaintive, little-girl cries while Uncle Devlin is spanking her!

He is being so unfair! What is he thinking?

He leans over beside her ear and she feels his warm breath on her neck. "I am going to spank your naughty bottom bright red, sweetie. Try to be a good girl and learn from this, all right?"

"But . . . but Uncle *Devlin!* I *promise* I won't tell fibs anymore! I don't *want* you to *eeeek!*"

His hand smacks hard on her firm behind, but then he squeezes for a second before he again raises his arm. Once more he clears his throat.

"I cannot emphasize this too much. (*Whack!* Owee!) The young women under your tutelage have very fragile psyches. (*Whap!* Yeow!) So it is imperative that you adjust the level of punishment to suit their sensibilities and level of experience. (*Whop!* Yike!) Young teachers, especially, should avail themselves of any and all documentation of a young woman's previous chastisements. (*Whashk!* Neeaah!) As mentioned in other chapters, a thorough reading of a girl's dossier combined with a review of any previous entries in the punishment log will aid the teacher, young or old, in correcting any student. (*Splat!* Eeyow!)

"Which brings me to the point of this chapter. (*Whisp!* Yowee!) There are certain transgressions that surpass all understanding. (*Crack!* Haaow!) One of these is lying. (*Whick, whump!* AyeeOW!) The instructor's first inclination, and understandably so, would be to paddle the girl purple. (*Swip!* Ouch! But I'm already . . .) Shh! Again, a young woman's previous record must be considered. (*Kerwhack!* Fowee!) As you know, some young ladies profit greatly from a single, bare-bottomed session across an instructor's knee. (Uh huh, I did! *Swap!* Yowchee!) But then there are the recidivists who must be dealt with. (*Whisht!* Naaieee!) Repeat offenders, especially those who lie to avoid responsibility, must be treated differently. (*Kerslap!* Deeyow!) After the second or third offense, when the girl has been well spanked on each prior occasion, another remedy may be indicated."

Teresa quivers and sobs when Uncle Devlin pulls her up to sit on his lap. His strong arms feel so good when they are wrapped around her, but she is so puzzled and so angry with him that she cannot enjoy the feeling of his smooth woolen trousers on her hot, sore behind.

"Uh . . . uh . . . Uncle Devlin?"

"Yes, sweetie?"

"Whuh . . . what are you *doing?*"

He kisses her damp forehead and smiles as he leans over and switches off the recorder. "Spanking my naughty girl's bottom, of course."

"No, I mean . . . you did not *scold* me while you spanked me, it . . . it sounds more like you are *writing* . . . writing out *loud.*"

"That's what I do. I write about naughty girls who need to be punished."

"But you . . . you must not write about spanking *me!* It is *one* thing in your stories because everyone thinks they are *fiction,* but to put me in a textbook that will be read by thousands of *teachers* . . . I will be so ashamed!"

Teresa weeps while Devlin holds her close. He kisses the top of her head and then reaches beneath to rub her sore bottom.

"Are you hungry? Do you want a bite of supper before we continue?"

"*No!* I . . . I don't want to *eat* and . . . and I don't want you to continue *anything!* I only want you to *hold* me."

"I would love to do that, but first I have to punish you for fibbing to me."

Tight ropes wrap her heart and squeeze. She gasps as she looks up into his eyes. They are so bright and so blue, but so scary that she squeals.

"But you . . . you already spanked me so *hard* and . . . and Jill will be hearing it all on the tape! How can you think to punish me even *more?*"

His muscles flex and he stands, just as if Teresa is not in his lap. She whimpers when he sets her down and hugs her.

"Go to your room and I'll be there shortly."

"But I don't *want* to, Uncle Devlin! What . . . what are you going to *do?* Don't spank me anymore, *please?*"

"I'm not going to spank you again tonight, sweetie . . . unless you defy me. Now do what I said."

She sobs and wipes her eyes on his starched cotton shirt. He smells so warm, like a pinewood in the Alps on a summer day. But she hears his heart beating fast, and she quivers when he reaches down to tug her pants up over her sore bottom. He gives her behind a few soft pats to tell her that time is up and she had better get going. Teresa whimpers as she unwraps her arms and then pouts over her shoulder while she stomps up the stairs.

Devlin sighs as he picks up the recorder and thumbs it on.

"Occasionally the professional instructor will be confronted with a particularly obstinate student. I make note here that the following instructions apply only to those teaching professionals who have the subject's parental approval as to the extraordinary measures he or she, the instructor, sees fit to employ. These disciplinary measures are not for the faint of heart, but if the reader has followed my arguments thus far, perhaps the next few pages will enlighten him or her further as to the efficacy of my methods." He shakes his head. "Jill, please type that as I said it. I'll go back and make it a bit less stilted in the rewrite, OK?"

The recorder clicks and clatters when he opens it and flips the tiny cassette over. A bottle gurgles as he splashes two ounces of Courvoisier into a crystal glass. He sips, then slurps, then drains the brandy.

• • •

Teresa whines while she twists to look at her image in the closet door mirror. Finger-sized red smudges highlight the overall pink-ness of her firm, round bottom. She frowns as she pulls up her pants, leans over to start the computer, and grabs a pillow from her bed while the machine boots up. A painful squeak escapes her lips as she sits on the pillow and flicks the mouse to initiate the server. Two more mouse flicks and she is in the chat room. Lindsey, the girl with the very strict Daddy, is there, and just as worried as she had been that morning. She is chatting with another person, but her complaints sound exactly the same.

> <<I do not know why this bothers me! He has whipped me with his belt so many times it should not be such a big deal but it is! >>

> <<Hi lindsey sorry to butt in! Its treezy. Does your daddy ever give you enemas when your bad? >>

> <<god no! does yours? jeeze treezy! :(>>

> <<well no but . . . wouldn't that be the worst? >>

> <<DUH! are you in trouble? >>

> <<yeah a little I got a ticket. >>

> <<oh god. will you get spanked? >>

> <<already did—but unc is being major weird about it like I robbed a bank or something>>

> <<so you know how I feel>>

> <<yeah BIG time and I don't think he's done with me>>

> <<yr gonna get a enema? shit treezy! sorry that didn't come out right O dam! that didn't either sorry>>

<<nevermind I gotta deal with it. be back in the am ok? >>

<<yeah. Daddy won't see the report until at least monday but I need you there after ok? >>

<<fr sure I gotta go>>

<<tell me about the enema? >>

<<maybe. bye lindsey>>

<<bye treezy good luck>>

Devlin climbs the stairs, the little recorder clutched in his fist. Teresa hears his footsteps in the hallway and hurries to shut down the chat windows. He pushes open her door and she pouts at him over her shoulder.

"Come along, Teresa. We need to discuss your behavior."

Her eyes fill with tears and she stomps her foot. "Uncle Devlin, you are being very unreasonable and. . . ."

She gasps when he stalks across the room to grab her arm. Mad, rampant butterflies zip through her tummy as he marches her down the hall to his room. His big, wide bed looks so inviting, but he drags her past it and into the bath. The final rays of sunset warm translucent windowpanes. Devlin flicks a switch and drowns the sunset in cool, white light. He sets the recorder on the shelf above a long, deep bathtub and presses a button.

"If all else fails, and it may," he says, "sometimes it is necessary to subject the obstinate pupil to more stringent discipline. As previously noted, punishment should be meted out in escalating doses, as the individual student requires. For example, a new enrollee should never be paddled on the bare bottom in front of her peers, regardless of her age or the offense. It is only after the young woman is exposed to this kind of discipline, perhaps with a long, strict spanking in the privacy of the instructor's office, that the instructor may decide to elevate the level of chastisement for subsequent bad behavior."

Teresa writhes and squirms while she gapes at Uncle Devlin and wriggles against the strong grip on her arm.

"Uh . . . Uncle Devlin?" she whispers. "You . . . you said you wouldn't spank me anymore!"

He smiles when he turns to hug her. "I won't. Let's have these clothes off, shall we?"

"But I don't *want* you to . . . !"

"Shh!"

She quivers when he reaches over to switch off the recorder. He thumbs down her loose pants and pushes them to the floor.

"Whuh . . . what are you going to *do?*"

He stands and pats her bare bottom while he gives her a stern look. "You may keep your shirt on."

Teresa squeals and grabs his neck. She screeches when he picks her up, flicks the sweat pants off her feet, and then lowers her onto the thick rug beside the bathtub. He stands and starts the recorder. Teresa sits on the mat and glares at him. Devlin takes a deep breath.

"It should be noted that a punishment enema is not a chastisement of last resort. Even if the student fails to respond to repeated spankings by hand, paddle or slipper, it is possible that the fault lies in the punisher and not in the punished. Embarrassment is key, even in the most perfunctory swat to the back of the skirt. Young women, especially in the presence of their peers, are very sensitive to perceived slights, and therefore vulnerable to any act of an authority figure that might accentuate this vulnerability. A case in point is the girl's fear of being exposed for a medical exam or procedure." He looks down at Teresa. "Roll onto your side."

"Uncle *Devlin!*"

"Hush, girl! Do it *immediately* or you will suffer the consequences!"

A shriek gravels her throat and she twists onto her side, a hand splayed over her rear cleft. Uncle Devlin has never shouted at her like this, and she prays very hard that it is only the book he is writing that makes him appear so angry.

"I am *sorry*, Uncle Devlin," she whispers as he leans over to caress her warm forehead. Teresa sighs. "Please do not be angry . . . sir."

He smiles and reaches down to squeeze her bottom. Teresa squeals as she glares at him. Devlin winks at her and then walks to the basin to fill a small red bulb with warm water. She grimaces

when he dribbles soap into it from a little tube, and then bites her lip when he scowls and turns toward the recorder.

"Although it may be obvious, I will state that a young woman in need of enema discipline will submit to it only if her teacher or mentor has previously exposed her, and, yes, her bare bottom, to a fairly stringent regimen of chastisement. The point and purpose of such discipline is embarrassment, much as it is in the classroom. But in the classroom, a paddling or spanking is as much about discomfort as it is humiliation. A punishment enema should cause little discomfort, let alone pain. If a spanking is to precede the enema, which in most cases it should, the spanking should be bare-handed on the bare bottom. Even if the instructor is quite put out at the student's behavior and has stung her behind ferociously, the instructor should make every effort to quell the sting in the pupil's buttocks before he or she attempts to administer a punitive enema."

Devlin looks down and shakes his head. Teresa is wriggling her bottom at him and trying not to smile.

"Yes, sir, Professor O'Neill, sir! You are quite correct and you had better put lots of lotion on my *buttocks* because they certainly are stinging!"

He frowns, picks up a lotion bottle along with the enema bulb and then kneels beside her. She bites her lower lip as he squirts yellowy goo into his cupped palm.

"Lotions, cold creams and other emollients, of course, may serve more than one purpose." His warm hand slicks creaminess across her bottom and Teresa moans. "The most obvious is to soothe and calm the student after an unpleasant punishment, but another, perhaps not so obvious, is to calm the punisher, who is understandably angry with the student, by allowing the teacher to massage the object of his or her anger and release pent-up emotion. This is very important, especially as concerns male teachers."

"No *duh*, Unca Devlin!"

"Be quiet, Teresa!"

She turns and sticks out her tongue. Devlin raises his hand over her bottom, then sighs and continues to rub lotion on it.

"The male faculty member . . . quit grinning, Teresa, that wasn't meant to be *funny* . . . must be especially careful during this procedure. Men under the age of fifty, regardless of sexual preference,

are strongly cautioned. A female student's naked buttocks can be extremely arousing when placed in this position, even to the most jaded individual, male or female, so the utmost decorum must always be observed. Male instructors of all ages should wear loose-fitting trousers during this procedure, as noted in other chapters regarding bare-bottomed punishment of females, so as not to exhibit their arousal, should such occur. Female instructors are of lesser concern, but no outward display at the sight of a young woman's anus or pudendum can be countenanced if proper discipline is to be maintained."

Teresa stifles a laugh. Male *members? Pudendum? Countenanced?* She knows he is not trying to be funny, but in spite of her situation, she simply cannot help being amused. Her shoulders are shaking and she gasps when he looks into her eyes. Devlin frowns and clears his throat.

"The most effective punishment enema is always given with the student in the knee-chest position."

"*Geeze,* Uncle Devlin!"

She whimpers when he nudges her, but she rolls, kneels, and pushes her bottom toward the ceiling while she glares at him over her left forearm.

"This position is not only humiliating for the student. . . ."

"You can say *that* again, Uncle Demon!"

"Hush . . . but it gives complete access to her anus and allows the instructor to administer the enema with a minimum of difficulty. Which brings up the issue of lubrication . . . and I think I'll have to rewrite this whole thing, Jill! A little green-eyed brat interrupted me earlier when I meant to talk about using lotion as lubricant. I'll fix it in the edit. *Ahem!*

"The student's anus must be thoroughly lubricated prior to the insertion of the enema, and the nozzle itself should be lubricated as well. A latex glove or finger cover must be used in all cases, to protect the student as well as the instructor. K-Y Jelly, Vaseline Petroleum Jelly, or any similar ointment will do nicely. Be sure to massage the lubricant all the way into the girl's rectum so that the nozzle slides in easily and without discomfort."

Teresa pouts and clenches her behind. "Yeah, right . . . *you* have no discomfort but I sure do!"

He chuckles, picks up the K-Y and leans over to kiss her pout.

"Yes, I *see* how you're suffering, sweetie." The tube squishes and Devlin coats his index finger with clear slipperiness. "You won't tell anyone if I don't use a glove when I slide this into your bottom, will you?"

"Oh, God! Mmmph! Neeeuhh! Ooh! *Geeze,* Devlin, I . . . oh, *God.*"

Tangy, tingly, nasty vibrations swirl through her anus, and she grabs Devlin's knee in her left fist. He cringes and then smiles as he withdraws the finger from her behind.

"The um . . . the naughty girl is now ready for her enema, which should be inserted into her rectum as quickly as possible once she has been fully lubricated. A small bulb syringe or Fleet's enema is all that is necessary for such a punishment, since the purpose of the exercise is embarrassment rather than a thorough cleansing of her bowels."

He squirts K-Y on the nozzle, smears it around the fluted plastic, then leans over to part her cheeks with his left thumb and forefinger. She squeals as plastic slides into her behind. Tight sphincter muscle clenches and quivers while Teresa pushes her back down and her bottom higher. Devlin squeezes warm water inside her. Heat fills her tummy and she longs to touch the hot node between her legs and quench the burning inside the puffy lower lips.

Devlin takes a deep breath. The delightful aroma of feminine arousal fills his nostrils. He blinks and swallows.

"If um . . . if the student still fails to respond in a positive manner, the instructor should remain in the room while the girl dispels the enema, in order to amplify her embarrassment. Let's end here, OK, Jill?"

Teresa quivers and moans while Devlin hugs her waist and slips the nozzle from her bottom. He pushes his thumb against the tiny hole while his fingers slide between her wet labia. Bright white sparks cascade behind her closed eyelids, and then deep, shuddery spasms blossom inside her vagina. He holds her tight against his chest while the spasms peak and then slowly subside. His hand remains, warm against her quivery bottom, his thumb tight against her rear vent. Teresa takes a deep breath.

"I . . . I have to go to the toilet, Herr Professor," she whispers.

"I would imagine so, Miss Wagner."

His arm slips beneath her bosom and he lifts her to her feet. She moans as she stumbles to the toilet. The seat is cold and Teresa shivers, but then smiles as Devlin closes the door behind him.

Well, I guess he thought that was embarrassment enough *for one day!*

Her guilt and humiliation drain into the bowl along with the enema, and Teresa sighs in contentment. Water gushes between her tingly lower lips and she gasps with orgasm aftershock. She blinks at the clock on a shelf . . . quarter to seven.

She washes, fore and aft, at the basin, then dries herself and glances at the wadded sweatpants on the floor. Her nipples tingle with wicked delight as she twists around to pat Tiffany after-bath powder on her pink bottom. The soft puff tickles and soothes the warm, quivery ache left by Uncle Devlin's hand, and she grins at her fanny's reflection. At seven-ten, Teresa brushes her hair before the mirror, then, still naked from the waist down, she opens the door and looks into his bedroom. He sits at a tiny desk and stares at a laptop screen, his back to the bathroom door. She creeps across the room and peeks over his shoulder.

<<and he said he would spank my bottom with a belt devlin! isnt that horrible? >>

<<Yes, your daddy is a very severe person, and it's just awful that he is going to do that to you. I wish I could kiss your little bottom afterwards>>

<<oh gosh thank you devlin. you are so sweet!! I wish you could to but my daddy would be real mad if I let a sweet guy kiss my sore little bottom—you know that don't you? >>

Teresa gasps and grabs his shoulder. "What are you *doing?* That is Lindsey! Why are you . . . ?"

Devlin pulls the bare-bottomed girl on his lap. She squirms and whimpers, and then pouts when he kisses her lips.

"Yes, that's Lindsey . . . and she has been telling that same story to anyone who will listen for at least a month. I pulled up the archive. I'm not sure she even *has* a daddy, except in her mind."

"But she seemed so *sincere* and . . . oh, shit!"

"Teresa!"

She jerks a hand to her mouth. "I am sorry, Uncle Devlin, but . . . it is all her *fantasy,* isn't it? She must need such attention very bad."

"Very *badly,* Teresa, and yes . . . she enjoys telling everyone how she suffers . . . or wishes she did. Do you tell your chat-room friends how Uncle Devlin makes *you* suffer?"

"Of course not! Such things are very private." She turns and coughs to hide a blush as she remembers what she wrote to Lindsey that evening. "It is terrible for her to fool people this way. Is . . . is she even a *girl?*"

He laughs and hugs her. "We can't be sure, can we?"

She huffs and reaches for the keyboard. "Can . . . may I have only a minute to tell her what I *think* of her? *Please?*"

Teresa squeals because Uncle Devlin is laughing again and picking her up. He dumps her onto his bed and turns down the covers. She rolls over and squirms between the sheets while she giggles. Devlin shakes his head and drops his robe. Teresa tugs her sweatshirt over her head as she watches him climb, naked, into the bed. Her heart pounds and her nipples burn his chest while she hugs him.

He turns her over and she sticks out her tongue at the computer while she rubs her bare cheeks on his hard belly. The computer screen goes dark as something even harder presses into the cleft of her soft, receptive bottom.

TERESA'S ILLNESS

This story is an early sketch for *Education at Red Blossom College*, Volume IV of *A Maid for All Seasons*, although it began as something else entirely. I had the new novel much on my mind when Teresa told me about her actual use of the liquid diet mentioned here. I hit the ceiling, then took her story start and launched into that which follows.

Felicia is Devlin's half-sister and also Teresa's stepmother. Teresa's father died in a plane crash a few years after he married Felicia, and named Devlin executor of his estate and Teresa's trust fund. Teresa is nineteen and Felicia is only eleven years older. When Felicia finds Teresa too much to handle, Devlin brings them both from Germany to the States where Teresa attends RBC. Lisa is Lisa Carlson, the title character in *A Maid for All Seasons*.

"Hi, Devlin . . . it's Felicia."

"Hi, Fel, what's up?" I stifle a yawn and switch the phone to the other ear. "You don't usually call at the crack of nine on Sunday morning."

"Well um . . . Teresa asked me to. She's been pretty wound up lately so I promised I'd do it right away."

"I see. What did she do *this* time?"

"She really didn't *do* anything, and that's the problem. She wants you to extend the deadline for her book summary."

"Oh? And why is that? It was due yesterday and she had plenty of time to write it."

"I know but. . . ."

"Procrastination is what got her into trouble in Hamburg and I won't put up with it *here*. I gave her those assignments so she would get used to the idea of homework before she starts school, but I suppose she was hanging around in those stupid chat rooms all night instead!"

"Would you please *listen* a minute before you go ballistic? First of all, she really intended to write the summary. She was very proud of her A on that first essay, and she's been working on the run-on sentence and sentence fragment problems, and she even tries to put in all the commas, which is really hard for a foreigner. Plus, she doesn't feel very well, but she panicked when I said you couldn't expect her to do an assignment when she's ill."

"Of course I wouldn't. I'm not an *ogre*."

"I know, but sometimes the girl is really strange. She started a diet on Friday and hasn't eaten anything since. She drinks some kind of protein shake and lots of water, but nothing else. Now she's in bed with a headache and generally feeling yucky."

"She's starving herself and you *allow* that?"

"Devlin! She won't take *no* from me. Our relationship was *never* that way. Gerhard didn't expect me to be her *mother* . . . he wanted us to be more like sisters, or at least friends."

"Hmm . . . I wonder which of the sisters was over his knee more often."

"That's none of your business. You embarrassed me *enough* when you gave that nasty belt to him as a wedding present. Oh, Dev! I miss him so much!"

"Sorry, Fel, I didn't mean to upset you. All right . . . tell Teresa you talked to me and I expect her summary by Tuesday. Also, I want her to stop that silly diet *immediately*. If she wants to lose weight she has to stop eating junk food and sweets and get more

exercise. I'll discuss it with her next time I see her, but I have to run now. You'll take care of her, won't you?"

"Sure, Dev. Thanks."

"You're welcome, little sister."

The phone clicks when Felicia hangs up.

• • •

Bright August sun bakes sweet odor from the honeysuckle vines that grow alongside the path to Red Blossom Cottage. Yellow butterflies dance among the scarlet azaleas and a dozen more dance in your tummy as you think about your first day at a new school. You take deep breaths, frown, and twist the door handle. The hallway smells of honeysuckle and old books. You glance at a shelf and run your finger over one of the spines . . . *Oliver Twist*. You smile and follow the sound of my voice to the classroom.

I smile. "Good morning, Teresa."

"Good morning, Herr Professor." You slide into a chair. Your heavy satchel clomps the hardwood floor and you blush at the noise. "Sorry," you say, and lean over to dig out a notebook and pen.

"That's all right. Class, this is Teresa Wagner. Teresa, say hello to Brittany and Ashley. You know Lisa, of course."

You turn and nod to the two girls you haven't met. They glance at you and smirk. Lisa leans toward you.

"Hi, Teresa. Are you OK?"

"Yes. I am fine."

I clear my throat and tap the chalkboard with a wooden pointer. "You're a bit late, Teresa, so I'll go over the objective case again, all right?"

A Mont Blanc pen scratches paper as you scribble notes while I discourse on the fascinating difference between *who* and *whom*. You yawn and I shake my head.

"Teresa, am I boring you?"

"No, I . . . I was only stretching my jaws. Sir."

"I see. Perhaps we all need a break. Ten minutes, girls." I drop my piece of chalk into the tray.

You sigh and follow the other girls into the kitchen to get a bottle of soda from the refrigerator and then all four of you wander into the back garden.

"That guy is *such* a drag." Brittany leans against the gazebo rail.

"No *duh.*" Ashley slurps from her bottle of Diet Coke.

Brittany grins and looks at you. "So . . . what are *you* in for?"

"I . . . I am here to improve my English."

The two girls laugh.

"That's what our moms told *us,* too," Ashley says. "But we're from California and English don't get any better than that, huh, Brit?"

"Damn straight . . . the old guy's got his head up his. . . ."

Lisa coughs and glares, then turns to you. "Hey, I hear you're on that protein diet."

"Yes, and it works very well."

"I could stand to drop a few pounds, myself."

"Perhaps one or two, Lisa, but I do not think you need this diet for so little. It is for losing 10 pounds or more." You watch the California girls wander away.

"That couldn't hurt."

"But ten pounds is almost ten percent of your weight. Your underpants would fall down!"

Lisa laughs, turns, and pats her round behind. "I doubt it . . . but maybe I'll just have salad for a few days and. . . ."

"He's not your private property, ya know!" Brittany glowers at her cousin as the two girls stand by an oak tree twenty feet away.

You and Lisa look at each other, then at Ashley and Brittany.

"Yours *either,* Brit, and besides, he thinks you're a *slut.*"

"You are *so* lying!" Brittany jams her fists at her hips.

"Oh, God." Lisa shakes her head. "Here we go again."

"What is it, Lisa?"

She bounces down the gazebo steps toward the girls. "Hey, you guys! Chill, OK?"

Ashley turns. "Shut up and mind your own business, Blondie."

Brittany huffs. "*You* shut up, Ash! Corbin's taking me to the mall tonight, so *deal* with it."

"Oh, yeah? Deal with *this.*" Ashley smacks Brittany's face with an open hand.

You gasp. Slender arms and legs flail as the girls tumble to the grass and squeal while they wrestle. Lisa runs and tries to grab one of them, but catches the heel of Brittany's loafer on her knee. I

hear the commotion through the open study window, run down the hall and out the kitchen door.

"Brittany! Ashley! *Stop* that!" I reach down and clutch two blouse collars.

"Oh, geeze," Brittany mutters, and dabs a spot of blood from her lip.

"She *started* it, Professor," Ashley whines.

"Did *not*. You hit me *first*."

"Quiet, *both* of you! What happened the *last* time you two got into a fight?" They play with their fingers and stare at the ground. "Brittany?"

She looks up at me. "Sir?"

"Tell me what happened last time."

"You . . . you p-paddled us."

"Ashley? Is that how you remember the event?" She nods but doesn't look up. "I see. Do you think it will be any different *this* time?" The girls shake their heads. "Well, you're mistaken."

They look at me, eyes wide, mouths open.

Ashley licks her lips. "You . . . you're not going to paddle us?"

"I didn't say that . . . but it *will* be different. Now both of you wait for me in the bathroom . . . the one in the bedroom, not the one in the classroom. You need first aid and your uniforms are a mess. Go on."

The girls glance at each other, at you, at Lisa, and then Brittany looks at me.

"Sir?"

"What is it, Brittany?"

"Whuh . . . what are you going to *do* to us?"

"Clean up your act . . . now *move*."

They amble away and then yelp when I swat their bottoms to hurry them toward the kitchen door. I turn to Lisa and take a small clasp knife from my trouser pocket. It snicks when I lock open the single blade.

"Lisa, will you cut a dozen twigs from the willow tree, please?"

The girls stumble and turn around.

"Nuh . . . not for *us*, Professor!"

"P-*please*, Professor!"

I whirl and glare at them. "*What* did I tell you to do?"

Skirts bounce as they run, and the door slams behind them. I

smile and turn to Lisa. She grins and flicks her thumb across the short, sharp blade. I nod.

"Only the green ones, Lisa, but not too many buds, all right?"

"OK . . . are you sure you want a *dozen*, Professor?"

"Hm? Well . . . perhaps six will do . . . about eighteen inches long, but make sure they're nice and flexible. You know what I mean."

Lisa blushes. "Yeah . . . the kind that really *sting*."

You chew a knuckle, watch Lisa skip toward a willow tree, and jump when I touch your arm.

"Sorry, Teresa. What was it all about? Do you know?"

"I um . . . I think it was about a boy they both like. Are . . . are you really going to switch them, Uncle Devlin? I mean . . . Professor?" I nod, take your hand and lead you toward the door. You frown. "But I thought you didn't *like* sticks."

"I don't . . . especially . . . but the paddle obviously made very little impression on them."

You bite your lip and look up at me as I shut the door behind us. I smile and you whimper as I lean down to kiss your damp lips. You squeal when I squeeze the rounded cheeks beneath your prim and proper pleated skirt.

"Uncle Devlin!" you whisper.

"What, sweetie?"

"Are you going to . . . to switch them *hard* . . . on their bare bottoms?"

I chuckle. "Why? Do you think that will be fun to watch?"

"No! I . . . I just wondered, that's all."

"Oh? Don't you want to know what I'm going to do to *your* bare bottom later on?"

"But . . . but you said you would not spank me for . . . for being so late with my assignment."

"No . . . but don't forget we need to discuss your diet. I won't punish you for *that* in front of the American girls, though."

"You . . . you won't?"

"As long as you help me with the dynamic duo in there."

You grin. "You . . . you will spank me *after* class?"

I nod and then frown. "Don't imagine it will be a day at the beach, Teresa Luisa."

A chill races up your spine. "Oh, God. Whuh . . . what do you want me to *do*?"

Your hand is cool and a bit damp. I hold it and lead you out of the kitchen, down the hall and into the bedroom. The bathroom door is open. Brittany and Ashley stand at the wide mirror and primp disheveled hair.

"Come here, girls." They turn toward me.

"We . . . we're all better now, Professor." Brittany's voice quavers.

"Oh, really? Let me have a look."

They walk slowly to me and I examine their faces and hands. Brittany's lower lip is split and Ashley has a round, knuckle-sized bump on her forehead. Both white blouses are smudged with grass and dirt. Dark water spots surround the stains where they tried to wash them out. Their skirts are wrinkled and grass blades cling to the light wool.

"All right, girls, remove your clothes, please."

"*What?*"

"Professor!"

I point to a dresser drawer. "There are oversized T-shirts in there. Take off your blouses and skirts in the bathroom and put one on, then I'll tend to your injuries."

You blush and they whimper as they bend to take squares of folded cotton from the drawer. I smile as the bathroom door clicks behind them.

"Teresa, would you go to the closet in the study for me, please?"

"Sure, but. . . ."

"Bring me two blouses and skirts . . . size four, I believe."

You grin. "You have extra uniforms for us?"

"I'd never let you girls go out in public wearing less than your best."

"I suppose not."

You lick your lips, kiss me quick on the mouth, and scurry out the door. Faded and frayed Dodgers tee shirts hang halfway down the cousin's thighs when they come out of the bathroom. I seat them on the bedside and dab Johnson's First Aid Cream on their battle wounds. They whimper when I make them stand so I can lift the T-shirts and examine them. You bring two fresh uniforms into the bedroom and smile as I smear unguent on an angry scrape to Ashley's rib cage. She holds up her shirt, bites her lip and stares at

the ceiling. Round, peach breasts quiver beneath a French brassiere. You glance at the plump, split mound at the front of her cotton panties, then blush and hang the clothes on the door handle.

"Thank you, Teresa." I wipe my hands on a tissue. "OK, girls, let's have your shoes and socks off. Just leave them by the door."

Brittany huffs. "*Please,* Professor, we won't ever. . . ."

"Hush! You *know* I don't allow fighting in this college. What in the *world* were you thinking?"

Ashley whimpers. "But you always just. . . ."

I scowl and raise a hand. They moan, flip away their loafers and tug off their cotton socks. You bite your fingertip and stand aside to let them pass into the hallway. Tears well in their eyes, and butterflies dance in your tummy. You watch them pad toward the schoolroom. Their tight bottoms look like live turtle shells under the threadbare shirts. Lisa peers around the doorway and winks at you after they walk into the classroom. You blush and look at me.

"Shall we?" I follow you down the hallway.

My desk is bare except for six willow wands. The switches glow deep, scary green against the polished oak. Lisa sits at her worktable and pretends to study a grammar book. You sit at yours and clench your fists in your lap while you watch Brittany and Ashley quiver beside the desk. The cousins stare at me, eyes wide and wet, as my heels click the hardwood floor. I stand in front of them and scowl.

"Apparently you two didn't learn your lesson last time so perhaps I can manage to be more convincing *this* time."

"No!"

"No *please*, sir!"

I bundle the wands in my fist and slap the desk. The damp *whunk* makes them squeal. Brittany bites her thumb and blinks at me. Ashley chews her little finger and takes two steps backward.

"*Where* are you going, young lady?"

"I . . . I just . . . *please* don't spank me with *those* . . . please?"

Brittany shakes her head furiously. "C-can't you just *paddle* us . . . like last time?"

"That had no effect as far as I can tell."

"But you didn't spank us very *hard!*"

Ashley stamps her foot. "For God's *sake,* Brit!"

The girl coughs. "*No,* I . . . I mean . . . the paddle really hurts a *lot* and. . . ." Her lips continue to move but there is no sound.

"She *means* we really *did* learn our lesson and . . . and this was just a . . . an *accident,* so . . . so if you just um . . . *remind* us with the paddle we won't *do* it anymore!"

"Thank you for the clarification, Ashley . . . but I don't intend to spank you with these."

They gape at me, then smile and look at each other. Brittany takes a deep breath.

"You . . . you're *not* going to spank us?"

I divide the bunch of willow twigs and lay them on the desk. "Of course I am . . . but not with these. Who started the fight?"

Each girl points at the other. "*She* did."

"I *see*. Then let me ask another way. Who threw the first *punch?*"

"Ashley did!"

"No way! You . . . you said I was a . . . and then . . . oh, *God.*"

"Ashley? Did you hit your cousin first?"

"Um . . . yeah . . . but she said I was a . . . a *slut,* Professor!" A fat tear drips from the corner of Ashley's eye.

"Brittany! Did you say that?"

"No! *Corbin* did!"

"He'd *never* say that!"

"Maybe not to your face!"

The girls square off, fists clenched, eyes ablaze. I grab neck napes and glare at them.

"Since you are *determined* to hurt each other, I'll give you the opportunity."

Brittany huffs. "*What?*"

"You heard me. Since Ashley hit you first, you will spank her bare bottom with the switches."

"No *way,* Professor!"

"Quiet, Ashley . . . I understand this wasn't an unprovoked attack, so you will repay her in kind."

They stare at me, their mouths open.

"But . . . but we're not *mad* at each other anymore, Professor."

"I find that *extremely* hard to believe, Brittany, and irrelevant in any case. Take off your panties and bend over the desk."

"Come *on,* Professor!"

"This is *so* not necessary!"

I bang the desktop with my fist and the girls grab each other's

hands and step backward. You look at Lisa and she grins. You blush and bite your fingertip.

"Do you want *me* to do it, girls?"

"Professor! *Please?*" Ashley whimpers and looks at Brittany.

"It's OK," Brittany whispers, and pushes her cousin toward the desk.

Ashley bites her lip as she watches Brittany pick up three switches, then she reaches under her shirt and yanks down white cotton panties.

"On the desk, Ashley."

She flicks the undies off her feet and drops them on the smooth oak. She grunts as she bends over and lays her palms flat on the desk, then looks back, eyes wide.

"Lift her shirt, Brittany."

"OK." She tucks the twigs under her arm and leans over to raise the frayed hem.

Ashley's tight bottom cheeks glow in the fluorescent ceiling lamps, pink and smooth as a strawberry malted. Brittany chews her lip and steps back a pace.

"All right, Brittany . . . give her three good ones and then stop."

The girl holds the wands like a racquet in a game she never played before. I nod and the wands bounce three times on Ashley's round pinkness. Ashley smiles at her cousin, then frowns at me as she rubs her uninjured behind. Brittany wipes invisible perspiration from her forehead and offers me the twigs.

"Set them down and remove your underpants." I tap the desktop with a fingertip.

Brittany drops the switches, thumbs down her drawers and tosses them next to her cousin's. She looks at you while Ashley rises from the desk and rolls her eyes. You giggle and put a hand over your mouth.

"Do you find this amusing, Miss Wagner?"

"No, I . . . I was only clearing my throat . . . sir."

"Lisa?"

"Sir?"

"Perhaps you will remind Teresa of proper classroom decorum while a classmate is undergoing correction."

"Yeah . . . um . . . we're supposed to . . . sit quietly and do our work while the professor sees that discipline and order are maintained in the college. Sir."

"*Very* splendid, Lisa. Do you understand what she said, Teresa?"

"Yes, *sir.* Perfectly well, *sir.*" You sneer at Lisa. "Only I did not know I was required to *memorize* the handbook."

"That will *do,* young lady." I scowl and you blush. "Any further impudence and you'll memorize the handbook while sitting on a blistered bottom." You stare at the floor and bite your lip as I turn away. "All right, Brittany, bend over. Ashley, bare her behind, please."

Her hand trembles as Ashley pulls up Brittany's shirt. Except for an extra centimeter of circumference, Brittany's round bottom is the twin of her cousin's. Ashley picks up the other set of twigs and flicks three light strokes across the firm cushions.

"Ow! I didn't hit you *that* hard!" Brittany glares at Ashley while she rubs.

"Uh *huh.* I did it just like *you* did."

"That's enough, girls . . . trade places."

Brittany grabs her switches and scowls at her cousin as she stands. Soft cotton slides down to cover her bottom and she grits her teeth as she yanks up Ashley's shirt. The twigs swish and bend across tender cheeks.

"Brit, *don't!* Ouch! *Ow!*"

"*That's* how you did it."

"No way! That really *stings.*" Ashley stands, twists and tugs up her shirt to examine the light pink lines that mar her perfect peach.

I cover a smile with my hand. "Your turn, Brittany."

She scowls at me, then looks down and bites her lip. Her hands slap oak as she bends and glares over her shoulder while her cousin lifts the shirt and raises the rod. Willow sings through the air and clacks naked skin.

"Ow! *Jesus! Ashley!*" Brittany jerks upright and grabs her bottom as she dances and rubs hot stripes.

Ashley grunts, bends, and yelps at each stroke of Brittany's supple wands. The marks on Ashley's smooth flesh are half a shade darker than the ones she left on Brittany's behind. The girl rises slowly while she caresses the sting and glares at her cousin.

Brittany yanks up her own shirt and clomps her elbows on the desk as she looks back and scowls. Ashley hisses through clenched teeth and twists her wrist when she whips into Brittany's warm,

pink mounds. The girl shuts her eyes and grunts as damp willow burns bright red pain across her soft behind. Brittany swipes an errant tear from her eye, pulls down her shirt and stands. The girls glare at each other from opposite ends of the desk. I take all six twigs, bend them in half and shove them into the trashcan by the chalkboard, then open a desk drawer and take out a sole cut from a size-twelve house shoe. Ashley squeals.

"You gotta be *kidding!*"

"*Yeah,* that's like *way* nasty and. . . ." Brittany whimpers when I smack the sole on my palm.

I twist the thin leather in my hands and step around the desk. The girls back away together and then stop when I snap my fingers and point at the floor a foot from the toes of my shoes. They grimace and shuffle to the spot.

"I am *very* disappointed with you two . . . but not at all surprised."

"Professor!"

"We . . . we did what you *told* us to so why do you gotta . . . ?" Ashley squeaks when I point the sole at her.

"I will *not* have your petty jealousies over a boy interfere with your education."

"But we're like *so* over that, Professor! She can *have* Corbin if she wants him."

Brittany nods hard.

"Or *she* can . . . it's like not a big *thing* anymore."

"I still don't buy that, girls . . . when just a minute ago you were determined to skin each other's bottoms."

"Nuh *uh!*"

"We were just messing *around,* Professor!"

"Well I'm *not,* Ashley." I slap the desk with the sole. "Sit right up here, *both* of you."

"*What?*"

"*Why?*"

"Because I *said* to, and be quick about it." The girls exchange puzzled glances, then turn and sit on the desktop. "Lie back."

"*What?*"

"*Why?*"

I give them both a sharp pop to the bare thigh. "*Stop* that . . . lie down and lift your legs . . . *now.*"

"But that's just. . . ."

– 90 –

"You *can't* make us. . . ."

"*Do* it . . . or I'll call your mothers to come and *help* you."

Hot blush reddens Brittany's face. "Don't call *her!*"

"Professor!" Ashley bangs a fist on the oak. "I . . . I'd just *die* if Mom saw me like this!"

Brittany swipes a tear. "Don't call Mama, OK? If I get in trouble anymore she'll send me to live with Aunt Ethel and Uncle Mike and I *hate* them!"

"Then do as I said."

"But . . . but if you spank us like . . . like *that*. . . ." Brittany looks at her cousin.

Ashley's eyes widen. She looks down at her legs, then at you, then at Lisa. "God, that's . . . that's *obscene!*"

"All right, then." I unclip the cell phone from my belt.

Both girls whine, lie back and raise their legs. Soft shirts pile at their waists and they clamp their thighs tight while they hold their knees with both hands. You keep your head bowed over your grammar book but your forehead wrinkles as you peer forward. Two firm, bare fannies jiggle while two pair of bare feet squirm high above them.

"*Please*, Professor . . . not real hard?"

"Hush, Brittany . . . and both of you keep you legs right *up*." I re-clip the phone while the girls strain their necks to watch me. "If *either* of you lets go and tries to cover or rub your bottom, I will start over on *both* of you. Is that clear?"

"Y-yeah." Brittany sniffles and tightens her grip.

"Ha . . . how *many*, Professor?"

"A dozen each . . . to start with."

"What does *that* mean?" Ashley's eyes fill with tears.

"That means if you're very good and take your first dozen well, the next twelve won't be as strict."

"Twenty-*four*? That's *way* harsh, Professor!"

"Would you care to try for thirty-six, Ashley?"

"Shut *up*, Ash!"

"Well *geeze*, Brit!"

"Knock it off . . . I . . . I'm ready, Professor." Brittany's fingers dig deep furrows behind her knees.

Ashley's nose wrinkles as she squeezes her eyes shut. "*God*, this sucks."

"All right . . . steady now."

I swing the sole and slap Ashley's pert bottom medium hard. You gasp and cover your mouth when a hot pink oval highlights the faint switch marks at the base of her cheeks. My jacket billows and you gaze at the front of my trousers while I paint ever-warmer shades of red on Ashley's smooth behind. She sobs, yelps, and flails her feet. Her bottom twists and the cleft opens and closes, like a mouth in prayer. You bite your fingertip when the puffy lower lips appear between her thighs. After six sharp smacks, I flex my arm and move half a pace to the right to color Brittany's behind a shade similar to her cousin's.

"Nah! Plah! Not so . . . ahh! *Hard! Ahhh! Professor!*"

You turn your head when Lisa's chair squeaks. Her chin rests in her left palm but her right hand is busy in her lap. She blushes and grins at you.

"Lisa!" you hiss.

Red embarrassment boils up your breasts and into your face when I look at you. Your fingers twine on the table and you stare at a book that might as well be written in Chinese. Ashley squeals as six more slaps echo through the room. The sound vibrates through the chair seat, up your thighs, and into your panties. You bite your lip and try to will the dampness away, but it is no use. Your eyes, of their own volition, steal away from the incomprehensible print to focus on Brittany's bright red cheeks and the soft pink slit between them, then shift to the pinstriped pleats at the front of my trousers. My arm flashes heat into the girl's squirmy behind, and you moan aloud as a drop of moisture, unbidden, unwelcome, squeezes between your labia and wets your knickers. You jerk backward and bite you knuckles when I turn to you once more.

"Teresa Luisa! Did you not understand when you were told how to behave during correction?"

"But I . . . I only *coughed* or . . . or something. Sir."

I point the sole at you, then at the corner between my desk and the window. "Stand over there and I'll deal with you in a moment."

"Uncle . . . *Professor* . . . no! I didn't *mean* to. . . ."

"Don't make me tell you *twice,* girl."

You whimper and push your chair back. Your knees wobble as you cross in front of Lisa. She looks up and winks. You scowl and

stick out your tongue, then look at me while you stomp toward the corner. I frown and you turn to face the wall.

Ashley and Brittany sob and squirm on the desk. Their knuckles are white, as is the taut flesh they clutch with stiff fingers. A blush the color of new roses covers their behinds. I sigh and fold my arms while I look at them.

"Brittany?"

"Wha . . . ? S-*sir?*"

"Ashley?"

"Yes, sir?"

"Will I *ever* have to remind you not to fight with each other?"

"No, sir!" they say at once.

"I had better *not*. You may get up now."

The girls moan as they lower their legs, roll off the desk and rub sore bottoms while they lean on each other. I smile, drop the sole on the desktop and open a drawer. Brittany looks at Ashley and covers her wink with a tear swipe as I pick up the bottle of baby oil, then she frowns when I hand it to her.

"Professor?"

"Since you threw the first punch, you may be the first to offer the olive branch . . . or would you rather not have any emollient today?"

"No! I mean *yeah* . . . but *you* usually. . . ."

"Then ask Ashley if she would like for you to tend to her."

I take a box of Kleenex from the drawer and both girls grab a handful when I set it on the desk. Brittany blows her nose and then shrugs at Ashley.

"So . . . um . . . you wanna?"

Ashley nods, glances at Lisa, then at you, before she lifts her shirt and turns her back to the girl. Brittany dribbles oil into her palm and smoothes it over the red behind. Ashley clutches soft cotton at her waist and bends forward so her cousin can smear relief along the crease where her buttocks and thighs join. Brittany wipes her hand on a tissue and gives Ashley the bottle, and she returns the oily favor.

"*Much* better, girls." I hold out my arms. "Come here." They whimper and cuddle close while I hug them. "We're all clear about the no fighting rule?" I kiss their foreheads when they nod. "Good . . . then you're forgiven. Now take your panties and go back to your seats."

"Professor?"

"What, Ashley?"

"Um . . . do we gotta sit on those hard chairs?"

"My butt's really sore, Professor." Brittany sniffles and dabs her eyes.

"You may get pillows from the sofa in the study, but come right back. I need to give you your assignments for next week."

The girls nod, squeeze my chest and pad out the door. You lick your lips and play with the stiff collar of your white blouse as you peer our shoulder at me.

"Come here, Teresa."

Butterflies dance in your tummy as you turn and shuffle to me. "I didn't *mean* to make noise while you were um . . . it was an *accident, I promise.*"

"You had to be told *twice* to pay attention to your work."

"But you . . . you *cannot* expect me to concentrate with all that . . . that *stuff* going on! It is not *fair!*"

"I *expect* you to behave like a mature young lady at all times and in all situations."

A tear drips from your eye and you bat it away. "But I *can't,* Uncle Devlin! You *know* this!"

"Teresa! Control yourself."

"You are just being *mean*. No!"

I grab you around the waist and sit on the desk. You kick, squeal and slap polished oak as I bend you over my left thigh. I lean back and clamp your legs between mine. You shriek when I pull your skirt up, and scream when I pull down your moist panties.

"Nooo! *Please!*"

"*Hush,* Teresa," I say, and spank your warm, plump bottom.

"But I didn't *do* anything!"

"You behaved very badly while I was trying to keep order in the classroom."

You yelp and squirm when I bounce a dozen sharp smacks on your quivery cheeks. Brittany and Ashley slink into the room, set fat round pillows on their chairs and sit. Lisa bites her lip and stares at her book.

"It is all *Lisa's* fault! Ow! She was *playing* with herself . . . ouch! While you were spanking those brats!"

"Teresa!" I slap hard across the center of your bottom.

You glare at Lisa. "*Tell* him!"

Lisa looks at me, eyes wide, moist, innocent. "I don't know what she's talking about, Professor."

"Yes you *do!*" You jerk your head toward me. "If you think *my* panties are wet you should see *hers!*"

"I *never* said your panties were wet, young lady."

"Well you can *see* them, can't you? Look at *hers*. I'll bet they are *soaking*."

I smack your bottom twice and then pull you up to stand in front of me. You wipe tears with your knuckles and stare at the front of my trousers.

"Teresa, I am *very* disappointed in you."

"But I . . . I did not do *anything*." You sob and lean over to whisk a handful of tissues from the box.

I stare at the ceiling for five seconds and then look at Lisa. She gazes out the window at a humming bird in the azaleas.

"Lisa, come here, please."

"*Sir?*"

She sighs when I crook my index finger, shuts her book and ambles to the front of the classroom, then stands and stares at a spot just above my head.

"Lisa Marie." She blushes and takes a half step back. "*Look* at me."

Small fingers fidget at her waist. "I didn't do anything *either,* Professor!"

I lean over, take her hand and pull her toward me. She whimpers when her thigh touches the desk next to my right leg.

"I'm sorry to have to do this, Lisa . . . but will you please raise your skirt?"

"I . . . I'd rather not. Sir."

"Oh? And why is that?"

"Be . . . because um . . . you don't have any *right* to look under my skirt!"

"Young lady, I have looked under your skirt, on average, six times a month since you have been at this college. Why do you suddenly object?"

"Um . . . because I have my *period. Sir.*"

"I see. Then I will call your gynecologist and make an appointment for you immediately. Something is obviously wrong, since you are so regular and your last one ended a week ago."

"No! I mean . . . it just came out of nowhere! I . . . I went horse-back riding and it. . . ."

"Lisa Marie, stop lying to me this *instant* and pull up your skirt."

"Oh, shit! I mean *shoot!*" She grabs the hem of the pleated wool.

"See?" You point to the wetness at the front of her demure cotton undies. "I *told* you."

Brittany and Ashley giggle and I lean to my left to glare at them.

"There are more switches on the willow tree, girls." They hide behind grammar books and I shake my head while I glare at the two of you. "I am *very* put out . . . this is *not* the way mature young ladies behave at my college."

Lisa drops her skirt and covers her eyes with both hands. You lick your lips and circle my neck with both arms.

"We're *sorry,* Uncle . . . Professor." You twist around to look at Lisa and your hip rubs the front of my trousers. I gasp and you grin at her. "We will never be naughty like that again, will we?"

She looks at you, wipes her eyes on the back of a hand and grins as she plucks tissues. "No *sir,* Uncle Professor."

I groan and push you away. "Brittany, Ashley. . . ." They look up as I glance at the clock. "Lessons are finished for the day . . . but I want a five-hundred word essay on the evils of fighting by next week. Put your clean uniforms on quickly so you can catch the three-thirty bus."

Ashley frowns. "We usually take the four-fifteen, Professor."

"Today you'll take the three-thirty and I'll call your mothers at five o'clock so you had better go right home. Understand?"

Brittany nods and pouts. "OK."

The girls walk out and Ashley turns at the doorway.

"They got to see *us* get blistered so how come we have to . . . ?"

Ashley shrieks and runs down the hall when I pick up the leather sole and smack it on the desktop. You both smile at me but your smiles fade when I scowl.

"Get to work."

"Yes, *sir.*" Lisa scurries to her chair.

"Uncle Devlin!"

"Teresa!"

"All right . . . *Professor* Devlin! Lisa got me in trouble and all you do is tell her to get to *work?*" You cross your arms and pout.

"I told *both* of you to get to work."

A hot blush rises from deep in your tummy as I stand and glower. You reach under your skirt, tug your panties into place and scamper to your seat. I take a small computer from the desk drawer and boot it up. Long minutes tick by, until, finally, the cottage's front door opens and shuts. You glance at Lisa, then at me. The laptop queeps when I shut it off, close the lid, and slide it into the drawer. You bite your lip while you pretend to read your book. I push back my chair.

"Go to the study, girls."

You pack your book bag while Lisa does the same, and you walk together down the hallway to the door on the left. Two heavy satchels hit the soft carpet at the same time as you and Lisa sit on the sofa.

"Sorry, Teresa."

"I have had worse from him."

Lisa grins. "Not *that,* silly. I mean I'm sorry you didn't get over the top when he was spanking those brats!"

"You . . . you had a *climax?*"

"Well, duh! I don't soak my panties for *nothing.*"

You blush. "I did not know."

"Do you get that wet and *not* have one?"

"I do not go *over the top* in such a short time."

"Usually I don't either, but you saw how *hard* he got when he was spanking them."

"Lisa! You must not *say* such. . . ."

You gasp and jump to your feet when I walk in. Lisa stands beside you, her arm tight against yours.

"All right, girls . . . let me have them."

"Have what?"

Lisa smirks. "Don't be dense, Teresa."

She hikes up her skirt and you stifle a moan as you tug your panties down your legs and step out of them. I shake my head and frown when you stuff your wet knickers into the plastic laundry bag I hold at arm's length.

"You behaved very badly today." I cinch the bag's neck and toss it into a corner. "Raise your skirts."

"Uncle Devlin!"

"I won't tell you again."

I lean forward and fist my hips. You whimper and drag your skirt, an inch at a time, up your smooth thighs. Lisa huffs and yanks hers to her waist. Her sex is a thin slit beneath short, light brown hair. Yours is plump and pink, with a trim triangle of damp, curly brown above. Lisa's hair sparkles with beads of moisture. You both squeal when I palm your vaginas.

"Professor!"

"Uncle Devlin, for God's *sake!*" A soft lightening bolt lances up your belly when my finger touches your labia.

"Hush, *both* of you . . . and keep your skirts right where they are." I grab Kleenex from the box on the end table and wipe moisture from my hands. "Go to the bedroom and get undressed. Now!"

You look over your shoulders as you scuff across the hall. I lock the front door and then lean against the bedroom doorjamb. Four clothes hangers lie on the bed where the cousins tossed them. Lisa shrugs off her blouse and looks at me as you do the same. A deep blush heats the creamy flesh above your bra as you drape your blouse over a hanger. Lisa pouts and unhooks her skirt's side vent. The light wool slides to a heap at her feet and she covers herself with a hand as she steps out of the woolen circle and squats to pick it up. You look at me for a few seconds and then stamp your foot.

"What are you going to *do* to us?"

"Punish you, of course."

"But . . . how can you be so *calm* about it?"

I stride over and take your hand. "Because I know I can count on you to display enough histrionics for all of us. Now take off your skirt and put it on a hanger."

"Uncle *Devlin!*"

"*Now,* Teresa." I turn to Lisa. "Shoes, socks and bras off as well."

A tear rolls down your cheek as you fumble with buttons. Plaid wool floats to the carpet when you drop your skirt, and you sob as you sit on the bed to take off your sensible footwear and soft cotton brassiere. Lisa drapes her bra over her blouse, hangs her uniform on the door handle and stares at the carpet.

"Back to the classroom, girls."

"Nuh-not *naked,* Professor!"

"*Quiet,* Lisa."

Your lips move but no sound emerges as you hug yourself and pad along the hallway. I follow and note that Lisa's firm rear cheeks are dotted with faded paddle marks, but your own plump behind glows a healthy, pinkish tan, with no sign of your recent spanking to mar its beauty. You sigh with relief when you see the schoolroom blinds are shut, and then look over your shoulder. I point to the door next to the desk and we walk through the cloakroom and into the bath.

"You may be first, Lisa."

She huffs, nods, and takes a dozen baby steps to stand in front of me. I smile when she half turns, bends and puts her palms on her knees.

"All in good time, Lisa." I take hold of her elbow. "Come along."

Lisa gapes when I lead her to the bidet. "But I . . . I never *used* one of these things!"

"About time you learned, then . . . especially if you insist on playing with your naughty bits in class."

"*Professor!*"

"Adjust the water temperature in the little fountain, just as you would in a wash basin . . . not too hot and *certainly* not too cold." She turns the spigot and glares at me while she tests the water temperature with her fingers. "Now sit astride the seat, as you would a motorcycle."

"But um . . . do you have to *watch?*"

"I want to make sure you do a good job. It's not pleasant for me to spank a girl whose nether regions are unclean."

"That's a *horrible* thing to say!"

"*Sit,* young lady."

She pouts and squirms as she straddles the bidet. "Ah! It's *cold.*"

"Then turn up the hot water . . . just a bit, or you'll find it very uncomfortable."

Lisa whimpers as she adjusts the knobs. Finally, she hunches forward and reaches between her legs to bathe herself in the fountain. I take a hand towel from the stack on a shelf and shake it out. A neon red blush glows on Lisa's face.

"Is . . . is that *enough?*"

"Scoot up and wash your bottom cleft as well."

She scowls and thigh flesh squeaks enamel as she moves forward, then she groans and bites her lip as water splashes her anus.

"All right . . . stand up and let me dry you."

I offer a hand and she shudders as she rises and stares at the ceiling, feet wide apart, while I towel her inner thighs and tender labia. I turn her and she bends forward so I can dab wetness from between her cheeks.

A pink haze clouds your vision and you shut your eyes to block the image of your uncle playing with another girl's bottom.

"That's good, Lisa."

You jerk like a wounded fawn and open your eyes when I give her a soft pat to indicate that I am finished. She stands straight and turns to me as she chews the tip of her thumb.

"Get a bath sheet and wrap it around you."

She hugs her breasts and hurries to the linen shelves. I hold out a hand and you blush as you cover yourself with both arms and shake your head.

"Do not make me *do* this, Uncle Devlin, *please?*"

"Stop being silly and come here."

Your knees quake and your heart pumps fiery blood through your erect nipples and up your neck. I stride across the tiles and take hold of your left wrist.

"*No,* Uncle Devlin! I . . . I did not play with myself, honestly!"

"That may be true, in a physical sense, but a good cleaning is indicated nonetheless."

"Nooo!"

You tremble as I seat you astride the bidet. The fountain dances a scant centimeter from your puffy, open slit. I push you down and you shriek when water floods the intimate folds. You try to stand but I hold your shoulders.

"Wash yourself, Teresa," I whisper.

"I . . . I *can't.*"

"Then I will."

I reach between your thighs and you clutch my arm. Tepid water burns your insides like live coals as my fingers caress the drippy slickness at the core of your being. Your clitoris feels like a river pebble when I slide a fingertip over it, around it, and then

over it again. You quiver, lean forward and bite hard into my suit coat. The quiver becomes a tremble, then a jerk, and you scream your release into Armani's finest woolen. I bathe your throbbing anus as you groan and squeeze tight on my upper arm.

"Get up, sweetie."

You nod but make no move to comply. I reach beneath your armpits and lift you. Lisa leans against the wall, wrapped in terrycloth from breasts to knees, and chews her thumb. I scowl and she snaps to attention.

"Stop smirking and bring me a hand towel."

She pouts and goes to the rack. "Here you go. *Sir.*"

I nod and reach down to dry between your thighs. "Open your legs a bit."

Bare feet squeak tile and you gasp as I dry your lower lips. I twist you to the left and you fold like a rag doll when I bend you over to dry inside your bottom. The tiny, wrinkled hole within throbs to the quick beat of your heart and you gasp when I dab moisture from it.

"OK . . . stand up." You moan and shake your head at the floor. "Come along now. You're all clean so I can spank you."

"*No!*" You spring straight up.

"No?"

"*Please?* We . . . I . . . don't be such a *tyrant*, Uncle Devlin!"

I cross my arms and stare as you cover yourself and back away. "You two behaved like children today so why on *earth* shouldn't I tan your naughty hides?"

"But I already *got* spanked!" You huff and lean on the wall beside Lisa.

"Yes . . . for creating an uproar during correction."

"Yeah . . . and that's *all* I did. You . . . you should spank Lisa because she um . . . she . . . . It was all *her* fault!"

"Yes, and you felt the need to tell the whole class of Lisa's indiscretion."

Lisa glares at you and slides away. You blush and bite your lip as I shake my head.

"Did you think I was unaware of her activity, Teresa?"

"I . . . I don't know . . . perhaps?"

"I disapprove of tattletales."

"But she got me in *trouble!*"

I shake my head and take another bath sheet from the cabinet. "Here . . . put this around you."

"Uncle Devlin, *please* do not spank me again! I *tried* to be good, only. . . ."

"Shh . . . come along to the study. It won't be as bad as all *that*."

"Um . . . Professor?"

"Yes, Lisa?"

"You . . . you're not gonna switch me, are you?"

"Why? Do you think I should?"

"*No!* I mean . . . no, *sir.* But what *are* you gonna do?"

"Punish you, Lisa." I push you both out the door. "Wait for me in the study."

You shuffle along the hallway and look at Lisa. She shakes her head and grunts.

"He is *so* aggravating."

"Very much so. I . . . I am sorry I told on you." Lisa shrugs as you both sit on the study sofa. "You are not angry with me?"

"A little . . . but he already knew what I was doing. He's got like eyes in the back of his head."

"I will not tattle tales of you ever again, Lisa."

She smiles, takes your hand and kisses your cheek. "Thanks. I get in enough trouble on my own. I just wish I knew what he was going to do to my heinie."

"I was very afraid when he took us to the bathroom, but it was not . . . hurtful . . . what he did."

Lisa giggles. "No, but I thought *you* were gonna bounce off the wall!"

You blush and squeeze Lisa's hand as I walk into the room and set the leather sole and baby oil bottle on the end table. You whimper, jump to your feet and clutch the towel to your bosom.

"All right, girls . . . turn around, kneel on the sofa and lean against the back."

"*Please*, Uncle Devlin . . . Professor . . . *sir* . . . not too *hard?*"

"Do what I told you, Teresa . . . Lisa?"

"Yes, sir?" She looks over her shoulder as she settles onto her knees.

"You know I have to be very strict with you, don't you?"

"I guess so . . . but you won't tell Michael . . . um . . . Mr. Swayne . . . or Ms. Weller, will you?"

I shake my head and she puffs a relieved breath. "Not if you promise to tell them the truth about *why* your behind is bright red and very sore, should they happen to see it."

She wrinkles her nose. "OK . . . but maybe they *won't* for a few days, huh?"

"One can only hope. Who gave you the paddle rash?"

"Darcy . . . Ms. Weller."

"Why?"

"I was um . . . Greg and I were uh . . . supposed to be doing homework and we were doing something else."

"I see. So part of your problem today was an interrupted amorous interlude?"

"No . . . Greg made sure I got over the . . . um. . . ."

Lisa stares at the wall and squirms her ankles. I sigh and fold the towels off your bottoms. Four bare, girlish cheeks clench and quiver in the cool half-light of the study. I pick up the sole and your shoulders jerk when I swish it through the air.

"Twenty-four for you, Teresa . . . Lisa, you will get forty-eight."

She jerks around. "*Geeze,* Professor! I . . . I *promise* I won't do it anymore so why can't you give me a break?"

"Would you prefer to go and cut more switches?"

"No! No, *sir!* I. . . ."

"Then stop arguing."

A wet sob burbles her lips as she bows her head on her fists. You hold her hand and glare at me over your shoulder.

"You have something to say, Teresa?"

"You are just . . . ! I . . . no. Sir."

"Lean forward, girls. I want your naughty bottoms well bended for this."

You squeeze Lisa's hand and push back with your hips. The sole swats your right cheek. You grunt and then squeak when I backhand a sharp smack to the left one. I shift to my right and swat Lisa's behind, forehand then backhand, just as I did yours. You grit your teeth to maintain a stoic silence until the leather cracks fifteen and sixteen. A guttural yelp tears from your throat and you kick the sofa with both feet.

"Not . . . ow! *Owee!* So *hard.*"

Lisa wails and kicks right along with you as I slap redness into your pert backsides. White noise roars in your ears and you wince

as the sole stings tender flesh. You sob and wail for several seconds until you realize that the slaps you hear don't hurt. Lisa's arms are flat against the wall behind the sofa and her wet face points to the ceiling. Her hips buck with each leathery crack. You look back at me as I fan the flames in Lisa's swollen cheeks, and pout as you rub harsh sting from your own behind. I ease off just a little but Lisa shrieks and babbles with each sharp swat. Since I doubt either of you will notice, I stop at forty-two.

"It's over, girls."

You scowl at me and peel Lisa off the wall. Her tears wet your bare legs as you ignore your own pain to sit on the sofa and lay the girl's head in your lap. I toss the sole away and pick up the bottle of oil.

"Should Lisa have this first?"

"Well, *duh*, Uncle Devlin!"

I frown, hand you the bottle and scoop Lisa from the sofa. You stand and your towel falls to the floor. I turn, sit and drape her across my lap as you kick the towel away and scurry to my left to sit and cradle Lisa's head on your thighs. I push away her rumpled bath sheet. My fingers burn when I touch the scalded behind. You yank a dozen tissues from the box, dab wetness from her face and glare at me.

"You are just a *meanie*, Herr Professor."

"Don't *start* with me, young lady."

You pout and hold Lisa's head up so she can blow her nose. I dribble oil on her ravaged backside and glide it across hot roundness. She sighs and smiles up at you.

"Thanks, Teresa . . . are *you* OK?"

"Yes . . . . he will wait until you go home to be mean to *me*." You look up and your tongue darts from between your teeth.

I ignore your impertinence and squeeze more oil. "How do you feel, Lisa?"

"Like I sat in a wasp nest. Sir."

"You rather look it, from this angle. I would prefer not to spank you this hard again."

"Works for me, Professor. Does that mean I'm forgiven for um . . . ?"

"Being exceptionally naughty in class today?" Lisa nods and you hand her fresh Kleenex. "Yes, you're forgiven . . . . full and free, and without let or hindrance."

Lisa smiles. "Michael said the same thing once . . . after he blistered my heinie. Did you guys go to the same school or something?"

"In a way I suppose we did. I hope you can stay out of trouble long enough for the marks to fade. I'd hate for him to call me for the details of um. . . ."

"My exceptional naughtiness? I'll drink to *that*."

"Excellent idea . . . sweetie, will you get the key to the liquor cabinet from the top desk drawer and pour Lisa about two fingers of brandy?"

"Can I have Scotch instead?"

I smile. "You've developed a taste for single malt, have you?"

"Yeah . . . kind of." Lisa snuggles into my stomach when you get up.

You open the cabinet and look at me as you pour Glenlivet. I smile and wink while Lisa's shiny red bottom squirms beneath my palm. You frown.

"Do you want one, too? *Sir?*"

"No thanks . . . but you may help yourself if you like."

The Courvoisier cork pops, moist and smooth, when you yank it out to pour a small snifter half full. You turn your back, guzzle most of it and then half fill it again before you bring the drinks to the sofa. The cognac burns all the way down to your tummy and you stumble as you turn to sit down. Lisa rises on both palms and whimpers as you plop onto the sofa. Whisky and cognac swirl in their glasses and mixed liquor splashes your bare breasts.

"Oh, shit!" You set the glasses on the end table.

"Are you all right, sweetie?"

"Fine!"

Lisa lays her head in your lap and you snatch Kleenex to take angry swipes at driblets of expensive liquor.

"Hey!" She lifts her head. "What's wrong, Teresa?"

"Nothing!"

She looks over her shoulder at me and I shrug.

You grab the whisky glass. "Do you want this?"

"Yeah, um . . . thanks."

Lisa sips whisky while you guzzle brandy. I fold the towel down over her oily bottom and pat it.

"Better?"

She squirms off my lap and onto her knees.

"Yeah. Um . . . yes, sir . . . but maybe I won't sit down right now."

I smile and Lisa grins as she leans on the sofa arm. You drain the cognac and then stomp over to retrieve your towel. I pick up the baby oil bottle and look at you.

"Teresa? Would you like . . . ?"

"No!" You swirl the bath sheet around your nakedness.

Lisa stands, sets down her glass and looks at you. "I better go."

"What*ever*."

"Professor . . . um . . . is it OK if I go home without any panties on?"

"Of *course* it's not OK . . . there are stacks of new undies in the closet. But you may want to take a pair that's a size or two larger than you usually wear."

"Yeah." She smiles and licks her lips. "Maybe I'll take a sofa cushion for the bus ride, too, huh?"

"That will be fine." I smile and stand up.

She grins, throws her arms around my neck and hugs me. "I'm *kidding,* Uncle Professor. I'll be OK."

The door squeaks when she opens the closet, grabs a pair of underpants from the shelf next to the rack of blouses and skirts and slips off her towel as she goes out the door. Her slick, red bottom bounces as she rounds the corner toward the bedroom. You glare at me from across the room. I sigh, take off my suit jacket and drape it over the back of the desk chair.

"Teresa?"

"What?"

"Are you trying to annoy me?"

"No!"

"Then why are you acting like such a spoiled, jealous brat?"

"I am *not.*"

"Oh, really? Then why on earth would I *think* that, do you suppose?"

"I have no idea."

"I see. Would it have anything to do with the fact that I have spent more time today spanking other girls than I have spanking *you?*"

"That is ridiculous! I *hate* to get spanked."

"Is that right?"

"Yeah, and . . . and you're just a big *meanie*. Lisa won't be able to sit for a *week*."

"She seemed well on the mend when she walked out."

"That's only because you spent more time rubbing oil on her bare heinie than you did spanking it in the first place!" You clap a hand over your mouth and turn away from me. I hug you from behind and you squirm in my arms. "Leave me *alone*."

I yank you around and the towel drops to the floor. You push against my chest, but I wrap you up and hold you close.

"*Stop* that, Teresa. I won't have you being jealous of Lisa."

"I am *not!*"

Your bottom quivers when I caress the angry red sole marks. "*Don't!*"

"Teresa Luisa, you are being *impossible*. What is the *matter* with you?"

"Nothing!"

"Young lady, if you say that once more I will blister you until your teeth rattle."

"I don't *care*. You are just *mean* to me."

"What? When have I ever . . . ?"

"You . . . you made me . . . *climax* . . . with your finger and . . . and then you *spanked* me!"

I smile and rub your back while you sob into my tie. "It's all right, sweetie."

"No it is *not* because then . . . then you rubbed oil on *her* bottom . . . be . . . because you think it is *prettier* than mine!"

"That is simply not *true*. I rubbed *her* bottom because it was twice as *red* as yours. I *wanted* to put oil on your beautiful fanny but you said *no*."

"But that was merely a . . . an afterthought!"

"Teresa! I'm ashamed of you for *thinking* that."

"I knew it! You are ashamed to be *seen* with me!"

I sigh, shake my head and glance at the doorway. Lisa peeks around the doorjamb, winks, hoists her book bag, and waves as she tiptoes to the front door. You jerk your head around when the latch clicks behind her.

"Lisa went home, sweetie."

"*So?*"

"Are you *quite* finished with your tantrum?"

"I did *not* have a tantrum!"

You stamp your foot and I yelp when the heel lands on my toe.

"That *does* it. I have had more of your nonsense than any sensible man should have to endure."

"I . . . I am *sorry*, Uncle Devlin, I didn't mean to . . . *no!*"

I grab your arm and you stumble as I drag you into the bedroom. You shriek and squirm when I sit on the side of the bed and toss you over my knees.

"Your adorable bottom is going to pay a *very* high price for this outrage."

"No, *please* . . . you already spanked me real . . . *owee!*"

My hand burns as I slip off my tie and toss it into the corner. You rub fresh sting atop the sole rash on your right cheek and turn your head to glare at me. I snug your waist hard against my stomach as I raise my arm high.

"I will! Not! Have! You! Act! Like! This! Teresa!" I land a crisp spank on your plump behind with each word.

"Naah! Owee! Devlin! *Please!*"

"Do you think I don't *love* you?"

"Nooo! Aiee! Auuu! Yes! You . . . auu . . . *love* me!"

"Then you will stop this nonsense?"

"Aaah! Naah! Yes! *Please!* Nooo mooore!"

I lay my hand on your scorched bottom and you sob into the satin quilt. You whimper when I lift you and roll you onto your back on the bed. Tears smear your vision when I lean over to kiss your lips.

"Is all the nonsense out of your system now?"

"It is *not* nonsense. You *do* like Lisa more than . . . *no!*"

Your arms flail when I scoop your legs up and bend your knees onto your breasts.

"Devlin, *please!* Don't spank me like *this!*"

"You thought it was very attractive when I did it to Brittany and Ashley."

"I did *not* I *swear.*"

You chew a fingertip and moan as I grab both your slender ankles in my left hand. Your knees part and you gasp when you look down to see your vagina. The lips are moist and the little nub of your clitoris peeks from beneath its hood. Your bottom cheeks glow like new sunburn.

"This is too *horrible!*"

"So was your performance the past fifteen minutes, so now you're going to *watch* while I spank your jealous little fanny!"

"Noooo!" You squeeze you eyelids tight.

"Open your eyes at *once,* Teresa Luisa."

"I don't *want* to!" You pout and quiver as I caress the tender flesh around your exposed anus with a fingertip. "*Ah! Don't do that!*"

You gasp, open your eyes wide and slide a hand down your belly to cover yourself.

"Take that hand *away.*"

"But Uncle *Devlin* . . . you *can't* make me watch my own bottom get spanked!"

"Young lady, either you watch me spank you or I'll get the hairbrush and you may keep your eyes shut as tightly as you like."

"Not the *hairbrush!*"

"All right, then."

I raise my arm and swat your left cheek with a cupped palm. You squeal and reach down to rub.

"Take that *away,* Teresa! The other one, too."

"But you might hit my . . . my *vagina.*"

"I have no intention of doing so and your arm is blocking your view so move it at *once.*"

"No!"

"I see! You want to *play* with your vagina while you're being spanked?"

"Oh, *God,* Uncle Devlin!" You yank both hands to your face and I lean over to slide another pillow under your neck.

"There . . . comfy?"

"How could I *possibly* be when you are . . . ?"

"*Hush* . . . and watch carefully while I punish your naughty behind."

"*Devlin!* Ow! Owee! Aiiee! Ohhh! Auuu!"

"Open your eyes, Teresa, I'm not *nearly* done."

"But it *hurts,* Uncle Devlin!"

"Much less than the hairbrush, now open! Your! Eyes!"

"Eeek! Aiee! Eyow!" My fingertips land on the sensitive flesh inside your cleft and you gasp. "*No!* Not in *there!*"

I twist a little to my left so I can flick my fingers on the tender skin around your anus. "Not *here,* Teresa?"

"Nuh . . . nuh . . . nuh . . . *noooo!*"

You stare through a veil of hot tears at the fingers that flash and send jolts of soft fire through your bottom and up your breasts. A bead of naughty moisture squeezes between your labia and you wail as you cover your eyes with both hands. Your legs drop and bounce when I release your ankles. I scoop you up, cradle you, and turn to sit on the bed. Your tears drench my collar.

"It's all right now. You were a brave girl."

"I . . . I . . . I am *sorry,* Uncle Devlin!"

"I know, sweetie, and I'm sorry I had to punish you so hard, but you've been very naughty today."

Your head bobs against my neck. "I . . . I won't be a . . . a brat anymore."

"Yes, well . . . let's not make promises we can't keep, shall we?"

You look up at me and your lips quiver as you smile. "I promise not to be a spoiled, jealous brat anymore . . . today."

Salty tears wet my lips when I kiss you. "*Much* better. You know I love you very much."

"More than Lisa?"

I frown. "Teresa!"

"I am *kidding,* Uncle Devlin."

"You'd better be. Now go get the cold cream from the bathroom cabinet."

"OK." You kiss me as you stumble to your feet, then look over your shoulder while you rub your red bottom.

"And wash your face while you're in there."

"I have to use the toilet, also."

"Don't be too long or I'll think you're doing something *else.*"

"Uncle Devlin! I would *never.*"

"Oh, *really?*"

"Of *course* not! I only want *you* to do that."

You giggle and skip away as I gasp. The bathroom door shuts and I undress while I listen to the water run. You yelp and I spring to my feet, dressed only in one sock.

"*Teresa?*"

"I am OK . . . but I forgot and tried to sit on the toilet."

"*Do* be careful, then."

"No *duh,* Uncle Devlin! You blistered my heinie pretty good."

"Pretty *well,* Teresa."

– 110 –

"Yes . . . it is *pretty* well done . . . more than medium rare, in any case."

I chuckle, yank off the sock and toss it at the hamper before I slip into my robe. The bathroom door opens as I turn down the bed covers. You hand me a jar of Pond's and I help you lie on your tummy. Your bottom's bright red has mellowed to a smooth ver-milion, with only a few violet semi-circles along the outer flesh from the sole's edge. I dip two fingers into the jar and you moan as I spread white coolness across your plump cheeks. Your blis-tered behind absorbs the cream, like rain in the Sahara. I slather more on and you grin at me as you open your thighs. The moist, hot crevice opens. I smile and you shudder as I dab unguent along the sensitive flesh inside.

"Mmm . . . that's nice."

"You're not angry that I spanked you there?"

"I *was* . . . not now, though. But I feel real sorry for those girls."

"*Really* sorry, Teresa."

You huff. "Can you *not* be a professor for a minute?"

"I'll try. Why do feel sorry for them? Because I spanked them in that embarrassing position?"

"No . . . because you spanked them in that embarrassing posi-tion and *then* did not put stuff on their bottoms with your own hands!"

"I didn't want to reward them for fighting."

"But I get rewarded for being a spoiled, jealous brat?"

"You're a special case."

"I am?"

"Of course you are and you *know* it."

"Yeah." You grin at me. "I just like to hear you say this."

I lean over, kiss your grin, then frown and put the back of my hand to your forehead.

"*What?*"

"You seem awfully warm. Do you have a fever?"

You shake your head. "Only you make me real . . . *really* hot!"

"Is that so?"

"Of course . . . you are a special case, too, you know."

"That's sweet. Would you crawl over and get me the K-Y Jelly out of the drawer so I can take your temperature?"

Your eyes bulge, your bottom tenses and the corners of your

mouth curl down. "Devlin, no! *Please?* You were being so *nice* to me and I *hate* that stupid thermometer!"

"I wasn't going use the thermometer."

"Then what . . . ?" You grab my ear and kiss me hard on the lips. I moan as your tongue darts along my teeth. Soft, naughty fire burns in your eyes when you lower your chin and look up. "How *will* you take my temperature, Uncle Devlin?"

"Well . . . the um . . . the male sexual organ is very sensitive to heat."

"Mmm . . . I have heard this." Your hand slides beneath my robe.

I gasp when warm, naughty fingers wrap my penis, and take a deep breath as it swells. "Yes . . . well . . . it's quite true."

"So . . . when you put this in my bottom you can tell if I have a fever?"

"Perhaps not the exact *degree,* but I believe you'll enjoy it more than the thermometer."

You bite your lip, loosen the robe belt with your free hand and gaze at my erection. "Uncle Devlin?"

"Hm?"

"If you want to fu. . . ."

"Teresa!"

"Um . . . put it in my bottom . . . you should merely *tell* me!"

I smile and fondle your creamy behind. "Sometimes even English professors are at a loss for the right words."

You grin and I groan as you squeeze my stiffness with both hands. "Then you need not *say* it . . . simply *do* it!"

"Out of the mouths of babes."

Spare batteries and other loose junk clatters when you open the nightstand drawer. Your sweet red bottom points at me as you search for the tube of jelly. I toss off my robe and lean on my elbow to admire the view.

"I have it!"

The bed quivers as you fall backwards and roll into me. Your behind burns against my hardness. I take the K-Y and flick off the cap. You bite your lip as I slick cool lubricant between your hot, rubbery cheeks. I frown when you turn over and grab the tube from me. Your hands sear my penis with cool fire as you slather clear, slithery naughtiness up and down the shaft.

"C-careful . . . that's a very sensitive instrument you're playing with."

You let go, lean over and kiss me, soft and sweet, on the mouth. "You just ended a sentence with a preposition, Professor."

I lick my lips and grab your waist. You giggle and toss the tube away as I turn you onto your side. I smile and you gasp as the hard, fat knob parts your cheeks and pushes at your rear entrance. You squeal and I moan as the head pops through your tight ring. I take a deep breath as sharp, hot darts zing up my belly to explode in my brain. You pant and bite my arm as you push closer to me.

"I think I died and went to heaven, sweetie."

"*Ah!* Ooh! Yeah, I just . . . *oh!*"

"Are you OK?"

"Uh huh . . . only . . . it is . . . much bigger than it *looks* when it is . . . *in* . . . so . . . go slowly, OK?"

I kiss your neck just beneath your ear. "Nobody's in a hurry."

You nod and swallow hard. I push forward a quarter inch into your liquid velvet sheath. Your back bows and you moan. I gasp as your cheeks part and my stiffness slides all the way inside, like a new piston in an oiled sleeve.

"Mother of *pearl,* Teresa!" I pant and you groan as you squeeze me. "Does . . . does it hurt?"

"Mmm . . . not . . . not really . . . but it feels . . . *ah* . . . like nothing I ever *felt* before!"

Your inner muscles caress me like soft, hot fingers. Thousands of tiny electric jolts tingle every inch of my body. We lie still while blood pounds in my penis and roars in my ears. I pull half an inch out and then push back in. You gasp and I groan, then I do it again.

"Oh, *God,* Devlin! Yes!"

Blue, red and purple tracers swarm before my eyes as I pull farther out, then slide all the way up your bottom. My ears ring and my fingers fumble down your smooth tummy to find the plump slit. Your clitoris is granite hard, and you shriek when I flick it with a finger pad. I pump quicker into you and my pelvis spanks your quivery cheeks. You shudder, whimper, and then stiffen like a statue before you scream like a banshee. I grit my teeth, thrust high up inside you, and yell at the ceiling as I release the flood. Waves of plasma fire bathe our bodies as bolts of sperm pulse from my organ. You yelp and I grunt as I anoint you with my tribute.

We lie together and enjoy the tingles for long liquid minutes. My penis slips from your bottom and you whimper. I hug you and kiss your shoulders. You roll over and cross your arms over your breasts while I cuddle you. I look down and kiss your pouty lips.

"Why did you wait so *long*, Uncle Devlin?"

"What? Well, we all know that nice guys finish last so I had to make sure you got over the. . . ."

"*No* . . . I mean . . . why did you not make love to my bottom a long time ago?"

"Oh . . . um . . . I wasn't sure you were ready."

"I've been ready for *ages* . . . ever since I *met* you."

"Sweetie, you were *four* when you met me."

"OK . . . perhaps not *that* long . . . but *too* long, I think!"

"Wasn't it worth waiting until we knew each other a little better?"

"I suppose . . . but you would laugh if I told you how many times you have done that to me when I was alone in bed."

"I might blush . . . but I doubt that I'd laugh. Was the real thing as good as your fantasy?"

You grin. "Not quite."

"Well, thanks very *much*."

"You really should have worn a suit of shiny armor."

I laugh and squeeze you hard. "I'll see if there's one in the attic . . . for next time."

"OK . . . but if there is not, that will be all right."

"My heart soars like a hawk to hear that."

You giggle. "That is *such* a strange saying."

"Perhaps . . . but true, nonetheless."

"So . . . are you going to shout at me about the diet now?"

"You *know* I don't shout at you."

"No . . . but you spank my poor little bottom all the time."

"Because you usually deserve it . . . but we'll postpone *that* discussion for another day."

"I wore you out, Uncle Devlin?"

"Yes you did, sweetie . . . and rest assured that I'll wear *you* out when we talk later."

"You are so *mean* to me." You cuddle your face in the hollow of my neck and shut your eyes.

"Only because I love you so much," I whisper.

SECTION II

DEVLIN'S CURE FOR GWEN

Gwen is a shy person and only recently admitted to herself how keenly she loves the idea of tender, erotic discipline. She enjoys my stories but never thought she could express her own desires and feelings in prose until I encouraged her to try. When she did, the talent and emotions she had kept inside for so long burst forth, to my utter delight.

Cure was our first complete story. We wrote several fragments in e-mail dialogue before she gritted her teeth and got serious. What follows is her leap of faith, in me and in her own ability.

It was a Saturday morning, the one I looked forward to for a month, the start of a rare, precious weekend with Devlin. He was coming to Boston to attend a conference at Harvard, but before his meetings began I'd have three whole days and three wonderful evenings alone with him. Nothing compared to the thrill and anticipation of the days just before these special occasions, except his actual arrival at my door.

I had set my alarm for 6:30 that morning because I wanted an unhurried bath and some time for extra-special attention to make

myself as perfect as possible for him. By 8:00 I was in the kitchen with the coffeemaker on. I wore my fluffy white terry bathrobe and nothing else except panties, but my makeup was complete, legs soft, shiny and smooth, toenails painted a pretty pink. My boy-short hair was still damp and I'd wear it the way it dried, in that *just out of bed* look Devlin said was so adorable.

Coffee steamed in the pot and I started to pour my first cup, then the doorbell rang and I jerked to look at the clock. 8:05? It *couldn't* be him! It was *way* too early and I wasn't *ready!* My heart pounded as I ran to the foyer and peeked out the curtained window beside the door. I was relieved but annoyed to see my girlfriend Amy grinning madly and waving to me.

"What the hell is *she* doing here? She *knows* he's coming this morning," I grumbled, then I unlocked the door and opened it about two you're-not-welcome inches. "Ames, your timing *sucks*."

She laughed. "I know, I know. Devlin's coming today . . . like you'd ever let me *forget* . . . but I've got news, Gwen. Just give me five minutes, OK? You've *got* to hear this."

I was afraid she would burst at the seams and she had one foot past the doorsill anyway, so I let her in. She carried a Tupperware pitcher full of sloshy yellow something, and giggled as we climbed the foyer steps toward the kitchen. I looked at the wall clock. 8:08.

"Amy, you gotta make this quick. What's up?"

She shook the Tupperware in front of my face. "Glasses first. We need to celebrate!"

"For *what?*" I whined, proud of myself when I didn't actually stomp my foot.

"He got the car . . . last night. Mike got the Jag!"

A sincere smile brightened my face. Good news, indeed, and yes, it *did* deserve a toast. I went to the cabinet and got glasses. Amy poured while she rehashed the prior week's events, most of which I was *more* than familiar with, but I couldn't spoil her fun. She told me again how her boss, almost at the last minute, decided to attend Christy's auction in NYC to bid on George Harrison's 1979 Jaguar. Amy had worked like a maniac for three days straight, exercising Mike's stock options, dealing with his bank and typing endless paperwork. I helped her with the shuttle tickets from Logan and arranged his limo, but that's as close to the deal

as I got. The auction was Friday, the night before, and Mike called that morning to tell her the Jag was his. His excitement leaped along the phone wire to light Amy up like New Year's in Las Vegas, and she in turn headed straight to my house, to celebrate with an eighteen-ounce glass of

. . . Vodka?

I coughed and almost choked. "What the hell *is* this?"

She laughed at my teary eyes. "It's a mimosa!"

"No *way*, Amy. I don't strangle on champagne. Try again."

"Then it's a screwdriver!"

"More like the whole *toolbox* and it's nasty! It needs another gallon of OJ."

"It's not *that* bad. Come on . . . be happy with me! Mike was so grateful . . . he couldn't say *thank you* enough. I'm thinking there'll be a big bonus coming my way!"

I took a baby sip and squeezed my eyes shut as I swallowed.

"Well he ought to give you *something* for everything you did. If you hadn't helped him he never would have made it on time. You got that money together in three days! The only other person who could have done such a great a job is . . . me!"

We laughed and I took another sip. She was right. It wasn't *that* bad, or else my taste buds had gone numb. We sat at the table and chatted while we enjoyed our drinks and celebrated her achievement, and then we got to the subject of Devlin. As we talked it dawned on me that I wasn't so nervous about his visit anymore. I just felt . . . good . . . and Amy's visit was . . . good . . . and my toenail polish was looking . . . very good.

Good. I love my grandmother's mantel clock. I counted the beautiful, mellow bells as it chimed eleven. What a lovely tone that old clock has. They don't make them like they used to.

Eleven?

I swore a string of the worst words I could think of as I sat straight up on the sofa and immediately got the spins. Where'd Amy *go*? That's right. She left. When did she leave? Did I tell her not to bring over any more screwdrivers? I *must* have! Didn't I? Oh no. No, no, *no*. This isn't happening! Devlin's supposed to arrive at . . .

Eleven.

The doorbell rang and a thought came to me. I didn't like it so

I don't know why I kept thinking it. He's gonna kill me . . . he's gonna kill me . . . he's gonna *kill* me. I haven't seen him in six weeks and I'm not even dressed! OK, maybe he'll be pleased that I'm only wearing a bathrobe and those lacy blue panties he likes so much, but I *don't* think he'll be thrilled that I'm looped at eleven am.

Ding-dong . . .

I stood up and fought the spins while I took deep breaths until I didn't feel like I was going to fall down, but I definitely felt . . . toasted. The floor was only a little uneven so I made it to the foyer without much trouble and glanced in the mirror. My makeup still looked good but he couldn't miss the bloodshot eyes. What a way to start our weekend! Could I have screwed it up any worse? Screwdrivered it up any worse? I giggled and then clapped a hand over my mouth. He's gonna *kill* me.

I leaned on the door and peeked around the curtain. Yes, it was Devlin on my doorstep this time, not that traitorous Amy. I opened the door and pulled it backward, the heavy wood a shield between me and his blue-steel eyes. He smiled, cupped my chin and bent to kiss my lips.

"Good morning, Princess."

His mouth lingered for a moment while I held my breath and wondered how long it would take him to taste or smell the alcohol. I stood on tiptoe, lost in his full, warm lips. Will I get away with it? Do I really *care?* He's *here,* that's all that matters. I sighed and he straightened his back. His left eyebrow arched and a bolt of pure dread lanced into my tummy and awakened those awful butterflies. Hot, salty tears welled in my green/red eyes. I *hate* it when his left eyebrow goes up like that.

He turned and took the two steps up to the living room. "I need to use your phone, all right?"

Not a good sign . . . kind of chilly, too, but maybe he's got work on his mind. He walked to the phone, dialed Information and asked for the Aujourd'Hui at the Four Seasons in Boston, my very favorite restaurant. He's taking me to lunch there today! Yes! Life is good!

"Hello . . . this is Devlin O'Neill. I'm afraid I must cancel a luncheon reservation for one o'clock this afternoon. Yes, that's it. No, I don't need to reschedule. Thank you."

My heart sank as he put the phone down and turned to me. He had *that* look in his eyes. They were such *nice* eyes, too; gray-blue with tiny black flecks in the pupils. But now, there was *that* look in them, the one that happened when he wrinkled his forehead just the tiniest bit. I called it his *professor* look, but never out loud, and it always made me feel like I forgot to do my homework. He held out a hand and crooked the index finger, but my feet refused to move. I opened my mouth and my lips worked, but no sound came out.

"Gwendolyn? What's wrong? Come here, please."

I *hate* it when he calls me that. Gwendolyn is my *in trouble* name and I didn't *want* to be in trouble. I just wanted to sit in his lap while he cuddled me and made up for all the long, lonely evenings when he's not here. But I needed to touch him, to feel his strong arms, so I didn't stomp my foot *very* hard before I went to him. He twined his fingers in mine while I put up my lips and whimpered when he didn't kiss me.

"Would you care to explain your condition, young lady?"

I pouted and blinked. "*What* condition?"

He sighed as he led me to the sofa. We sat down and I cuddled his shoulder while I gave him my best wide-eyed innocent smile.

"Let's start with your robe. I know it's Saturday, but shouldn't you be dressed by now?"

I licked my seriously unkissed lips as vodka swirled in my head. "I, um . . . there was an emergency . . . um . . . at work. So I was . . . I've been on the phone all morning but I'll go get dressed now, OK?"

His big, gentle hand clasped my shoulder when I tried to get up, so I gave in and bit my lower lip while I didn't look at him.

"Princess, what sort of *work* emergency could you have on Saturday morning?"

"It . . . it was a travel emergency . . . um . . . Amy's boss, he . . . yeah! He got stuck in New York and he needed a. . . ."

I stopped when he put a finger under my chin to raise my head. The stern look was gone but I nearly cried because he looked so sad.

"Gwen, please don't say anymore right now because you *know* how much I hate it when you fib to me."

"But I'm *not* . . . I mean. . . ."

"Shh . . . you didn't forget I was coming, did you?"

"*God,* no! Jesus, Devlin, I . . . I'm *sorry,* but Amy got Harrison's Jag for Mike, and then the mimosas and . . . and I was all *ready* for you and. . . ."

He nodded, wrapped his arms around me and picked me up. I wept drunken tears into his white shirt while he patted my back. Red, blue and green lights flashed behind my eyelids as I floated down the hall, through my bedroom and into the bath. He set me on quivery feet and I leaned against the counter. I opened my eyes just a slit and wailed when I saw the smudged and smeary face in the mirror. Strong, sure fingers untied my robe belt and I sighed as he slipped it off my shoulders. He turned me around and my nipples burned against his chest.

"Your panties are very nice, Gwen," he whispered.

I gasped when he tugged them down and let them drop in a blue puddle at my feet. "Devlin, I'm really, really. . . ."

"We'll start the day over, all right? I don't know what got into you this morning but it's not going to happen again, is it?"

"N-no! I . . . I know I shouldn't have dranken all those screwdrivers but Amy was so excited and. . . ."

"You *dranken* all those screwdrivers?"

And then he *laughed,* and that made me mad enough to stomp my little foot. Was it *my* fault his Italian wingtip got in the way?

"Ow! Gwen! For crying out loud!"

"Oh, God, I'm sorry! Devlin? Nooo! What are you . . . ? Ow!"

His hands are nice and soft when he hugs me or rubs my back or strokes my breasts so I don't know *how* they can be so hard when he spanks my bottom. It just doesn't make *sense.* But that swat felt like a very large, very hard paddle, and the sting brought tears to my eyes. And then he didn't even rub the sting, he just pushed me into the shower stall and turned on the spray!

"Devlin!"

"*Hush.* Pick up the soap and wash off that distillery smell."

The cool water cut into my breasts like tiny knives. I turned and the knives attacked my quivery bottom. "But *Devlin.*"

"Now, young lady! Unless you want me to scrub the skin off your fanny with the loofa!"

"*No!* You're just being a sh. . . ."

He glared at me. "I'm just being a *what?*"

"Nothing! OK? Geeze!"

I grabbed the Ivory bar and lathered while I watched him go into the bedroom. The spray felt good on my hot face and I scrubbed away the soggy makeup. I shut off the water and sputtered as I groped for a towel and wiped my eyes. Where did he go? What's he *doing?* Did I hear the front door shut? Is he still mad that I stomped on his foot? That was like mega-stupid, Gwen! He really *was* OK that I got drunk this morning so why the hell did I have to do *that?* I mean it wasn't even my *fault* I got drunk. He should spank Amy. Yeah! No! No, no, *no!* He's not going to see *her* fat fanny bare, no way! I peered through the ribbons of steam, then tiptoed over and put my head around the doorjamb. Devlin stood by the closet door and shrugged into the burgundy terrycloth robe he keeps here. He turned, smiled at me, and my heart skipped a beat. God, I love his hairy chest!

"Feel better, Princess?"

"Uh huh. Devlin, I. . . ."

He put a finger to his lips and strode toward me. I quivered when he took the towel, turned me around at the sink and patted my back with it. He picked up my comb and we looked at each other in the foggy mirror while he parted my hair in the middle. He chuckled.

"What?" I said.

"You look like Alfalfa."

"Nuh *uh!*"

I jabbed a gentle elbow into his ribs. He grinned and gathered a handful of short hair just above my right ear, then opened a drawer and found long-forgotten hair bands. I gasped as he twisted one around the hair to make a spiky pigtail.

"OK . . . now the other side."

"Devliiiin," I wailed while I tried not to laugh. "This is *ridiculous.* You can't. . . ."

He bent me over the sink and swatted my bottom three times really quick. His spanks really, really *hurt* when my butt is wet, so I pushed my lower lip out when he let me up, to show him how mad I was. He didn't seem to care how hard I pouted, but he never does. He's like that. I made faces at him in the mirror while he tied another pigtail on the left side.

"There, Princess . . . you're adorable."

"For Pete's sake, Devlin! I look like I'm *twelve.*"

His lips pressed my neck and a hot, quivery blush flowed down my breasts and into my belly.

"I'll bet you were cute at twelve."

I hated my new hairstyle so I took a deep breath and reached for the right-side pigtail. He pushed my hand away, which didn't really surprise me, but I gasped anyhow.

"Don't you want me to get *dressed?*"

"Of course. I laid your clothes out on the bed so go put them on."

"But not with these *things* in my hair. You can't be serious! Ow! Devlin!"

You'd think after all this time I'd learn not to argue with him, especially when I've got nothing on to protect my tushy, but obviously I haven't. So I rubbed the new sting, let him kiss me (let him? Ha!) and stomped into the bedroom.

I couldn't believe it, so I rubbed my eyes and looked again. Where on earth did he find *that*? No way! This is over the top even for *him!* His warm hands rubbed my shoulders and I sighed, then I leaned backward into his chest.

"Very funny, Devlin." I turned to wrap my hands around his neck.

He rubbed my bare bottom and warm tingles flashed into my tummy. I leaned back so he could bend and kiss me. Mmmm. His tongue is *so* soft. It tastes like satin sheets and candlelight.

"Put your jammies on, Princess," he whispered into my mouth.

I squeezed my eyelids tight and shook my head. "You're kidding, right? They're little girl baby doll pajamas! You can't really expect me to . . . ow! Jesus, Devlin! Ouch! Don't! Please!"

Damn! His hand just gets harder and harder every time he smacks my bottom!

"Put them *on*, Gwen!"

"OK, *OK!* Don't yell at me . . . geeze! Where'd you *get* these, anyway?"

"A friend in LA. Now put them *on*."

"Ow! OK!"

How can he be so sweet one minute and so bossy the next? I picked up the lace-trimmed top and matching panties. The soft cotton had a little ballerina pattern that *was* kind of cute. I huffed and put on the top while I glared at him. I didn't glare long because

he had *that* look in his eyes, and it wasn't even my fault! It was Ames. He should spank her! Little brat. He should use a hairbrush and . . . what?

"I *said,* button the front, Gwen. Are you still loaded?"

"Nooo, I just . . . OK! There! Happy?"

He frowned and nasty butterflies danced in my tummy while I pulled on the pants, then sat on the bedside and wriggled my bottom. The material felt really good, but Devlin still had that stern look so I fluttered my eyelashes and tried to look contrite. I'm not very good at contrite and he knows it, dammit! He smiled but that only made it worse.

"Come here, Gwendolyn." He held out a hand.

Oh, geeze! *Gwendolyn* again. Devlin was going to spank me and there was nothing I could do about it, so I got up to face the music. My legs felt like they were made of shaving cream but I managed to stumble to him. He took my hands while I leaned on his hard chest. His heart pounded under my ear, low, slow and steady.

"Princess, I'm very disappointed. You know that, don't you?"

That voice! It's always so deep 'cause it starts *way* down inside and . . . what did he say?

"What?"

He sighed, held my shoulder and made me lean back so he could look into my eyes. "I *said* I'm going to blister your bottom, little girl."

"You didn't say *that!* I'd've *heard* that! Why are being so *mean* to me? I thought we were going to have *fun* this weekend."

"We will . . . after you sober up. You're still about two sheets to the wind."

"Nuh *uh!* And anyway it's all *Amy's* fault! She should've told me . . . *no!*"

I don't know how, but all of a sudden I was across his lap with his arm on my back, and all I could do was kick and scream while he yanked my pants down. I felt warm and cozy in those silly panties, so it was just *awful* when he pulled them to my knees and my butt nearly *froze* . . . and then he *spanked* it, which didn't help at all!

"Owee!"

"Hush, Gwen! I've hardly started."

"Uh *huh!* It hurts *very* hardly! Neeeah! Ow! *Devlin!*"

His awful, nasty, hard hand just kept on smacking my bare bottom, which was *so* unfair because it wasn't even my fault, but I couldn't tell him that because I was crying so much. I mean, it really did *sting,* but he didn't care. He just kept on spanking me, like I was a little girl or something. And he kept on talking to me while he smacked my bottom, like I could even *listen!*

"Young lady, what in the world possessed you to get loaded and greet me at the door without any clothes on? Hm? Tell me!"

"Ouch! Fwee! Baaah! Neeenoooh!"

"The very idea! Plastered at eleven in the morning, when you *knew* I just flew in from LA on the red-eye. Do you have any idea how tired I am?"

"Yaaah! Ohoo! Heezooo! Prreee!"

"Not to mention *hungry.* Do you know what United serves for breakfast on the red-eye? Lie still, you little brat! There's a spot on your right cheek that isn't . . . quite . . . scorched . . . enough! There! There! *There!*"

"Yeeeoweee! *Devlin!*"

I'm not sure exactly when he turned me over, but it sure felt good when he hugged me. *God,* did my bottom burn! I was glad he left my panties down, and even gladder when he kissed me. Mmmm. He's such a good kisser, but I was so *mad* at him.

"Feel better, Princess?"

It was easy to pout because my lips were all wet with tears. "No! You were very harsh to me and I *hate* you!"

He hugged me real hard and smiled. "No you don't. You had that coming and you know it."

"I did *not* . . . it was all *Amy's* fault. She *made* me drink all that screwdriver junk so I'd be a mess when you got here and. . . ."

"I love you, Gwen," he whispered in my ear.

"Oh, *geeze.*"

Yeah. I folded. How can I stay mad at him when he says stuff like *that?* Then he took off those silly PJs and put me back over his lap so he could smear cold cream on my bottom. I really like it when he does that, especially when he smears it down in the crack while he kisses me. I had to twist my neck halfway around to give him my lips, but I really wanted to give him something *else,* later on, after our nap.

• • •

I woke up three hours later with a heavy head, a sore bottom and a queasy stomach. Worse, I was alone in bed. Devlin's side was cold and I heard water running in the bathroom. It annoyed me that he wasn't in bed to comfort me because I needed a hug! The clock on the nightstand told me that the afternoon was almost over. I was *so* disappointed that it flew by like that, and even more disappointed that I felt like *crap*.

"Devlin!" Ow. I tried again, but softer. "Devlin?"

He came out of the bathroom, dressed in Loden green denim slacks and a blue-and-green pinstriped shirt, both pressed crisp. I sighed. He always looked handsome but I really liked it when he didn't have a suit and tie on.

"Nothing like a good nap to refresh a person, right, Princess?" The look on my face told him I was anything *but* refreshed. He came and sat on my side of the bed. "Why don't you get dressed? You can show me The Grist Mill at the Wayside Inn."

"Not right now," I whined. "I don't feel like it."

"No? You liked the idea a few days ago."

"Maybe later." I flopped against the pillows.

"Don't you feel well?"

"I'm OK . . . really."

"Then I suggest you get your cute little buns in gear and get *dressed*."

His tone of voice inspired me to sit straight up before he finished speaking. It was his *you're pushing me* tone, so I knew he was almost out of patience. I wanted to tell him that I was annoyed because he was out of bed and dressed while I'd rather stay in bed, with *him*, preferably, but the way I felt, *without* him would have been acceptable. Then my sore bottom reminded me that I should at least *try* to be a good girl, so I rolled out, took a few deep breaths and then slipped on a pair of my favorite worn, Lauren jeans and a faded tee shirt. I stuck my bare feet into a pair of loafers and ran my fingers through my hair while he watched.

"I'm ready, Devlin."

He shook his head. "For what? Painting the garage?"

"*No* . . . I'm ready to *go*. Come on! It's getting late."

"I get the sense that your heart isn't in this outing."

I pouted. It wasn't *fair* to make me feel guilty on top of everything. "I really *do* want to go . . . I *love* being with you. I've been counting the days until you got here. I just feel a little sleepy, that's all, and . . . and my stomach isn't quite right."

"Oh, is *that* all? Would the gallon of alcohol you consumed this morning have anything to do with that?"

"It wasn't a *gallon,* Devlin." Then I smiled. Sounded good to me! "Yeah, it's the alcohol. It's still in my system. Nothing a big cup of coffee won't fix. Let's go to Starbucks."

He walked over and cupped my chin in his warm palm. "I know something that'll work better. I'll have you fixed up in no time, Princess."

I didn't much like the look of the grin he gave me, but then I forgot about it because he kissed me. When he kisses me I forget a lot of stuff. Sometimes I think I should worry about that, then he kisses me again and I forget to worry about it.

• • •

He parked his rented car in the pharmacy lot, switched off the engine and patted my thigh.

"Let's go, Gwen."

"I don't *want* to go in. I'll wait here."

"Excuse me?"

"Devlin, I can't *do* this. I really *can't!*"

"Yes, you really *can.* Come along now."

He squeezed my leg, opened the door and put one foot out. I didn't budge. He looked at me and sighed. I didn't look at him, but I could feel his eyes on me.

"You're trying my patience, little girl. I'll allow for the fact that you're not yourself today, but I have plans for this evening and I'm not about to let your poor judgment spoil them. Now . . . we're *both* going into the store to buy a few items to clean the toxins out of your system, so get your sore little behind out of the car. *Now.*"

"But it's just so. . . ." It was hard to pout with his finger on my lips, but I did my best.

"Shh . . . I promise you'll feel better afterward. If you find this humiliating, it's no more than you deserve. Now march!"

My cheeks burned, front and rear, when I looked into his eyes,

and my tummy quivered because he had switched them into stern-mode overdrive, so I turned to stare at the airbag sign.

"Devlin, we don't *need* to do this. I don't *feel* that bad, honest! I'll just have extra coffee today. Really. I'll be OK!" I knew it was useless, but I tried to sound as pitiful as I could. "I don't *want* to go in there."

"It's part of your punishment. Naughty girls get punished and you *know* that."

"Yeah, but . . . but it's *embarrassing.*"

He smiled and that scared me even more than his stern look. "Just think of it as a warm-up for when I get you home. You have five seconds to open the door. Five. Or I'll take you in the back seat. Four. Put you over my knee. Three. Pull down your panties. Two. And spank your pink little bottom. One."

"OK!"

I sobbed as I jerked the door handle, then pushed it open and just sat there. He did that to me before . . . spanked my butt in the backseat of a car . . . so I knew he wasn't kidding. I sniffled as he walked around to help me out. He held my hand and led me into the store, and I yanked on his arm as I lagged a step behind. As we passed the cash registers, a thin, haggard woman dragged a six-year-old girl behind her going the other way. The girl whimpered and slapped her shoes on the worn tiles as she tried to wriggle her hand from her mother's grasp. The woman looked at me, raised her eyebrows and smiled. I looked away, straight into a mirror on a sunglass kiosk, and realized I wore the same expression as the little girl. That just made me *madder.*

"Devlin, *please?* Let's just get *out* of here."

He ignored me, except to tighten his grip on my hand, as he scanned the shelves. I bit my lip while I glanced around for friends and neighbors who might see us in *that* aisle. He picked up a box, a combination hot-water bottle/douche/enema bag, and turned it over to look at the back.

"Oh, good grief! Don't *read* it. Let's *go* already."

"You know, for a girl who is *still* in a lot of trouble your behavior leaves a lot to be desired. You need to settle down. Go get that empty basket at the end of the aisle."

"What do you need a *basket* for? You're only getting that *one,* right?"

"The basket, please."

My feet felt like lead as I went to fetch the damn basket. When I tried to give it to him he just put the box in it and made me hold it. Then he picked up *another* box, this one smaller, with a picture of a bright-blue bulb syringe on the front.

"Devlin, *no!* We don't *need* that!" I whispered.

He didn't say anything, just nodded, dropped the second box in the basket and then led me by the arm to the next aisle. I huffed and pouted because he was so damn *casual* when he tossed a huge tube of K-Y Jelly on top of the boxes. Then he smiled and that *really* annoyed me. How could he take so much pleasure in my anxiety?

"You're *horrible*."

"No . . . *horrible* would be if I used Vick's Vap-O-Rub instead of K-Y. Count your blessings, little girl."

I blushed and stared at him. Could he be *serious?* Then he winked and I *really* couldn't tell. I hunched over the basket to hide the naughty medical supplies while I kept watch for nosy neighbors. He searched more shelves, added a box of latex gloves, I couldn't *believe* it, to the collection, then stood and stared at the basket for ten seconds before he snapped his fingers like he just remembered something. He dragged me over to the baby aisle and I sighed with relief when he picked up a thermometer. Finally. Something harmless.

"I have one at home. You don't need to buy a *new* one."

"Really?" He held up the package and smiled. "One of *these?*"

"*Yes*. Two, actually, but one doesn't. . . ."

He grinned when I focused on the package and my eyes went wide. For Rectal Use Only. My lips moved but nothing came out, and the thermometer clunked into the basket like a brick.

"Come along, Princess. Register's that way."

"But I *can't*."

"Don't start, Gwendolyn."

Oh, God! Not *Gwendolyn* . . . not here in the *store*. He wouldn't! Would he? I looked around but couldn't see anyone. He had never actually spanked me in public, just a swat on my jeans a few times.

Then he walked away! Just left me *standing* there, holding the basket! I bit my lip and hurried to catch up.

"*Devlin!*"

"Hm?"

"What are you *doing?*"

He looked at me and lifted just the left corner of his mouth. "It's customary to pay for one's purchases before leaving the store."

I stomped my foot and the woman at the register looked at us. He smiled at me when I blushed, which just made me blush harder as he took my arm and led me to the checkout lane. I stood on tiptoe to whisper in his ear.

"I'll go wait in the car, OK?"

"Put the basket on the counter and take everything out," he said in a normal tone.

My cheeks burned and I wanted so bad to run out the door, because the woman just *smirked*. I glared at Devlin but he ignored me while he counted twenties from a wad he took from his pocket. The basket clanked when I set it down and I scowled as I unloaded all his nasty toys.

"How are you folks this evening?" the woman said as she swiped packages across the scanner.

"Just fine . . . and you?" Devlin smiled at her.

"Just fine, thanks. Did you find everything you needed today?"

"Yes, thank you."

The woman leaned across the counter and winked at me. "You know, honey, if you take milk of magnesia regular, about a table-spoon a week, you don't get so backed up."

"Oh, but I . . . I just. . . ." I closed my eyes, let a new blush wash over me, then took a deep breath. "Thanks. I'll keep it in mind."

She patted my arm, picked up Devlin's money and gave him the change. He took the plastic sack and led me to the car. I stared out the window while he drove home. He didn't say anything and I didn't either, but I wanted to yell at him, bawl him out, scream my head off, except I couldn't think of anything *bad* enough to say. And he just drove, like nothing had *happened*. My tummy hurt even worse but *he* didn't care. I think he looked at me, but I didn't look at *him*. I mean, how humiliating! Some woman I don't even *know* told me I was backed up!

He stopped in the driveway and opened the car door for me, and I pushed him away when he tried to help me out. I probably shouldn't have done that.

– 131 –

"Gwendolyn!"

I got out of the car really quick because I *hate* that tone of voice, and I *really* hate it when he pulls his hand back like that.

"March yourself into the house this *instant,* young lady. The very idea!"

"I'm sorry, Devlin. *No!*"

He held the sack and my left arm with his left hand and swatted the seat of my jeans with his right hand all the way to the front door. I tried to fit the key in the lock while I looked around to see who was watching me get my behind spanked in the front yard, and keep from yelping at every smack, so of course it didn't work.

"Give me that, Gwen."

I rubbed my bottom while he opened the door, then I ran and threw myself on the bed. He came in a few seconds later and sat beside me. I squirmed away, but he picked me up and cuddled me while I cried into his shirt.

"It's OK, Princess. Let it all out."

"It . . . I . . . how *could* you?"

"How could I what?"

"Muh . . . make me buy all those awful *things,* and then . . . then *spank* me, right in my own front *yard?*"

"Shh . . . you know you get spanked when you act like a brat."

"But I *didn't!*"

He sighed and hugged me. "You gave me the silent treatment all the way home, then you shoved me when I tried to help you. If that's not being a brat I don't know what *is.*"

"But I . . . I was so mad! That wuh-woman at the register . . . sh-she *knows* what those things are for!"

"Of course she does . . . that's her job. She knows they're to help my little girl feel better."

I looked up at him and pouted and that was *another* mistake, because he kissed me and then I wasn't nearly as mad. Damn! I wish he couldn't *do* that to me. He kissed me again and I kissed back, and hugged him, too. Then he rubbed my bottom with the same hand he just spanked it with, and I wasn't mad at all. Well, maybe a little, but I had to try really hard because it felt so good.

"I . . . I'm sorry I was a brat."

He smiled. "How's your tummy?"

"It still kinda . . . um . . . it's fine . . . *lots* better, in fact! Are you hungry? I could make some scrambled. . . ."

"Gwendolyn!"

Oh, *man!* My tummy hurt like hell and he knew it.

"Sir?"

"Get up so I can take your clothes off."

"Can't we just cuddle for a few . . . ?"

"*Now.*"

"OK! I'm *up.*"

He switched on the lamp by the bed while I took off my leather jacket and tossed it at the closet. I giggled when he pulled my tee shirt over my head.

"Don't tickle, Devlin! That's mean."

"Oh, hush. I barely touched you."

"Yeah, but I'm kinda sensitive right now, OK?"

He shook his head and reached down to take off my shoes. That tickled, too, but I bit my lip until he unbuttoned my jeans.

"I'm *cold,* Devlin. Can I have a . . . ?"

"You can have a spanking if you don't stop complaining and let me undress you."

"Why are being so . . . ?"

I clapped a hand over my mouth when he glared at me. My white bikini panties sagged when he pushed my jeans down. I grabbed the waistband to pull them up, but he glared again so I let them sag. They didn't sag for long because he yanked them right down to the floor about two seconds later. He stood up and pushed me to the closet to get my robe. I sighed when he held it out so I could put it on and wrap it tight.

"Where are your slippers, Gwen?"

"Um . . . I think they're in the bathroom. "

"Go find them while I get ready."

"I really feel a *lot* better. Maybe if I just sit on the toilet for a while. . . ."

"Gwendolyn!"

"OK! Geeze!"

I went to the bathroom and looked over my shoulder while I groped beside the hamper for my slippers. Devlin dumped everything from the sack onto the dresser. I put on the fuzzy mules then leaned against the doorjamb to watch him. He didn't look grouchy

anymore, and even kind of smiled as he opened boxes and peeled plastic wrap off his nasty new toys. There were three nozzles that came with the big bag, and he lined them up beside my jewelry box. I whimpered when he ripped open the thermometer package, took it out and shook it. He glanced at me and I ducked inside the bathroom, leaned against the wall and panted.

"Did you find your shoes, Gwen?"

"Um . . . yeah . . . sorta. I mean um . . . I don't really like *these* ones. I like the ones in the spare bedroom better, OK?"

"OK *what?*"

"I mean . . . can I go get those *other* ones? I'd rather have those other ones, OK?" I jerked when he stuck his head around the door-frame. "*Jesus,* Devlin! You nearly scared me to. . . ."

"Quit stalling."

He held out a hand and I whimpered and pouted but I took it. It was *so* warm. Maybe he was only trying to scare me. He wouldn't *really* put all those nasty things in my bottom, would he? I mean he embarrassed me half to death in the drugstore, wasn't that *enough?* But he had the thermometer and that big tube of K-Y gunk in his other hand. Maybe he'd just take my temperature and tell me I didn't *need* any of that other stuff. Yeah. All those other things were just for show. I know Devlin and he'd never be mean enough to put icky nozzles and things in my bottom. He just wanted to scare me. It even felt kind of good when he sat on the bed and put me over his lap. I moaned when he pushed the robe up and patted my bare fanny.

"Spread your legs a little, Princess."

"OK. I'll be good. I'm a good girl now, huh?" He squeezed my bottom and then pulled a rubber glove out of his shirt pocket! "Devlin! Do you have to put *that* thing on? I already *had* my checkup."

"It's for your own protection. Standard AMA hygienic protocol."

The thin latex snapped when he tugged it on.

"That's ridiculous! What do you think you are, a *doctor?*"

"No, but I like to *play* doctor. Now quit wiggling."

He flipped open the tube cap. The jelly kind of squished when he squirted it on his gloved fingers and smeared it with his thumb. I took a deep breath and licked my lips. His left thumb and index

finger pushed my cheeks apart, and then he dabbed warm jelly on my bottom hole and that felt really *weird*. I mean, not bad weird, like when my GYN does it before she puts her finger in there to poke around, but not *good* weird, either, like when he touches me there when we . . . .

"Oh, *hey!* Devlin!"

"Shh . . . it's only my finger. It's been in there before. Just relax."

"I . . . I *can't*. I didn't know you were going to . . . um. . . ."

"I'll use lots of lubricant so you're comfortable."

"Yeah? Ooh! OK. Um . . . thanks . . . I guess."

Comfortable? How *comfortable* can it be when he pushes a glass rod inside my tushy? But I didn't say anything because I knew if I just let him play with my bottom he'd be OK. He's not unreasonable, even if he has this *thing* about my butt. I mean I know I've got a cute one but he's like *fascinated* with it. Even when we make love he always has to . . . . .

"Ooh . . . that's *cold*."

"We'll just leave the thermometer in for a few minutes to make sure it's only the hangover from your massive dose of alcohol that's making you feel sick."

I pouted and turned to look at him, trying to forget I had that thermometer sticking out of my fanny. "I didn't *mean* to get drunk this morning. I really, really *wanted* to be ready for you. It was all *Amy's* fault!"

He squeezed his lips together and shook his head. "You have to take responsibility for your own behavior, Princess. Blaming Amy will *not* get rid of your guilt."

"But I'm not *guilty* . . . I just . . . um . . . showed bad judgment, that's all!"

I quivered and gasped when he smiled and patted my fanny because his finger touched the thermometer. A thousand naughty hands caressed the inside of my bottom when the glass vibrated.

"Only another minute, then I'll take it out and see if I need to call the paramedics."

"That's *not* funny."

"Oh? How about this? A duchess, a priest and a Ferengi go into a bar . . . no?"

Sometimes he can be so *silly*. I rolled my eyes and stared

straight ahead, and hoped he knew I was ignoring him. The thermometer slid out of my bottom and I whimpered, then he turned toward the lamp and rubbed my fanny while he squinted at it.

"A fraction high but no penicillin shot for you today, little girl."

He smiled when I squirmed around and sat on his lap to hug him.

"I *told* you I wasn't sick. Now where are we going? You said we had plans."

I quivered and moaned when he kissed me. He kissed me for a long time, or maybe it just *felt* like a long time because he took off the glove and rubbed my bottom while we played with each other's tongues, and all that hot, gooshy stuff between my cheeks kind of slid between my legs. I giggled and hung on when he tried to break the kiss, and then I stuck my tongue right between his teeth.

"You're just a little *weasel!*"

He laughed and I rested my head on his shoulder. It's a *nice* shoulder, firm and soft, like a brand new pillow. I sighed as his hand patted my bottom. It's a *nice* hand, when it isn't spanking me. Then it happened. I got a really sharp cramp down deep in my belly and I grunted as I doubled over.

"Devlin, I. . . ."

"Shh . . . it's all right. Your tummy is still upset. We'll fix it."

"*No!* Not with those . . . those *things! Please?*"

I hate it that I'm so little, because he picked me up like a rag doll and carried me over to the dresser to get the blue bulb. Then he squeezed it and it whistled like a dog toy while he took me into the bathroom. I shut my eyes tight and held onto his neck, but he just let go of my legs and made me stand beside the sink while he turned on the water and adjusted the knobs.

"Devlin, *please?*" I whispered.

"It's just a starter, Princess. You won't even feel it."

"Uh huh I *will*. I don't *want* it in my bottom, OK?"

He *chuckled*. I couldn't *believe* it. He chuckled and held onto me while he filled that stupid blue bulb with water!

"Quit squirming, Gwen. I have to put the nozzle back on."

"But *Devlin!*"

I quivered when he leaned down to kiss me. Damn! I wish he wouldn't *do* that. He fitted the gigantic, two-and-a-half-inch

nozzle into the bulb and screwed it down. It was almost as big as my finger! He couldn't possibly expect me to . . . .

"We'll do your first enema on the bed, all right?"

How could he sound so *reasonable?* He was going to stick that horrible thing in my *bottom* and . . . what did he say? *First* enema? No way!

"Um . . . I have to pee, OK?"

He grabbed three towels off the shelf and shook his head. "This will only take a minute, then you can go."

"But I really have to . . . !"

"You're stalling, Gwen. Come on."

I stomped all the way to the bed while he held my arm. He sat down and draped a towel across his lap, then draped me across the towel. I shivered when he lifted my robe again, then I moaned when he rubbed my bottom. He put a towel over my legs and I didn't shiver *quite* so much . . . until he put another glove on and picked up that stupid K-Y stuff. Yuck! It squirted and I looked over my shoulder at him.

"Do you really need to put more of that *goop* in me? Eeeyooo!"

My bottom wriggled and I scrunched my nose while he mushed K-Y between my cheeks and around my little hole. It wasn't as bad this time, when his finger slid inside. I mean, it's not like it hurt but I just feel so *helpless* when he does that.

"Now scootch up so your tummy isn't lying on my legs."

He made me wriggle forward until just my hips and thighs were on his lap, which made my fanny stick *way* up. I closed my eyes and took a deep breath. He opened my bottom again and I squealed when the nozzle touched my little hole.

"Don't clench, Princess . . . let it go . . . right . . . *in.*"

"Nuh . . . ooh . . . I'm *trying* but this is so . . . awful!"

Then that stupid nozzle slid right down *inside* me, until I could feel the round part of the bulb between my cheeks. The nozzle and the bulb were warm so it wasn't *too* bad, but I still wailed and wriggled my legs. He just patted my behind with his left hand and kept on squeezing water into me.

"Tha . . . that's *enough.*"

"Hush, Gwen. We're nearly done. Only a little . . . bit . . . more. There."

I gasped as he took the nozzle out, then I reached back to cover

my crack with my hand. There was slippery stuff all over *everywhere.*

"It's so icky! I don't *like* this!"

"Here."

He took the towel off my legs and wiped my hand, then wiped the goop off my behind. The other towel under me slid off when he got up and stood me on my feet. I clenched my cheeks together really, really tight and kind of scissor-stepped into the bathroom with Devlin right behind me. He took off his glove, tossed it in the trash, then stood in the doorway and *watched* as I yanked up my robe and sat on the toilet!

"A little *privacy,* please?"

"Oh . . . sure."

Then all he did was turn to the left, lean against the doorjamb and look straight ahead! Ooh, that *man!* No *way* was I going to let him watch me. I reached forward and took a swipe at the door, closing it on him just seconds before the enema ran out of me. I sat on the toilet for a while until my belly felt OK. I had just flushed and was standing at the sink to wash when he opened the door.

"*I'll* do that, Princess."

"What? *No!* I can wash my own . . . for crying out *loud.*" He made me lean over the counter and then he put on another one of those damned gloves and lifted my robe. "*Devlin!*"

"Hush and spread your feet a little . . . that's a good girl."

He soaped up a cloth and washed inside my cheeks while I wailed. I never thought there could be *anything* more embarrassing than for him to give me an enema, but I was wrong. When he reached between my legs and washed me *there,* I wanted to faint. Well, not *entirely* from embarrassment. Like I said, he *does* have the nicest hand, even if it *was* all covered in latex. I tried to stand up but he just leaned his elbow on my back to hold me bent over.

"Stay put . . . we're nearly done."

"Ooh! That's *hot!*"

"Glad you like it."

"I didn't *say* I . . . ah! Mmmm."

God, he can be a rat, but it's hard to stay mad at somebody who knows how to wash my 'gina with hot water and give me chills at the same time! I kind of melted into the counter while he slid the cloth up and down my crack and all over between my legs. After

about a minute I managed to look up and there he was, grinning at me in the mirror. I stuck out my tongue and then yelped because he swatted my poor little butt kind of hard. You'd think I'd know better, especially when my bottom's wet.

The glove popped when he took it off, then he started the water and threw the washcloth into the sink. He washed his hands, then wrung out the cloth. He finally dried me, let me up and hugged me for a really long time.

"Feel better, Princess?"

"Uh huh . . . all kinda warm and fuzzy . . . maybe we should go to bed, huh?"

He kissed me and I just melted. "Don't you want to go dancing?"

"We're going *dancing?* I'll get dressed!"

"After your enema."

"*What?* You just *gave* me one. I don't *believe* you!"

He just smiled and grabbed more towels while I stomped my foot. I really, really wanted to yell at him some more, but my bottom still stung and he had that *stern* look again, even with the smile, so I didn't . . . not even when he took off my robe and laid me down on the bathmat, stark naked. He made me lie on my left side with my knees bent, and put one of the towels under my head for a pillow, then put another one over my legs and one from my neck down to my bottom.

"Comfy, Gwen?"

"As *if!* It's *cold* down here. If you just *have* to give me another . . . um . . . why can't you do it on the *bed?*"

"Because there's no hook to hang the bag from." He kissed me but I didn't kiss back. "I'll only be a minute."

I lay there for a few seconds and just glared at the side of the bathtub, and then I twisted my neck to watch him run water into the clear plastic bag. It swelled like a balloon and got all sudsy.

"What did you put *in* there, for Christ's sake?"

"A few drops of Ivory hand soap . . . it's perfectly safe."

"But that's too *much.* You can't put a gallon of water in. . . ."

"Shh! There's barely a quart. You'll have no problem with it."

"Well, I'm thinking I've got a *big* problem with it. See how *you* like putting that much water up *your.* . . ."

I'm not sure why I can't keep my mouth shut sometimes, but I

can't. He didn't seem to move, then all of a sudden he was kneeling on the floor beside me, the towels were flipped out of the way, and he was smacking my bottom kind of hard while he held me down with his other hand. I yelped but I didn't say anything. He was mad enough without me smarting off anymore, and it was a lot warmer on the floor after he put the towels back over me. And besides, he didn't say anything when I rubbed my fanny, which is usually like a big no-no, so I decided to cut my losses.

"Do you think you can behave for a few minutes, Gwen?"

"I didn't *do* anything," I muttered.

"*What?*"

"OK! I will . . . *geeze.*"

He went back to the sink to get the bag and hose and then hung the bag on a towel hook next to the tub. The water was still cloudy but not sudsy anymore, but *man,* was there a lot of hose! And at the end of it . . . oh, *no!*

"Um, Devlin?"

"What, Princess?"

"I'm not lipping off or anything, but um . . . you've got the douche nozzle on it."

"I know."

That's all he said! *I know.* Like that was perfectly *normal* or something. He knelt down and kissed my lips, then patted my bottom, which would have been a lot nicer except it still stung a *lot.*

"I'll get the K-Y and be right back. Just relax."

I bit my lip to keep from screaming at him. *Relax,* he says! I tried not to stare at the white nozzle, but it was like trying not to stare at a car wreck. It had a hole in the tip and little holes all around toward the end, and it was *huge* . . . almost as big as his thumb. I couldn't *believe* he was really going to put that in my little . . . .

"Here we go . . . this won't take long."

"But, Devlin!"

"Just relax."

"Stop *saying* that! How can I relax when you're going to force that . . . that *thing* up my behind?"

"You can because I *say* you can. Now quit fighting me."

"But I'm not! I've done every nasty, icky, awful thing you *told* me to and all I did was have a little too much . . . *ouch!*"

Another big Devlin handprint stung my fanny and he pushed my arm away when I tried to rub, and then folded the towel off my bottom. Even though only my head and butt weren't covered up, I felt nakeder than if I didn't have anything on at *all*. And even *worse,* I could have *sworn* he dried my 'gina after he washed it, but now . . . it was kind of damp again. OK, no . . . it was *wet.* I shuddered when he reached under the towel to straighten my left leg, then pushed my right leg, the one on top, up and kind of over, so my right knee was on the bathmat, and I blushed because the wet between my thighs made kind of a slishy noise when he did that.

"I'll put a little more lubricant in, Princess. Stay real still."

"OK, but not too ooh *much* . . . Devlin!"

"Shh."

He gooshed about half a pint of that slippery stuff all inside my cheeks and swirled it around my hole with his fingers. It was like *major* icky and I wanted to tell him that, but then he put his finger inside and all I could do was squeeze my eyes shut and take deep breaths, because it almost felt like his finger was inside the *other* place, and I didn't mind *that* too much. But I didn't want *him* to know that so I just whimpered a lot so he'd think he was making me miserable . . . like he *cared* or anything.

"I'll ease the nozzle in now. Try not to clench."

I *did* try not to clench. I *tried* to relax . . . but when he pushed that garden hose up my bottom I kind of lost it.

"Aieeee! It's too *big!"*

But he held onto my shoulder while the nozzle slid all the way inside. I gasped and panted, but then I got used to it. He leaned over and I turned my head a little so he could kiss me. No idea why I did that. He didn't *deserve* a kiss, the way he was treating me.

"Tell me if you start to cramp when I start the flow."

"Oh, yeah, you'll be the *first* to know . . . *count* on it."

The little plastic clip squeaked and water gushed into my bottom. He reached under the towel with his left hand to massage my tummy while he held the nozzle with his right.

"D-Devlin? I need to go, OK? Can I go now? I really gotta *go!"*

"Only a little more, Princess. You're doing fine."

"But I really, really gotta . . . *ooh!"*

The cramp wasn't that bad . . . I just didn't expect it.

"Can you get up on your knees, Gwen?"

"No *way* . . . you have to let me . . . I gotta *go!*"

He wrapped his left arm around my hips and lifted. "Keep your head way down, so your pretty little bottom is way up in the air, all right?"

It wasn't like I had a *choice*. Both my knees were on the bathmat and so was my face, and there was like a *barrel* of water inside me. His right hand was on my butt, holding the nozzle in, and his left arm was pushing down on my back. I wasn't going *anywhere* until he said I could, so I just grabbed handfuls of the bathmat and held on while he rubbed my tummy. The cramp went away and I wasn't cold at all, even though I had no idea where those towels went. I was bare naked with my fanny in the air on my bathroom floor, but somehow it seemed OK. Maybe it was because Devlin had both his hands on me. Maybe it was because my left hip was right against his chest and I could feel his heartbeat. Maybe he put some weird drug in the water . . . I don't know, but I felt safe and warm. I even tried to feel humiliated, or even mad, but I couldn't.

"Good girl. It's all in so I'll take the nozzle out now, OK?"

I whimpered and curled my toes. It *wasn't* OK to take it out because I sorta *liked* it in my fanny, but I *said* it was so he did. I shuddered when it slipped out of me and even *that* felt good. Then he cupped his hand on my crack to help me hold it while he stood me up. I wanted to hug him but all the water gurgled downhill and I just barely had time to shoo him out the door before I rushed to the toilet.

A long time later, Devlin came back in and washed me, same as before. This time he even wet a hand towel and patted my face and neck with warm water. I was just exhausted, so I was actually glad that he was there to help me. When he finished, he carried me into the bedroom. The sheets felt cool/warm when he tucked me in.

"Aren't you coming to bed?"

He smiled and kissed my lips. "You rest while I make supper, OK?"

"Nooo . . . I want you in *bed*."

"Princess, I am *starving*. You're not going to argue with me, are you?"

I gave him my best smiley pout. "No, sir. Oh! I got some of that Havarti cheese you like."

"Mmm. Cheese omelets. I'll come get you when they're ready."

"OK. Devlin?"

"Hm?"

"I um . . . thanks."

"You can thank me if I don't burn the omelets. Now take a nap."

He kissed me and went to the kitchen. I listened to pans and dishes clatter for almost a minute before I dozed off and dreamed of Devlin's big, hard hand on my sore, tender, satisfied little bottom.

A DOLL STORY

Our first complete story opened the floodgates of Gwen's naughty imagination and *Doll Story* followed soon after. She is very good with set-up but says she has trouble with the *squirmy parts,* as she calls them, so my job is to edit the multitude of pages she writes and then bring it all home. I doubt if there is a better job anywhere in the world.

I fidgeted while Devlin pulled my panties down. He had me on the bed, on my tummy, with my skirt up to my waist while he arranged my Olga Scoops neatly at the backs of my knees. I dug my bare toes into the duvet and I guess I wriggled too much because he reprimanded me and told me to lie still. He gets that awful *professor* tone in his voice when he does that and I just want to run away. Yeah, right! As if!

My bottom still stung from the spanking he gave me a minute before but I couldn't help but whine when he told me to raise my hips. He ignored my protests and snaked a strong arm around my waist to lift me up and wedge a folded pillow underneath me. I sobbed because I could feel how high my bare bottom was raised and the view it showed him, and I sobbed again when I felt his

hand at my knees, nudging them as far apart as my panties would allow.

His big hand patted my sore, red bottom. "Hush, Gwen, and get off your elbows. You know better than that. Put your chest on the bed . . . your head too. That's my girl. Offer me your naughty bottom, and I want you to *stay* like that. I'll be right back."

Of course he didn't come *right back*. He made me lie there and wait for him, so I could contemplate the night ahead of me and the day that just passed; the day that got me into this horrible predicament!

• • •

The day itself couldn't have been any lovelier. It was warm autumn in New England, with the leaves just past peak. Devlin and I went to an antique fair at the Littlefield town common. It should have been the perfect place to spend a romantic, lazy afternoon together, holding hands while we browsed dusty old goods.

We hadn't been there long when Devlin struck up a conversation with a man who sold antique watches. He'd always wanted an old timepiece to display on his desk. The guy was good and kept Devlin's interest with his sales pitch. I pulled on his arm several times but he ignored me. I wasn't *even* interested in watches, and we still had miles of booths to see, but the man would *not* shut *up*, so I yanked again, a little harder. Devlin just patted my hand and carried on talking. I sighed as loud as I could, then pouted and peered toward the booths we hadn't explored yet.

About fifty feet way a wooden sign read *Dolls*. My weakness! I yanked Devlin's arm again, harder than I intended. Both Devlin and the salesman looked at me and Devlin's eyebrow shot up, which told me we'd be having a *talk* later about my rudeness.

"I'm sorry, Devlin, but I . . . I have to go check something out, OK? I'm just going farther down the row."

"Give me another minute and I'll come with you." His voice sounded smooth, like Bailey's Irish Cream.

But I didn't *want* to wait and I pulled his hand like an impatient child. "No, that's OK . . . you guys finish up. Meet me at the doll booth when you're done, OK?" He did that eyebrow thing again. *"Please?"*

He nodded and let go of my hand. "I'll be there in a couple of minutes."

The doll dealer acknowledged me and I smiled as my eyes roamed over the merchandise. Most of the dolls weren't true antiques but they were still beautiful. I browsed until I was satisfied there were no special finds, but as I turned to go something caught my eye. There was a doll tucked under the back table, and from what I could see of her pretty face she appeared to be a nineteenth-century Jumeau. Pale blue glass eyes stared at me from under a mop of red curly hair and I knew I was in love.

I pointed to her. "Has that one been sold?"

The woman said the doll had been on hold since early morning but no one had returned to pay for her. When she brought her to me I couldn't get my hands on her fast enough, and I was right! She was a bisque Jumeau, probably made in the early 1880s, who wore a faded but *gorgeous* cream silk dress with tiny daisies embroidered on the bodice and a lace-trimmed cloak to match. I turned her over and over as I admired every little age flaw. Oh, she was beautiful!

"How much are you asking?"

"Three fifty."

Nuts! I *knew* $350 was a lot of money, I truly did, and I *tried* to negotiate but the woman wouldn't budge. Did I care? Nah. A Jumeau was worth that, so I took a nervous peek at Devlin, who was still at the watch booth. Of course I *knew* he would kill me if he found out how much money I was going to spend on a doll, but I simply *had* to have her. It was one of those things in life that a girl *must* have, so before I could talk myself out of it I handed over my credit card and asked the woman to hurry. She nodded, winked, and in less than a minute the doll was mine, paid for, wrapped and bagged. I thanked her, tucked the package under my arm, turned and . . . bumped into Devlin, who was standing behind me.

"Oh, hi! You um . . . snuck up on me. So . . . um . . . did you buy anything from the watch man?"

"No . . . everything was overpriced."

Sometimes I think Devlin has antennas.

"Oh, gee . . . that's too bad. I'm sure you'll find a watch eventually."

– 146 –

"Yes, but I'm in no hurry. You know I don't make rash decisions with pricey baubles."

I definitely did *not* like the way this conversation was going. Time to change the subject.

"So . . . are you hungry for lunch yet?"

His head turned just an inch. "Ah, no . . . thank you. Eleven o'clock is a little early for me." He nodded at the package that was half-hidden behind my back. "What did you buy?"

I pretended not to hear him as I strode away from the doll booth. "Oh, look . . . hot apple cider. Want some?"

"Sure smells good. What did you buy?"

I could feel his eyes on the back of my head. "Oh, the cutest little doll you ever *saw*. She's old, though . . . needs to be cleaned up. It'll be a lot of work but she'll be so pretty!"

"You know, Princess, you don't get the best bargains at places like this. If you wanted a doll you should have told me. The wise thing would have been to check out the dolls on Ebay."

Yes, that would have been the wise thing to do, except Ebay didn't have *this* doll.

He cleared his throat and I trembled. "You *do* remember the promise you made about sticking to your budget, don't you?"

Oh, no, *please?* Not the promise! I bit my lip and clutched my doll tighter.

Devlin shook his head. "Have you already forgotten last month's discussion?"

Discussion? That was *not* a discussion . . . that was him lecturing me on the evils of high-interest credit cards while I laid across his knees, wriggling and kicking to get loose while he spanked my bottom *red*.

"No . . . I remember."

"And do you recall saying you'd curb your spending on unnecessary luxuries until you paid that card down?"

That card? Wow. I was glad he thought there was only *one* card.

"Uh huh . . . and I've tried really, really hard to. . . ."

"So correct me if I'm wrong, but your sudden reticence leads me to believe that the purchase you're clinging to so desperately would likely *not* be considered an inexpensive luxury . . . *would* it, Gwen?"

I looked at him and opened my mouth but nothing came out. I

didn't *want* to lie to him. Well, yes, actually I *did* want to lie, but I couldn't think up a believable fib *fast* enough. I couldn't even stammer because he was looking straight at me, and I got that awful *tight* feeling in my belly because I knew I was caught.

Devlin knew it too. He took me firmly by my elbow and escorted me to a quiet spot next to a big oak tree, away from the commotion of the booths. My heart was pounding in my throat as he bent down toward my flushed face and asked quietly in his deep, Devlin voice, "How much did you pay for that doll, young lady?"

My first inclination was to deny that I was even *holding* a doll. At that moment I wanted nothing to *do* with her. I wanted to get rid of the evidence and if Devlin had been looking the other way I would have been tempted to ditch her in the big green trash barrel!

"Pay?" I was about half a breath from desperation.

"Yes . . . pay . . . what was the *cost?*"

Oh, I *really* didn't want to tell him that! My bottom twitched when I remembered how badly he had me squirming over his knee the last time. When he finally allowed me to stand up, but before he banished me to the corner so he could admire my scarlet tushy for half an hour, Devlin had made it very clear what I could expect if I was irresponsible with my credit card again. It was something I had understood perfectly and remembered . . . until today.

"I'm waiting, Gwen."

I tried to look calm while my head swirled and my eyes looked up, down, left, right, anywhere but at *him*, because I knew his eyebrow would be arched, and seeing that would only make my belly tighten more . . . but then . . . a miracle! An answer came to me while I studied the bark on the oak tree.

"I paid th-thirty-five dollars for her, Devlin. I thought that was reasonable."

Strong fingers lifted my chin, making me look into his narrowed, skeptical eyes.

"You paid thirty-five for the doll?"

"Uh huh."

"Really?" He couldn't have sounded any more doubtful.

"Uh huh."

Devlin can usually sense when I'm not being totally up-front about things, but he's a gentleman and he'd *never* call a lady a liar. He studied my face and gave me one last chance.

"You're *positive* about that."

Arrgg! How many times would he make me *say* it? "Yes . . . thirty-five American dollars."

"Then it sounds like you found yourself a bargain, Princess. She'll make a nice addition to your collection."

It took all of two seconds for guilt to kick in, because he was being nice to me and I didn't deserve it. He took my hand and we continued to wander the fair, but it wasn't fun anymore. I was mad at the doll, I was annoyed at Devlin, and I felt very sorry for myself that I couldn't even enjoy this treasure I found, or rather this treasure that cost me $350! That sounded like an *awful* lot of money all of a sudden. He put his arm around me and was just beginning to give me a hug that I *also* didn't deserve when we were interrupted by a female voice, calling to me.

"Excuse me, Miss? Miss!" I turned and my stomach lurched when I saw the doll booth woman heading toward us, waving a piece of paper. "You were in such a hurry you forgot your receipt! I'm so glad I spotted you!"

Devlin turned, glanced at me, and then smiled at *her.* I moaned because the woman's eyes glistened when she saw Devlin's smile. It has that effect, especially on older women. OK, me too, but old ladies kind of melt when he looks at them a certain way, like he's their long-lost son or something, and she just shoved the receipt into his hand without another look at me. I tried to snatch it from him, but he read it while he held it up and out of my reach. And then . . . things didn't go so well after that. He thanked the woman and she left, but she kind of sighed as she looked over her shoulder. I quivered when he gave me the Visa slip.

"I don't understand . . . there *must* be a mistake! I thought the price tag said thirty-five, not three fifty! Where'd that extra zero come from?"

"You probably should run after her then, don't you think?"

"No! I mean . . . well, I . . . see . . . um. . . ."

A hot blush covered my cheeks. My desperate ploy only made Devlin's eyebrow go up higher than I've ever seen it before.

He leaned down and whispered. "Do you know what happens to little girls who fib? Especially to *me?*"

I could only shake my head.

"Well then, Princess . . . I believe it's time you learned."

Of course I *did* know what happened to little girls who fibbed to Devlin, or I could guess. I'd never done it before. Well, I hadn't been *caught,* anyway, until then. My guess turned out to be pretty accurate, because my fanny was really sore already and I didn't dare rub because I didn't know where he'd gone and I couldn't see the bedroom door without turning my head, and if he was standing outside watching me, he'd spank me again for moving when he told me not to. And heaven help me if I *rubbed* my bottom after a spanking before he said I could! I really, really wanted to be a good girl and show him how sorry I was that I spent all that money on the doll, especially after we had that *long* discussion just the month before. He must have spanked me for half an hour that time, before he sent me to the corner. I *hate* standing in the corner. It's *so* embarrassing to have my red bottom on display, and having Devlin sitting behind me somewhere. And I never know if he's reading or watching TV or admiring his handiwork. I *hate* standing in the corner.

When we got home from the fair, I was over his lap for almost an hour while he *reminded* me of that discussion. I'm always amazed how he can scold me for so long and never say the same thing twice. At least I don't *think* he does. Of course, I'm kind of distracted by his hard hand smacking my bottom every six seconds. That's part of what makes his spankings so awful. He leaves plenty of time for the sting to get all the way into my cheeks before he gives me the next swat, so by the time he's finally done my fanny feels absolutely on *fire.* But there's no rubbing allowed, not unless Devlin does it himself.

He didn't say, but I had to assume that now he was going to *talk* to me about the fib. Where'd he go, anyway? What's he *doing,* for crying out loud? Well, I knew *one* thing he was doing, and that was giving me time to think about what he'd do *next,* which scared me half to death. I mean, there I was with my fanny in the air, *so* vulnerable, *so* wide open, and the cool air could get all inside, especially down low, where my lips were kind of damp. OK, that's another fib. They were *wet.* And the more my bottom cooled the wetter they *got.*

Where *was* he? Not that I *wanted* him to come back and look

inside my behind and then spank me for fibbing, but my tummy was getting pretty nervous and all those nasty butterflies were flapping around like *crazy*. Maybe he wouldn't spank me again, after all. Maybe he just wanted me to get really scared and embarrassed so I wouldn't fib to him anymore. Hah! Maybe the moon is made of Monterey Jack!

"Gwen!"

I jerked and my belly did flip-flops. "What? Um. Sir?"

"Didn't I tell you to stay the way I put you?"

"I *did*."

"Then why is the pillow scrunched between your legs?"

I looked down. "Oh, *God*."

"You were rubbing your naughty parts against it, weren't you?" He lifted me by the waist so he could put it back where he left it.

"*No* . . . I . . . I don't *know* how that happened."

"Then why is there a wet spot on the pillow case?"

A tear dripped from my eye. "But . . . but you were gone so *long*, I just . . . I guess I wiggled a *little* bit but I didn't really *move*, honest!"

"We will discuss the issue of your honesty in a moment. Now spread your knees the way I had them before."

I blushed but opened my legs for him. "OK. See? I'm being good. We don't have to *discuss* anything right now, do we? You already spanked me real *hard* and I'm *awful* sore. Devlin? What are you going to *do*?"

"Teach you not to fib to me, Princess."

"But . . . but I already *know* that, honest! I mean . . . I *do* know that! You don't have to punish me anymore 'cause I already *learned* my lesson!"

"Obviously you haven't or you would have been too overcome with shame to masturbate against the pillow."

"But I *didn't!* How can you *say* that to me?"

I felt the sting an instant before I heard the crack of his hand on my bottom. My hand jerked back to rub before I could stop.

"*Gwen?*"

"I'm sorry but that *hurt!*"

He pushed my hand away and sat on the edge of the bed. I folded my arms above my head and stared at the duvet. My cheeks still quivered, both from the spank and from trying not to clench,

and I could *feel* his eyes as he inspected the insides of my cleft. Why does he *do* that? Doesn't he know how embarrassing that is? I sighed and curled my toes. Of *course* he knows. What was I *thinking?*

"You're just dripping, Gwen."

"Am *not.*"

"*And* you're arguing!"

"Ow, ow, *ouch.*"

I couldn't *help* it! He smacked my sore tushy about a dozen times, and I just *had* to clamp my legs together because his fingers kept landing *inside,* and it really *stung!*

"Spread your thighs and open your bottom!"

"Devlin, *no! Please?* I . . . I *hate* it when you look inside!"

He tapped the back of my knee and I whined, but I spread my legs like he wanted.

"That's better, little girl."

His voice was so calm, so deep, so soft. I'm always afraid I'll make him mad but it doesn't seem like I ever do. And I love it when he calls me his little girl, because I know he'd never hurt his little girl, not really. The stinging on the sensitive skin in my cleft kind of glowed and I took a deep breath when he stroked me there, and then when his fingers went deeper it was like a bunch of warm firecrackers went off in my tummy!

"Ooh, Devlin! Mmm *yes.*"

"Princess?"

"Hm?"

"Do you remember when we talked about what happens to extra-naughty girls? Girls who don't mind me, or defy me . . . or *fib* to me?"

The soft, liquid voice turned to frozen hydrogen when he said *fib,* and the warm glow in my tummy turned to a block of ice. He was referring to a late night conversation we'd had months ago.

"But, *Devlin,*" I whispered. "You . . . we were just *talking.* You didn't *mean* that, did you? You . . . you had your finger on my . . . um . . . *button* and . . . and you just wanted me to *imagine* that . . . didn't you? You wouldn't really *do* that to me!"

"Do what, Princess?"

"*You* know! S-spank me . . . um . . . in *there!*"

"But you remember what I said, don't you? When I told you

– 152 –

what would happen if you enrolled in my college, and you misbe-haved? Remember?"

"*Yes* . . . but it . . . it was just a *story*. We . . . you were just *playing*."

His hand rubbed my sore behind, and his thumb slipped between the cheeks and caressed for just a second. I gasped and bit my lip.

"But you told me what *you* would do," he said in that liquid voice. "If I made you bend over the desk in the classroom, lifted your little schoolgirl skirt and took down your little white school-girl panties. Do you remember what you said?"

"*No!* Ow! Devlin! OK! *Yes!* I *remember!*"

He didn't swat very hard but I didn't expect it, so I kicked the mattress.

"Be *still*. Now . . . tell me what you said."

"*No*," I whimpered.

I squealed when I felt his arm rise up.

"*Now*, Gwendolyn." The soft voice had a really scary edge to it.

"OK! I . . . when we were *playing* that, um, schoolgirl fantasy, I said something about . . . how very extra-naughty girls get spanked . . . inside their bottoms." I took a deep breath. "Then . . . then I said . . . uh . . . I said, 'Ooh, I *am* pushing it out, Professor! I *am* offering! Oh, don't spread my bottom like that! *Please*, it's so embarrassing to know you're looking back there! *Don't!*' Or . . . or something like that."

And I *did* push it out then, because I remembered *exactly* what I said that night. I could just *see* that classroom he writes about in his naughty stories, and me dressed like a schoolgirl, bent over the desk while the other girls watch me get punished. It doesn't matter that I'm fifteen years older than them . . . when Devlin's got his finger on my trigger I could be Madonna on-stage at the Hollywood Bowl, except it isn't fake when I explode like a ton of dynamite!

Then he *chuckled*. I swear! The man actually *laughed!* I jerked my head around and glared at him, which was probably a mistake. Damn! I *wish* I'd ever learn. At least I didn't *say* anything, which I was going to until I saw his left eyebrow go up. At least he didn't scowl, which was a good sign, but he did squeeze my sore bottom pretty hard, and that made me whimper really loud.

"That was *very* good, Gwen. So you know what you have to do now."

"No, Devlin! I don't *want* to! It was just a *fantasy!* You can't expect me to *really* . . . owee! Ouch! Ow! OK! I will! Uh! I'm *doing* it, OK? See? I . . . my bottom's all spread out, and . . . and I'm sticking it up, see? But *please* not too hard, OK? Don't spank me real hard inside my fanny, *please?*"

"*Much* better, Princess," he said, and leaned over.

I nearly had a heart attack because he *kissed* me, right between the cheeks, about an inch from you-know-where!

"Ooh, *Devlin!* That feels so . . . mmm!"

Then he rubbed my tushy with both hands and I thought I'd died and gone to heaven. But he stopped, dammit, and *then* he said something I did *not* want to hear.

"How many times did you fib to me today, Gwendolyn?"

Oh, *God!* Not *Princess* . . . not even *Gwen. Gwendolyn* . . . my in-trouble name.

"I . . . I'm sorry I fibbed, Devlin. Sir."

"That's *not* an answer, young lady. How many times?"

I tried to ignore the awful, icy butterflies flapping in my belly. "I . . . um . . . just once . . . sir."

"Oh? Didn't I ask you *twice* how much you paid for the doll?"

"I . . . I don't remember. Owich! Ooh! *Yes!*"

He swatted my right cheek, pretty hard, but at least his fingers didn't land inside, then he rubbed the sting away while I nodded.

"And when the lady came with the receipt, didn't you try to fib to me *again?*"

"Y-yes, sir," I whispered.

"Better . . . and how many times did you put me off before you even *told* the first fib?"

"I . . . um . . . twice. Sir."

"At *least* that. So . . . that's two prevarications and three outright fibs. How many fibs can a girl tell me before I consider her *extra-naughty*, Gwendolyn?"

I couldn't *believe* it! He was gonna make me *say* it! I cried because it was too awful to *admit* I'd been extra-naughty. His hand felt *so* good on my hot fanny when he rubbed it while I sobbed, and I sobbed for a *long* time. Just not long enough or hard enough, I guess.

"Gwendolyn? I asked you a question."

"I . . . I *know!*"

"I expect an answer . . . now!"

"Geeze, Devlin! Um . . . five?"

He squeezed my sore tushy and I yelped.

"Not even close. Try again."

"Oh, God! Three?"

"*One* is the correct answer, young lady!" He smacked my fanny and I squealed. "So that makes you *what* kind of little girl? Hmm?"

"A . . . a v-very extra-naughty l-little girl."

"And what happens to very extra-naughty little girls, Gwen?"

My bottom hole was just *throbbing* and I really *wished* he couldn't see it, but I took a deep breath and shut my eyes tight.

"They . . . they get spanked?"

He sighed. "Where, Gwendolyn?"

"In . . . inside their bottoms?" I whispered.

"What? I couldn't hear you."

Dammit, of *course* he could hear me! It was so quiet in the bedroom I could hear the Canada geese honking at the pond a mile away!

I huffed, kind of loud. "Inside their bottoms, *OK?*"

He smacked me again. "You're in *enough* trouble so watch that sassy tone."

"But . . . this is so *awful!*"

"I hope it's *awful* enough that you remember it the next time you even *think* about telling me a fib."

"But I *will!* You don't have to *do* this! I'll never fib to you again, I swear!"

"Push your tummy down so your bottom lifts more."

"Devlin, *please?*"

"Hush and do what I said."

It was *horrible,* lying there with my panties around my knees, my bottom way up in the air, all spread out, and my boobs mashed on the duvet. My nipples were hard as rock and they just *burned.* I tried to concentrate on *them* so I wouldn't think about how wide open my fanny was, but then he started spanking me in between my cheeks, not too hard at first, and it wasn't long before I forgot all about my nipples.

"Owee! Devlin! That *stings!*"

"It's going to sting a lot more in few minutes. Stay *still.*"

"But it's *nasty!*"

"So is fibbing, young lady."

"But I'm *sorry!* Ow! Ooh! Not right *there!* Don't spank me *there!*"

"Are you going to fib to me ever again?"

"Neeeooh! Owitch! I . . . I *promise!*"

"You promised you wouldn't spend money on frivolousness, but you *did.*"

"Nooo *ow!* Eeek! *Devlin!*"

"Push your bottom up more, girl. I've hardly begun."

"Nahahahah noooo!"

It was just his fingertips at first, smacking the soft skin inside my crack, and that was more embarrassing than painful. He kept up the light swats for five minutes, but then he started to swat pretty hard, with all of his big, hard fingers and that *really* stung. I'm pretty sure he scolded me about something or other for the next ten minutes, and I *think* I said whatever he wanted to hear. All I knew was how much the inside of my bottom burned, and how he was leaning over, pushing down on my back, looking right *inside* my most private spot, while he spanked and spanked and *spanked!*

After forty or fifty swats on one side, he'd twist around and lie across my legs so he could spank the inside of the *other* cheek, then he'd go back and start on the *first* side again. I was screeching and pounding on the bed with my fists, and then I tried to put my legs together. Why can't I ever *learn?*

"Gwendolyn! Extra-naughty girls do *not* get to close their bottoms!"

I have *no* idea what I said, and I'm pretty sure it was gibberish anyway, but the next thing I knew my panties were gone and my knees were spread out about a *mile.* That's when he knelt behind me and slapped straight down into the crack! It made kind of a *pop* every time he smacked me, and my little hole just *quivered.* That went on for *hours,* or maybe only a minute or two, and then all of a sudden I wasn't lying on my tummy over the pillow anymore.

"Shh . . . it's all right, Princess. I've got you."

And he did, too. He sat on the edge of the bed and cradled me

in his arms so my sore, humiliated little tushy was on his lap. That was even better than him rubbing me, when I'd sit and wiggle my hot bottom on his pants to take away the sting. I clung to his neck and sobbed while I told him how sorry I was, and I'd never do it again, and I would be the best little girl in the world, and I can't remember what else. Finally I looked up at him and realized *none* of what I'd said came out anything like English, but his smile made me feel better.

"I . . . I . . . I love you, Devlin."

"That's all I need to hear. You're still my girl, even when you're naughty."

"Uh huh . . . I know." I adore having his arms around me after a spanking. There's no better place to be, and that's why his next words hit me like ice water.

"OK . . . be my good girl and stand up for me."

I was *so* comfy and cozy, cuddled on his lap, but he didn't let me hesitate for long, just stood up and I had no choice but to get up too, then I gave him the biggest, angriest pout I could muster.

He chuckled. "Any more of *that* attitude, young lady, and you'll find yourself with a bottom full of soap suds."

The pout disappeared real quick. "*No*, Devlin, I'm *sorry*. See? Look . . . a big smile for you, OK?" I gave him a nervous fake grin, and then hid my face in his shirt, praying I hadn't blown my redemption.

He hugged me and rubbed the back of my head. "I don't *want* to give you a nasty enema, but that's one naughty-girl procedure that always gets your attention, isn't it? So be on your best behavior while we finish up or I'll add a soapy enema to the agenda. Is that clear?"

"Yes, sir . . . I . . . I understand." But I was *so* disappointed. Here I thought I was free and clear after that awful spanking and now I had to worry about an *enema?*

"That's my girl. Here . . . let me see you."

Warm palms held my face while he looked at me, then he pressed the back of his hand to my forehead. I closed my eyes, enjoying his soft touch.

"You feel a bit warm, Princess. Get the thermometer and Vaseline, please."

My eyes shot open. "Devlin, *no!* I'm *not* warm!"

"Go into the bathroom and bring them to me *now*. One more syllable and I promise you a fanny full of soapsuds within five minutes."

Then I *was* warm . . . and sort of scared . . . so I turned around and walked to the bathroom. It felt like *miles*. I *hated* having my temp taken that way and my bottom started clenching in anticipation. When I finally made it past the door and reached for the cabinet, I saw that he had already put the Vaseline, thermometer and a white hand towel on the counter by the sink. Ooh, that *man!* He had planned to take my temp even *before* he spanked me! I should have *known* this would be part of my punishment because he *knew* how much I hated it.

Once, during a vacation down the Cape, we got into a petty argument about the sailboats that skimmed across the bay. I should have known better than to argue, but I'd had three mimosas after breakfast and felt pretty sure of myself, so I kind of got in his face about the difference between a lateen and a spinnaker, and even though I was right he said I was *way* too smarty-pants about it. He *really* doesn't like to be shown up about nautical stuff, so he spanked me before breakfast, lunch and dinner every day, followed by the rectal thermometer. I had that damn thing hanging over my head our entire vacation and he had me squirming the whole *week*.

I picked up the items and turned to leave but stopped in midstep. There, on the towel rack, hung the red enema bag. I couldn't *believe* it! He had taken it out, assuming he'd be using *that* on me, too! I was *so* angry and *so* frustrated and *so* determined not to give him any excuse to put that nasty nozzle in my bottom! I'd just keep very quiet no matter *what* he did. Yeah, right! As if!

"Don't keep me waiting, young lady!"

My feet dragged as I went back to him. He made me stand in front of him while he rolled up his shirtsleeves, then he took the hand towel and laid it on the bed. Next he took the Vaseline jar and popped off the lid. I don't think *anyone* hates that sound as much as I do. It's a noise like nothing else in the world, and it makes my belly flip-flop. He put the jar on the towel and then took the thermometer from my hand, gave it a few shakes and stuck it in the pale jelly.

Then he patted his knee to tell me it was time to lie over his lap. My bottom still stung and I didn't relish the thought of an enema

on top of everything *else,* so I didn't say anything. I knew what I had to do, except I couldn't budge, so after a few seconds he took me by the elbow and pulled me across his knees. He didn't waste any time, just pushed my skirt up to my waist to expose my bare, red bottom. I whimpered a little when he spread my cheeks and held them wide open for about a dozen seconds while he looked inside. I huffed and wriggled to let him know I wasn't real happy about it, but he only spread my bottom wider, like he didn't particularly *care* what I thought!

"Be a good girl and stop wriggling. You know this won't hurt."

No, but it was *humiliating,* and I had to bite my tongue to keep from telling him that. Then he touched my little hole with the thermometer and I twitched.

"I *said* to lie still. Don't make me tell you again."

He slicked Vaseline around my anus with just the tip of the thermometer, and I couldn't do *anything* but lie there and wait until he was satisfied my bottom hole was thoroughly greased. When he hugged my waist tighter, I knew it was time, and the cold glass slipped into my behind. Ooh, it was almost *icy,* like it had been in the refrigerator! I wriggled, trying to get accustomed to the awful sensation.

"That's not quite right, is it, Princess?"

The thermometer slid out, only to slide back in, but this time he twisted it to the right, then to the left, then pulled it out a bit before pushing it all the way back in. I gasped and struggled to keep still. He always has to make such a *production* when he takes my temperature! *Still* he wasn't satisfied, so I had to suffer through the process one more time, him pushing, pulling, twisting, withdrawing the rod almost completely before pushing it back inside. I sobbed and wiggled in protest, and got a sharp slap on my fanny.

Then I guess he figured he had tormented me enough and left the nasty thing where it was, but he kept the end between his fingers while his hand rested on my sore behind. Every so often he'd spread my cheeks to make sure it was still properly inserted, or he'd give it a nudge to make sure it wasn't slipping out, as if he'd let it!

The minutes ticked by slowly while I lay across his lap with the thermometer stuck in my bottom, and I was really proud of myself for keeping quiet, and still determined not to let my mouth get me

in trouble. Devlin loves my fanny, and sometimes at night when we're in bed I don't mind so much when he plays with it, but I really *hate* these punitive sessions. Well, almost nearly hate. I mean, sometimes he embarrasses me so much I want to *die* but so far I haven't.

Finally he decided time was up. He spread my cheeks wide again and I whimpered because he didn't need do to *that*. Then, ever so slowly, and I mean *painfully* slowly, he withdrew the thermometer.

With his hand still on my blushing fanny he announced, "Marginally high temp but nothing to be concerned about." He patted my bottom, a signal for me to stand up. "We're nearly finished. Let's go into the bathroom."

I took his hand when he held it out, but I couldn't move my feet to follow him. Something told me we *weren't* going in there to wash up. I couldn't *see* the enema bag, but I could *feel* it, and I didn't want to be anywhere *near* that thing.

"Come along, Princess."

He dragged me several miles across the bedroom, then he went straight to the towel rack to unhook the enema bag and I nearly went into shock! I hadn't made a *peep* for the past fifteen minutes and I didn't *deserve* an enema! I was a breath away from shouting at him, but thank God I saw that he was only putting it away, back in the cabinet. Phew! That was close! Devlin never goes back on his word so I couldn't understand why I'd be getting an enema if I hadn't disobeyed him. My heartbeat slowed almost to normal, but then he turned around and I saw the blue bulb syringe in his hand. No *way!* He smiled when he saw my eyes go wide in awful surprise.

"I'll just give you a little washout . . . nothing major. You'll be more comfortable if you're nice and clean when I put the bottom plug in, won't you?"

What? Bottom plug? He chuckled at my panicked expression and I wanted to yell at him, but I was speechless! I shook my head back and forth. Not the *bottom plug!* I definitely didn't deserve *that*. I opened my mouth to argue, but he quickly put a finger over my lips.

"Shh . . . you've done very well so far . . . don't spoil it now. No argument, no pouting. You'll get a little-girl enema and the plug

for the rest of the evening. Any backtalk and you'll get the soap-suds, a spanking with the hairbrush and the *bigger* fanny plug. The choice is yours."

I stomped my foot. "That's not a *choice!* What did I do that was so *terrible?*"

"You fibbed to me."

"But I won't ever do it again, I *swear!* And . . . and you already spanked me really hard, and all inside my. . . ."

He wrapped his arms around me while I cried. "Take off your clothes . . . all of them. Now."

"But, Devlin!" I gasped when he let go of me and went to open the cabinet. "No! *Please?* Don't get the hairbrush, *OK?* I'll take off my clothes, *see?*"

My fingers didn't work very well, but he waited patiently while I fumbled and whimpered and finally got my skirt and blouse off. My bra hooked in the front and I nearly climbed the wall when my hands touched my nipples. I shut my eyes and let all the won-derful, wavy quivers run up my neck and down my tummy. Water started to splash in the sink so I leaned against the wall and watched him rinse out the bulb and fill it. He looked at me in the mirror and I blushed really hard. I whimpered and stomped my foot again, because he chuckled when I put my hand down to cover my vagina.

"Don't do that, Gwen. You have nothing to be ashamed of."

"How can you *say* that?"

Nothing to be ashamed of? I was standing there, stark naked, and he was about to put me over his lap, open my bottom, and put all kinds of nasty things right in my *hole,* for crying out loud! And he just *smiled* about it!

"No tantrums now. Come here."

He held out his hand and I stumbled over to him. I moaned and grabbed his shirt when he leaned down to kiss me. His lips felt *so* warm, and I was just shivering. I licked his tongue for as long as he let me, which wasn't nearly long enough. He started to raise his head and I whimpered.

"No, *please?*"

"Shh . . . come on. Time to wash out your little fanny."

I blushed really red. How could be so *calm?* My feet felt like ice on the tiles, and then suddenly they weren't *on* the tiles anymore

because he was sitting on the vanity stool and I was draped over his thighs with my hands on the floor and my tushy straight up in the air!

"Devlin!"

"Open your legs a little."

"But I don't *wanna* . . . ow! OK! Not so *hard*."

"Then *behave*. You know better than to tell me *no* when you're across my knee."

Oh, God! I wanted to reach back and rub the sting where he swatted me, but instead I opened my thighs. He parted my cheeks again and I wailed. It was still really slick with Vaseline inside the cleft, and his finger slid right into my anus. I clenched and he grunted.

"I'm sorry, Devlin, but I . . . I wasn't *expecting* it."

"It's all right . . . I wanted to be sure you were still lubricated. I'll take my finger out now, then put the nozzle in your bottom hole, OK?"

Did he just *have* to say that? And how could it *possibly* be OK? But I just bit my lip and nodded. His finger slipped out, but then he spread me even wider and I felt the plastic tip. He made little circles around my anus while I gasped for air and tried to keep my legs apart. Then he did the same thing with the enema nozzle that he did with the thermometer, except more and slower! It took him five minutes to get it all the way in, and all I could do was stare at the floor while waves of awful, squirmy, delicious shudders flowed through my bottom. I whimpered and bit my fingertip when a little drop of moisture squeezed between my lower lips, and I *knew* he could see it!

"Ready for the water, Princess?"

Like I had a choice or *what?* "OK."

He pressed the bulb and I moaned as warm wetness trickled inside me. It was awful and terrible and icky, especially when he leaned his elbow on my back to push my head toward the floor. The enema ran downward, into my tummy, and spread even more heat through my vagina. He took his fingers out from between my cheeks and massaged my belly with his left hand as he emptied the bulb. I tingled from head to toe as he pulled the nozzle out an inch, pushed it back in, pulled it out again, over and over until I thought I'd explode! Finally, he took it all the way out and set it on the counter.

"You're a very good girl, Gwen."

I sighed as he patted my fanny. My tummy gurgled when I slid off his lap and stood in front of him. He got up and hugged me while I squirmed in his arms.

"Um, Devlin? I need to um . . . you know?"

He looked at me with the strangest expression, and then snapped his fingers. "I left my briefcase in the trunk."

"Yeah, OK. Go get it while I. . . ."

"Come along."

"What are you . . . ?"

I couldn't *believe* it! He dragged me by the arm into the bedroom. I sputtered protests as I kept my cheeks clamped tight and hoped nothing *awful* would happen while I tried to figure out what his *problem was!*

"Here . . . put this on."

"Devlin, are you *crazy?*"

He grabbed one of my old tee shirts from the bureau top and made me raise my arms while he slipped it on me. It was nice to have *some* kind of clothes on, but the hem reached only about an inch below my bare butt. I didn't remember putting the shirt on the bureau, and I *sure* didn't remember putting my house shoes on the floor beside it, but there they were, and suddenly they were on my feet!

"This will only take a minute, Gwen."

"Are you out of your *mind?* I have to *go!* You're *not* taking me. . . ."

"The car's right outside in the driveway. Come on."

"Devlin!" I took tiny scissor-steps and gaped at the madman who wore Devlin's face as he pushed me through the living room. "I *can't* go outside! I'm half-naked and my bottom's full of. . . ."

He yanked open the front door and flipped on the porch light. I squirmed and panted but he curled his right arm around my shoulders as we walked the brick path to the driveway. The water inside me fought to get out while I peered up and down the block to see who might be watching. All my neighbors' lights were on but I didn't see anybody. Something in his hand chirped and the Lincoln's trunk lid popped open. I stared into Mrs. Frazetti's lighted picture window to make sure she wasn't staring back at *me*.

"It's right there." He pointed inside the trunk. "Would you get it for me, please?"

I wanted *so* bad to stomp my foot and scream at him, but I knew neither one was a good idea under the circumstances, so I just glared.

"*Now,* little girl." His voice was like molasses tinged with acid. "The longer you defy me the longer it will be before you get back inside."

"How can you *do* this to me?"

Shameful tears burned my eyes as I leaned over to grab the briefcase, then I felt cool night air on my bare bottom. Both sets of my cheeks flushed bright red as I clutched the handle with one hand and reached back with the other one to pull the shirt down over my fanny. Devlin grunted when I swung the leather bag into his chest.

"There! Can we go now?"

He scowled and I wanted the earth to open up and swallow me.

"Yes. Right after I cut a switch from the mulberry bush."

"*No!* I . . . I'm *sorry,* Devlin! Can we *please* go inside now? *Please?*"

I sighed with relief when he smiled, put his arm around me and reached up to close the trunk lid. It hissed and snicked shut as I pulled him toward the front door. My butt muscles throbbed from holding the water in, but I felt warm in spite of the fall night air. Finally we were in the foyer and he was closing the door behind us. I danced from one foot to the other while water sloshed.

"*Now?* Now can I? *Please?*"

He looked at me and squinted. "Can you what, Princess?"

"Aaagh! Go to the bathroom! What do you *think?*"

"Well, of course. You don't need my permission to use the. . . ."

I screamed several words that I *know* he doesn't like me to say as I ran to the toilet. The enema was less than a pint but it was in me so long it loosened up *everything.* I leaned forward and sat for a *very* long time. Finally it felt safe to get up. I was completely empty and *really* hungry, but not for food. I took off the tee shirt and soaked a washcloth with warm water and Yardley's Lavender Soap. It really felt good on my sore bottom, and even better someplace else, but I must have been kind of loud when I washed *there* because the next thing I knew Devlin was knocking on the door.

"Are you OK?"

"Yeah, fine! I . . . um . . . it feels so good when it stops hurting, that's all."

"I see. Well, hurry up. We're not done yet."

"Devlin! How can you even *think* about . . . ?"

"That mulberry bush is still in the yard, Gwen."

I chewed my lip for a few seconds and then took a deep breath. "Yes, sir. I'll be out in a minute."

Drat that man *anyway!* I couldn't *believe* he was going to put that *thing* in me after he dragged me out of the house and embarrassed me nearly to *death*. But my little 'gina still tingled from a *huge* orgasm, so it was tough to be mad at *anything* right then. I knew I'd change my mind as soon as he had me over his lap again, but I didn't think about it as I patted myself dry down there and enjoyed the little aftershocks. Finally I put the tee shirt back on and opened the door. He was lying on the bed in his robe, his back against the headboard, the current Cosmo folded to the letters section. His eyes lit up when he smiled and my 'gina got all quivery again.

"Feel better, Princess?"

"Uh huh . . . but you were really *mean* to make me go outside with the enema in me and I think that was punishment *enough* for fibbing."

His smile disappeared as he threw his legs off the bedside and stood up. "Oh, you *do,* do you?"

I took two steps backward and bit my fingertip. I didn't want to look at him, and I *sure* didn't want to look at the hope chest because that nasty pink plug was on it, sticking straight up. And if *that* wasn't bad enough, his briefcase was open on the floor by the bed and I could see the tip of that huge, horrible *black* one in a zipper pocket. Devlin had only *showed* it to me once, to scare me, thank God, because the pink one was *plenty* awful!

"*Gwendolyn.*"

I blinked at him. "Huh? Um . . . sir?"

"Stop gawking and come out of the bathroom."

"But I really don't think you should put that in me!"

"Ordinarily I value you opinion but you haven't yet been punished completely for fibbing, so come here."

He held out a hand and I shook my head. My feet wouldn't move, and I wanted to slam the bathroom door in his face but I *really* didn't want to find out what he'd do then, so I just stood there until he came and got me. He didn't say anything, just leaned over and put his shoulder right up against my 'gina and picked me

up so I hung over his back with my head down and my tushy pointed at the ceiling. I grabbed his robe belt and wailed because he held my legs and spanked my bare tushy while he walked across the room! He wasn't in any hurry either, and I must have got about thirty really hard smacks with his left hand by the time he dumped me on the bed.

"You're not making this any easier on yourself, Gwen."

That was *so* true, because riding with his hard shoulder pressed against me down *there* had lit up that fire again, and all I wanted to do was put my hand on it.

"I . . . I'm *sorry*, Devlin. I'll be a good girl, I promise. I'll stay real still while you spank me as hard as you want, but *please* don't put the plug in me, OK?"

He sighed and shook his head. I whimpered and hugged my knees while he sat on the bedside. He opened the robe and patted his bare thigh.

"Now, Gwendolyn."

His voice was so soft, so deep, so *demanding*, I just huffed and crawled across his lap. My hot little lips barely touched his leg when a really fierce swat crashed into my fanny.

"Owee!"

"*Other* side, Gwen. When have I ever spanked you with my left hand?"

"Just a minute ago you . . . OK! Geeze!" I scurried around his knees. "I'm *trying* to be good, Devlin. See? I did what you told me and . . . and you can spank me real hard now, huh?"

He smiled and I nearly melted when he bent over to kiss me real softly on the lips while he rubbed by sore tushy.

"I'll tell you when you're a good girl. Can you behave if I give you a really hard spanking?"

"Yeah . . . um . . . yes, sir, and then you won't . . . ?"

"Shh . . . lie still."

And I tried! I really, really *tried!* But he just spanked and spanked and *spanked* my sore bottom for like *hours*. Or maybe ten minutes, but it stung like crazy every time his hand landed, and my arms and legs just *ached* from being still when all I wanted to do was kick and scream and pound on the bed. Well, I *did* scream . . . and wail . . . and cry . . . but I didn't move hardly at *all*, and I was so proud of myself when he finally stopped, and I was *sure* he

– 166 –

wouldn't do anything else. Sometimes I'm so naïve I amaze myself.

"I . . . I . . . I was really g-good, wasn't I?"

"Yes you were, Princess."

He rubbed my achy, fiery bottom while I sobbed and wiped tears. *Then* he reached over and got the K-Y Jelly out of the nightstand!

"Devlin, no! You *promised!*"

"I promised nothing . . . that was wishful thinking on your part."

"But *Devlin!*"

"Hush and spread your legs."

"Noooo!"

I whined, I whimpered, I gasped, but I did what he said. He just opened my bottom wide and started to smear goop on my little hole. It was *so* tender and *so* sensitive, and I just couldn't *help* but kick. Boy, was *that* ever a mistake, because he spanked me about a dozen times, right in the crack, before he even *said* anything!

"So much for your being good, Gwendolyn!"

"But I *tried,* Devlin! I *did!* You *know* how much I hate that thing!"

"I know you do . . . and that's why you have to have it. Now. Can you be good for me?"

"I . . . I'll *try.*"

He pressed his fingertip into my little hole and I wailed. "That wasn't the right answer. *Will* you be a good girl while I put the plug inside your bottom?"

"Oh, *God. Yes.*"

"What?" His finger slipped in another half inch.

"Yes, *sir!*"

"Then push up with your knees so you're spread nice and wide and I can make the little hole all slick and ready, OK?"

"*Geeze,* Devlin!"

"Excuse me?"

The finger slid *all* the way in and I gasped as I lifted my fanny for him. "I mean, yes, *sir!*"

"Better . . . just a bit higher. That's good. Now I can see *all* the inside of your bottom, and those pretty pink lips, too."

My face turned *bright* red. It was so *awful* when he inspected me like that, and I felt so *vulnerable,* because I knew I wasn't

going anywhere until he said I could. And what was worse, the more I thought about his finger in my tushy and his eyes on my 'gina, the hotter I got!

"D-Devlin?"

"Hm?"

"Could you . . . ? Would you just . . . um . . . touch me a little bit? Please?"

His hand twisted around and he chuckled. "You mean . . . down *there?*"

"Uh huh. It would make my punishment easier to take. *Please?*"

I sighed when he leaned over and kissed my right bottom cheek while his finger slid in and out of my rear end.

"First of all, young lady, it looks like somebody *already* touched herself down *there.*"

"No! I wouldn't. . . ."

"Gwendolyn, don't say another word! Why are you being punished?"

"Be . . . because I fibbed."

"And didn't you just compound the offense?"

I panicked. "No way! I mean no *sir* way! No way, *sir!* I did! I mean I *didn't!* It was an accident! It just. . . ."

"*Hush,* Gwen." He slipped his finger out of me. "I find it hard to believe you *accidentally* gave yourself an orgasm, but you should know by now that your fun comes *after* your punishment, not during."

"But it's been like . . . *hours.*"

"That is totally irrelevant." He let my cheeks close and I whimpered when he raised his arm. "I think you need another spanking for impertinence."

"No, God, *please!* I . . . I'm already *blistered!* Just . . . just . . . oh, *God!* Just *do* it, OK?"

He rubbed my bottom with his right hand while I moaned. His finger was still slick with jelly.

"Do *what?* What do you want me to do?"

I sobbed and bit my finger. I couldn't *believe* he was going to make me *say* it!

"Put it in," I whispered.

"Put *what* in *where?*"

My heart pounded like a jackhammer. "In . . . in my *bottom*."

"Put my finger in your bottom? Is *that* what you meant?"

I nodded and pushed up with my fanny. He shook his head while he rubbed it.

"That's *not* what you meant, is it? Now stop this foolishness and tell me."

"Oh, *geeze!* Put the damn plug in my bottom and get it over with! Oweee! Ow! Ow! Ow! *Devlin!*"

God, I can be so stupid sometimes! His big, hard hand whacked my soft, sore butt and I didn't even *pretend* to be good. I kicked and screamed and thrashed around like a fish on a boat deck, but he just held me around the waist and whacked my fanny, over and over, like he planned to make a career of the job! It really, really burned, and I almost jerked right off his lap, but then he stopped spanking and started to rub. I cried and sniffled and wiped my nose on my sleeve for five minutes while he stroked my pitiful little tushy and made some of the sting go away.

"Gwen?"

"Y-yes, sir?"

"Can you ask me nicely now?"

I only hesitated long enough to take a deep breath, because I knew if I stopped I'd never be able to say it all.

"Would you please put the plug in my bottom hole?"

He leaned over and cupped my chin in his hand. Hot, shameful tears drenched our lips while he kissed me.

"That was very good, Princess. I'll be happy to."

I didn't *want* to watch him stretch to the end of the bed and pick up the plug. I didn't *want* to watch him spread jelly all over the nasty thing. I didn't *want* to watch him open my sore cheeks again. And I *sure* didn't want to watch him bite his lower lip as he poked the tip right into my anus! But I *did,* and I hated every second of it! It was so *cold!* Cold and *icky!*

My toes curled up and I spread my legs as he slid in the first inch, then the second, then he pulled it out again. The first two inches aren't *too* bad, but I really, really *hate* that third inch because that's where the big bulge is. After the bulge, it's really tiny, with a flat disk at the end, so your sphincter ring kind of clamps down on the skinny part. Devlin says that's so naughty girls can't push it out before their punishment is over. All I know

is, that bulgy part is *major* nasty! It's like *twice* as big around as Devlin's finger, and he *always* stops right when it gets to the fattest part to make sure I really feel how big it is.

"See? That's not so bad, is it?"

Yeah, like *he'd* know! But all I said was, "No, sir."

He went in and out with the first two inches for a long time; long enough for me to get used to it and maybe even enjoy it a little. But I knew what was coming next, and it was awful and scary and I *hated* it. Except, tell *that* to my stupid hormones!

"It appears you don't detest this nearly as much as you claim, Princess."

I wailed when he touched my wet, quivery 'gina with his fingertips, then he kept on pumping that first two inches, in and out; fast, then slow; then slower, then fast again. Somewhere off in the distance I could feel my scorched bottom cheeks, but all that mattered at the moment was right in between them.

"Mmm, Devlin! That's so . . . so. . . ."

"Vile? Heinous? Horrible?"

"Wonderful!"

"Good. Let's go on then, shall we?"

"Nooo!" My sphincter clamped tight on the soft rubber.

"Shh . . . it's all right. Push up your fanny and take deep breaths."

I tried, I really did, but that third inch *always* makes me squirm. It wasn't *quite* as bad this time, but it was *still* yucky, and I whimpered the whole time he held it *right* at the fattest part. *Then* he pulled it out! Not all the way, just down to like the first inch, and then started all over! A couple more in and out, then all the way in to the bulge again! I moaned and quivered and spread my knees even farther apart, but it was *still* icky when it got to the bulgy part. He must have done that five or six times, I'm not really sure, because after the second time he put his fingers on my 'gina, not inside or anything, but kind of cupped it while he did those terrible, unspeakable, absolutely thrilling things to my bottom hole.

When he finally pushed the plug all the way in, my ring hugged it like an old friend. It filled me with warmth, like hot oatmeal in front of the fire on a snowy day. I could feel the pulse in his fingertips as they rested on my vagina. His breath tickled my ear when he leaned over to kiss my neck. A single, hot fingertip

slipped between my lower lips, touched the button and I exploded in a shower of red and blue sparks. Soft, bright lightening bolts zipped through my body and shot out the top of my head.

My tee shirt was drenched and I shivered as I clung to Devlin's neck a thousand years later. I opened my eyes while he cuddled me in his lap and kissed my forehead, my cheeks, my chin, my neck. I sat on his bare thighs, vaguely aware of the dull ache in my bottom and not in the least worried about it. I grinned and clamped my lips to his.

"Don't you have something to tell me, Princess?" he said when the kiss finally ended.

I nodded. "I'm very sorry I was a naughty girl and fibbed to you. I'll never do it again."

He squeezed me hard and I sighed as we kissed again.

"Then you're forgiven. Are you hungry?"

"Yeah. I kinda feel like some hot oatmeal. Is that OK?"

He shrugged. "I don't know why not."

"I'll put some clothes on and make it. You want raisins and cinnamon?"

"Yeah . . . and butter. Lots of butter."

I turned to stand up, then shrieked and grabbed my fanny with both hands.

"Oh, my *God!*"

He chuckled. "What's the matter?"

"You didn't take it *out!*"

"Did you want me to?"

"For Christ's sakes of *course* I. . . ."

Then I just grinned and rubbed my bottom, and the sweet little plug jiggled inside. Devlin smiled and patted my sore tushy. I squealed and grabbed my robe on the way to the kitchen.

PREPARING THE WAY

Gwen and I knew each other for several months before we decided to have intercourse, odd as that may sound to some people. We talked about it from time to time, and of course the act occurred only in written form, but neither of us likes the idea of quick, casual sex, soon accomplished and soon forgotten. Shyness or antiquated social mores had nothing to do with postponed gratification, only that the pleasure of anticipation often exceeds the pleasure of the event, a fact we both appreciate.

I really love Bullfinches. It's such a romantic restaurant, with pillar candles on tables set with vintage china and crystal. Potted trees and antique room dividers screen the diners from one another, and that evening I was grateful for the privacy. Any other time I would have cuddled close to Devlin in our favorite booth, but that night I sat stiff and straight and tried to keep my distance.

"How's your lobster bisque, Princess?"

"Fine."

Devlin hates one-word answers but I didn't care. I wanted him to know I was still pouting so I just swirled my spoon in the thick stew.

"You're not eating. Don't you like it?"

"It's OK."

He sliced off an inch of baked tentacle and held it on his fork. "Would you like some of my calamari instead?"

"Ick, no! That stuff is gross!"

"You shouldn't insult other people's food, Princess."

I licked my lips and felt even worse. I knew better. "Sorry." My fanny squirmed on the seat as I tried to find a comfortable spot.

"Would you *please* sit still? I feel like I'm having dinner with a five-year-old."

"But I can't *help* it. No matter how I sit . . . this . . . this *thing* . . . I can't . . . ooh, it *hurts*." I blushed at my own outburst. Too embarrassed to look at him, I stared at my dish.

The *thing* was a pink rubber plug that filled my fanny, and it didn't actually *hurt* but it was uncomfortable as *hell*. I couldn't concentrate on anything, could barely keep a thought in my head because it was such a *torment*. There was no escape from its invasive, probing pressure and the feeling that my little bottom hole was being stretched. It nagged me with every little movement I made. Worse, I felt as though everyone in the restaurant knew *exactly* why I was fidgeting, like I had a note posted on my forehead that read Fanny Plug In Place.

Devlin took my hand and leaned his handsome face close to mine. "Is it painful?"

I shrugged. "Not *exactly* but. . . ."

"Then stop fussing and behave."

Stop *fussing*? Easy for *him* to say! He didn't *know* how embarrassed I was to sit in public with a rubber tool invading in my bottom, and he *couldn't* know how uncomfortable I was! And it wasn't just the plug . . . I could still feel the *spanking* he gave me before we even left for the restaurant!

• • •

Well . . . I guess the spanking *was* my fault. I got pretty indignant when he told me I had to submit to the plug in the first place, and *then* he told me I had to have it in when we went out! I was all dressed up for him in my little black DKNY number with black hose and pumps, and he wanted me to have my bottom stretched

all evening by a *plug?* I just stared at him while he said he'd noticed a willful streak in me on his last visit, whatever the heck *that* meant, and although this wasn't for punishment, he thought a few hours of having the plug in my bottom would help adjust my attitude. Ooh! I was so angry I wanted to *strangle* him, and I told him so, which was *not* a very good idea. The look on Devlin's face when I stomped my foot for emphasis said louder than any words that I had gone too far. You'd think a smart girl like me would have learned not to argue with him, but it's only *after* he hauls me over his knee and my bottom is raised and bared that I remember to be smart.

He took hold of my wrist, pulled me to the ottoman, and in a flash he had me across his lap, wriggling to get free. I wriggled a *lot* for the next twenty minutes while Devlin held me tight and spanked my poor bottom until it was bright pink. While I kicked and squirmed, he calmly lectured me on how tired he was of my uncooperative attitude, that he expected me to be on my best behavior during his weekend visits because he knew what was best for me, and that he intended to make certain I behaved like the good girl he knew I was.

I sobbed that I was sorry, that I really, really *did* promise to behave, and I begged him not to make me wear the plug because he *knew* how much I hated it. It didn't matter to him, though. He just rubbed some of the fire out of my fanny while he told me that was why I needed to wear it, to teach me discipline. That made me squirm even more, and then he said he was looking forward to a nice, long evening of making love to me when we returned from dinner, which made me feel pretty good . . . until he told me he didn't want to hear any whining when he took my bottom!

OK, yeah . . . that stunned me. Devlin had *talked* about doing it in my behind, but this time he sounded serious. My first inclination is always to say no to him when he even touches me there with his *finger.* Once I give in, usually after a pretty hard fanny warming, and he puts it inside . . . well, that's heaven, pure and simple. It's the *getting-there* part I have a problem with. So I really didn't need to hear that he wanted me to be a big girl about it when he made love to my bottom, *or* that the plug would make me better prepared . . . that only made me sob harder.

But he *does* seem to know what I need, and after he was done

scorching my fanny with his hard hand, his fingers roamed all over my bottom, soothing the burn in my cheeks. After a while they dipped down between my legs to play with my 'gina. He stroked and tweaked the slick little button, and for a heated minute I forgot about the nasty plug he was going to stretch me with, and what *else* he would stretch me with later, if he wasn't just talking to make me squirm. His finger was one thing, but I didn't even want to *think* about his hard penis in my bottom! I'm a *good* girl and good girls are *supposed* to worry about the anal sex taboo, aren't they?

So there I was, across his lap, my poor fanny all red and scorched, and Devlin toying with my 'gina, and the next thing I knew he was pushing my legs apart and spreading my bottom cheeks. He continued to scold me, and said if I had accepted the plug then the spanking wouldn't have been necessary. I sobbed when he massaged K-Y around my anus with his finger, and I *tried* to close my bottom but he's too strong. His index finger slipped slowly inside and I shrieked. Devlin tightened his grip around my waist as he worked the finger in and out of my hot little hole. He told me I needed to be fully lubricated before he inserted the plug, like I wanted to hear *that*.

"Devlin! It . . . it's horrible! Please take your finger out! Please *stop!*"

He chuckled as his thumb dropped down between my wet lips. "You *poor* thing! This must be torture for you, Princess."

Well, of *course* I was dripping! A girl's body doesn't lie at moments like those, but I blushed anyway when his thumb made kind of a gooshy noise in the wetness down there. He took his finger out and quit playing with my lower lips, which I didn't like at *all,* and then he kept me over his knee while he lubricated the plug, his elbow pressed down on my back to keep me still. Once he was satisfied it was slick enough, he opened my cheeks wide and pressed the tip of the plug against my puckered hole.

"Noooo!"

"Relax, Gwen. This'll only take a minute, then we'll be on our way."

Ooh, he was so nonchalant I wanted to slap him! I squealed as my little hole gave way and the plug slipped farther and farther into my bottom. Devlin controlled the insertion very carefully and when the plug began to widen at the base, he stopped.

"All right, Princess, here comes your favorite part. We'll go nice and slow."

"No, please, it's too *big!*"

It wasn't, of course, and I knew that, but the damn thing always widened so *much* before it narrowed again, and felt *enormous* for the first minute or so.

"Hush . . . you know it's not too big for you. Hold still."

I knew not to squirm then because that could be dangerous, so I gritted my teeth as my anus stretched wider and wider to accommodate the plug.

"*Devlin!* Please?"

He shushed me again and I took sort of normal breaths as he pushed it all the way in and my anal ring clamped on the narrow end of the plug. He let go with his fingers and I clamped my cheeks around the flexible base of the plug. It felt so *rude,* wedged inside my tushy like that.

"You can't *possibly* expect me to . . . it's *horrible!* Don't leave that nasty thing in my bottom! Why are being so *mean* to me? Take it out! Don't think for one second that I'm leaving this house with that nasty, horrible, icky . . . owee! Okaaay! Don't . . . don't spank me anymore, *please?* I'm getting up!"

I don't know *how,* but I managed to stand still while Devlin pulled my panties up and straightened my dress and hose. He even handed me a Kleenex and helped me with my coat, despite the fact that I whimpered and moaned the whole time we were getting ready to go. I glared at him as he walked me to the car and opened my door. The leather seat felt cool at first but it warmed up pretty quick with the heat from my well-spanked fanny, and I don't think I could've pouted any harder if I tried.

A very long ten minutes later we arrived at Bullfinches and pulled into the parking lot. I absolutely, positively did *not* want to go into that restaurant! Desperate for an excuse, I told Devlin that the plug felt like it was slipping out and I didn't want to embarrass him. He just shook his head.

"Nonsense. It won't come out until I take it out."

"Devlin, please? I *can't* go in there . . . I'm afraid! It doesn't *feel* right! Let me take it out and I promise . . . I *promise* I'll put it back in later."

He nodded, but his left eyebrow went up, so he knew I was fibbing.

"You're afraid it'll come out, Princess?"

"Uh huh, it . . . it *might.*"

"All right, let me have a look. We'll make sure it's still snug. Slip down your panties."

"No!"

"Then lean toward the window and lift your bottom so I can take them down."

"Devlin, *please,* no! I . . . I guess I was wrong. It's really still in my bottom all the way . . . you don't need to check! *Please?* What if someone *sees?*"

"There's not a soul around. Hurry, now, or we'll miss our reservation."

He took hold of my ear and pulled until I lifted my bottom off the seat. I shrieked, but he reached right up under my dress with his left hand and tugged my panties to my knees. I glared at him as I plopped back down with my arms folded under my breasts.

"Pull up your dress and lift your pretty cheeks so I can make sure the plug is where it should be. Go on."

I stared straight ahead, so furious with Devlin that his next comment took me by surprise.

"Gwendolyn! Obviously your bottom has cooled sufficiently that you think you can defy me, so it appears I need to take you into the backseat and reheat your impertinent fanny!"

He wasn't joking and I knew it, so I sobbed, clutched my dress to my waist and lifted my bottom off the seat. But he didn't check my fanny . . . he reached under my skirt in front and put his big hand on my tummy.

"Spread your legs so I can see about the plug in your bottom hole."

"Don't *say* that! Someone might *hear* you!"

My panties stretched tight around my knees as I spread for him. Long, warm fingers slid down my 'gina and I fought the urge to tell him how good they felt but he didn't *deserve* that! I mean, he stuck that nasty fanny plug in me and made me wear it in public! What kind of awful ogre would make me *do* such a horrible . . . but he leaned across the console and I trembled when I felt his breath on my neck, and my little lips down there were so *wet* there was no mistaking how much I enjoyed what he was doing. I *hate* being such an open book to him! His fingers teased their way

lower, in between my bottom cheeks. He pried them apart and I squealed when he touched the base of the plug, and then prodded and tested the plug's security.

"Devlin, *don't*."

"It's quite firmly in place, Princess. No need to worry."

I *still* don't know how I managed to walk into the restaurant, but I did.

• • •

The waiter refilled our glasses from the Chianti bottle on the table and I gulped sour, red wine. Devlin's eyebrow rose half an inch, then he smiled at the young man.

"We'll have the chocolate strawberries for dessert . . . and you may put the lobster bisque into a container."

The man nodded to Devlin and looked at me. "It was not to your liking, ma'am?"

"It was fine, I . . . I'm just not hungry."

He bowed and took my dish while I blushed. Devlin chewed the last of his calamari while I drained my glass and poured the last of the wine into it. Three waiters pushed a trolley past our booth. A cake with white frosting and a fizzy sparkler sat in the middle of a linen cloth, and the waiters sang "Happy Birthday" to someone across the room. Devlin smiled and I bit my lip.

"Yours is coming soon, Princess."

"My what?"

"Your birthday, of course. May the . . . twenty-sixth, I believe."

"Oh, yeah . . . um . . . but you don't have to do anything special. It's just another day."

"Yes, I know how much you hate it when I make a fuss over you."

I quivered and blushed because I knew he was teasing me. He patted his full lips with a napkin, smiled and raised his wine glass. My hand shook when I picked up mine and clinked. The waiter put a plate in front of us. Ten fat strawberries slathered with thick coats of deep, rich brown sat on the plate. Devlin picked out the biggest berry and handed it to me.

"Thanks . . . can we um . . . ?"

"What, Princess?"

"Can we go pretty soon?"

"Finish your dessert first."

"But, Devlin! How can you . . . ?"

He scowled. I pouted and nibbled chocolate off the strawberry. It was obvious he wanted to enjoy his dessert, and even *more* obvious that he didn't care that I was so uncomfortable. The birthday party got really loud and Devlin finally signaled for the check as I slurped the last strawberry. I've never been so relieved in my *life* to leave a restaurant.

I moaned while he caressed my thigh all the way home. By the time we got to the bedroom my panties were just drenched, and he hadn't even *kissed* me.

"Hang up your dress, Gwen."

"But . . . but what are you going to *do?*"

"About what?" He looked truly puzzled.

"Are . . . are you going to um . . . do what you said before?"

"Make a fuss for your birthday? Well of course I'll. . . ."

My foot hit the floor kind of hard, which was a mistake because it made that stupid plug just *wriggle* inside me. "*No* . . . what you said about muh . . . making love."

He hung his suit jacket in the closet and loosened his tie, but he didn't say anything, just wrapped me up in his arms and kissed me for like an hour. Well, maybe not a *whole* hour, but long enough for that little pilot light between my legs to heat up again. He has the nicest lips and most talented tongue, and all those special muscles down *there* started to flick and twitch, and that made my bottom hole flick and twitch around the plug, but honestly, I didn't mind. But *then* he put his hand on my tushy and started to squeeze my cheeks together and push the plug in and out, so I gave up on the kiss and just buried my face in his chest and whimpered.

"What's the matter, Princess?"

I muttered that he ought to stop doing that, but he didn't seem to hear. He just kept squeezing while he unzipped me, then stopped long enough to pull my dress up over my head and toss it at the bureau. It landed in a black puddle on top of my hairbrush. I don't know why but I took that as a good sign. He rolled my hose down while I kicked off my pumps, then I couldn't think anymore because he started in on my cheeks again, *and* put his other hand on the front of my panties! God, they were so wet, and they just

kept getting wetter the more he squeezed. His middle finger was right between my little lips, and he kind of pushed and rolled it over the top of my button until I thought I was going to climb the wall! I clung to his neck and let the squirmy, hot waves build and build, until I had to shriek and push away from him. I didn't get far because he picked me up and carried me to the bed.

He put me down so my head was on the pillows, and I moaned and squirmed while I watched him take off all his clothes and hang them up. His penis was already pretty hard, and it kind of wobbled when his pushed his underpants down. I got a really nice twinge when I saw that and put my hands over the front of my panties to help it along.

"Gwendolyn!"

I yanked my hands away and jammed them under my arms. "Sir?"

"You *know* better than to play with yourself while I'm here."

My face turned even redder, which I didn't think was possible. "I *wasn't!* Honest, it . . . it was an accident! I didn't *mean* to. . . ."

"Stand up, young lady."

He had *that* look in his eye and he already called me *Gwendolyn,* so I knew better than to disobey. It was kind of weird for him to be stark naked and me to still have clothes on, but that didn't last long. I got up and faced him, and then he turned me around and unhooked my bra. His penis rubbed my fanny while he did that, and it felt so hot against my rear end that I thought it had burned through my panties! He made me stand there while he sat on the bedside and looked at me. The frown on his face made me quiver, but his eyes were so soft, so blue, so tender, that I really wasn't scared. Well, until he said what he said.

"You *know* what happens to extra-naughty girls who play with themselves, don't you?"

"*No,* Devlin! *Please?* I wasn't extra-naughty! Not *tonight* . . . not after the plug! I couldn't *stand* for you to. . . ."

"Hush! Turn around and bend over."

My mouth just hung open for a few seconds. "*What?*"

His scowl got even scarier. "Which part of the instructions did you not understand, girl?"

Oh, geeze! He couldn't be *serious,* could he? Would he spank me bending over? He nearly *always* spanked me on his lap. I

– 180 –

really, really wanted to stomp my foot, but for once I was smart. I didn't like that scowl one bit and I *sure* didn't want to make it any worse, so I turned around and leaned forward a little.

"I said *bend,* young lady, not *tilt.* All the way over and put your hands on your knees."

"But, Devlin, the plug might. . . ."

"Bend *over . . . now.*"

Oh, God, it was the *professor* voice. I really *hate* that voice because it reminds me of his schoolroom and that nasty paddle, and I *really* hate the paddle because he doesn't put me over his knee when he uses it. Surely he didn't bring *that.* I glanced at his open suitcase on the hope chest and was relieved not to see it, but sometimes he keeps special *surprises* in the car trunk. I couldn't worry much about it, though, because I was trying to bend over and be a good girl for him, but the farther I bent the more the damn plug tried to get *out.*

"That's better. Now lower your panties."

"But *Devlin.* . . ."

"*Now,* Gwendolyn."

Not *Gwendolyn* again! I started to cry because I knew he'd be able to see inside my crack when I pulled down my panties, and that icky, embarrassing pink plug ring right in between my cheeks. My hands shook as I slipped my thumbs in the waistband of my Olgas and pushed them halfway down.

"Gwendolyn, do you think I'm kidding?"

"Oh, *God!*"

I pushed them the rest of the way off my fanny and sobbed because I just *knew* his eyes were glued right to the plug base. It was so shameful I could hardly *stand* it.

"Move your feet a little farther apart."

"Nooo!"

"I *said.* . . ."

"OK! Geeze!"

Hot tears dripped from my eyes as I spread my feet about two inches.

"A little more, Princess . . . then push your undies all the way to the floor, and *no* backtalk."

It was awful! I whimpered while I wriggled my feet apart, and then gasped because when I bent all the way down to shove the

panties to my ankles, the plug nearly escaped! I shut my eyes and clenched to hold it while I rose back up, and managed to keep it in, but I *knew* what he was looking at. With my feet spread he could see my 'gina! But that was kind of OK, since if he was staring at *that* he wasn't looking at my soppy-wet Olgas. Then the bed squeaked and I felt him right *behind* me.

"Devlin?"

"Shh. You were a good girl and kept the plug right where it belongs."

I sighed when his fingers slid down my crack and touched the plug's base.

"Whuh . . . what are you going to *do?*"

"Don't you want me to take it out?"

"Uh huh! Please!"

"All right. Raise up just a little and I will."

"*No*, I . . . I want to be over your lap when you take it out! Owee!"

I wasn't *even* expecting that slap on my tushy and it really stung!

"Extra-naughty girls do *not* tell me how to take out a bottom plug."

"But . . . but you said I was a *good* girl!"

"Yes, but you're an *extra-naughty* good girl. Now keep still while I remove the plug from your extra-naughty bottom hole."

"*Devlin!*"

I panted and squirmed and whimpered, but he just wrapped his arm around my waist and held me bent over while he tugged the hideous, nasty thing *out of* me. It came out a little easier than it went in, but I *still* hated that wide part. I did relax some when it was finally gone, and I nearly fell over when he let go of me to take the plug into the bathroom. I *so* wanted to reach back and soothe my poor little hole, but I didn't dare. Suddenly he was back and had his arm around my waist again.

"Do you remember what happens to extra-naughty little girls, Princess?"

"No, *please?*"

"*No*, you don't remember? Or *no*, you don't want me to punish you for touching yourself in my presence?"

"Yes! *No!* I mean . . . please don't spank me *there.*"

"Where, Gwen? *Where* do extra-naughty girls get spanked?"

Huge sobs made it impossible for me to talk.

"Gwendolyn, I asked you a question."

"I . . . I . . . I don't *want* you to!"

"You know you have to tell me. Now say it. Where do extra-naughty girls get spanked?"

I couldn't tell him, I just *couldn't*. How could he *do* that to me?

He sighed. "I *thought* the plug would improve your attitude, but I can see I didn't leave it in long enough. Stay right here and I'll go get it."

"*No!* OK! In . . . in their *bottoms*."

"What?"

"Eh . . . extra-naughty g-girls get spanked in . . . inside their bottoms, OK?"

My knees sort of gave out and I wailed while I sagged against his arm.

"That's *almost* it, but that last *OK* sounded rather impertinent."

"I didn't *mean* it! I'm sorry! I'm *trying* to be good, but I don't wanna get spanked like *that!*"

"Gwen, Gwen, *Gwen* . . . you are only digging yourself in deeper. Now put your hands on your knees and straighten your legs."

"OK. I mean . . . yes, sir!"

I felt pretty wobbly and nearly fell on top of him when he knelt to pull my panties off my feet. His organ was all swollen and I gasped when I glanced at it. The head was just *purple*. I wailed and shut my eyes because I didn't want to *see* what he was going to put in my tiny little hole, *after* he spanked all in between my cheeks! Somehow I managed to stay bent over while he wrapped his arm around my tummy again. He stood a lot closer and I could feel his hardness against my thigh.

"Spread your legs a bit more, Princess, so your bottom opens wide."

"*Devlin!* Ow! OK! Yes, sir! *Please* not too hard, OK? *Sir?*"

My feet burned when I squiggled them across the carpet, but it was nothing like the burn of that first, nasty swat right in my crack! *God*, I hate that feeling. I'm just so *exposed*, and he can see *everything*, and when he *spanks* me there it's just *awful*. I wriggled and squirmed and yelled and cried for like *hours* while he smacked

and smacked and *smacked* right inside where it's really, really *tender.* I have *no* idea how many swats he gave me, but finally he picked me up like a baby and carried me to the bed. He gave me a whole bunch of Kleenex right away, because he didn't have a shirt on for me to cry into, and I *really* missed his trousers because I like to wriggle my sore bottom on the soft wool after a spanking, but also because his stiff penis was like *right* up against my leg, as a reminder.

But he was *so* sweet, and kissed me all over my face and neck, and rubbed some of the sting out of my tushy while he cuddled me. It didn't take very long for me to feel a lot better, but I wasn't about to tell *him* that. It was real easy to look pitiful when I pouted at him.

"You're very cruel to me, Devlin O'Neill."

He smiled and kissed my pout, and I couldn't help but kiss back. "I know, Princess. I can't help it and you wouldn't have me any other way."

"Nuh *uh* . . . you didn't have to spank me so *hard* in such an icky *place.*"

"Yes . . . I know you suffered terribly."

I gasped and whimpered when he slid his fingers between my cheeks and caressed my little hole. Lightening just *shot* all the way up through my breasts and then back down between my 'gina lips and set me off *again!* I really *wanted* to be mad at him, but I didn't have a chance!

"Oh, *God,* Devlin!"

He held me real close while he played inside my bottom until I thought I was going to *faint,* then he rolled me over on my tummy on his lap and reached for the jar on the nightstand. I thought I heard angels singing when he slathered cool, slick skin cream all over my cheeks and *way* down inside. My fanny didn't sting at *all* anymore, but it felt like an itch I couldn't scratch, especially when his fingers would touch my 'gina, so I spread my legs to make sure he touched it a *lot.*

"Better, Princess?"

"Uh huh. Feels good."

"OK. Hop up and let me turn down the covers. It's bedtime."

"But I want some more . . . *ow!* OK!"

"What?"

– 184 –

"I mean yes sir! *Geeze*, Devlin!"

I rubbed a hot new handprint as I rolled off his lap. He stood up and kissed me, then pushed me toward the bathroom with a gentle swat.

"Go clean up and brush your teeth. You won't need a nightie."

"OK. Sir!"

The bathroom door clicked behind me and I looked in the mirror. My face was bright red, but my tushy was barely pink. I bit my lip and spread the cheeks as I looked over my shoulder. K-Y glistened all inside, but I couldn't really tell if it *looked* like it had been spanked, or if it was my imagination. When I sat on the toilet I had to turn my head because that *thing* was sitting right by the sink, pointed straight up, so when I went to wash I threw a hand towel over it. I dabbed on a little perfume, then grinned and dabbed a little more between my bottom cheeks.

Devlin sat in bed, his back against the headboard and his lower body under the covers. He smiled when I ran over and jumped in beside him. We cuddled for a few minutes without a word. I was a little disappointed because there wasn't much of a pup tent under the duvet. A couple of times I tried to reach underneath, just to check, but he grabbed my hand and kissed it when I did that. Finally he kissed me on the lips and raised an eyebrow. My heart nearly stopped.

"*What*, Devlin?"

"Do you think you can behave yourself while I get ready for bed?"

"Don't be mean."

"I want your naughty parts *under* the covers and your hands *above* them, all right?"

"Devlin, that is *so* . . . uuuh!"

He chuckled and kissed me again but I didn't kiss back. Who did he think he *was*? But I scrunched the covers up over my boobs and held them there while I pouted at him. Then he was gone for *such* a long time, and I really *did* kind of feel like, um, *you* know, but I didn't. Well, not with my hand, anyway. I mean, *honestly,* how can a girl keep her thighs still after all *that*? They just *naturally* squeeze together. And besides, my bottom was *so* tingly, especially inside, and I was *so* wet. But as usual, I overdid it. I shut my eyes for just a second, I *thought,* while those special feelings

washed over me, and I didn't *even* hear him come out of the bathroom, so I kind of squeaked when I opened my eyes and he was standing right by the bed!

"Gwendolyn?"

"Um . . . sir?"

"What are you doing?"

"Nothing! I . . . I'm just being *good* . . . like you *told* me to."

"Then what was all that moaning about?"

"Whuh-what moaning?"

"You know very *well*, young lady! Let go so I can pull down the covers."

"No, Devlin! *Please?*"

My hands trembled and let go of the duvet. I closed my eyes so I couldn't see him lean over to inspect me *down there*. It was just so awful because I *knew* what he would see!

"Open your legs, Gwen."

"Nooo. . . ."

"Gwendolyn!"

I just *wailed* when he pushed my knees apart and cold air nearly froze my wet little 'gina!

"But I didn't *do* anything, honest! It . . . it's just that you're so big and strong and sexy and you make me so horny I can't *help* myself!"

His thunderous scowl quivered a little, then his chest shook, and finally he burst out laughing and pushed me over so he could crawl in beside me. I hugged his neck while he laughed.

"Princess, that is the biggest load of bull feathers I've ever heard come out of your mouth."

"Nuh *uh!* It's *true*, Devlin. Every word!"

He chuckled and rubbed my back and bottom while I hung on for dear life. "I really ought to spank you, you know."

I shook my head and kissed his neck. "No, *please?* I really *did* try to be good. Can't we just cuddle?"

"All right . . . for a while. But don't you want to make love?"

Oh, man, was *that* ever a loaded question! "Uh huh, but um . . . just regular, OK?"

He leaned back, cupped my chin in his hand, and his eyes bored into me like watery blue drill-bits. "As opposed to what? Premium? Calcium fortified? Extra heavy duty?"

"You know what I mean. Don't um . . . do *that*."

"Did you take some sort of vagueness lessons that I don't know about, because I truly don't follow. Come closer so we can cuddle."

I really wanted to say something else, but he hugged me and shut my mouth with his lips. After a minute I forgot what it was I wanted to say. It must have been something about him having his way with my bottom, but when he slipped two fingers inside my cleft and put another finger in front to toy with my slippery little button, it was impossible to remember if I was for it or against it, so I just held onto his neck while he made me squirm.

"Princess?" he whispered.

"Huh?"

"Did you like it when I made you bend over to be spanked?"

"Nuh-*no!* It . . . it was *awful*. I . . . I hate it whuh-when you suh-spank me in there."

"Do you?"

"Uh huh. It . . . it's *nasty*."

"Do you hate it when I touch these wet little lips while I'm spanking you?"

"Ah . . . ah . . . of *course!* Yuh . . . you're just t-teasing me!"

"And you *hate* that, don't you?"

"Yuh-*yes!* Oh, *God*, Devlin!"

And he just kept *on* like that, touching and testing and prodding, all the while he was talking to me, until I didn't know *which* end was up. *God*, he loves to make me squirm. And I love it too, but I'm not going to tell *him* that, so I argued with everything he said. At least I *think* I did, but the next thing I knew I was bottom up with my tummy on a pillow and he was on *top* of me. I could hardly move! Not that I *wanted* to but I just felt so *helpless*, especially when he opened my cheeks to push himself inside my little hole!

I squealed and he stopped as soon as the tip was in, then he asked if I was OK. It did kind of hurt, but not much more than the wide part of the plug, so I sort of grunted and pushed up with my bottom. He was so *hard* that he just slid into me, like a knife in a sheath, and then he was lying on my back, his belly pressed against my hot fanny. I could feel his breath on my neck and he groaned when he pulled out a little, and then slid all the way

inside. He started a slow, strong rhythm, back and forth, back and forth, and I whimpered because I felt so *full* of him, and he kept calling me his good girl, his good girl with the burning fanny. And it *did* burn, inside and out, a delicious, delirious burn that fed the raging furnace in my 'gina. I felt his body begin to tense and knew he was about to come, and then he plunged and groaned, and emptied himself into me. I moaned and squirmed wildly as his heat filled me up inside, and squeezed my fanny to milk every last drop out of him. His full weight slumped down on me and we lay together as I fell asleep. He was still nestled in my behind, and I have a vague recollection of his lips covering the back of my neck with soft kisses.

Forgetfulness

The neglected grocery incident that inspired this story actually occurred, but there was no such satisfactory real life resolution. Further, Gwen *did* spend that outrageous amount for a concert ticket, so I decided that *this* tale had to be told from Devlin's point of view in order to make sure she understood that my exasperation was *not* fictitious.

A breeze blew in from the harbor and ruffled the leaves on the big white birch tree in Gwen's front yard. It was just after five o'clock when I opened the rental car door and stepped out into soggy New England swelter. All my fatigue from seven hours of blather-filled academic meetings vanished in an instant. It had been three weeks since I had seen her, touched her, tasted her lips, and I felt like a kid in a candy store. The squirmy, naughty, politically incorrect emotions that I have to keep dammed at work flowed to the surface, but I did manage to walk, not skip, along the path to the front porch. I rang the bell and heard bare feet slap foyer tiles. She yanked open the door and my face almost burst apart when I grinned. My pulse quickened as I stretched out my arms and she leapt into them.

She wore a deep-blue chemise nightgown, silky and smooth, that hugged her own silky, smooth contours while I hugged her. Gwen is always beautiful, but the look on her face when she greets me melts my heart. She doesn't use a lot of makeup, doesn't need it, but she knows I love her big green eyes so she highlights them a little, just to tease me. They sparkled with a mixture of school-girl glee and womanly abandon when she looked up at me. She nearly always looks up at me. Not that I'm that tall, five-eleven, but she's not quite five-two. She used to resent the difference in our heights, until she learned to like being Devlin's little girl.

Her hair is short, too, which only adds to her adorable waifish-ness, especially when it's still wet from the shower. She calls it *boy-short,* but any boy who would wear a wispy, feathery style like hers would do it to look like a girl. Her mouth is small but her lips are full and soft, like down pillows if down pillows had minds of their own. I bowed my head to kiss their soft fullness.

I inhaled her aroma, part Amariage perfume and part pure Gwen, an indescribable scent that makes me think of rumpled sheets and a quivery red bottom. After the soft kiss I looked into her eyes and smiled. Her lips trembled and I opened my mouth to cover them. She whimpered when I sucked her tongue between my teeth to caress and toy with it. Her breasts quivered and she moaned. Our lips parted and I looked into her eyes.

"I've missed you, Princess."

"Not as much as I've missed *you.*"

She grabbed my hand, slammed the door and pulled me up the foyer stairs toward the bedroom, but I tugged her into the living room instead. I sat on the sofa and she straddled my lap, facing me, and loosened my tie. She unbuttoned my collar while she kissed my neck. I chuckled.

"I think you *have* missed me."

"I mished you alod," she mumbled.

Her warm lips fluttered and mashed just under my ear, and shot icy warm tingles all the way down my belly. I stroked her back with both hands, and then slid my palms down to caress her firm round bottom beneath its silken sheath.

"Come on, Devlin . . . let's go to bed."

"But I've only been in the house a minute and half."

"*Way* too long for us not to be in bed yet!"

I laughed when she crawled off of my lap and yanked on my hand, like a child anxious for the next ride at Disneyland.

"All right, all right, I'm coming."

She grinned the bad-little-girl grin I love so much. "God, I *hope* not . . . not yet, anyway."

I tried to look stern, but even as I reached around to smack her fanny I could tell she was going to push me to the limit.

"Owee!" She rubbed her bottom and pouted. "*That* wasn't very nice."

"Neither was the joke, young lady. Now could you at least *try* to show a bit of restraint?"

She frowned for a second and then giggled. "Restraint? You wanna tie me up? I didn't think you were into that kind of. . . ."

I grabbed her arm and gripped it softly while I give her a serious smack on each silky cheek, and one straight across the deep cleft.

"Ow! Ow! *Ouch!* OK, OK, *geeze!* What did you do . . . leave your sense of humor in the car?" She grinned and pushed off my jacket.

"Yes . . . it's in a bag in the backseat."

Her grin faded for a second, then flashed again. "It must be a pretty small bag if *that's* all that's in it."

I gave up and let her drag me to the bedroom. A dozen candles glowed on the antique hope chest and the nightstands. The shades were down and the ceiling fan was set to a slow whirl. White sheets were drawn back and reflected the golden candlelight.

She managed to strew half my clothes on the carpet in the hallway, but I felt so drained from the long day that I knew if I lay down in her soft, warm bed right then I'd go to sleep.

"How about a bath before bed, Princess?"

"Sure . . . that sounds great. You go ahead and fill the tub and I'll get you a drink. Don't use too much bath oil, though, or we'll get too slippery."

Warm water foamed the capful of peppermint oil I dribbled into the tub, and I tossed what little clothing my adorable brat had left me at the hamper. I sighed and sat with my feet under the stream, then leaned over to turn up the temperature. Gwen came in with two frosty glasses and set them on the tile ledge next to my head.

"Ooh, look at you in there . . . all furry and big and wet. Very sexy, if you don't mind me saying so."

I smiled and crooked a finger. Gwen shrugged and her night-gown slithered to the floor. My little girl can make overalls look sexy if she's in them, but when she's naked I just have to wonder what I did in a previous life that I got so lucky in this one. She has a little mole on the right side of her left breast that reminds me of the ancient Greek sculptors. They always put a tiny flaw in their masterpieces so as not to offend the gods by creating perfection. And perfection she is, from her boy-short hair to the pale pink enamel on her toenails. Her no-more-than-a-handful breasts with their soft, pink aureoles and hard, tight nipples sit high on her bosom, like impertinent eyes that tease and demand attention. She thinks her hips are too wide, but I tell her that narrow hips are for boys, and that they have to be wide to support the firm, round bottom I adore. Her waist is slender and her thighs are trim but not skinny, and the hair on her *mons veneris* is clipped and shaved to a cute, clean triangle just above the top of her sweet lower lips.

She blushed as she stepped into the tub. "Don't *do* that!"

"What?"

"When you look at me that way I feel like you're undressing me with your eyes."

"Princess . . . you're stark *naked*."

"I know . . . that's why it's so *weird*." She put her feet on either side of my thighs and sat down facing me. "I love a hot bath . . . especially with *you*. Isn't this just heaven? The tub is kinda small for two, but it's cozy, isn't it? I could stay here all night. Would you pass me my drink?"

I handed her a glass, then took a sip from the other one and gasped. The little minx *grinned* at me.

"What's the matter, Devlin? Is it too strong? It's supposed to be a Cape Codder . . . vodka and cranberry."

"I don't notice any cranberry in here, Princess."

"There is *too* . . . see? It's pink . . . sort of . . . kinda *clear* pink, I guess. Just take little sips and relax."

"I don't think anyone at Ocean Spray will retire on *your* contribution to the company."

"It's not Ocean Spray, it's the other stuff . . . and they were out of the red Smirnoff so I got blue instead."

I shook my head. "So this is four ounces of hundred-proof vodka on the rocks with a pink tinge?"

She sipped, nodded and giggled as she leaned forward. Hard, hot nipples burned against my wet chest while firm thighs squeezed my legs.

"Uh huh . . . you got a problem with that?"

"Not yet . . . but you'd better go easy on this stuff or you'll have a hangover tomorrow, and you *know* what happens to my little princess when she doesn't feel well."

"Devlin! Don't be mean. I know you're talking about a . . . a . . . *enema*, but you can just forget it 'cause I'll be *fine* tomorrow, I promise. Right now I'm just really, really hot, and I'm not talking water temperature." She took a healthy sip of her drink, set the glass on the ledge, and then scooted backward. "Lift up your knees so I can kneel between your legs, OK?"

I dribbled a cubic centimeter of liquor over my tongue and nodded as I set down the drink and did as she asked. Hot water sloshed as she squiggled forward.

"What are you doing, Princess?"

"I just want to soap up your chest, that's all."

"Be careful down there, OK?"

"OK, OK, I *know.*" She took the Ivory bar and twisted it in her hands. "I'll be careful, but you just relax. You're so *tense.* Now doesn't that feel good?"

Angelic fingers worked up a thick lather and massaged my chest. She grinned and I gasped.

"Hey, Devlin, your nipples are hard." She snickered and I rolled my eyes. "Can I play with them a little bit? Is that OK? I'll just give them a little . . . pinch . . . and pull . . . and roll them between my. . . ."

"Um, Princess?" I swallowed hard as her fingers shot tremors all the way to my toes. "Do you have a *thing* for men's nipples I didn't know about?"

She blushed and blinked as she squeezed. "Yes, actually I *do.* Can't help it . . . and if you weren't always so busy driving me up the wall when we're together, you would of *known* that."

"Oh, I *see* . . . so it's *my* fault you never told me about this?"

"Yes, it *is.* I can barely *think* when you're spanking me and putting your big hands all over me and making me squirm, let *alone* tell you anything important."

I stared at her for a few seconds. It really *did* feel good when

she played with me like that, and I felt guilty that I never knew about her little quirk, and even guiltier that she was giving me those lost-kitty-cat eyes, the ones I get when she thinks I'm angry at her. I chuckled and felt relieved when she sighed.

"OK, Princess. Tell me about it now . . . and don't stop doing what you're doing."

"Well . . . I like the way they feel when they're hard . . . and I like to run my fingertips over them . . . so lightly . . . but I like to *squeeze* them, too . . . and I've always wondered if men's nipples are as sensitive as women's. Here, Devlin, let me rinse you off so I can lick them . . . for a minute . . . tease them with my tongue." It felt like a cat's lick, rough and slick at the same time, and I panted as warm, fuzzy tremors lanced through me. "Shh . . . I won't bite, Devlin. Not very hard, anyway."

"*Gwen?*"

She sat back, grinned and picked up my glass. "Just *joking* . . . here . . . have another sip and chill. Then hand me the loofa and I'll do your legs."

"Gwen." I stretched the word and gave it the Professor O'Neill warning tone as I reached behind my head for the hard sponge, and she huffed to tell me she got the message.

"I won't do it hard, I *promise*. I know it hurts when I rub too hard. I'll just run it up and down your leg, nice and slow." The loofa wasn't wet through and it tickled so I put my hand on it. "Yes, I know . . . don't push it away. The inside of your thigh is very sensitive so I won't use too much pressure."

"Careful . . . *he's* very sensitive, too."

"I promise I won't go any higher than that. This thing is too rough to use on your um . . . there, see? I was careful. Now scootch forward and I'll sit behind you and wash your big strong back."

Soapy water ran down her thighs and sparkled in the short curls on her *mons* when she stood. She looked like a wet, pink seal and I grinned as she picked up the soap and swiveled around to sit on the rear ledge. Her fingers kneaded, slithered and caressed while I leaned forward and tried not to whimper like a dog getting a belly rub.

"Now you're nice and soapy for the bath brush. Mmm . . . I love it when you're all slippery and wet. I wish we could do this every day."

"You would spoil me."

The brush scritched my back like a thousand kittens' claws and I felt the tension drain from my shoulders.

"That's the *idea,* Mr. Knots In Your Neck." She cupped her hands in the water and sluiced lather away. "OK, I just need to do your pretty face now."

"Um . . . Gwen?"

"Don't panic, Professor. I won't use the bath brush on your *face.* I'm not an amateur, you know." She doused a flannel in the water as she turned to sit on my thighs. "Here, feel how soft this is. See? Soft enough for a baby's face. Don't shut your eyes. I won't get soap in them, I promise, and I really like to see those big, soft blues."

I chuckled. "What do you mean *soft?* My eyes are steely hard and gun-metal blue, and scare naughty girls so much they wet their panties."

She squinted. "Nuh *uh* . . . your eyes don't scare *me.* I love them . . . and my panties are none of your *business.*"

"Oh? They don't get wet when I glare at you with my steely, gun-metal eyes?"

"No!" She grinned. "They just get wet when I read those naughty stories you write about me. Now hold still while I wash right down here between your . . . oh, Devlin! You're hard as a *rock.*"

I gasped when she touched me, and sweet, quivery demons danced on my penis as I took a deep breath. "And whose fault is *that?*"

Her eyes gleamed while she blushed. "Um . . . maybe mine?" I nodded. "That's nice to hear . . . glad I could help. Now sit up so I can wash you off, then we'll get out of this tub and into bed."

My erection bobbed against her thigh while she sponged soap from my face.

"What's your hurry, Princess?"

"I, um . . . I just . . . seeing you like *that* . . . I'm hot as hell, Devlin! OK . . . all clean and very, *very* erect. Let's go!"

We were still damp and slightly oily when she pushed me backward onto the bed and jumped on top of me. She slithered down my chest and I gasped when she took me in her mouth. Down-pillow lips squeezed and teased the tip of my erection, and her

naughty, angelic tongue flicked divine sparks that exploded behind my eyelids. I took hold of her shoulders and she squealed when I lifted her and tossed her onto the sheet beside me.

"Devlin, I just wanted to. . . ."

"Hush . . . I know what you want."

She moaned when I twisted her around on her side and hugged her from behind. My rigid member snugged tight within the deep crevice that separated her warm, round cheeks. I kissed her neck and ear while I squeezed her left breast with one hand and slipped the other down her smooth belly to cup her vagina.

"Oh! Oh, *God* . . . don't *tease* me! *Please?*"

My middle finger slid between puffy lower lips and flicked the hot, hard button. She wailed, pushed back with her hips and opened her thighs. I groaned as her cheeks squeezed my penis, then took my hand off her clitoris long enough to guide my erection between the lips and into her tight, electrified canal. She squeaked when I slid all the way inside her, and then pressed my hand once more to her vagina. I slipped in and out of the fluttery, molten core while she whimpered and wailed, and then grabbed my butt cheek with her hand.

"Faster!"

"Don't be so impatient, little girl."

"But I want you to fuh . . . make love to me *harder.*"

Her fingers squeezed like little crab claws and I stopped, still buried deep within her hot clinginess.

"Do you want to go over my lap and get your naughty, impatient fanny *spanked* harder, young lady?"

"Nuh . . . *no,* Devlin!"

"Then behave."

I flicked her clitoris with my finger and she gasped.

"Oh, *OK.* I'm sorry . . . it's just been so *long.*"

"So hush and enjoy the ride."

She quivered and twisted her neck to look at me, and then sighed as I twirled a finger pad over her wet bud. I kissed her lips and she moaned. The quivers became tremors, and then quick jerks while she climbed toward the summit. She closed her eyes and nodded.

"Whuh . . . whatever you say-*aay!*"

I slid back and then plunged forward, deep inside, and her

special muscles contracted in time with the quivers I coaxed from her clitoris. Backward and forward I stroked, slow at first, then faster as her moans and squeals intensified. She let go of my butt and grabbed my arm. My hips pounded her bottom as the climax approached. Gwen screeched, her body went rigid and I rammed hard and released the flood. A deep, animal howl escaped my throat as I thrust the final drops of passion into her depths.

Her special muscles squeezed my diminishing manhood and quivery aftershocks shot through us for a long minute, then she grunted, pulled away from me, twisted around and pushed me onto my back as she lay on top of me. Cool peppermint sweat coated our bodies. Her nipples pressed into mine as she licked my lips. I smiled and kissed her.

"I love you, Princess."

"I love you too . . . but you were very mean to say you'd spank me while you were making love to me."

"Yes, I *know* how much you hate to be spanked. I'm sure that didn't make you hot at *all*."

"I couldn't have *been* any hotter, that's why I was *ow!*"

I shook the sting out of my palm and she caressed the red hand-print on her bottom.

"I'm not going to argue with you, little girl. Let's just cuddle a while, OK?"

Gwen pouted, blinked, and then smiled. "OK . . . but I'm not moving."

"Whatever you say, Princess."

She cradled her head on my chest. I shut my eyes, cupped her adorable bottom in both hands and drifted away on a misty sea of peppermint.

• • •

I opened my eyes and glanced at the clock. Nine-thirty already. She still lay on top of me, her legs tight along my thighs, her breasts mashed into my chest. My hands never left her smooth, round behind, even while I dozed. If I had my way, I'd never stop caressing it, never leave off spanking it, never cease making love to it. I let a finger slide into her warm crevice and she wriggled in response. She was awake but pretended not to be, so I did too.

Her wet vagina rubbed my belly. I moaned, as if still asleep. She lay quiet for a moment and then flicked a fingernail against my nipple. I growled a sleepy, unlikely threat and told her to be still. The little brat scratched my nipple again, hard, and the quivery tingle awakened more than just my mind. She squealed when I clenched an arm around her waist, then she squirmed downward until her slippery lower lips hugged my manhood. It couldn't resist the invitation and grew strong again. Her bare bottom stretched wide as she arched her back. She whimpered when she felt my hand rise, then gasped when my palm slapped firm, warm flesh and my fingertips flicked inside her open cleft. I gave her a little-girl spanking, slow and methodical, not too hard, but steady, while she mewed like a kitten and wrapped her arms around my neck.

Warm moistness turned hot as she squirmed her vagina against my erection. I spanked harder and she squealed when my fingers landed just millimeters from her anus. She tried to push away, but I held her close while I whispered dire and thoroughly lascivious threats in her ear.

"Nuh-nuh-nooo . . . please don't spank so hard inside my bottom! I'll be good!"

"You were very naughty to wake me up like that, and you *know* what happens to very naughty little girls."

I felt the quiver in her tummy when I scolded her, the quiver that said I couldn't stop now, that she wanted me to take her over the top, up to the stratosphere, and make her explode in horrid, heavenly bliss. She squealed and wriggled as I coated her tender bottom with soft pain. Bright sting lanced through my hand, up my arm and into my heart, heating the blood that rushed to my penis. I spanked harder, right between her cheeks and she screeched when she pushed her bottom up so the hard tip slid between wet, open petals.

She sobbed when I let her go, and then leaned backward. I moaned as I slid upward into slippery moist infinity. She rocked her hips and her hot-spanked fanny burned my thighs. Then all was lost, because every atom of my being thrust into her. I yelled and she screamed as lightening and thunder surrounded us. We pulsed to a single beat and my entire selfness shot into her. She collapsed on my chest, exhausted, and covered my sweaty body with hers.

Minutes . . . hours . . . days later, I summoned enough energy to turn on my side and found her cuddly bottom waiting for me. I spooned against her and she wriggled her adorable tushy into my belly. She sighed, reached for my hand and brought it around to hold against her breast, as we both, finally, fell asleep.

• • •

We slept until two-thirty in the morning and woke up famished. I put on the blue Polo pajama pants she gave me for Christmas. She didn't give me the matching shirt because she liked to see my chest, which was OK with me, in the summer anyway. I watched her slip a big, soft tee shirt over her head and followed her to the kitchen.

"How about omelets, Princess?"

"Sounds good to me."

She yawned and clattered eggs, milk and cheese out of the fridge and onto the center serving counter. I tied on the canvas apron that read "Kiss the chef," and smiled because she kept grinning at a printed slip of cardboard held with a magnet to the refrigerator door.

"What's that, Gwen?"

"Um, it's . . . it's a ticket to the Aerosmith concert next month."

"Really? That's great. You love those guys."

"Uh huh . . . and it's just once a year, you know . . . it's not like I. . . ."

"Gwen!" I chuckled and hugged her when she threw her arms around me. "It's OK if you go to a concert. Just because I'm an old geezer and had my fill of loud rock and roll thirty years ago doesn't mean *you* can't go have fun."

She pouted at me. "You are *not* a geezer so stop saying that."

"All right . . . but I *do* want you to have fun, and if watching Jim Perry cavort around the stage in leather pants while your eardrums break is your idea of fun. . . ."

"It's *Joe* Perry and why are you *teasing* me?"

I kissed her pout and smiled. "Because it's my job."

"Nuh uh! *Your* job is to make omelets and quit making fun of Aerosmith 'cause you *know* how much I like them."

"Just another band out of Boston."

"Devlin O'Neill, don't you *dare*. . . ."

She moaned as I wrapped her in my arms and our tongues played together, then she whimpered when I let go.

"OK . . . no more teasing." I grinned and switched on the stove, then dug a griddle out of the cabinet. She scowled as she watched me crack eggs into a bowl with one hand. "See? It's all in the wrist."

"Show-off! You know I can't do that so why do you have to rub it in?"

The eggs bubbled and frothed as I whipped them with a fork. "Would you get the mushrooms, please?" I turned and saw that she had taken the eggshells to the garbage disposal. "Never mind . . . I'll get them." I opened the refrigerator and stood a moment in stunned silence.

Gwen shut off the disposal and looked at me. "The mushrooms are in the drawer."

I stared at almost-empty shelves. "Did you get the grocery list I faxed?"

She huffed. "That wasn't a grocery list . . . it was a supply requisition for the Ninth Armored Division . . . and *yes*, I went yesterday morning. Took me an *hour* to get everything and it wasn't cheap, by the way. You owe me just over two hundred and ten bucks. It was the lobster meat and shrimp that was so hefty, but the pine nuts were kind of pricey, too, come to think of it. I don't know what you're making for dinner tomorrow night but I bet it'll be delicious."

"I don't know what I'm making, either . . . because I don't see any food in here."

"What are you *talking* about? I schlepped a twelve-bag order out of that store! I could barely fit them all in the trunk of my. . . ."

Gwen gasped. Her mouth hung open, her eyes stared into space like they had just witnessed a train wreck, and her face was the color of milk.

"Princess? Are you OK?" She nodded. "You schlepped them out of the store and put them . . . where?"

"In . . . the trunk."

I licked my lips and took light, slow steps over to her. She didn't seem to see me, and she jerked when I put my hand on her arm.

"Gwen?"

"Huh?"

"You put them in the trunk of the Jetta, right?"

"Um . . . yeah."

"And then you drove home, right?"

"Uh huh."

"Then you parked the car in the garage . . . and then what?"

"Well, I . . . she . . . um . . . Deb was here . . . in the Mustang convertible and we . . . we went to. . . ."

I put my arm around her shoulders and the dam burst. She wouldn't look at me while she cried, but she clung to my neck like she would never let go. I rubbed her back while I leaned over to turn off the burner under the griddle.

"Did you forget to take the groceries out of the trunk before you took off with Deb?" She looked up at me and sobbed while she tried to form words. "Shh . . . it's OK, but um . . . did you get everything on the list?" She wailed. "So . . . eighteen pounds of fresh seafood has been sitting in your trunk, in the garage, since yesterday morning, in ninety-five degree heat?" Her sobs ripped my heart as she nodded her head on my chest. "I think we need to talk."

She gasped, looked up and took a deep breath. "*No!* I . . . I'm *sorry!* I . . . I just. . . ."

"It's *OK* . . . I'm not angry."

"Yuh-you're *never* angry . . . but you . . . you're just gonna blister meeee!"

I hugged and shushed her while I stroked her neck. The reason I sent the grocery list was so I could stay up all night and play with her and not have to worry about grocery shopping for the college faculty dinner I planned for the next night, but I could deal with that. She cried and cried, and I felt worse and worse because it isn't Gwen's job to entertain a bunch of stuffed-shirt professor types. Well, except for one, and she always tells me I'm not as stuffy as most of them.

"Come on, Princess. Let's go sit down, all right?"

"O . . . OK. Um . . . you're not going to spank me?"

I looked straight into her wet, green eyes. "Shouldn't I?"

"*No!* I . . . I didn't do it on *purpose!*"

"And yet . . . two hundred and ten dollars worth of food is rotting in your trunk."

She wiped tears as she huffed. "I *know* and I *said* I was sorry! I'll go first thing in the morning and get some more but. . . ."

"We'll discuss the situation first."

"But I don't wanna *discuss* it and that's a *horrible* way to tell me you're gonna blister my fanny! Why do you *do* that? I'm not a little girl, dammit!"

"Gwendolyn! You're being ridiculous. Let's go have a chat."

"Devlin, *no!*"

"*Hush*, Gwen."

Tears streamed anew and she trembled in my arms when I scooped her up and carried her to the bedroom. The covers, so clean and tidy a few hours before, looked like a couple of wild animals had nested in the bed, which wasn't far from the truth. I tossed the sheet and quilt out of the way and sat down to cuddle her on my lap. She squealed and wriggled for a minute, then wrapped both hands around my neck.

"Devlin, *please?* I know I was stupid but don't spank me!"

"You are *never* stupid but sometimes you're careless . . . and when that happens I need to remind you to pay attention to what you're doing."

"But I *know* all that and I'll fix *everything*, I promise!"

I smiled and peeled her fingers off my neck. "We'll fix it together . . . but you know what I have to do first, don't you?"

"You don't *either* have to and I don't *want* a spanking! I feel bad enough as it *is*, for Christ's sakes!" She took a deep breath. "You . . . you're just being unreasonable!"

"I'm *not* being unreasonable, because if I don't punish you I can't forgive you."

"Yes you *can!* I *said* I was sorry and . . . and I won't be any *sorrier* if you spank me!"

She scowled when I chuckled.

"We both know better than *that*, little girl."

"Nooooo!"

I picked her up and turned her across my lap. The tee shirt rode up to bare her hard thighs and the adorable under swell of her bottom. She screeched and tugged at the hem to cover herself, but her wriggles and kicks didn't feel right. I pushed her hand away and slid the soft cotton up to reveal her perfect little tushy, then shook my head because all she did was whimper and squirm.

"Devlin, this isn't *fair!*"

"You know I have to spank you so you might as well keep still."

"But I don't *want* to!"

"That doesn't matter, though, does it?" I caressed her magnificent fanny for ten long seconds while she sniffled, and while I tried to determine what felt so *wrong.* "You were very naughty to forget about the groceries and go running off with Deb, and now your little bottom is going to pay for that mistake."

"You don't have to be so *mean* to me," she whispered.

Her voice didn't sound quite right, either. I have never been at a loss for a reason to spank her, even if it's only *because of your attitude, Princess.* She needs the warm, crisp attention to her bare behind, although she will never admit it, but she's always much more vocal with her protests when she really *has* been bad than if I'm spanking her just because I want to. Something else was going on and I was determined to find out what.

She cupped her hands over her eyes and wept when I raised my arm. I licked dry lips and swatted, not very hard, and she squeaked but didn't move. A vague, pink handprint glowed on her creamy smooth behind. I slapped again, and again, a bit harder, but she only whimpered.

"Gwen? Are you very sorry for what you did?"

"I already *told* you that! Why don't you ever *listen* to me? Ow!"

Her cheeks quivered when I slapped hard across her deep, shadowy cleft.

"I *want* to listen to you, Princess, whenever you're in the mood to tell me what's really going on."

"Nothing! Ow! Owee! Stop! Ouch! Not so hard! Neeeek! *Devlin!*"

I spanked her bottom a warm, light red while she yelped. She wept on my neck when I turned her over and put her on my lap. I kissed the top of her head but she didn't look at me, didn't wriggle her sore fanny on the canvas apron that covered my thighs, didn't even dig her fingertips into my back.

"Princess? Do you want to tell me?"

"I'm sorry and I'll never do it again."

The words gushed like a waterfall. I cupped a palm under chin and looked into her sad, wet eyes.

"You've been a very bad girl, haven't you?"

She bit her lip and nodded. "Yes sir, and I'm very sorry. I'll go first thing in the morning and get some more seafood, OK?"

I shook my head. "Not until you tell me what this is all about, young lady."

Her lip trembled. "Whuh-*what?* I left the food in the trunk and it's all icky now and. . . ."

"Where were you off to in such a rush? What was so important that you forgot about the groceries? Where were you going with Deb?"

Tears streamed and she hid her eyes in my neck. I sighed and patted her quivery behind.

"All right, it's time to come clean. We both know there's more to this than just forgetfulness. Gwen? Look at me."

"I *can't!*"

"Gwendolyn! Look at me right *now.* Where did you go with Deb when you got home from the store?"

She sobbed like her heart would break. "Oh, *God,* Devlin!"

"*Now,* Gwen."

"Oh, *geeze* . . . we . . . we went to . . . to get the tickets!"

I blinked. "The concert tickets? You drove into the city to get them?" She nodded and swiped wetness from her eyes. "Why didn't you just order them on the phone . . . or the web? Why did you . . . ?"

My eyes widened and she cried even harder.

"I . . . we . . . it seemed like . . . oh, *geeze!*"

"You went to a scalper, didn't you?"

"Oh, Devlin, I'm *sorry!*"

Hot blood rushed to my face and I took two long breaths before I spoke. "Young lady, *what* have I told you about spending money irresponsibly?"

"But . . . they're third-row seats!"

"And how much did you *pay* for those third-row seats?"

I held tight when she tried to leap off my lap.

"I . . . I can't *tell* you and . . . and *besides,* it's only once a year and . . . and I wasn't even going to buy a new *outfit* like Deb wanted me to 'cause I *knew* you'd get mad if I did, so I was just going to wear my. . . ."

"*Gwendolyn!* How much did you pay for the ticket?"

She grabbed me and buried her face in my neck again. I

unwrapped her arms, tossed her across my lap and smacked her bottom hard.

"Nowee! Yow! Nowitch! Deaaahevliiiin! Doooon't!"

"Tell! Me! Right! Now!"

"Ow! Ow! Ow! Okaaaay! Pleeeease! It huuurts!"

"It's going to hurt a lot *worse* if you don't! Tell! Me! Now!"

"Eeeyah! Aieee! Sheeeeaah! Okaaay, I *will!*"

I rubbed a bit of the sting out of her very sore bottom while she sobbed into her hands. Round cheeks jiggled while she kicked.

"Gwen? *Now.*"

"O . . . O . . . *OK!* Tuh . . . two hundred! But I wasn't going to buy new clothes or *anything,* even if we *were* going to be twenty feet from Joe Perry and . . . and Deb said we had to look sexy and. . . ."

She wailed when I picked her up, and this time she squirmed her bottom on my thighs while she wept into my neck. I stroked her hair and held her close.

"You were a very bad girl not to tell me that to begin with, and I can see why such excitement would make you forget about a mundane thing like taking the groceries out of the car."

"I'm so *sorry!* I didn't *mean* to be a flake! I . . . I don't *know* what happened to me!"

"No, I'm sure you don't . . . but I know you'll understand why I have to be very strict with you now."

Bright green eyes stared at me through a veil of tears. I nodded and she screeched when she wrapped her arms around my neck again.

"*No!* Don't spank me anymore! My bottom really, really *hurts!* Why do you have to be *strict* with me? You . . . you *already* spanked me real hard so you don't have to. . . ."

"Hush, Gwen. You know you were very naughty, very silly and very careless to leave the food in the car, so I'm going to make sure you never do anything that thoughtless again."

"But . . . but I *won't* 'cause it . . . it was an *accident* and it won't ever, ever happen again, I *swear,* so you can't *treat* me like this!"

I smiled as she pleaded with me to spare her fanny any further indignity. The words were right, the tone was right, and all seemed right with the world when I picked her up, turned, and put her down on the bed.

"You *know* better, little girl. Now lie on your back and lift your legs."

She gasped. "You . . . you can't be *serious!* Not like *that!*"

"*Just* like that, young lady." I scowled, reached down and took hold of her ankles.

"Don't lift my legs! *No!*"

I pulled her feet up and back until her knees nearly touched her shoulders. Her buttocks clenched and she dashed both hands down to cover her pubis.

"Take those naughty hands away right *now,* Gwendolyn."

"Devlin! You . . . you can see *everything!*"

She squealed when I swatted her right cheek and let my fingers sting the inside of her cleft. The little rosebud within pulsed and quivered.

"Move them *now.*"

"Oh, God!" She slid her hands up her tummy and over her breasts, and bit the tip of a pinky finger. "I . . . I'm really *sorry* I was bad but you *know* I don't wanna be spanked like this!"

Her hands jerked when I slapped the left cheek, but she only whimpered and kept them where they were. Rosy bottom skin stretched tight and smooth, and strong muscles rippled beneath the flesh when she wriggled.

"Well this! Is the way! You're going! To be spanked!"

"Ow! *Ow!* Ouch! Oweee! Buh . . . buh . . . but *Devlin!*"

"*Not* bent over the bed!"

"Owee!"

"*Not* standing and touching your toes!"

"Aieee!"

"*Not* lying over the chair!"

"Yeeeoww!"

"*Not* kneeling on the bed with your *bare! Naughty! Thoughtless! Fanny! High! Up! In! The! Air!*"

She screeched at each sharp spank and I aimed every second one into her widespread cleft. Her hands sneaked down her bosom and onto her tummy, but she managed to stop short of covering her vagina. Tears puddled her eyes and moisture of another sort sparkled on her puffy slit. She panted and whimpered as I rubbed her bottom and let my fingers stray into her cleft.

"*Please,* Devlin? Nuh . . . *nobody* gets spanked like this! It's *awful!*"

"Only very, *very* bad girls get spanked in the diaper position, Princess."

Her eyes opened wide. "How can you *say* that? That . . . that's just a *nasty* thing to call it!"

"And quite accurate . . . now put your hands behind your knees and hold on. My arm is getting tired."

"*What?* Haven't you embarrassed me *enough?*"

"Do what I told you. Hold your legs up high so I can complete your punishment."

She closed her eyes tight as she clasped her legs with quivery fingers. I let go of her ankles and her feet dropped.

"Gwendolyn! Keep them *up.*"

I flicked her cleft with my fingertips She squealed and then pointed her toes at the ceiling.

"You . . . you're just *awful* to make me display everything!"

I leaned over and kissed her moist pout. "Stay like that and don't move while I fill the enema bulb."

Her whole body jerked but I was ready. I wrapped her legs with my right arm while I pressed down on her right shoulder with my left hand. She gripped the back of my neck as she stared into my eyes. Her voice was remarkably calm when she spoke.

"Devlin. Sir. I really don't think this is a good position to get an enema in."

She moaned and shut her eyes when I kissed her, long and soft. Our tongues played for a minute as her legs squirmed against my elbow. I caressed her neck, smiled, and broke the kiss.

"Don't end a sentence with a preposition, Princess . . . and keep your legs right where they are or I'll get the hairbrush."

"Devlin, *please!*"

"Gwendolyn!"

"But I *hate* this! You can't . . . it's worse than the *doctor* and you *know* how much I hate going to the doctor! Can't you just . . . ?"

"I can just scorch your impertinent fanny unless you do what I told you."

"But it's *already* scorched . . . it just *burns* and . . . and it's all open and *everything!*"

I sighed and shook my head. "All right . . . I'll get the enema *and* the hairbrush."

"Noooo! OKaaaay! Geeze, you're being such a . . . I don't even know *what!*"

She swiped tears from her face and glared at me as she cupped her palms at the backs of her thighs. I kissed her but she didn't kiss back, and I didn't look around when I got up and went into the bathroom. The blue bulb syringe was right where I left it in the cupboard. I could hear her petulant whines and whimpers until I turned on the water to let it run warm.

"Where are your legs, Princess?"

"*What?*"

I smiled and filled the bulb, and then shut off the water. "You *heard* me, young lady."

"They're . . . right over my head like you told me, *OK?*"

The bed squeaked so I knew she was fibbing, but I just shook my head and cleared my throat.

"They had *better* be!" I dribbled a teaspoon of Ivory hand soap into the bulb, screwed the slender black nozzle on, and shook it as I picked up the tube of lubricant.

Gwen stared at me and twisted her ankles when I walked into the bedroom. Her knees were jammed together, which made the damp, pouty lips at the apex of her thighs that much more adorable as they peeked above her bottom cleft. I sat beside her and opened the K-Y cap.

"Devlin, *please?*"

I leaned over as if to kiss her mouth, then turned and kissed the pouty lips above her firm bottom. She gasped and squirmed, and almost smiled, then glared again.

"Knees farther back so I can put lubricant on your little bottom hole."

She whimpered but pressed her legs closer to her bosom. "I can't *believe* you're doing this to me!"

"Shh . . . relax while I make you ready for the nozzle."

"But it's so *icky!* Why do you . . . ? Eeewww!"

I slicked a dollop of jelly around her anus while she huffed. Her tiny rear opening resisted for a moment and then pulsed to allow my finger inside. The tight sheath throbbed and I took a deep breath while it caressed me like a moist, electric glove. I pushed inside to the hilt and reveled in the tight embrace.

"That's a good girl . . . almost done. Then I'll put the little nozzle inside to clean all the naughtiness out of you."

"Buh . . . but I . . . I'm *not* naughty! I just *forgot,* is all! Whuh . . . why do you have to do such horrible thuh . . . *things* to my fanny?"

"To help you concentrate." I withdrew my finger and patted her bottom. "Are you going to be a good little girl while I put the nozzle in your heinie?"

"Devlin, I *hate* that word! Isn't it bad enough I gotta show you *everything* without . . . *ow! OK!*"

She whimpered and scowled as I rubbed new sting from her behind, but her eyes were far away, lost in the zone where she goes when I stimulate her most sensitive erogenous zone. Her tiny orifice throbbed to my touch and she moaned as the nozzle's tip prodded the dainty hole. It slid inside, like it had been invited, and she squealed.

"Shhh . . . keep still, Princess."

"Oh . . . oh, *Devlin!*"

A sweet, mellow huskiness tinged her voice, and she lifted her bottom higher to receive the sacrament. I smiled and let the warm water dribble inside her while I slipped a thumb between her wet lower lips and found the hard nub between them. She jerked her arms, grabbed hold of her elbows, and clasped her thighs to her breasts to push herself into the nozzle. I squeezed the bulb and twisted it left and right.

Warmth anointed her rectum and she moaned. Wet fire from her clitoris bathed my thumb and I grinned as she mounted the heights. I emptied the bulb, drew it from her with great care and tossed it aside, then lay next to her while my thumb caressed the volcanic heat at her core and the tip of my middle finger pressed against the rosebud between her cheeks. She screamed at the ceiling and I held on while long, quivery pleasure waves crashed over her. Her toes pointed straight up, then she rolled toward me and wrapped her arms around my neck. I lifted my thumb from the burning node, but kept my fingertip tight against her rear vent.

"*God,* Devlin! I . . . I'm sorry but I gotta. . . ."

"It's all right. I'll help you stand up."

"OK, but I . . . what did you *do* to me?"

I smiled and kissed her. "Nothing you didn't *deserve*. Now let me help you off the bed."

A deep groan quivered her bosom as I edged backward and pulled her with me. She whimpered when I put my feet on the floor, and then squealed as I picked her up and stood her beside me, my finger still lodged between her hot cheeks.

"Devlin, you don't have to keep your finger in my. . . ."

"Come on . . . time for the bathroom."

"You are just *evil*, you know that?"

I grinned when she glared at me and pushed my hand from her bottom. She blinked, huffed, and then kissed me as she ran and slammed the bathroom door behind her. I took off the apron, piled pillows against the headboard and opened a Vogue that I found on the shelf.

Ten minutes later she emerged. Her hair was combed, her eyes bright and shimmery in the candlelight, and she was naked. She ran and jumped on top of me. I dropped the magazine and hugged her.

"Hi, Princess. Feel better?"

"*Better?* You nearly killed me!"

"Nonsense."

We kissed and her sharp little teeth tortured my tongue for a long minute. Finally she sighed and pillowed her head on my chest.

"Uh huh, you *did*. That was *horrible* and you had no *right* to put me in that awful position to spank me *and* give me an enema. I mean *really!*"

"Yes, I see how you suffered."

She looked at me and pouted. "Well I *did*."

I stroked her smooth, damp bottom and smiled. "Are you still hungry?"

"Well, *duh* . . . ow! Devlin!"

She pouted even harder while I rubbed new sting. "Then put some clothes on and go get the groceries out of the car."

"*What?* You can't be serious! Ouch! *OK!* Geeze!"

"I'll make supper while you put it all in the trash can, and I mean *everything* . . . and then spray the trunk with Lysol and leave it open."

"OK." She sighed and cuddled into my chest. "I really am sorry, Devlin."

"I know. We'll go shopping tomorrow . . . well, later today . . . together. Now scoot."

Her eyes gleamed when she looked at me. "You forgot something."

"Hm?" I blinked and then grinned. "Yes, you're forgiven. You were a very bad girl but it's all right now."

I kissed her. She sighed, bit her lip and then licked it as she fluttered her eyelashes. I moaned.

"Very well, Princess. You may buy a new outfit for the concert, on my credit card, but no more than a hundred dollars, and *no* new shoes."

She squealed and kissed me hard, then rolled off my chest and scampered to the closet.

THE UNFORTUNATE DISAGREEMENT

We wrote the first partial draft of *Disagreement* from Gwen's point of view, and I switched to Devlin's POV about five pages along to make it a *he said/she said* piece. She told me she liked the new way better and wanted it *all* to be a Devlin story. It took some serious mental gearshifts to flip around everything *she* wrote, but I managed. Tell *me* I don't suffer for my art.

Gwen screeched and yanked me out of the car by my Abboud necktie. I braced myself against the rear fender as she hugged my neck and locked her legs around my hips. She covered my mouth with hers before I could even say hello and plunged her tongue inside, staking claim. The deep, fierce kiss went on and on as we tasted every bit of each other. I hadn't seen my princess in nearly a month and I was ravenous. Her bottom wriggled in my hands as she clung tight. Long, warm minutes later she let go and slid down the length of my body, and then looked up at me, her arms wrapped around my ribs in a smooth bear hug. I hugged back, smiled at the naughty glimmer in her green eyes, and then gasped when she reached down to unzip my fly.

"Bad *girl*," I growled.

"What did you expect . . . a handshake?"

My lips twitched as I stifled a grin, grabbed her wrist and pulled her along the brick walk to her front door. Inside, I managed to pull off my coat and tie before she grabbed me again. Soft bare legs wrapped my waist once more, and we resumed our kiss as I leaned back against the foyer wall. I tugged her jeans skirt up and staked a claim of my own. She moaned when my fingertips slipped beneath panty legs to find her warm, moist vagina. Her knees trembled as I gently stroked and probed. She took a deep breath and buried her face in my neck. I smiled and teased while she chewed my collar and squirmed her heavenly bottom. Hard, hot bullets atop soft, firm breasts burned my chest. She lifted her mouth to be kissed, but I pressed her lips with mine for only an instant. Liquid emerald eyes pleaded for more. She is so adorable when she gives me that look, and my heart melts every time I see it.

"Devlin? Can we . . . ?"

"Hush, Princess," I whispered. "I think we've beaten our record. I was on your property for an entire two seconds before you started to maul me."

She gasped and her mouth opened wide. "Nuh uh, I didn't . . . *Devlin!*"

I laughed when she swung her legs down, pushed against my chest and spun around. She giggled when I scooped her slender waist beneath my arm, bent her over and unzipped her skirt as I carried her up the steps into the hall. Rumpled denim fell to the carpet and she wriggled around to unfasten my trousers. We wrestled and laughed all the way to the bedroom. She knew what I was going to do and it wasn't exactly what she wanted at the time, but I figured she had it coming.

• • •

Pale orange sunshine flickered behind the shades in Gwen's bedroom. A late autumn Sunday afternoon faded to a warm, New England memory. I leaned against the headboard, reached over and picked up a wine glass from the nightstand. Gwen sighed, opened her eyes and wriggled beneath my arm. She hugged my chest while I sipped and then shook her head when I offered her the glass.

"Are you gonna tell me what the hell is going *on*, Devlin? Why are you *here?*"

"That can wait. Don't you want lotion on your bottom?"

She pouted. "Yes! You were a nasty, evil man to spank me so hard and I can't *believe* you punished me for just being glad to *see* you."

I chuckled and handed her the wine. She stuck out her tongue and then drained the merlot before she scrambled across my bare thighs. I grabbed the glass as it tumbled from her fingers, set it on the nightstand and picked up the Jergen's bottle.

"Young lady, I would *never* spank you for being glad to see me. I spanked you for ambushing me in the driveway and nearly breaking my neck when you grabbed my tie."

"Same thing," she muttered, and then sighed when I smeared lotion on her delectable fanny. "And anyway, you didn't even tell me you were *coming.*"

Her smooth behind quivered, then relaxed as I massaged. She has the most adorable bottom, and I quivered while I played with it. I wore only my blue dress shirt, unbuttoned, and undershorts, and Gwen had on just a pink tee shirt and white ankle socks. The rest of our clothes were strewn through the hallway. I had fully expected her to complain about the spanking, but it was something we both needed after four weeks apart. Of course, it wasn't really punishment, more of a *hi, glad I'm back,* and her bottom wasn't even pink.

"I *did* call from the airport, Gwen."

"Yeah, from *Logan.* You didn't give me time to get my nails done or go to the grocery store or . . . ouch! Devlin!"

She pouted at me over her shoulder and rubbed sting from a warm new handprint. I tried not to smile as I bent over to kiss her sweet pout.

"Hush, little girl, and stop squirming. I didn't know I was coming until late last night and I didn't want to wake you."

"Yeah, right . . . you just wanted to freak me totally *out* when you showed up on my doorstep. I don't hear from you for days, and I'm thinking maybe AOL shut off your service 'cause you didn't pay your bill, and all I get is your answering machine when I call . . . what's it all *about,* anyway?"

"Push up a little so I can rub lotion inside your cheeks."

"Devlin, I . . . oh, *God* . . . stop that! You . . . you *know* I can't

think when you do that! Will you tell me what's going on and quit *teasing* me?"

I laughed and turned her over. She whimpered and fought, but finally settled down on my lap.

"OK. I got a new book contract."

She almost shrugged. "Uh huh. I mean . . . that's great, but . . . you're *always* writing books."

"This one's a textbook."

"Yeah, OK . . . but I *still* don't see what that has to do with you showing up out of the clear blue sky."

I grinned and kissed her. "I wanted to make sure it was OK with you if I did book research at the campus library for a couple of weeks."

Her eyes widened and her jaw moved, but no sound came out for ten seconds, then she squealed and hugged me. "You're gonna do research in the library *here?* Why didn't you *tell* me? What are you . . . ? How are you . . . ? *Devlin!*"

She twisted around, straddled my legs and covered my face with kisses while she babbled. Her hot lower lips wetted my shorts as they pressed against my erection. I panted, blinked, and rolled onto my side, not quite pushing her away in the process. She scrambled her arms and legs around me as I lay across the bed.

"Princess? Can . . . can we talk?"

I gasped when she grabbed my ears and clamped her lips to mine. Her tongue pushed between my teeth and I moaned while we kissed. A long time later she let go of my lips and scowled.

"Devlin, I ought to just . . . *ooh* you make me so mad!"

"So it's OK if I park it in Boston for a couple of weeks?"

She huffed and her lips pursed. "*God,* I wish I was bigger! I'd spank *you* until you couldn't sit down! Why didn't you *tell* me?"

"Because I wasn't sure until last night. The grant finally came through, and Jill called me about nine o'clock Pacific time. I didn't want to disturb you that late."

"You could have sent an e-mail, you know! Why haven't you been answering my e-mails, anyway?"

"I *told* you . . . last Tuesday. Didn't you get the message?"

"Yeah, yeah . . . you said you'd be busy for a few days and I shouldn't worry, but dammit, Devlin! You were too busy to answer your damn phone?"

I scowled and she blushed as her hand darted back to cover her bottom.

"Gwendolyn?"

"I . . . I'm *sorry*, Devlin. My bottom's real sore already, OK? I didn't *mean* to swear but I was *worried* about you. So . . . so um . . . when are you coming to do the research?"

She cuddled her face into my chest. Her lips tickled my nipple and I swallowed hard.

"Three . . . three weeks from now . . . the twelfth through the twenty-ninth. I need to go to the library tomorrow and pick up my guest badge."

"Mmm . . . this is just *wonderful*. We'll have *such* a good time." She laughed as she pushed me onto my back and straddled my stomach. "But I'm still mad at you for not telling me. Did you think I wouldn't *want* you to stay with me while you do your research?"

"Of course not. I just didn't want to say anything until it was a done deal. Now that we have the grant we're good to go. But uh . . . I won't be staying here. I arranged for a residence suite near the campus."

Gwen didn't take the news very well. Her jaw dropped and she sat straight up. I grimaced when she scrunched her face like a little girl who broke a favorite toy.

"Don't . . . don't you *want* to stay with me?"

My heart nearly broke and I hugged her. "I'd like nothing better, Princess, but you *know* I'd never get any work done here. You understand, don't you?"

"No I *don't*. You're just being *unreasonable!*"

She twisted out of my arms, and her shiny little bottom bounced as she stalked to the closet and grabbed a pair of sweatpants from a basket. I leapt off the bed, grabbed her arms and spun her around.

"Young lady, you do *not* take that tone with me. Now let's sit down and talk about this."

"I don't *want* to talk about it. If you already got someplace else to stay you can just go stay there *now!*"

"Will you please calm *down?* I'm not coming to Boston for a vacation, I'm coming to do a *job!* You're acting like a five-year-old."

Her face turned bright red and she stomped her foot. "Am *not* . . . but you're being a total *creep!*"

I gritted my teeth and the breath I didn't know I held escaped in a loud hiss. "That *does* it, Gwendolyn."

She gasped and clutched the sweatpants to her bosom. Her shriek nearly deafened me when I picked her up by the waist and carried her to the bed. Slender bare legs scissor-kicked, and her right fist beat against my knee as I sat down, held onto her with my left arm and secured her across my lap.

"This isn't *fair!* I have every *right* to be mad so you can't spank me*eeow!* Ouch! *Ouch! Devlin!*"

My hand stung after the first five swats, all of which landed right at the center of her round fanny. The pain dispelled my aggravation and reminded me that I only wanted to get her attention. I shortened the strokes and distributed more moderate smacks across the lotiony smoothness of her bottom.

"All! Right! Young! Lady! If! You! Don't! Want! To! Sit! And! Talk! You! Will! Just! Have! To! *Stand!* And! Talk!"

"Ow! Ouch! Owhoo! Nooo! Daa-Daa-Devleee! Ouch! Naaah! *Please!* Not! So! *Hard!* I'm *sorry!*"

She covered her face with her hands and wept while I rubbed her bright pink behind. When her sobs diminished I swatted her again and she yelped.

"Are you *really* sorry or are you just saying that to get out of a good blistering?"

"I . . . I'm ruh . . . really *sorry,* OK?"

I gave her four crisp swats, two on each cheek. "I'm not convinced, Princess."

"Oweeech! *Devlin!* What do you *want* from me?"

The room echoed with hollow pops as I cupped my hand and clapped three times, straight across her deep cleft.

"I want you to lose that defiant attitude for one thing!"

"*God,* I *hate* it when you spank me like that!"

"How's *this*, then?"

She screeched, kicked and flailed the duvet with her fists while I rained dozens of quick spanks at the base of her sore cheeks with just my fingers. When my fingertips began to sting, I stopped and rubbed. I let her wail and wriggle for a minute, then leaned over and kissed the back of her neck. She jerked and then moaned as she turned wet, sorrowful eyes to me.

"I . . . I'm suh . . . sorry I thuh . . . threw a fit, honest!"

I reached over and plucked a handful of tissue from the box on the nightstand. She wiped her face, blew her nose, and then closed her eyes and twisted toward me. I smiled as I kissed her swollen lips. Her sweet, sore bottom clenched while I massaged some of the sting away, and then she rolled over, sat up, and threw her arms around my neck.

"You're a good girl now, Princess."

She nodded and whispered, "Thank you."

"Are you ready to talk about some things? Without the histrionics?"

"Yes, sir. Whatever you say, sir."

I leaned back and wiped a stray tear from her eye as I squinted. "And without the sarcasm?"

"I *wasn't*, Devlin! You . . . you already made up your mind so I'm not gonna argue with you."

"I know you're disappointed, but really it's the only way this will work. I'm too used to coming here to play, and you would be a constant distraction. Plus, it's an hour's drive to the campus and I wouldn't want you to worry if I came home late at night."

"But . . . um . . . can I say something?"

"Of course. All I wanted to do was talk about it."

"Well . . . OK. If . . . if you *did* stay here, I'd keep out of your way and you could have the spare bedroom for an office and . . . and I work all day anyway, so I'd hardly ever be around and . . . and it's only about forty minutes to campus, 'cause I go there for concerts all the time! If you stay in some hotel I'll never get to *see* you even though you're right across town, and that would just drive me *crazy*."

I sighed and hugged her while I racked my brain for a compromise. "It would probably drive *me* crazy, as well, so . . . how about this? You want a part-time job as a research assistant?"

She gasped and her eyes lit up like the first day of spring. "OhmiGod! I could take vacation time and. . . ."

"No, Princess, just a couple of evenings a week. I'll stay on campus and we can play on weekends. Would you be willing to do *that*?"

"Oh, Devlin!"

I fell backward onto the bed. She laughed and covered my lips

and face with warm kisses while her slender fingers tugged at my shorts. I groaned and she sighed as her lower lips engulfed my hardness in wet fire.

• • •

I arrived at the residence hotel late on a Sunday night, unpacked my gear and phoned Gwen. She surprised me when she didn't make a fuss that I had gone straight there, and said she'd be over Tuesday evening to help with the research. I spent the next two days in the library and amassed an armload of copies. She arrived on time, for Gwen, only a half hour late, and waited while I shut the door behind her before she leapt into my arms.

"I missed you, Princess," I said when we came up for air.

She pouted and huffed, then grinned and squeezed my neck harder. "Serves you right!" I raised my left eyebrow and she bit her lip. "I missed you, too, Devlin. Did you have any supper?"

"I grabbed a sandwich at Subway about four o'clock."

"Uh huh . . . if I know you, that was lunch."

"Well . . . yes . . . technically. . . ."

"Geeze, Devlin!" She shook her head as she pushed away from me. "I'll be back in a minute, OK?"

"But I thought you came here to *work*."

"I did!"

She dashed out the door and left it wide open. I sighed and looked out as she clattered down the outside stairs to her car. She came back ten minutes later with hot food from a Chinese restaurant down the block. I was surprised again when she insisted I show her what I wanted done, even as we ate lemon chicken and shrimp fried rice. We made visible progress and I wanted carry on, but at 10:30 I stood and lifted her from the chair.

"Time to go home, Princess." I kissed her and she pouted. "You need to get some sleep."

"But I'm not *sleepy* . . . and anyway, if I don't get these graphs in the right order you won't know where the. . . ."

"Shh. I said it's bedtime, young lady."

She grinned and squeezed my chest. "OK, Professor. I'll go get my bag out of the trunk."

I sighed and hugged her. "Gwen, I thought we agreed . . . we'll play this weekend. Now go home. You have a *real* job, remember?"

Angry green kitty-eyes burned into mine when she looked up. "So you're kicking me *out?*"

"Of course not. I'll even walk you to your car."

"Devlin!" A little doe-hoof stomped the carpet. "You can't be *serious* . . . I mean. . . ." She grinned as she rubbed her tummy against the front of my jeans. "I don't think *he* wants me to leave."

"Young lady, you just. . . ." I took a deep breath and she whimpered when I pushed away the soft temptation. "We had a deal . . . so be a good girl and go get some rest, OK?"

"But I *hate* being sent away! Don't you love me anymore?"

I gasped, grabbed her and hugged her hard with my left arm while I swatted the seat of her short black skirt.

"Don't *ever* say that to me, Gwen!"

"Ow! Ow! Ouch! But . . . but you want me to go home! *That's* not very loving!"

She squealed when I picked her up, carried her to the over-stuffed couch and plopped her across my lap. I bunched the skirt at her waist and held her while she kicked. Her loafers flew off and sailed over the sofa arm. Just for a second, I admired the curve of her behind beneath a pair of tight blue boy-leg briefs, and then remembered what she said to me. My open palm cracked the plumpest part of the blue curves a half-dozen times.

"Princess, I love you more than life itself, but you're being an unmitigated *brat* about this."

"Am *not!* If you loved me you wouldn't treat me like the hired help!"

"Like the . . . ? Young lady, you just . . . ! I can't *believe* you said that!"

I told myself I wasn't angry but I knew it was a lie. Gwen remained stoic for the first forty or fifty crisp swats on the seat of her knickers, but then put her hands over her eyes and wept. I stopped spanking just long enough to wipe a drop of moisture from my own eye, and then gave her another dozen hard smacks. Her little body trembled when I scooped her up, set her on my lap and let her cry into my neck. I stroked the back of her head with one hand, and her fiery panty-seat with the other.

Long minutes ticked by while she sobbed. I felt like the champion heel of all time. Finally she looked at me.

"I . . . I'm sorry, Devlin. I'll go home now."

"Yes, well . . . I . . . I think there's some lotion in my bag. I'll just go and. . . ."

"No . . . that's all right. Good night."

She jumped off my lap. I stood and reached for her, but she ran to the kitchen and grabbed her purse.

"Princess, I. . . ."

"G'night, Devlin."

"Call me when you get home, O. . . ." The door slammed behind her. "K?"

I took a deep breath and looked around. The huge suite, with its high windows and vaulted ceiling, so bright and cheerful moments before, had become a dreary cell in a dank prison. I sat at the desk and shuffled papers, but none of the words made sense, so I went and washed the dishes Gwen had stacked in the sink, even though the hotel staff always did them when they cleaned.

The TV blinked as I flicked through the same forty or fifty channels a dozen times. Finally I picked up the phone and called her house. The machine picked up.

"Hi, Princess. I, um . . . I trust you made it home all right. Call me when you get a chance."

I switched off, then grunted and redialed, got the machine again, smiled into the receiver. "Oh, I almost forgot!" The smiley voice sounded false, even to me. "You're a good girl now . . . g'night!"

• • •

She finally called me from work Thursday afternoon and said she didn't feel well and would I be terribly disappointed if she just went home to bed and didn't come over to help with the research? I asked if there were anything I could do but she said no, and then got evasive when I wanted to make plans for the weekend so I told her I'd call her on Saturday. I already had the book outline and research plan, so I set myself on autopilot and dug what I needed out of the library stacks, thankful that I didn't have to be creative. The piles of Xerox copies became unmanageable, so I packed some boxes and shipped them home.

When I called Friday night I got the machine, but I didn't leave a message. Saturday morning, the same thing happened, so I drove to her house. I sat in the driveway for a while . . . ten minutes? Two hours? I don't know. It was nearly noon when I pulled myself together enough to get out of the car and go to the door.

I was about to knock when a cold chill dashed up my spine. A black cashmere sweater sleeve was stuck at the base of the jamb, and the latch rested against the weather stripping. I pushed the door open and looked around. Black, patent-leather pumps sat, one at the top, one at the bottom, of the steps that went up and into the hallway. A black bra and a black miniskirt hung from the rail. I gathered the clothes, shut and locked the door, and went to her bedroom. A wad of black, micro-fiber panties and charcoal stockings lay tangled on the hope chest.

Tousled boy-short hair peeked from a crevice in a rumpled blanket and I smiled as I tossed the clothes on the hope chest and then dropped the shoes on top of the pile with a thunk. The blanket shifted and moaned. I raised the window shade, sat on the bedside and hooked a finger in the crevice. Gwen grimaced and blinked when I tugged the cover from her face.

"Good morning, Princess."

"Oh, *God!*" she whispered, and pulled the blanket over her eyes.

"I take it you had an interesting Friday night."

"What are you *doing* here? I can't talk to you right now."

"Yes you can." I kissed the top of her head. "And you *will*, young lady. Did you go out and get plastered with Amy?"

"No!" The blanket wriggled. "I just . . . I wasn't too smart last night."

"I see. So you have a raging hangover?"

"Noo! I didn't *drink* too much. I . . . I had my usual two and a half . . . plus a Philly cheese steak sandwich . . . with extra mushrooms . . . and loaded potato skins."

"Good heavens!"

"Devlin! Bartender Mike said if Amy and I said *wow* when he presented the skins to us they'd be on the house, so naturally we did and we got them for free, but . . . ugh! What I *should* have done without was the coffee with um . . . whipped cream and . . . something else . . . some kind of alcohol in it. Mike called it something, I don't know what . . . but . . . *ugh!*"

"*Ugh* is right . . . and since they were free, I assume you felt obligated to eat every bite of the stuffed potatoes."

She glared at me for a second and then blinked. "Well . . . yeah . . . and after that my stomach just said *enough already*. I woke up at three am, *so* hot . . . with a headache, and my stomach feeling so sickly, and I couldn't sleep after that, I felt so nauseous. Then I dozed 'til six, took some aspirin and went back to sleep. What time is it?"

"A little after noon."

"Oh, *God!* I have to go *grocery* shopping today . . . I *hate* that."

I smiled and Gwen wriggled while I rubbed her back. "But you *always* hate it."

"I really, really *do*." She whined for a few seconds and then yanked the covers down and glanced around the walls. "How did you get *in* here, anyway?"

"You left the door open."

"Nuh *uh!*" Her under lip trembled as she glared. "I'm still mad at you, I don't *care* what Amy says, and anyway I have a bellyache so please go *away*."

"I'm sorry you're ill and I'll go away soon. But I'm curious . . . what *did* Amy say?"

She huffed and pulled the blanket over her head. "None of your *business*. Now go *away* . . . I'm sick."

"I see that, and it makes me very sad . . . and even sadder I wasn't here to hug you and kiss you and make you feel a little calmer. You just rest while I get the enema bag."

The blanket bundle jerked and thrashed. My little princess scrambled her head out and moist, green eyes stared. Her lips moved as she squirmed backward across the bed, but there was no sound for five seconds.

"You *can't* . . . I *don't* want you to . . . *nooo!*"

"Hush, young lady! I would have been stunned if you *hadn't* got sick from last night's excess."

"But it *wasn't* excess, not *really!* Just don't even *say* that!"

I shook my head and leaned over to kiss her warm lips. "You said you had a fever, didn't you? That's not a good sign."

"Did I say *fever?* Um . . . I didn't *mean* to say fever! I . . . I was just really *warm*, that's all. Maybe I fell asleep with my sweatshirt on. I think maybe I *did* . . . and I . . . um . . . maybe I forgot to turn

off the heating blanket, too! Yeah! *That's* why I was so hot . . . and you never *told* me what you're doing here, anyway!"

"Never mind that . . . I need to take your temp."

"Devlin, you're not *listening* to me!"

Long fingernails dug into my forearms as I tossed away the covers and pulled her to me. Her heart thudded against my chest when I hugged her quivery body close.

"Yes I am, Princess, and you sound like a naughty little girl trying to cover up a fib. I have to take your temperature so stop fussing."

"But you *know* I hate it!"

I smiled and hugged her tighter. "You *do* tend to wiggle and complain, don't you?"

"Because it's *embarrassing!* I could just *die* when you do that to me!"

"Shhh. I want you to lie still while I get the thermometer, OK?"
"*Nooo!*"

I kissed her moist pout and pulled the sheet over her, then glared when she tried to throw it off. "I said to *wait* for me, Princess."

She huffed and clutched the wrinkled linen to her chin. "I don't *want* to."

"All right . . . then get up and make me a Santa Fe omelet with braised onions and extra red pepper."

"Oh, *Gaahd!*"

She disappeared beneath the sheet and I grinned while I went into the bathroom. I glanced over my shoulder as I rummaged in a cabinet, but the Gwen bundle barely moved until I sat back down on the bedside.

"Come along, Princess. Let's have you."

Her head popped out like an angry gopher. "I'm OK, honest! Just . . . just put that stupid thing away!"

"Don't annoy me, little girl. Come on."

"*Devlin!* For crying out loud!"

She kicked and whined and complained as I rolled her across my lap. She wore only a faded Dodgers tee shirt that she had stolen from my bureau a half-dozen years before. It was five sizes too large for her and she looked totally adorable in it.

"Hush and quit wiggling. I'll hold you really tight, with your bare tushy up in the air. . . ."

"Nooooo!"

"And your plump little cheeks spread really wide so I can see where everything is."

She kicked and squeaked. "This is *so* not fair!"

I clicked my tongue. "You wouldn't want me to stick anything in the wrong place, would you?"

"I don't want you to stick anything *anywhere! Please?* I *hate* to be so embarrassed and I promise . . . I *promise* . . . I'll be a very, *very* good girl if you don't use *that!*"

"Young lady, you *know* there's no negotiating when it comes to your health or your hygiene . . . or your punishments, for that matter. A nice, big bagful of peppermint soap and warm water will do you a world of good."

"Oh, nooo!"

"Hush and keep still while I put Vaseline on your bottom hole." She wailed when I snapped the lid off the jar. "There. Now be still, Princess . . . it's only my finger."

"But it's so . . . so *awful* when you . . . *ow!*"

"Shhh . . . your anus is very tight and I don't want to hurt you. Now just relax so I can get your bottom hole ready."

"Would you stop *saying* that? It's . . . it's *nasty!*"

"I *said* quit squirming. I don't want to spank you but I will if you keep this up."

"*No!* Duh . . . *don't* put that nasty thing in my bottom, *please?*"

Her tight rear vent squeezed my finger as I pulled it out. She panted and whimpered while I shook the thermometer and dipped it in Vaseline. The puckered entry throbbed as she gasped.

"Be *still*, Gwendolyn . . . this is for your own good."

"Nuh-nuh-*nooo!*"

I pushed the cold glass into her behind. She quivered, yelped, and clutched the sheet.

"There now . . . is that so bad?"

"I don't . . . don't *wanna* have that thing in my bottom!"

"Yes, so you say . . . now be quiet for a few minutes so I can get a good reading."

"*No!* Take it out, OK?"

"Hush, little girl . . . you know better."

She wriggled, whined and almost called me a very bad name while I patted her round fanny, but mostly she just wriggled and

whined for four minutes. Her sweet, round behind quivered beneath my palm, and I had to keep an eye on the bedside clock or I would have forgotten to check the thermometer. She squealed when I pulled it out.

"Hmm . . . ninety-nine point four . . . perfectly normal." I dropped the thermometer onto the nightstand. "Feel better now?"

"*Geeze,* Devlin! You're just a. . . ." She scrambled around and hugged my neck. We kissed, long and hard and deep for a half-minute and then she squirmed, let go the kiss and pouted at me. "That was really *icky* and . . . what are you *doing* here?"

"I told you . . . you left the door open for me. How's your tummy?"

"Never *mind* my tummy! Did you use the key under the rock?"

"*What?*" I chuckled and she huffed. "You keep a key under a *rock?* That's interesting . . . but you may need to have your black cashmere sweater re-knitted."

"My *sweater?* What did you . . . ? Oh, *God.*"

She pressed her face into my shoulder and sobbed. I hugged her and patted her soft, bare bottom.

"Is it all coming back to you? You didn't drive home in that condition, did you?"

"Of *course* not . . . Amy picked me up and I took a cab home."

I pulled her close and kissed her while she whimpered. After two seconds, her hot little tongue caressed mine, and I moaned as she flicked it around my mouth. She giggled when I pushed away.

"I was a good girl to take a cab, huh?"

Her naughty, gamin smile nearly melted me, but I managed a scowl.

"Yes, but I expected no less. How does your tummy feel now?"

"Devlin, for crying out loud! Oooof!"

She leaned her head on my chest and took deep, ragged breaths. I rubbed her back while she moaned.

"It's OK, Princess. I'll take care of that."

"Nuh-*no* . . . I'm fine, honest! Do . . . do you want some breakfast?"

"Shh . . . rest for a minute, OK?"

"I . . . I'll make you some eggs or some pancakes or . . . eeesh!"

Her shoulders quivered as she clutched her tummy and writhed. I tugged the blanket over her, reached down to switch off the heat

control, kissed her warm cheek, and then went into the bathroom. Everything was just as I left it in our special cabinet.

I closed the little clamp on the clear hose, twisted a nozzle to its end, and then half-filled the red rubber bag with warm water and a few drops of liquid peppermint soap before I replaced the stopper and shook it. The bag sloshed when I set it on the basin counter. The smaller curve of a white plastic double hook hung from the eyelet hole at the top of the bag. I crooked a finger around the larger curve of the hook and went back to the bedroom. Gwen moaned when I sat beside her. I hooked the heavy bag over the head rail and stretched the hose to lay the nozzle on the nightstand beside the Vaseline jar.

"It's time, little girl."

Her eyelids fluttered as she stared at the nightstand. "Not *that* one!"

I pulled her across my lap. "We have to use the big nozzle so it won't take *hours* for all the water to flow into your tushy."

Green eyes glared back at me and burned with panic-stricken yearning. "Oh, please, not the *black* one! Not the really *wide* one! It's too *big*, Devlin! It's too big and it . . . it *stretches* me when you put it in! Oh, *please* not that one! It feels *awful*."

"I'll put lots of Vaseline on it, and more inside your bottom so you won't be uncomfortable when I push it in."

She sniffled and whimpered and wriggled her adorable fanny while I spread pale jelly on the nozzle.

"I *hate* that one! It makes me feel full even before the enema starts! It makes my . . . my bottom hole . . . sore! Why can't you just use the little skinny one?"

"Oh, dear . . . I can see you're going to give me a hard time. All this complaining, fussing and whining. . . ."

"I am *not* whining!"

"The black nozzle isn't too big for you, Gwen. My penis is much larger than this and I know you enjoy having *that* in your bottom, so I'm not too concerned about any *stretching* during your enema."

She kicked the mattress, grumped and huffed, angry because she knew I was right.

I sighed and caressed her warm, quivery cheeks. "It makes me wonder, Kitty Eyes, how you *really* feel when I invade your

– 227 –

private spaces like this. You put up such a fuss, but I know what happens between your legs when I discipline you."

"That . . . that's a *horrible* thing to say! I'm a *good* girl! I don't *like* you touching and looking at my. . . ."

"So I may as well tell you now . . . I will have to spank you even before the enema, just to be certain I have your full cooperation."

"*What?* A spanking too? But *why?*"

"Not a very hard spanking, though, because you feel so bad."

"*Yeah!* I *do* feel sick! *Remember?* So . . . so maybe you shouldn't spank me!"

"I'll only spank you until you're more agreeable and your little bottom is a nice, warm pink, and it stings enough to make you a little bit sorrier for yourself."

She squealed. "I can't *possibly* feel any sorrier for myself! I feel miserable already! And there's no *way* I'm going to be happy about having to take that . . . that . . . enema!"

The final word came out in a snarl, and I clamped my left arm around her waist.

"All right, then . . . if you won't cooperate, I'll just have to spank you."

"Noo! Ouch! Not so *hard!* Owee! OKaay! Geeze, Devlin! I said *OK,* all right?"

I smiled, rubbed sting from my palm, and reached over to the nightstand. She whimpered as I dipped a fingertip into the Vaseline jar and then coated her rear dimple. The little bud blossomed and she moaned when I pushed inside. I massaged her tightness for a dozen seconds before I removed my finger and picked up the nozzle. The bag gurgled when I opened the clamp to let the water force the air from the last foot of hose. A tiny jet of soapy water sprayed the carpet before I stopped it with my finger.

She buried her face in her hands when I pressed the rounded cylinder against her quivery anus, and jelly glistened around the tiny pink hole as it reluctantly opened to accept the nozzle. My heart throbbed while black plastic sank deep into her bottom. She gasped and spread her legs as I unhooked the bag from the bed rail, lifted it high and opened the clamp all the way. Warm, soapy water flowed and she bent her knees to raise her fanny. Her tender cleft spread like a tulip that opens its petals to a spring rain. She panted and squeaked, and told me how much

she hated to be so embarrassed, and what a horrible man I was to make her do this.

Her bare cheek pressed my erection as she leaned into me. I wriggled the nozzle and smiled at the dampness between her thighs. Plump, pink lower lips sparkled with feminine dew. She babbled complaints, but pushed her fanny up while I reached around to massage her hot, swollen tummy. I squeezed the last of the water from the bag and then hung it on the bed rail and slowly pulled the nozzle out. She squealed and I pressed my thumb to her moist rear vent as I leaned over and whispered in her ear.

"You may have some time alone in the bathroom . . . after the peppermint soap stays in your tushy for a few minutes."

She gasped and wriggled. "But the soap *stings*. Do I really have to *hold* it?"

"Yes . . . and once you've composed yourself we'll have a talk about your overindulgence."

"But . . . but I . . . I think the mushrooms on the sandwich were bad! I *didn't* overindulge."

I kissed her neck and she shivered. "We'll talk about that later, Princess . . . a long, kind of loud and ouchy talk."

"Noooo. . . ."

"The kind where your bare bottom begins to feel like you sat in a wasp nest."

"Devlin, *please,* I'm so, *so* sorry . . . I promise I'll be good!"

"The kind where my calm, reasonable scolding goes pretty unheard beneath all the yelping and whining."

She sniffled and pushed her bottom into my thumb. "You're not *listening!* I don't think I *deserve* another spanking!"

"Then I'll put a nice, cozy sweat suit on you so you'll be warm."

Moist, green eyes blinked when she turned to me. "*That* sounds sorta nice."

"While you stand in the corner. . . ."

"Not *fair!*" She huffed and pouted.

"With your pants pulled down just enough so I can admire my handiwork on your adorable behind."

"Nuh *uh!* You *know* I hate it when you make me stand in the corner! I don't want you to look at my spanked fanny! I just want to *hide* after you spank me! How can you be so *mean* to me?"

– 229 –

She wailed when I pushed my left arm beneath her breasts, and then whimpered when I lifted her and set her feet on the carpet. My thumb slipped from between tight cheeks. She clapped both hands to her bottom as she ran to the bathroom and slammed the door. I curled the plastic hose and buried the enema equipment amid her clothes on the hope chest.

I went to the kitchen, cleaned a couple of potatoes, put them in to bake, then poured a glass of wine and sat in the living room with a Günter Grass novel I found on a shelf. Gwen spent the next hour in the bathroom. I looked up when she pouted at me from the hallway. Her hair was dry and finger-combed, and she had on just a touch of makeup. I smiled, put down the book and held out my arms. A short, billowy skirt flounced as she ran to me; a thin brassiere, visible through her cream silk pullover, pushed her tight, round breasts up and out. Her feet were bare and her legs glistened with lotion. She sat on my lap and cuddled my chest. The aroma of fresh soap and gardenias in full bloom filled my nostrils.

"Feel better, Princess?"

"Uh huh. I, um . . . I guess I really *did* need that. You're a very wise man and you take care of me real good."

I laughed and kissed the top of her head. "You're still getting that spanking, Kitty Eyes."

"Noooo! I just . . . I want to *talk,* OK? And not that ouchy kind of talk, either! Can we just *talk* . . . like *people?*"

"Sure." I hugged her close and she wriggled her bottom on my thighs. "So . . . what did Amy say to you last night?"

She blinked and bit her lip for a second. "About what?"

"About me, I assume. Whatever it was you refused to tell me earlier."

"Um . . . I forget. Nothing important. You know Amy."

I glared and she squirmed. "Gwendolyn?"

"Don't *do* that, Devlin! She . . . she just said, um . . . that you were the best thing that ever happened to me and I should quit being a butthead about you kicking me out the other night." She whimpered and blushed when I hugged her hard. "But she was half loaded and. . . ."

"Shh . . . she was also only half right."

"Huh?"

— 230 —

"*You* are the best thing that ever happened to *me*, and I may have forgotten that for an instant."

"Then . . . why are you so *mad* at me?"

I lifted her chin and looked into deep green pools as she blinked. "I'm *not*, Princess. I thought you were mad at *me*."

"*No!* I mean, well . . . kinda. You were really awful to me the other night."

"I suppose I was . . . but *you* went back on our deal."

"No I *didn't!* Not *really!* And anyway, is that any reason not to take my panties down when you spanked me? You *never* spank me like that!"

"That's true. I was angry and I owe you an apology. I promise not to do that ever again."

"OK." She shut her eyes while our lips met in a long, soft kiss, and then she whimpered and looked at me. "Wait . . . do you mean you won't get angry, or you won't not take my panties down?"

"Both. Either." I smiled and she moaned as I kissed her again, a bit harder. "And don't you owe *me* an apology . . . for snubbing me the past few days."

She leaned back and looked at the ceiling. "Nope. Don't think so."

I laughed. "Then it's carpet-inspection time for *you*, little girl!"

A girlish squeal pierced my ears and she giggled as I picked her up and turned her over my lap. Both hands darted back to protect her rear end. I flicked her fingers with mine and she moaned as she put her palms flat on the floor. The little skirt rode up to reveal a plump under curve of smooth flesh. Her toes wriggled in the deep carpet and she turned her head. Green kitty-eyes pleaded with me, but a naughty smile curved the corners of her full lips. I huffed and shook my head.

"Would you care to rephrase your response, young lady?"

"Um . . . well . . . not *really*. I mean it *was* all your fault and . . . eeeek! Devlin! Don't lift my skirt!"

Her legs scissored and I grinned as I pushed the light cotton up and off her bottom. Firm, high cheeks glimmered in the lamplight.

"So you were just making sure, were you, Princess?"

She glared, but the naughty smile remained. "Sure of *what?*"

I smacked the center of her bare behind. "No panties for me to leave on, *that's* what!"

– 231 –

"Owee!" She grinned and wriggled her hips. "I guess I forgot to put some on."

"Oh, you *did,* did you?"

She yelped only twice while I swatted, not too hard, a few dozen times all around her quivery cheeks, then she lowered her head and pushed up her fanny. I snugged her waist tightly, shortened the strokes, and peppered the soft base of her behind with quick, sharp spanks. Her legs twisted and her toes curled, but she kept her bottom still while I turned the tender flesh bright red. When she began to wail, I stopped, rolled her over and held her on my lap.

"My . . . my bottom just *burns,* Devlin!"

"I know it does, Princess. Now . . . don't you have something to say to me?"

Her damp under lip pushed even farther out. "I . . . I *guess* so."

"Well? Go on."

"You were very mean to me but . . . I guess I shouldn't of . . . reacted the way I did."

I kissed her pout and her tongue darted inside my mouth. Her arms squeezed my neck and I moaned as a warm hip pressed my erection. After a long minute I gasped and leaned back.

"Well . . . under the circumstances. . . ." I lifted her legs to relieve the pressure on my hardness. "I suppose I'll accept that as an apology."

She grinned and kissed me again. "Then I'm a good girl now?"

"Yes. Yes you are."

"And I took my spanking real good, even if I *didn't* deserve it?"

I shook my head. "You took it really *well,* and you deserved every swat."

"Hmph! OK, Professor." She sniffed and glanced toward the kitchen. "You made lunch? I smell something cooking."

"I put some potatoes in the oven. We'll broil those little sirloins in the meat compartment and . . . *what?*"

"You baked *potatoes?* Ugh! I never want to *see* another potato skin as long as I live!"

"Oh! Well . . . yes. Possibly that was a poor choice."

"*Possibly?* Ooh! Men!"

She jerked off my lap, grabbed my hand and pulled me into the kitchen. I took the potatoes from the oven and tossed them into the

garbage while she held her nose, then I followed her flouncy skirt to the bedroom and undressed her while she pretended to complain. She moaned and wriggled as I held her across my lap and smoothed lotion over her sweet, sore behind. Her legs spread and my fingers slid inside the deep cleft. She squealed when a fingertip invaded the tight recess inside, and I moaned as her puffy anus clenched like a vise.

"Are you hungry?" I whispered to her ear.

"Uh huh. I . . . I'm *really* hungry for . . . *you* know."

I swallowed hard and picked her up. My finger never left her rear vent as I slid her around to lie on the bed. She whimpered but lifted her bottom to let me push pillows under her hips with my free hand.

"Do you want something *besides* my finger in your little fanny?"

"Oh, God, *yes!*"

"Then stay there like a good girl, with your naughty bottom in the air, while I get undressed."

"But . . . but . . . how can I be a *good* girl if I have a naughty *bottom?* Huh?"

I leaned over and kissed her, then smiled and drew my finger, very slowly, from her anus. She grunted and kicked the rumpled blanket. I smiled.

"That's *always* been a mystery to me, but you do it so well."

"Devlin! You're just teasing me!" She squeezed her legs together and scowled as she clapped a hand over her cleft. "And quit looking inside my naughty bottom, you naughty man! The very idea!"

Her scowl exploded into a grin as I laughed and fumbled with shirt buttons. "If you keep stealing my righteous-professor catch-phrase, I'll do more than *look* inside your naughty bottom, young lady."

"Yeah . . . that's what I'm counting on." She gaped at the front of my pants. "Oh, my *God!*"

I sighed as I pushed trousers and shorts off my feet, along with my socks. My manhood bobbed its head in the air and warm blush covered my face.

"Flattery will get you . . . well, you're about to find *out* what it will get you, little girl."

She wriggled her hips and grinned harder. "I am *not* a little girl . . . good thing, too, huh? If I was I'd *never* be able to take your enormous. . . ."

"Gwendolyn!"

"Sir?" She blinked and licked her lips.

I lay beside her, wrapped her in my arms and kissed her. "Always use the subjunctive of the *to be* verb when the relative clause begins with the word *if*."

"Mmmm . . . if you *were* through with the lecture, would you quit being a righteous professor and make love to my bottom?"

"Only with the greatest of physical and spiritual pleasure, you adorable brat." She jerked, quivered and parted her thighs as I dipped my finger once more into her hot, velvety sheath. "Your little brat bottom hole is very tight, Princess. Should I exercise it first?"

"N-noooo! You . . . you already put that . . . that big old *nozzle* in me, and . . . embarrassed me almost to death with that stupid thuh-thermometer! I . . . I want *you* in me!"

"So do I. Can you stay still while I get the K-Y?"

"No I *can't!* I . . . I want to do it."

I pushed my finger into her bottom as far as it would go. She yelped when I squeezed her cheek.

"Ask nicely, Princess."

"Ooh! Okaaay! Can . . . can I put the . . . ?"

"*May* I . . . ?"

"Devlin! *May* I put the K-Y on your penis? God, you are such a. . . ."

"Shh . . . you're about to get yourself into trouble."

"*Please?*"

"Of course you may. Is there some in the nightstand?"

"Yeah, but . . . don't take your finger out of my fanny, OK? It feels really nice."

I smiled and kissed her. "You want to see how agile I am, right?"

Her sphincter ring clamped hard as she grinned. I twisted and fumbled in the nightstand drawer with my left hand. She snatched the tube when I turned around, and then straddled my thighs as I lay on my back. My arm ached and stretched, while my finger burned inside her, but I kept her nether hole plugged

as she dribbled clear fluid into her hand. She grinned as she rubbed her palms together, and then anointed the shaft. I gasped while hot fingers caressed me. She bent down and her pink tongue darted between her teeth to tease the taut, purple head.

Moist lightening bolts flashed through my belly and I grabbed her chin. She giggled and slid upward. Her flat tummy pressed my erection, and diabolical teeth teased my right nipple. Smooth, squirmy muscles inside her bottom squeezed my finger, and I groaned as I rolled over and dumped her, facedown, onto a stack of pillows. She whimpered when my finger slipped out of her anus, then spread her thighs and pushed up with her hips.

"Puh . . . please, Devlin?"

"Please what, Princess?" I covered her nakedness with my own and pressed my stiffness lengthwise into her hot, moist cleft. "Please don't violate your tender bottom hole with my rampant manhood?"

Her back quivered as she giggled. "No! Please *do! Now!*"

"Oh, really? All right."

I reached down and guided the head to her tight vent. She gasped and bowed her back as she pushed her hips into me. The tiny portal throbbed as it yielded and I slid into soft clinginess. Her little fingers clawed sheets. I reached out to grab her wrists and held them above her head while I pushed farther into her.

She wailed and flexed her knees. Her bottom stretched wider and drew me all the way inside. The wet, open mouth of her vagina heated my testicles and fire bathed the head of my penis, a thousand miles beneath the surface of her smooth behind. I kissed the damp hair at the back of neck and whispered in her ear.

"You are *mine* now . . . your naughty, adorable fanny is all *mine* . . . and there's nothing you can do about it, Princess. I'm going to hold you completely still while I ravage your sweet little bottom hole and you're helpless to stop me."

"Nooooo!"

The long, shrill negative lilted through two full octaves as I pulled out a few inches and then slid back inside her. She trembled and gasped, then clutched me hard with her sphincter.

"Hush, Gwen. I want you . . . and I shall *have* you."

"Ohhh! *Devlin!* I . . . I . . . oh, *God! Yes!*"

I pulled back, pushed in again, and slick, shivery electricity

lanced through me. She yanked a hand from my grasp, thrashed her arm for a second, and then whimpered and found my fingers with her wrist. I panted, held tight, and nuzzled her ear.

"Don't do that again, Princess, or I'll have to spank you."

"I . . . I'm sorry, Devlin! I won't . . . just. . . ."

"Shhh! Push your bottom into me."

"O . . . OK. I . . . *Jesus,* Devlin!"

She squeaked and squealed as I pulled her arms farther over her head. I took a deep breath, drew back, and then set a slow, even pace that quickened as her squeals rose in timbre. Her bottom clenched and relaxed as she matched my rhythm, and sheets of icy fire covered me from forehead to kneecap. Deep, shuddery quivers rolled down her back and I exploded inside her like a trainload of dynamite.

Long, gaspy minutes later, I turned over and lay beside her. Gwen whimpered and climbed on top of me. The short curls at the base of her tummy tickled and tormented my spent manhood. She kissed me and I licked her tongue.

"Hi, Princess." I swallowed the hoarseness in my throat and smiled.

"Mmmm . . . hi. You absolutely destroyed me, you know?"

I hugged her while she trembled. "Sweet of you to say so."

She giggled, and then squirmed downward to bite my nipple. "I'm hungry."

"Yow! Gwen! Male breasts are completely devoid of nourishment and you *know* that."

Her laugh filled the room as she sat up and hugged herself. "Yeah, but I still *like* them. So what are we gonna have for lunch?"

I grabbed her waist, twisted her around and flung her across my lap. "Broiled rump of princess!"

My Secret Life
Anonymous

Over two million copies sold!

Perhaps the most infamous of all underground Victorian erotica, *My Secret Life* is the sexual memoir of a well-to-do gentleman, who began at an early age to keep a diary of his erotic behavior. He continues this record for over forty years, creating in the process a unique social and psychological document. Its complete and detailed description of the hidden side of British and European life in the nineteenth century furnishes materials for the understanding of the Victorian Age that cannot be duplicated in any other source.

The Altar of Venus
Anonymous

Our author, a gentleman of wealth and privilege, is introduced to desire's delights at a tender age, and then and there commits himself to a life-long sensual expedition. As he enters manhood, he progresses from schoolgirls' charms to older women's enticements, especially those of acquaintances' mothers and wives. Later, he moves beyond common London brothels to sophisticated entertainments available only in Paris. Truly, he has become a lord among libertines.

Caning Able
Stan Kent

Caning Able is a modern-day version of the melodramatic tales of Victorian erotica. Full of dastardly villains, regimented discipline, corporal punishment and forbidden sexual liaisons, the novel features the brilliant and beautiful Jasmine, a seemingly helpless heroine who reigns triumphant despite dire peril. By mixing libidinous prose with a changing business world, *Caning Able* gives treasured plots a welcome twist: women who are definitely not the weaker sex.

The Blue Moon Erotic Reader IV

A testimonial to the publication of quality erotica, *The Blue Moon Erotic Reader IV* presents more than twenty romantic and exciting excerpts from selections spanning a variety of periods and themes. This is a historical compilation that combines generous extracts from the finest forbidden books with the most extravagant samplings that the modern erotica imagination has created. The result is a collection that is provocative, entertaining, and perhaps even enlightening. It encompasses memorable scenes of youthful initiations into the mysteries of sex, notorious confessions, and scandalous adventures of the powerful, wealthy, and notable. From the classic erotica of *Wanton Women*, and *The Intimate Memoirs of an Edwardian Dandy* to modern tales like Michael Hemmingson's *The Rooms*, good taste, passion, and an exalted desire are abound, making for a union of sex and sensibility that is available only once in a Blue Moon.

With selections by Don Winslow, Ray Gordon, M. S. Valentine, P. N. Dedeaux, Rupert Mountjoy, Eve Howard, Lisabet Sarai, Michael Hemmingson, and many others.

The Best of the Erotic Reader

"The Erotic Reader series offers an unequaled selection of the hottest scenes drawn from the finest erotic writing." — *Elle*

This historical compilation contains generous extracts from the world's finest forbidden books including excerpts from *Memories of a Young Don Juan*, *My Secret Life*, *Autobiography of a Flea*, *The Romance of Lust*, *The Three Chums*, and many others. They are gathered together here to entertain, and perhaps even enlighten. From secret texts to the scandalous adventures of famous people, from youthful initiations into the mysteries of sex to the most notorious of all confessions, *Best of the Erotic Reader* is a stirring complement to the senses. Containing the most evocative pieces covering several eras of erotic fiction, *Best of the Erotic Reader* collects the most scintillating tales from the seven volumes of *The Erotic Reader*. This comprehensive volume is sure to include delights for any taste and guaranteed to titillate, amuse, and arouse the interests of even the most veteran erotica reader.

Confessions D'Amour
Anne-Marie Villefranche

Confessions D'Amour is the culmination of Villefranche's comically indecent stories about her friends in 1920s' Paris.

Anne-Marie Villefranche invites you to enter an intoxicating world where men and women arrange their love affairs with skill and style. This is a world where illicit encounters are as smooth as a silk stocking, and where sexual secrets are kept in confidence only until a betrayal can be turned to advantage. Here we follow the adventures of Gabrielle de Michoux, the beautiful young widow who contrives to be maintained in luxury by a succession of well-to-do men, Marcel Chalon, ready for any adventure so long as he can go home to Mama afterwards, Armand Budin, who plunges into a passionate love affair with his cousin's estranged wife, Madelein Beauvais, and Yvonne Hiver who is married with two children while still embracing other, younger lovers.

"An erotic tribute to the Paris of yesteryear that will delight modern readers."—*The Observer*

A Maid For All Seasons I, II – Devlin O'Neill

Two Delighful Tales of Romance and Discipline

Lisa is used to her father's old-fashioned discipline, but is it fair that her new employer acts the same way? Mr. Swayne is very handsome, very British and very particular about his new maid's work habits. But isn't nineteen a bit old to be corrected that way? Still, it's quite a different sensation for Lisa when Mr. Swayne shows his displeasure with her behavior. But Mr. Swayne isn't the only man who likes to turn Lisa over his knee. When she goes to college she finds a new mentor, whose expectations of her are even higher than Mr. Swayne's, and who employs very old-fashioned methods to correct Lisa's bad behavior. Whether in a woodshed in Georgia, or a private club in Chicago, there is always someone there willing and eager to take Lisa in hand and show her the error of her ways.

Color of Pain, Shade of Pleasure
Edited by Cecilia Tan

In these twenty-one tales from two out-of-print classics, *Fetish Fantastic* and *S/M Futures*, some of today's most unflinching erotic fantasists turn their futuristic visions to the extreme underground, transforming the modern fetishes of S/M, bondage, and eroticized power exchange into the templates for new sexual worlds. From the near future of S/M in cyberspace, to a future police state where the real power lies in manipulating authority, these tales are from the edge of both sexual and science fiction.

The Governess
M. S. Valentine

Lovely Miss Hunnicut eagerly embarks upon a career as a governess, hoping to escape the memories of her broken engagement. Little does she know that Crawleigh Manor is far from the respectable household it appears to be. Mr. Crawleigh, in particular, devotes himself to Miss Hunnicut's thorough defiling. Soon the young governess proves herself worthy of the perverse master of the house—though there may be even more depraved powers at work in gloomy Crawleigh Manor . . .

Claire's Uptown Girls
Don Winslow

In this revised and expanded edition, Don Winslow introduces us to Claire's girls, the most exclusive and glamorous escorts in the world. Solicited by upper-class Park Avenue businessmen, Claire's girls have the style, glamour and beauty to charm any man. Graced with super-model beauty, a meticulously crafted look, and a willingness to fulfill any man's most intimate dream, these girls are sure to fulfill any man's most lavish and extravagant fantasy.

The Intimate Memoirs of an Edwardian Dandy I, II, III
Anonymous

This is the sexual coming-of-age of a young Englishman from his youthful days on the countryside to his educational days at Oxford and finally as a sexually adventurous young man in the wild streets of London. Having the free time and money that comes with a privileged upbringing, coupled with a free spirit, our hero indulges every one of his, and our, sexual fantasies. From exotic orgies with country maidens to fanciful escapades with the London elite, the young rake experiences it all. A lusty tale of sexual adventure, *The Intimate Memoirs of an Edwardian Dandy* is a celebration of free spirit and experimentation.

"A treat for the connoisseur of erotic literature."
—*The Guardian*

———

Jennifer and Nikki
D. M. Perkins

From Manhattan's Fifth Avenue, to the lush island of Tobago, to a mysterious ashram in upstate New York, Jennifer travels with reclusive fashion model Nikki and her seductive half-brother Alain in search of the sexual secrets held by the famous Russian mystic Pere Mitya. To achieve intimacy with this extraordinary family, and get the story she has promised to Jack August, dynamic publisher of *New Man Magazine,* Jennifer must ignore universal taboos and strip away inhibitions she never knew she had.

———

Confessions of a Left Bank Dominatrix
Gala Fur

Gala Fur introduces the world of French S&M with two collections of stories in one delectable volume. In *Souvenirs of a Left Bank Dominatrix*, stories address topics as varied as: how to recruit a male maidservant, how to turn your partner into a marionette, and how to use a cell phone to humiliate a submissive in a crowded train station. In *Sessions,* Gala offers more description of the life of a dominatrix, detailing the marathon of "Lesbians, bisexuals, submissivies, masochists, paying customers [and] passing playmates" that seek her out for her unique sexual services.

"An intoxicating sexual romp." —*Evergreen Review*

Don Winslow's Victorian Erotica
Don Winslow

The English manor house has long been a place apart; a place of elegant living where, in splendid isolation the gentry could freely indulge their passions for the outdoor sports of riding and hunting. Of course, there were those whose passions ran towards "indoor sports"—lascivious activities enthusiastically, if discreetly, pursued by lusty men and sensual women behind large and imposing stone walls of baronial splendor, where they were safely hidden from prying eyes. These are tales of such licentious decadence from behind the walls of those stately houses of a bygone era.

The Garden of Love
Michael Hemmingson

Three Erotic Thrillers from the Master of the Genre

In The *Comfort of Women*, the oddly passive Nicky Bayless undergoes a sexual re-education at the hands (and not only the hands) of a parade of desperate women who both lead and follow him through an underworld of erotic extremity. The narrator of *The Dress* is troubled by a simple object that may have supernatural properties. "My wife changed when she wore The Dress; she was the Ashley who came to being a few months ago. She was the wife I preferred, and I worried about that. I understood that The Dress was, indeed, an entity all its own, with its own agenda, and it was possessing my wife." In *Drama,* playwright Jonathan falls into an affair with actress Karen after the collapse of his relationship with director Kristine. But Karen's free-fall into debauchery threatens to destroy them both.

The ABZ of Pain and Pleasure
Edited by A. M. LeDeluge

A true alphabet of the unusual, *The ABZ of Pain and Pleasure* offers the reader an understanding of the language of the lash. Beginning with Aida and culminating with Zanetti, this book offers the amateur and adept a broad acquaintance with the heroes and heroines of this unique form of sexual entertainment. The Marquis de Sade is represented here, as are Jean de Berg (author of *The Image*), Pauline Réage (author of *The Story of O* and *Return to the Château*), P. N. Dedeaux (author of *The Tutor* and *The Prefect*), and twenty-two others.

"Frank" and I
Anonymous

The narrator of the story, a wealthy young man, meets a youth one day—the "Frank" of the title—and, taken by his beauty and good manners, invites him to come home with him. One can only imagine his surprise when the young man turns out to be a young woman with beguiling charms.

___

Hot Sheets
Ray Gordon

Running his own hotel, Mike Hunt struggles to make ends meet. In an attempt to attract more patrons, he turns Room 69 into a state-of-the-art sex chamber. Now all he has to do is wait and watch the money roll in. But nympho waitresses, a sex-crazed chef, and a bartender obsessed with adult videos don't exactly make the ideal hotel staff. And big trouble awaits Mike when his enterprise is infiltrated by an attractive undercover policewoman.

___

Tea and Spices
Nina Roy

Revolt is seething in the loins of the British colonial settlement of Uttar Pradesh, and in the heart of memsahib Devora Hawthorne who lusts after the dark, sultry Rohan, her husband's trusted servant. While Rohan educates Devora in the intricate social codes that govern the mean-spirited colonial community, he also introduces his eager mistress to a way of loving that exceeds the English imagination. Together, the two explore sexual territories that neither class nor color can control.

___

Naughty Message
Stanley Carten

Wesley Arthur is a withdrawn computer engineer who finds little excitement in his day-to-day life. That is until the day he comes home from work to discover a lascivious message on his answering machine. Aroused beyond his wildest dreams by the unmentionable acts described, Wesley becomes obsessed with tracking down the woman behind the seductive and mysterious voice. His search takes him through phone sex services, strip clubs and no-tell motels—and finally to his randy reward . . .

The Sleeping Palace
M. Orlando

Another thrilling volume of erotic reveries from the author of *The Architecture of Desire*. Maison Bizarre is the scene of unspeakable erotic cruelty; the Lust Akademie holds captive only the most debauched students of the sensual arts; Baden-Eros is the luxurious retreat of one's most prurient dreams. Once again, M. Orlando uses his flair for exotic detail to explore the nether regions of desire.

"Orlando's writing is an orgasmic and linguistic treat." —*Skin Two*

Venus in Paris
Florentine Vaudrez

When a woman discovers the depths of her own erotic nature, her enthusiasm for the games of love become a threat to her husband. Her older sister defies the conventions of Parisian society by living openly with her lover, a man destined to deceive her. Together, these beautiful sisters tread the path of erotic delight—first in the arms of men, and then in the embraces of their own, more subtle and more constant sex.

The Lawyer
Michael Hemmingson

Drama tells the titillating story of bad karma and kinky sex among the thespians of The Alfred Jarry Theater.

In this erotic legal thriller, Michael Hemmingson explores sexual perversity within the judicial system. Kelly O'Rourke is an editorial assistant at a large publishing house—she has filed a lawsuit against the conglomerate's best-selling author after a questionable night on a yacht. Kelly isn't quite as innocent as she seems, rather, as her lawyer soon finds out, she has a sordid history of sexual deviance and BDSM, which may not be completely in her past.

Tropic of Lust
Michele de Saint-Exupery

She was the beautiful young wife of a respectable diplomat posted to Bangkok. There the permissive climate encouraged even the most outré sexual fantasy to become reality. Anything was possible for a woman ready to open herself to sexual discovery.

"A tale of sophisticated sensuality [it is] the story of a woman who dares to explore the depths of her own erotic nature."—*Avant Garde*

www.ingramcontent.com/pod-product-compliance
Ingram Content Group UK Ltd.
Pitfield, Milton Keynes, MK11 3LW, UK
UKHW022254280225
455674UK00001B/16